BIRD OF PREY

BY ROBERT CRUISE

Copyright ©, Robert Cruise, 2024

Disclaimer

Any events or characters depicted in this work are entirely fictional.
Any resemblance to actual people or event is purely coincidental.

All rights reserved.

For more information, contact the publisher at
AdlerSealPublishing@Gmail.com

First Edition 2024

IBSN 978-1-998497-40-9

TABLE OF CONTENTS

CHAPTER ONE: (1786)
NOBILITY'S VEIL

The waning light of 15 March 1786 filtered through the grimy windows of the once-opulent Corbeau mansion, casting elongated shadows across the faded tapestries and tarnished gilt frames. Étienne Corbeau stood in the grand salon, his gaze fixed upon the dust motes swirling in the slanting rays of the setting sun. The air was heavy with the scent of neglect—a mélange of stale perfume and the lingering mustiness of unused rooms.

He traced his fingers along the edge of a mahogany escritoire, its polished surface dulled by a thin layer of dust. Memories flickered at the periphery of his mind: lavish *soirées* filled with laughter and the clinking of crystal glasses, his father's booming voice regaling guests with tales of distant travels, his mother's silken gowns rustling as she moved gracefully among their esteemed company. Those days seemed a lifetime ago, lost in the chasm that had swallowed his family's fortune.

Étienne's reflection wavered in a tarnished mirror above the fireplace. At thirty-two, his once-youthful features had hardened—a sharp jawline framed by dark hair that curled just above his collar, eyes a shade too weary for a man of his years. His dwindling resources were revealed by the signs of careful mending on the well-made tailored coat he wore.

He turned away from the mirror, his gaze sweeping the room that had been the heart of the Corbeau legacy. The grandeur remained, but decay tainted it—the fraying edges of an Aubusson rug, the threadbare upholstery of a chaise longue, and the chandelier hung precariously with several missing crystals. It was a physical manifestation of his family's descent, a silent reproach that gnawed at him daily.

The sound of hesitant footsteps drew his attention. Cécile, his wife, stood at the doorway, her hands clasped tightly before her. She was a vision of subdued elegance—her auburn hair pulled back modestly, a simple muslin dress that stressed her slender frame. The vibrancy that once lit her hazel eyes had dimmed, replaced by a quiet resignation.

"Étienne," she began softly, her voice barely above a whisper. "I have prepared dinner. Will you join us?"

He hesitated, the weight of unspoken tensions settling between them. "I'm not hungry," he replied tersely, returning to the window where the last vestiges of daylight clung to the horizon.

Cécile stepped further into the room. "The children have been asking after you. Henri wishes to show you his latest drawings, and Sophie—"

"Not now," Étienne interrupted, a hint of irritation colouring his tone. "I have matters to attend to."

She sighed quietly, the lines at the corners of her eyes deepening. "They miss you. We all do."

"Do you think I have the luxury of idle time?" he snapped, at once regretting the sharpness of his words. He softly said, "I am trying to find a way forward for us, our family."

Cécile regarded him for a long moment. "We can endure much, Étienne, but not your absence. Your children need their father."

He clenched his jaw, the conflict within him mounting. "And what would you have me do? Pretend all is well while our world crumbles around us?"

She approached him tentatively, placing a delicate hand on his forearm. "We can face these challenges together. You don't have to bear this burden alone."

He pulled away, moving towards the fireplace where cold ashes lingered from a fire long extinguished. "Together?" he echoed bitterly. "Were we together when my father gambled away our fortune? When the so-called nobility shunned us as pariahs? They left me to salvage what remains."

Cécile's eyes glistened with unshed tears. "We are your family, Étienne. We stand with you."

He shook his head, his gaze fixed on the empty hearth. "Standing with me does not restore our name, nor does it fill our coffers."

A heavy silence settled between them, punctuated only by the distant chiming of a clock marking the hour. Finally, Cécile spoke, her voice barely audible. "Very well. I shall leave you to your thoughts."

As she turned to leave, a pang of guilt pierced through his defences. "Cécile," he called after her.

She paused, her back still turned.

"I didn't mean to—" he began, searching for the right words. "It's just… difficult."

She glanced over her shoulder, offering a faint smile that didn't reach her eyes. "I know," she whispered. "Goodnight, Étienne."

He watched as she disappeared down the dimly lit corridor, the echo of her footsteps fading into the depths of the mansion. Alone again, he sank into a worn armchair, sagging under his weight.

The silence pressed in on him, oppressive and unrelenting. His thoughts drifted to his father, the late Marquis Philippe Corbeau, whose reckless ventures and ill-fated investments had decimated the family's wealth. Promises of prosperity through speculative endeavours had turned to ash, leaving debts and disgrace in their wake. The creditors had been relentless, stripping away properties and possessions piece by piece.

The aristocracy, with whom they had once shared laughter and camaraderie, had recoiled as if the Corbeaus carried a contagion. Invitations ceased, acquaintances avoided eye contact in the streets and whispered rumours circulated through the salons of Paris. The sting of betrayal and humiliation festered within Étienne, a simmering resentment that threatened to consume him.

He recalled the words of Voltaire, whose writings he had devoured in his youth: *"Dans ce pays-ci, il est bon de tuer de temps en temps un amiral pour encourager les autres."* In this country, it is wise to kill an admiral from time to time to encourage others. He couldn't help but notice the irony—the aristocracy had sacrificed his family to preserve their illusions of stability.

The mantelpiece caught his eye, adorned with trinkets that once held sentimental value: a miniature portrait of his mother, a silver clock frozen at the hour of his father's death, and a delicate porcelain figurine of a dove—cracked and imperfect—symbolising a life fractured.

Étienne stood abruptly, the chair scraping against the floorboards. He could not continue in this state of inertia. Action was required, but what form should it take? The established avenues barred him from taking action.

A sudden thought struck him—the murmurs of discontent he had overheard in the taverns and marketplaces. The common people spoke of injustice, of the widening chasm between the monarchy's opulence and the masses' desperation. Philosophers like Rousseau championed the idea of the general will and the people's sovereignty.

There may be an opportunity.

He strode towards his father's old study, which he seldom entered. Dust coated the shelves lined with leather-bound volumes; the air tinged with the scent of aged paper and forgotten ambitions. Rifling through the desk drawers, he found what he sought—a cache of letters and documents detailing connections to various figures within the city.

One name stood out: Madame de Staël, a formidable hostess whose salons were renowned for intellectual discourse and radical ideas. An invitation to one of her gatherings could open doors to new alliances.

Étienne retrieved a fresh sheet of parchment and penned a letter, his quill scratching deliberately across the page. He wrote of shared interests in philosophy and the arts, hinting at a desire to contribute to the vibrant discussions for which her salons were famed.

As he sealed the envelope, a sense of purpose steadied his hand. If the aristocracy would not accept him, he would find another path that might surpass the traditional corridors of power.

The grandfather clock in the hallway chimed midnight, resonant tones echoing through the silent mansion. Étienne extinguished the candle, the room plunging into darkness save for the faint glow of moonlight seeping through the window.

He went to his bedchamber, the weight of his decision settling upon him. As he lay upon the silk sheets that had once symbolised luxury but now felt like a relic of a bygone era, his mind churned with possibilities and uncertainties.

His children's faces drifted into his thoughts—Henri, with his curious eyes and penchant for sketching the world around him, Sophie with her melodic laughter and fondness for stories. Guilt pricked at him for his earlier brusqueness, but he rationalised his efforts were ultimately for their benefit.

"15 March 1786," he whispered into the darkness. "The day everything begins anew."

Sleep eluded him as plans unfurled in his mind—a tapestry of strategies woven from ambition and necessity. Change was happening in the world;

perhaps, amidst the shifting tides, there was a place for a man like him to reclaim what had been lost.

The distant sounds of the city—carriages rattling over cobblestones, the faint strains of music from a nearby tavern—lulled him into a restless slumber. Dreams and reality blurred, the shadows of his past entwined with future uncertainties.

As dawn's first light crept over the rooftops of Paris, Étienne awoke with an unwavering determination. He rose from his bed, the chill of the morning air invigorating. Peering out the window, he watched as the city stirred to life—the vendors setting up their stalls, the labourers beginning their toils.

"Change is coming," he murmured. "And I won't stay behind," he murmured.

He dressed swiftly, choosing attire that was refined yet understated. There was no need to flaunt fineries he no longer possessed. Making his way to the breakfast room, the surprised gazes of Cécile and the children met him.

"Papa!" Henri exclaimed, a smile lighting up his face.

"Good morning," Étienne greeted them, a genuine warmth softening his features.

Sophie giggled, her eyes sparkling. "Will you join us today, Papa?"

He nodded, taking a seat at the table. "Yes, I believe I shall."

Cécile offered a tentative smile, hope flickering in her expression. "It's good to have you with us."

As they shared the simple meal, Étienne felt a momentary peace settle over him. Yet beneath it lay the undercurrents of his resolve. While engaging with his family, he remained steadfast on his newfound path.

After breakfast, he excused himself and informed Cécile of his intention to visit the city. She did not question him, but the concern in her eyes was unmistakable.

Stepping out into the crisp morning, Étienne inhaled deeply. The streets beckoned, filled with both the familiar and the unknown. He set off towards the heart of Paris, the rhythm of his footsteps matching the steady beat of his ambitions.

"Today," he thought, "marks the beginning of my return."

As he disappeared into the bustling thoroughfares, the Corbeau mansion stood silent behind him—a monument to past glories and the crucible from which his aspirations would rise anew.

•••

The evening of 23 April 1786 draped Paris in a mosaic of twilight hues, the sky a gradient of lavender fading into deep indigo. Étienne Corbeau stood before an ornate wrought-iron gate, the entrance to the townhouse of the Vicomte de Brissac—a minor noble known for his unorthodox gatherings. The soft glow of lanterns spilt onto the cobblestone street, casting flickering shadows that danced at Étienne's polished boots.

He adjusted the cuffs of his charcoal-coloured coat, ensuring that the lace trimmings were impeccable. Though his attire was modest compared to the extravagance of his past, he wore it with an air of confidence that belied his diminished circumstances. Taking a steadying breath, he ascended the steps and rapped the brass knocker shaped like a lion's head.

A liveried footman opened the door, his expression neutral. *"Bonsoir, Monsieur."*

"Étienne Corbeau," he announced. "I am expected."

"Bienvenue, Monsieur Corbeau." The footman stepped aside, allowing Étienne to enter the foyer, where the warmth of the interior embraced him.

Conversation filled the salon, creating a melodic hum occasionally interrupted by bursts of laughter and the sound of clinking crystal glasses. Rich tapestries depicted pastoral scenes, and the scent of beeswax mingled with delicate floral perfumes. Chandeliers overhead cast a golden light upon the assembled guests, whose attire ranged from the wealthy to the austere.

Étienne surveyed the room with a practised eye, noting the eclectic mix of attendees. Intellectuals in simple garb conversed animatedly with nobles draped in silks and brocades. A sense of camaraderie that transcended social boundaries charged the atmosphere—a novelty in these stratified times.

"Ah, *Monsieur* Corbeau!" a voice called out, drawing his attention. The Vicomte de Brissac approached, his demeanour affable. He was a man of middling years, with a shock of silver hair and eyes that gleamed with intelligence. "I am delighted you could join us."

"*Merci* for the invitation, Vicomte," Étienne replied, inclining his head.

"Please, call me Henri," the Vicomte insisted with a dismissive wave. "Titles are so tiresome, don't you agree?"

Étienne offered a subtle smile. "As you wish, Henri."

"Come, there are some individuals I must introduce you to." Henri guided him through the crowd, pausing occasionally to exchange pleasantries with guests.

They arrived at a cluster of people engaged in lively debate. At the centre stood a young man of slight build, his piercing blue eyes alight with enthusiasm. His attire was modest—a plain waistcoat and breeches—but he carried himself with quiet authority.

"*Messieurs,*" Henri interjected smoothly, "allow me to present Étienne Corbeau. Étienne, this is Maximilien Robespierre."

Robespierre extended a hand. *"Enchanté, Monsieur Corbeau."*

"The pleasure is mine," Étienne replied, grasping the offered hand. He had heard whispers of Robespierre—a lawyer from Arras gaining notoriety for his advocacy of the ordinary people.

"And this," Henri continued, gesturing to a man beside Robespierre with tousled dark hair and a mischievous grin, "is Camille Desmoulins."

"Always a delight to meet a new face," Desmoulins said, his eyes sparkling with mischief.

"Likewise," Étienne responded, sensing the man's sharp wit.

"Étienne has recently joined our little gatherings," Henri explained. "I trust you will make him feel welcome."

"Of course," Robespierre assured, his gaze assessing.

As Henri excused himself to attend to other guests, the circle drew Étienne in. The conversation resumed, centring on Rousseau's writings and the principles of natural rights.

Robespierre declared that "the social contract" must be the foundation for building a just society. Without it, the people's sovereignty remains only a dream.

Desmoulins nodded vigorously. "And yet, the monarchy remains deaf to the cries of its subjects. How long before the dam bursts?"

Étienne interjected cautiously, "Do you truly believe that such radical change is possible within our lifetime?"

Robespierre regarded him thoughtfully. "Change is not only possible, *Monsieur* Corbeau; it is inevitable. Whether we steer it towards justice or allow it to descend into chaos."

"A fair point," Étienne conceded. "But the mechanisms of power are deeply entrenched. The nobility and clergy hold sway over the courts and the coffers."

"All the more reason to challenge them," Desmoulins asserted. "The pen is mightier than the sword, or so they say."

Étienne arched an eyebrow. "Do you place such faith in words alone?"

Desmoulins grinned slyly. "Words ignite minds, and minds move mountains."

Robespierre said, "We cannot suppress enlightenment indefinitely; the dissemination of ideas is our greatest weapon."

As the evening progressed, Étienne listened more than he spoke, his keen mind absorbing the nuances of the discourse. He observed the passion that animated these men—their unwavering conviction that a better France was within reach. Yet, he remained sceptical. Ideals were admirable, but he questioned their practicality.

A servant circulated with a tray of wine glasses. Étienne accepted one, swirling the ruby liquid thoughtfully.

"Tell me, *Monsieur* Corbeau," Robespierre inquired, "what brought you to our gathering this evening?"

Étienne chose his words carefully. "I have long harboured an interest in philosophical matters. The winds of change seem to stir, and I wished to engage with those at the forefront of such discussions."

"A noble pursuit," Robespierre acknowledged. "Change requires the collaboration of all who will contribute."

Desmoulins leaned in conspiratorially. "And perhaps a dash of audacity."

Étienne allowed a small smile. "Audacity can indeed be a catalyst."

From across the room, a melodic voice captured their attention. A woman stood upon a small dais, reciting verses that weaved imagery of liberty and fraternity. Her presence commanded the room—a blend of grace and enthusiasm. Étienne recognised her as Olympe de Gouges, the playwright known for her progressive views.

"She speaks beautifully," Étienne remarked.

"She writes with equal eloquence," Robespierre noted. "Her plays challenge societal norms, particularly regarding women's rights."

"A daring endeavour," Étienne commented.

"Daring but necessary," Desmoulins asserted. "Voices like hers broaden the scope of our cause."

Étienne sipped his wine, contemplating. The salon was a microcosm of burgeoning revolutionary thought—a convergence of minds intent on reshaping the fabric of society. Amidst the idealism, he perceived opportunities.

"Maximilien," he began, "you mentioned the people's sovereignty. How do you envision this manifesting in practical terms?"

Robespierre's eyes brightened at the question. "Through representative assemblies elected by universal suffrage. Laws created for the benefit of all, not just the privileged few."

"Ambitious," Étienne mused. "But would those in power relinquish it so readily?"

"Unlikely," Robespierre admitted. "But history favours those who persevere."

Desmoulins chimed in, "And sometimes, history needs a push."

Étienne regarded them thoughtfully. "Forgive my honesty, but have you considered the risks? Those who challenge the status quo often face severe repercussions."

"Change is seldom without sacrifice," Robespierre said solemnly. "But to do nothing is to accept the perpetuation of injustice."

Desmoulins raised his glass. "To change and those bold enough to pursue it."

They toasted, and Étienne joined them, the clink of crystal punctuating the moment. He felt a stir of something akin to admiration for their conviction, yet he remained detached. They could harness and direct their enthusiasm.

As the night wore on, the gathering dispersed. Robespierre and Desmoulins bid Étienne farewell with promises to reconvene.

"Until next time," Robespierre said, clasping his hand. "Your insights were most valuable."

"Likewise," Étienne replied.

Stepping out into the cool night air, Étienne descended the steps of the townhouse. The streets of Paris stretched before him, lanterns casting pools of light amidst the darkness. He walked at a measured pace, his mind a labyrinth of thoughts.

The salon had revealed much. The revolutionary ideas circulating among these thinkers presented both a challenge and an opening. Étienne recognised that the old structures were weakening, and cracks formed in the *ancien régime's* foundations. But while others sought to rebuild anew for the collective good, he contemplated a different path.

"Liberty, equality, fraternity," he murmured, the words rolling off his tongue with a hint of irony. Noble ideals, yet human nature was rarely so generous.

He envisioned the potential to reclaim his stature, not through the traditional avenues barred to him, but by navigating the undercurrents of this rising tide. If he could position himself advantageously, he could shape events to serve his ends.

Reaching the Seine, he paused on a bridge, gazing at the river's dark waters, which reflected the shimmer of the moon. The city was a living entity, pulsating with its inhabitants' hopes and frustrations.

"23 April 1786," he reflected. "A turning point, perhaps."

A carriage rattled by, the clatter of hooves echoing against the stone. Étienne watched it disappear into the night, its destination unknown.

He resumed his walk, his newfound determination solidifying. The path ahead was uncertain, fraught with risks and ripe with possibilities.

Returning home, he entered the quiet mansion. The household was asleep, save for a solitary candle flickering in the hallway. He ascended the staircase silently, passing the doors behind which his family slept.

In his study, he lit a lamp and sat at the desk. Unfolding a sheet of parchment, he wrote—notes on the evening's discussions, observations of key figures, and potential strategies.

He paused, the quill hovering over the page. A pang of hesitation flickered—was he straying too far from his principles? But the thought dissipated as quickly as it had arisen.

"Survival requires adaptation," he reminded himself.

Extinguishing the lamp, he sat in darkness, the weight of his choices settling upon him.

The die was cast. Étienne Corbeau, once a mere observer, was now a participant in the unfolding drama of his time. How he would shape his role remains to be seen, but one thing is sure: he would not remain idle while the world transformed around him.

Thus, with the quiet resolve of a man embracing his destiny, Étienne retired for the night, the echoes of the salon's debates lingering in his thoughts.

• • •

The rain had subsided by the morning of 7 May 1786, leaving Paris refreshed under a pale blue sky. Étienne Corbeau navigated the bustling streets with a purposeful stride, the cobblestones still damp beneath his polished boots. The city's energy thrummed around him—vendors hawking their wares, carriages rattling over uneven roads, and the ever-present murmur of conversations in cafés and alleyways.

He approached the modest building on Rue Saint-Honoré that housed Maximilien Robespierre's law offices. Étienne paused briefly outside, adjusting his cravat and smoothing the lapels of his charcoal-coloured coat. A calculated smile played on his lips as he entered the foyer, where the scent of parchment and ink mingled with the faint aroma of roasted coffee.

A junior clerk looked up from his desk. "*Bonjour, Monsieur.* How may I assist you?"

"Étienne Corbeau to see *Monsieur* Robespierre," he announced. "I believe he is expecting me."

The clerk consulted a ledger. "Ah, yes. *Monsieur* Corbeau. This way, *s'il vous plaît.*"

He led Étienne down a narrow corridor with shelves overflowing with legal tomes. They arrived at a door slightly ajar, through which the sound of quill on paper was audible.

"*Monsieur* Robespierre," the clerk called softly, tapping lightly. "*Monsieur* Corbeau is here."

"*Entrez,*" came the measured response.

Étienne stepped inside to find Maximilien Robespierre seated at a cluttered desk, his attire simple but immaculate. A pair of spectacles perched on his nose framed his quiet, intense eyes. He looked up, removed the glasses, and rose to greet his visitor.

"*Monsieur* Corbeau," Robespierre said with a courteous nod. "A pleasure to see you again."

"The pleasure is mine," Étienne replied, extending his hand. "I appreciate you taking the time to meet with me."

Robespierre gestured to a chair opposite his desk. "Please, have a seat. How may I be of service?"

Étienne settled into the chair, adopting a posture of earnest interest. "Our conversation at the Vicomte de Brissac's salon intrigued me greatly. Your perspectives on justice and the rights of citizens resonated with me."

Robespierre offered a modest smile. "It's encouraging to find others who share a concern for the welfare of our nation."

"Indeed," Étienne agreed. "I've been reflecting on the role individuals like ourselves might play in fostering meaningful change."

Robespierre leaned forward slightly. "Change begins with awareness, challenging the accepted norms perpetuating inequality."

"Precisely," Étienne responded. "I must admit, I haven't experienced the realities faced by many," Étienne responded. "Recent circumstances have… opened my eyes."

Robespierre's gaze softened. "Awareness is the first step towards action. May I ask what spurred this shift in perspective?"

Étienne hesitated, feigning a touch of vulnerability. "My family's fortunes have waned, as you may have heard. The loss has afforded me a clearer view of societal disparities."

"I'm sorry to hear of your hardships," Robespierre said sincerely. "But adversity often illuminates truths we might otherwise overlook."

"Very true," Étienne conceded. "I am eager to contribute but unsure of the most effective means."

Robespierre regarded him thoughtfully. "There are many ways to engage. Public discourse, legal advocacy, supporting educational initiatives…"

Étienne seized the opportunity. "I've considered that perhaps my limited resources could support endeavours aligned with these ideals."

"That is a generous offer," Robespierre acknowledged. "We are organising a series of lectures and pamphlets to raise awareness. Help in that area would be invaluable."

Étienne replied with a hint of enthusiasm, his tone tinged with colours as he said, "I would be honoured to assist. Perhaps you could elaborate on the specifics?"

Robespierre outlined their plans—the distribution of Rousseau's works, forums for open debate, and efforts to petition the crown for reforms. His passion became apparent as he spoke, his words measured yet fervent.

Étienne listened attentively, his expression thoughtful. He noted the meticulousness with which Robespierre approached each initiative and the idealism underpinning his strategies.

"Your dedication is admirable," Étienne remarked when Robespierre paused. "But do you ever worry about opposition from those who benefit from the status quo?"

A shadow crossed Robespierre's features. "Resistance is inevitable. But we must remain steadfast. The greater good outweighs the comfort of a few."

"Spoken like a staunch advocate of the people," Étienne said appreciatively. "Your conviction inspires confidence."

Robespierre offered a humble smile. "I am but one voice among many. It is the collective effort that will affect change."

"Nonetheless," Étienne continued, "leadership is essential. People rally behind those who articulate their struggles and hopes."

Robespierre's gaze held a hint of scepticism. "Leadership should serve, not command. We must avoid replicating the hierarchies we seek to dismantle."

"Of course," Étienne agreed smoothly. "I merely meant that guidance is necessary to channel the energies of the movement effectively."

"That is true," Robespierre conceded. "Clarity of purpose is vital."

Étienne shifted in his seat, adopting a more candid tone. "If I may be frank, Maximilien, I believe your voice carries significant weight. Your peers respect you, and your words resonate."

Robespierre appeared taken aback. "I… appreciate your confidence. But I am wary of personal ambition overshadowing our goals."

"A noble sentiment," Étienne acknowledged. "But perhaps humility should not prevent one from embracing the influence one naturally wields."

Robespierre considered this. "I shall reflect on your words."

"Forgive me if I overstep," Étienne added. "I only wish to see the cause flourish."

"No apology necessary," Robespierre assured him. "Your perspective is valuable."

They continued their discussion, delving into the nuances of proposed reforms and the challenges they faced. Étienne contributed thoughtfully and carefully, aligning his remarks with Robespierre's principles while subtly probing his convictions.

He watched the man—the earnestness in his eyes, the measured cadence of his speech, the undercurrent of determination. Robespierre was an idealist, perhaps to a fault. His unwavering adherence to principles made him admirable and susceptible in Étienne's estimation.

As their conversation drew to a close, Robespierre stood. "I must attend to some matters at the courthouse. But I am grateful for your visit."

"The gratitude is mine," Étienne replied, rising as well. "I feel our collaboration could yield meaningful results."

"I agree," Robespierre said warmly. "Shall we reconvene soon to discuss the details of your involvement?"

"Certainly," Étienne affirmed. "I look forward to it."

They shook hands, and Étienne took his leave. Stepping out onto Rue Saint-Honoré, he inhaled the crisp air, tinged with freshly baked bread from a nearby boulangerie.

He began walking, his mind methodically analysing the encounter. Robespierre's influence among the reformists was considerable, and his moral rigidity, while commendable, could be advantageous for someone with the right approach.

Étienne mused to himself, "I can redirect an unwavering compass. Provided one understands its bearings."

He continued through the lively streets, the chatter of merchants and the clatter of horse-drawn carts providing a vibrant soundtrack. The city was a mosaic of contrasts—wealth and poverty, tradition and innovation, complacency and unrest.

Arriving at a quaint café overlooking a bustling square, Étienne sat at an outdoor table. He ordered a coffee, savouring the bitter aroma as he contemplated his next moves.

A familiar voice interrupted his reverie. "Étienne! What a pleasant surprise."

He looked up to see Camille Desmoulins approaching, his expression as jovial as ever. "Camille," Étienne greeted with a genuine smile. "Join me."

Desmoulins settled into the chair opposite. "I trust you're enjoying this fine day?"

"Indeed," Étienne replied. "I've just come from a meeting with our mutual acquaintance, Maximilien."

"Ah, Robespierre," Desmoulins said with a chuckle.

Étienne observed, "He certainly shows commitment to his ideals."

"Sometimes I think he carries the weight of France upon his shoulders," Desmoulins quipped. "But we need his steadfastness, I suppose."

"How about you, Camille?" Étienne inquired. "What occupies your thoughts these days?"

Desmoulins leaned back, his eyes dancing with mischief. "Oh, the usual—plotting the overthrow of oppressive regimes, penning scathing critiques, stirring the pot."

Étienne laughed lightly. "Always the provocateur."

"Someone has to keep things interesting," Desmoulins declared. "But tell me, what brings you deeper into our circle?"

"I find myself increasingly aligned with the need for change," Étienne said carefully. "Our society teeters on the brink of something significant."

Desmoulins regarded him shrewdly. "And where do you see yourself within this impending shift?"

Étienne met his gaze steadily. "I wish to contribute where I can. Perhaps my experiences afford me a unique perspective."

"Undoubtedly," Desmoulins agreed. "An insider's view from the corridors of the *ancien régime.*"

"Precisely," Étienne affirmed. "Understanding the mechanisms at play could be advantageous."

Desmoulins tapped his fingers thoughtfully on the table. "You know, some might question your motives."

Étienne raised an eyebrow. "And you, Camille? Do you question them?"

Desmoulins smiled disarmingly. "Not yet. I prefer to form my opinions based on actions rather than suspicions."

"A wise approach," Étienne remarked.

"One must be cautious, though," Desmoulins continued. "These are volatile times. Alliances shift like the wind."

"Agreed," Étienne said. "But I assure you, my intentions are sincere."

"Then welcome aboard," Desmoulins declared, raising an imaginary glass. "To new comrades."

Étienne inclined his head. "To progress."

They chatted amiably for a while longer, exchanging anecdotes and observations. Étienne subtly steered the conversation, gauging Desmoulins's perspectives and influence.

As they parted ways, Étienne felt a sense of satisfaction. Engaging with both Robespierre and Desmoulins provided valuable insights. Each man wielded influence within different spheres—the austere idealist and the charismatic agitator. Understanding their dynamics would be crucial.

He returned to his residence, the late afternoon sun casting long shadows across the cityscape. The bells of Notre Dame tolled in the distance, a solemn melody that resonated through the streets.

"7 May 1786," Étienne reflected. "A day of promising developments."

Upon reaching home, he found Cécile in the garden, tending to a cluster of lavender. She looked up as he approached, a flicker of surprise flickering across her features.

"Étienne," she greeted. "You're home earlier than usual."

"I thought I'd enjoy the evening here," he replied.

She smiled softly. "It's a pleasant surprise."

He joined her with the lavender; the scent was soothing. "How have you been?"

"Well enough," she said. "The children are inside, practising their letters."

He nodded, a pang of guilt surfacing briefly. "Perhaps I'll join them later."

Cécile regarded him with a mixture of hope and caution. "That would please them."

They stood in companionable silence for a moment, the gentle rustle of leaves filling the air.

"I've been considering becoming more involved in… civic matters," Étienne ventured.

Cécile looked at him curiously. "What sort of matters?"

"Discussions on societal reforms, ways to improve conditions for all," he explained.

"That's admirable," she said thoughtfully. "I wasn't aware you held such interests."

"Recent events have prompted reflection," he admitted.

She reached out, touching his arm lightly. "I hope it brings you fulfilment."

He placed his hand over hers briefly. "Thank you."

Later, as twilight settled, Étienne sat in his study, penning notes and drafting correspondence. His mind was a whirlwind of strategies and considerations.

He contemplated Robespierre's steadfastness, Desmoulins's charisma, and his ambitions.

"Influence is a subtle art," he mused. "One must navigate carefully."

He recognised that it required delicacy while aligning with these figures could advance his position. Overplaying his hand could arouse suspicion.

"Patience," he reminded himself. "Each step deliberate."

As the candles burned low, Étienne leaned back, gazing into the flames. The path he had chosen was fraught with uncertainties, but the potential rewards beckoned alluringly.

He thought of his family's legacy, tarnished yet salvageable of the possibilities ahead if he manoeuvred astutely.

"Fortune favours the bold," he whispered into the quiet.

Extinguishing the candles, he retired for the night, his resolve firm. The calculated encounters of this day were but the beginning.

Thus, with the city settling into slumber around him, Étienne Corbeau embraced the unfolding chapters of his design.

• • •

The opulence of Versailles shimmered under the golden glow of the late afternoon sun on 15 June 1786. Étienne Corbeau approached the grand palace with a mix of trepidation and disdain. The sprawling gardens, meticulously manicured and adorned with fountains and statues, seemed to mock him with their extravagance. He adjusted his attire—a well-tailored but modest suit that hinted at former glory—ensuring that every crease was impeccable, even if the fabric was not of the finest quality.

As he entered the Hall of Mirrors, the splendour of the surroundings was almost overwhelming. Crystal chandeliers cast a kaleidoscope of light across gilded walls and marble floors. The air was thick with the scent of expensive perfumes mingling with the subtle aroma of freshly polished wood. Nobles adorned in silks and jewels drifted through the room, their laughter a tinkling chorus that echoed off the high ceilings.

Étienne held his head high, his gaze steady as he navigated the sea of aristocracy. Whispers trailed in his wake, muffled comments barely concealed behind decorative fans and gloved hands.

"Is that not the Corbeau heir?"

"Indeed, fallen from grace, I hear."

"How bold of him to appear here."

He clenched his jaw but maintained his composure. He was determined not to show any sign of the irritation that simmered beneath his calm exterior.

A familiar voice interrupted his thoughts. "*Monsieur* Corbeau, what an unexpected pleasure."

Étienne turned and faced Vicomte Lucien de Rochefort, a tall man with sharp features and a perpetual smirk. His powdered wig was perfectly styled, and he donned attire resplendent in deep burgundy and gold, boasting the latest fashion.

"Vicomte," Étienne replied evenly. "It has been some time."

"Indeed," Lucien drawled, his eyes flickering over Étienne's attire. Lucien expressed surprise upon seeing Étienne's name on the guest list.

"An oversight, I'm sure," Étienne remarked dryly. "I am here."

"Well, one must seize opportunities where one can find them," Lucien said, a hint of condescension colouring his tone. "Tell me, how fares the Corbeau estate?"

Étienne met his gaze steadily. "It endures."

"How fortunate," Lucien replied. "In these trying times, many find it challenging to maintain their… standings."

"Adversity tests the mettle of a man," Étienne retorted. "And reveals the true nature of those around him."

Lucien's smirk widened. "Quite so. Do excuse me; I see the Comtesse de Valois requires my attention."

As the Vicomte sauntered away, Étienne felt a surge of bitterness. The thinly veiled disdain and subtle barbs were reminders of his altered status among the nobility.

He went to the refreshments, where crystal goblets of champagne and trays of delicate pastries awaited. Reaching for a glass, his hand brushed against another's.

"Pardonnez-moi," a soft voice said.

He turned to see a young woman with piercing green eyes and a cascade of auburn curls. A sapphire gown adorned her, complementing her striking features.

"The fault is mine," Étienne replied, offering a slight bow. "Étienne Corbeau."

She hesitated before responding, a flicker of recognition in her eyes. "Geneviève Laurent."

"A pleasure, Mademoiselle Laurent," he said.

"Likewise," she replied. "I believe I have heard your name before."

"Not all tales are worth repeating," he remarked wryly.

She studied him thoughtfully. "Perhaps not, but they often hold a kernel of truth."

"Then I hope the truths you have heard are not entirely unfavourable."

A hint of a smile touched her lips. "That remains to be seen."

Before their conversation could continue, a group of young nobles approached their expressions, which were a mix of amusement and scorn.

"Geneviève, dear, are you acquainting yourself with Monsieur Corbeau?" one of them asked, feigning innocence.

"Indeed," she replied coolly. "We were just discussing the merits of truth in storytelling."

"Ah, well, be cautious," another interjected. "One wouldn't want to be led astray by fanciful tales."

Étienne felt the weight of their collective disdain but maintained his poise. "I assure you, mademoiselle can discern fact from fiction."

Geneviève met his gaze, an unspoken understanding passing between them. "I appreciate your confidence, Monsieur Corbeau."

The group exchanged glances before one of them addressed Étienne directly. "Tell us, how does one find life on the periphery of society?"

Étienne smiled tightly. "It offers a unique perspective—one unclouded by excess and pretence."

"How quaint," the noble sneered. "Perhaps you might regale us with tales of simplicity."

"Another time," Étienne replied. "I fear my experiences may be too… complex for casual conversation."

"Come now," Geneviève interjected, her tone sharp. "Must we engage in such trivialities? We are here to enjoy the evening."

"Of course," the first noble conceded, though his eyes fixed on Étienne with thinly veiled contempt. "Forgive us."

As the group drifted away, Geneviève sighed softly. "I apologise for their rudeness."

"No apology necessary," Étienne assured her. "It seems some take pleasure in reminding others of their misfortunes."

"Not all share their sentiments," she whispered.

He inclined his head, acknowledging her kindness.

She hesitated before speaking again. "Perhaps we might continue our conversation elsewhere, away from prying eyes."

"That would be most agreeable," he replied.

They moved towards a quieter corner of the hall, near a grand window overlooking the expansive gardens. The sounds of the gathering faded slightly, offering a semblance of privacy.

"I must confess," Geneviève began, "I admire your composure in the face of such treatment."

"One grows accustomed," Étienne said. "Though I admit, patience wears thin."

"Have you considered seeking alliances elsewhere?" she asked. "There are those who value substance over status."

He regarded her curiously. "Are you referring to the rumblings of reform?"

"Perhaps," she said enigmatically. "Change is on the horizon. Opportunities may arise for those willing to embrace them."

Étienne contemplated her words. "And you, *Mademoiselle* Laurent, where do you stand?"

"I believe in positing justice," she replied. "And in the potential for renewal."

"Then we share common ground," he said.

A moment of silence was settled between them, filled with unspoken possibilities.

"Geneviève!" a voice called out, breaking the spell. An older woman approached, her attire opulent and her expression stern. "There you are. I have been looking for you."

"*Madame*," Geneviève acknowledged. "I was just—"

"Yes, yes," the woman interrupted, casting a dismissive glance at Étienne. "We must depart."

Geneviève offered Étienne an apologetic smile. "Until we meet again."

"Until then," he replied, watching as they led her away.

Left alone, Étienne felt the weight of isolation more keenly than before. The grandeur of the hall now seemed oppressive, the laughter hollow. He took his leave, making his way towards the exit.

The gathering sounds faded behind him as he stepped out into the cool night air. The sky was a tapestry of stars, unmarred by clouds. He walked along the gravel path, the crunch beneath his feet echoing his turbulent thoughts.

The disdain he had faced reignited his simmering resentment. The aristocracy, with its layers of hypocrisy and superficiality, had no room for those who did not conform to its expectations.

He paused at the edge of a grand fountain, the water glistening in the moonlight. His reflection stared back at him—a man caught between worlds, neither accepted nor entirely rejected.

A resolve hardened within him. The revolution that brewed beneath the surface of society was more than a distant concept—it was a vehicle. Not merely to dismantle the existing order but to reshape it.

"If they will not have me," he thought, "then I shall surpass them."

He envisioned a new hierarchy where merit and cunning triumphed over birthright. He could harness the revolution and direct its chaos towards his ascent.

Étienne straightened, a newfound determination coursing through him. The path ahead was uncertain, but he was no stranger to adversity.

He allowed a faint smile as he approached the carriage that awaited him. The nobility's disdain would be their undoing.

"Let them cling to their illusions," he whispered. "I shall rise above them all."

The carriage door closed behind him, and as the horses set off, Étienne gazed out at the illuminated palace receding into the distance. The lights flickered like distant stars, oblivious to the shifting tides.

He leaned back, the wheels turning beneath him, a metronome marking the beginning of his journey towards power.

• • •

The summer heat lingered over Paris on 27 July 1786, casting a hazy veil over the bustling streets near the Palais-Royal. Étienne Corbeau navigated the labyrinth of vendors and pedestrians, the air thick with the scent of freshly baked bread mingled with the stench of refuse left baking in the sun. The city pulsed with restless energy, whispers of change rippling through the crowds like an undercurrent waiting to surface.

He approached the Café de Foy, a modest establishment favoured by intellectuals and agitators. Its unassuming façade belied the spirited discussions that brewed within. Pushing open the door, a cacophony of voices and the rich aroma of strong coffee and tobacco greeted Étienne.

"Étienne!" Camille Desmoulins called from a corner table, his eyes alight with mischief. "Over here!"

Étienne weaved through the crowded room, nodding politely to familiar faces. Seated with Desmoulins were Maximilien Robespierre and Georges Danton. Robespierre sat upright, his attire modest yet immaculate, his gaze contemplative behind wire-framed spectacles. Danton, in contrast, lounged comfortably, his robust frame and hearty laughter commanding attention.

"Mes amis," Étienne greeted them, taking a seat. "I trust the day finds you well?"

"Well enough," Danton rumbled, pouring a red wine. "Though the heat tests one's patience."

"Indeed," Étienne agreed, loosening his cravat slightly. "But it seems to have stirred the spirits of the city."

"Change is in the air," Desmoulins remarked, his fingers drumming eagerly on the table. "The people grow weary of empty promises."

Robespierre nodded thoughtfully. "Their grievances are justified. Bread prices soar while wages stagnate. The monarchy remains indifferent."

"Justice must prevail," Étienne said, carefully measuring his tone. "But how do we turn discontent into meaningful action?"

"Education," Robespierre asserted. "We must enlighten the masses about their rights. An informed populace is the cornerstone of a just society."

Danton scoffed lightly. "Education is vital, but the people need more than pamphlets and speeches. They need leaders who will act."

Étienne leaned forward. "Action guided by principle. Without moral integrity, any movement risks descending into chaos."

"Precisely," Robespierre affirmed, casting a grateful glance at Étienne. "Virtue must guide us."

Virtue alone doesn't fill bellies," Danton countered, taking a hearty sip of wine. "We need practical solutions."

Desmoulins grinned. "Perhaps a balance of both? Idealism tempered with pragmatism?"

Étienne observed the interplay, noting the subtle tensions. "If I may," he interjected, "might there be a way to unify these approaches? Mobilise the people with compelling ideas and decisive leadership?"

Robespierre regarded him curiously. "What do you propose?"

"A series of assemblies," Étienne suggested. "Gatherings where citizens can voice concerns, and we can offer guidance. It shows solidarity and fosters organisation."

Danton stroked his chin thoughtfully. "Not a bad notion. Gives the people a sense of agency."

"Furthermore," Étienne continued, "it positions us as the movement's vanguard, those who can translate unrest into reform."

Robespierre adjusted his spectacles. "We aim to empower the people, not to seek power for ourselves."

"Of course," Étienne agreed smoothly. "But effective coordination requires leadership."

Desmoulins tapped the table. "He's right, Maximilien. Without direction, the momentum could dissipate."

Robespierre hesitated. "Leadership must serve the common good, not personal ambition."

"Agreed," Étienne said, meeting his gaze steadily. "Our intentions align with justice and equality," Étienne said, meeting his gaze steadily.

A moment of silence settled over the table, the ambient noise of the café filling the gap. Étienne sensed Robespierre's internal conflict—a man torn between his ideals and the practicalities of effecting change.

"Very well," Robespierre conceded. "We can explore this approach, provided our motives remain pure."

"Excellent," Danton boomed, raising his glass. "To the people's assemblies!"

They toasted, and Étienne allowed himself a discreet smile. Someone had sown the seed.

As the conversation shifted to logistics, Étienne subtly steered discussions towards establishing a network of supporters. "We should identify key individuals in each district," he proposed. "Those who can rally others and disseminate information efficiently."

Desmoulins nodded eagerly. "I know several artisans and shopkeepers who are sympathetic."

"I can reach out to the legal circles," Robespierre added. "The corruption in the judiciary frustrates many people," Robespierre said.

Danton grinned. "Leave the taverns to me. Nothing stirs revolutionary spirit like a good drink."

Étienne sipped his coffee, the bitter taste grounding him. "Our combined efforts will create a formidable foundation."

As plans took shape, Étienne's mind churned with possibilities. Aligning himself with these influential figures granted him access to the movement's core. He noted Robespierre's moral rigidity, Desmoulins's charisma, and Danton's pragmatism—each a valuable asset.

"By the way, Étienne," Desmoulins said suddenly, "you've been rather quiet about your journey. What fuels your passion for change?"

Étienne feigned a reflective sigh. "Personal experience, I suppose. Witnessing the indifference of the elite has been… enlightening."

Danton raised an eyebrow. "Care to elaborate?"

"My family's decline exposed the fragility of status," Étienne explained. "I realised that privilege often masks injustice. The system serves few at the expense of many."

Robespierre regarded him with newfound respect. "Transformation often begins with such revelations."

"Indeed," Étienne affirmed. "I am committed to building a more fair society."

"Then we are fortunate to have you among us," Robespierre said earnestly.

"To shared purpose," Étienne toasted, lifting his cup.

As the afternoon waned, the group dispersed, each tasked with specific preparations. Étienne lingered, watching as his companions departed into the crowd of Parisians.

"Étienne," Robespierre called back. "Walk with me a moment?"

"Of course," he replied, falling into step beside him.

They navigated the bustling street, the din of merchants and city life enveloping them. "I wanted to express my appreciation for your insights," Robespierre began. "Your perspective enriches our discourse."

"I am glad to contribute," Étienne replied. "Our collaboration strengthens our cause."

Robespierre hesitated before speaking. "I must admit, I sometimes grapple with balancing idealism and pragmatism. It's reassuring to have voices that bridge that gap."

Étienne seized the opportunity. "Our strength lies in unity. Diverse approaches can complement rather than conflict."

"Wise words," Robespierre acknowledged. "We must remain vigilant against the corrupting influence of power."

"Accountability is key," Étienne agreed. "Together, we can ensure our integrity remains intact."

They parted ways at a crossroads, Robespierre offering a rare smile. "Until our next meeting."

"Au revoir, Maximilien."

Alone, Étienne's expression hardened. Robespierre's trust was both an asset and a vulnerability. "He underestimates the complexities of power," Étienne mused.

He strolled towards the Seine, the river's languid flow mirroring his contemplations. The sun cast a golden hue across the water, and the silhouette of Notre Dame loomed in the distance.

His thoughts turned to the assemblies. Steering their direction would position him favourably. By subtly influencing agendas, he could shape the movement's trajectory.

A street vendor's cry broke his reverie. "Fresh fruit! Sweet as a summer's kiss!"

Étienne approached, purchasing an apple. As he bit into it, the crisp tang reminded him of his hunger—not for food but ascendancy.

He recalled the disdain of the aristocracy, the hollow platitudes of nobility who dismissed him. Their obliviousness would be their downfall. "They cling to a decaying order," he thought. "I will forge a new one."

Returning home, he found the house quiet. Cécile was tending to the children in the garden, their laughter carrying softly through the open window of his study.

He sat at his desk, quill in hand. Drafting letters to potential allies, he outlined strategies and contingencies. Each stroke of the pen was a step towards consolidating his influence.

A gentle knock interrupted him. "Yes?"

Cécile peeked in, her eyes reflecting concern. "You've been busy of late."

"Important matters require attention," he replied without looking up.

She lingered. "Is everything alright?"

"Perfectly," he said curtly.

She sighed softly. "Dinner will be ready soon."

"I'll join you shortly."

As she closed the door, Étienne allowed himself a moment of reflection. His detachment from family weighed lightly compared to his ambitions, and he justified making sacrifices.

He sealed the letters, calling for a messenger. Watching as the courier rode off into the fading light, he felt a surge of determination.

"Justice, equality, fraternity," he mused. "Noble ideals ripe for exploitation."

He descended to the dining room, where Cécile and the children awaited. Their faces brightened at his arrival.

"Papa!" Henri exclaimed. "Will you tell us a story tonight?"

"Perhaps," Étienne replied absently, seating himself.

Throughout the meal, he engaged minimally, his mind elsewhere. Cécile observed him quietly, her expression tinged with sadness.

Later, as twilight deepened, Étienne stood by the window of his study, gazing at the stars emerging in the velvet sky. Above, the city's sounds blended together, creating a vivid depiction of life unaware of the turmoil brewing beneath.

"Let them sleep in ignorance," he thought. "I will awaken a new dawn."

He recalled Robespierre's earnest face, Danton's boisterous confidence, and Desmoulins's eager wit. Allies for now, perhaps pawns later.

Extinguishing the candle, he embraced the darkness. "The game begins," he whispered.

In the quiet that followed, the only sounds were the distant echo of a city poised on the brink of revolution and the steady beat of a man intent on bending its course to his will.

• • •

In the waning days of summer, the heat clung stubbornly to the air on 2 September 1786 as Étienne Corbeau rode through the sun-dappled lanes leading to his family estate. The once-proud manor loomed ahead, its silhouette marred by neglect. Vines twisted around the crumbling stone, and the gardens, once a tapestry of colour and life, lay wild and overgrown. The carriage wheels creaked beneath him, mirroring the fatigue etched upon the very bones of the house.

Étienne dismounted at the entrance, his boots stirring up small dust clouds from the gravel path. The heavy oak doors groaned in protest as he pushed them open, and he stepped into a grand hall that echoed with the ghosts of former glory. Faded tapestries hung limply from the walls, and a film of dust dulled the chandelier above.

"Monseigneur," a voice called hesitantly.

He turned to see Pierre, the ageing steward, his wrinkled hands nervously clasped. "Welcome home."

Étienne offered a curt nod. "Thank you, Pierre. Is everything in order?"

"As much as it can be," Pierre replied cautiously. "The repairs you requested… funds have been scarce."

"Yes, I am aware," Étienne said sharply, brushing past him. "I will attend to it."

He climbed the sweeping staircase, each step creaking underfoot. The weight of the estate's decay pressed upon him, a physical manifestation of his family's decline. Reaching his study, he closed the door behind him, shutting out the world. The room was a sanctuary of sorts, lined with shelves of leather-bound volumes and maps unfurled across a massive oak desk.

He moved to the window overlooking the untamed grounds. Children's laughter drifted faintly from the gardens below—Henri and Sophie, oblivious to the burdens that consumed their father. For a fleeting moment, guilt tugged at him, but he pushed it aside. There was no time for sentimentality.

Étienne sat at his desk, his fingers tracing the contours of a map of Paris. Pins marked various locations—cafés, meeting halls, and residences of critical figures. His encounters with Robespierre, Desmoulins, and Danton had been enlightening. Their enthusiasm for revolution was palpable, but their naiveté was a tool he could exploit.

He unfurled a letter from Robespierre, inviting him to a gathering of like-minded individuals. "Your insights have been invaluable," it read. "We believe your involvement could advance our cause." Étienne allowed himself a thin smile. The door was open.

A soft knock interrupted his thoughts. "Enter," he called.

Cécile stepped in, her delicate features framed by wisps of auburn hair that had escaped her coiffure. "You're back," she said softly.

"As you can see," he replied without looking up.

She approached cautiously. "Will you join us for supper?"

"I'm occupied," he said briefly, shuffling papers to emphasise his point.

She hesitated. "The children miss you. Henri has been asking when you'll spend time with him."

"I have important matters to attend to," Étienne snapped, his patience fraying.

Cécile's eyes hardened slightly. "More important than your family?"

He met her gaze finally. "Everything I do is for this family."

"Is it?" she challenged. "We see so little of you; when we do, you're distant. The estate is falling apart, Étienne. We need you here."

He stood abruptly. "What would you have me do? Sit idly by as everything crumbles? I'm securing our future."

"By involving yourself with radicals and agitators?" she retorted.

His expression darkened. "Be careful, Cécile. You know nothing of these matters."

"I know you're slipping away from us," she said quietly. "From me."

He turned away, dismissing her with a wave of his hand. "I have no time for this."

She lingered momentarily before leaving, the door closing softly behind her.

Alone once more, Étienne exhaled slowly, attempting to rein in his tumultuous thoughts. His family's concerns were an unwelcome distraction. The revolution was gaining momentum, and he needed to position himself strategically.

He recalled his last conversation with Danton, the man's booming voice echoing in his memory. "The people are restless, Étienne. They need leaders who can harness their energy." Danton had clapped him on the shoulder, a gesture of camaraderie. "We could use men like you."

Robespierre, ever the idealist, had spoken of justice and equality. "We must be the change we wish to see," he had declared earnestly. Étienne had nodded along, masking his true intentions behind a façade of shared conviction.

He reached for a quill and parchment, drafting a message to a contact within the Jacobin Club. He drafted the language carefully, expressing solidarity while probing for weaknesses. Information was power, and he intended to wield it deftly.

As he wrote, the distant sound of piano keys reached his ears—Sophie practising her scales. The melancholy notes resonated through the empty halls, a haunting backdrop to his machinations.

Time slipped by unnoticed for hours until the light outside waned, shadows stretching long across the floor. Étienne lit a candle, its flickering glow illuminating the determined set of his features.

A knock sounded once more. Suppressing a sigh, he called out, "Yes?"

Henri peeked around the door, clutching a wooden toy soldier. "Papa?"

"What is it?" Étienne asked, striving for patience.

"Will you read me a story tonight?"

"Not now," he replied, returning his gaze to the papers before him.

"Please? Just one chapter."

"I said no," Étienne snapped, the sharpness of his tone causing Henri to flinch.

The boy's eyes welled up. "You never have time anymore."

"Henri, go to your mother," he ordered firmly.

With a wounded expression, Henri retreated, closing the door behind him.

Étienne rubbed his temples, annoyance mingling with a pang of regret. Distractions, he reminded himself. He could not afford them.

He turned back to his maps, plotting routes and considering the placement of troops should unrest escalate. His military background, though limited, provided him with a tactical mindset. If he could anticipate the moves of the revolutionaries and the monarchy, he could manoeuvre himself into a position of influence.

"Fully embrace the revolution," he murmured. "Become indispensable."

The nobility had cast him aside, but the revolution offered a new arena—a chance to reclaim and surpass his former status. He envisioned himself rising through the ranks, his contributions recognised and rewarded.

A knock came yet again, this time more hesitant.

"What now?" he barked.

The door opened slowly to reveal a maid, Marianne, "*Pardon, Monsieur.* Shall I bring you some supper?"

He realised he had not eaten since morning. "Yes, fine. Leave it outside."

"Very good, *Monsieur,*" she said, withdrawing quickly.

Étienne leaned back in his chair, gazing into the candle's dancing flame. The shadows it cast seemed to flicker in time with his thoughts—dark, elusive, ever-shifting.

He pondered the steps to ascend within revolutionary circles. Aligning with Robespierre would grant him moral legitimacy, while Danton's connections could open doors to the movement's more pragmatic elements. Desmoulins's talent for persuasion was another asset to be utilised.

But trust was a scarce commodity. He must tread carefully, revealing enough to gain confidence without exposing his true ambitions.

A faint creak signalled the supper tray outside his door. He retrieved it, the aroma of stew reminding him of his hunger. Eating mechanically, his mind remained elsewhere.

He considered contacting Jacques-Louis David, the influential painter whose depictions of revolutionary themes stirred public sentiment. An alliance could prove beneficial, as art is a powerful tool for propaganda.

Finishing his meal, Étienne returned to his desk. He drafted letters late into the night, the scratching of quill on parchment the only sound in the silent house.

As the first light of dawn tinged the sky, he sealed the final envelope. Exhaustion tugged at him, but satisfaction overrode it. He achieved progress.

He stood, stretching stiff muscles, and moved to the window. The estate sprawled before him shrouded in the pale glow of morning. In the distance, workers began their day, toiling in fields that yielded less with each passing year.

A figure moved below—Cécile, wrapped in a shawl against the dawn chill. She glanced upwards, perhaps sensing his gaze, but he remained hidden behind the glass.

He felt a fleeting desire to join her, to share a moment of quiet companionship. But the distance between them had grown insurmountable. His path diverged sharply from hers, and he accepted it with a bitter resignation.

Turning away, Étienne extinguished the candle. There was much to do, and sentimentality was a luxury he could not afford.

Descending the staircase, he encountered Pierre once more. "Prepare my horse," he instructed.

"Yes, *Monseigneur.* Will you be away long?"

"As long as necessary," Étienne replied.

He donned his coat and hat, stepping out into the crisp morning air. Mounting his horse, he cast a last glance at the manor. The shutters remained closed, the household still unaware of his departure.

He urged the horse forward, the hooves striking a steady rhythm against the dirt road. As he rode towards Paris, the landscape shifted from rolling fields to the city's outskirts, the air growing thicker with each mile.

The revolution awaited, a tide he intended to ride to its crest. His family, estate, and former life had become secondary to his pursuit of power.

The city skyline emerged through the morning haze, a mosaic of rooftops and spires. Étienne felt a surge of anticipation.

"Let the others chase ideals," he thought. "I will seize the opportunity."

He envisioned the faces of those who had dismissed him—the nobles with their sneers, the radicals with their self-righteousness. They would all bear witness to his ascent.

As he entered the city streets, already alive with activity, Étienne blended into the crowd. He was one among many, yet set apart by his purpose.

He headed directly to a discreet lodging he maintained, a modest apartment that served as his base in the heart of Paris. Here, he could operate without the encumbrance of familial obligations.

After settling in, he arranged meetings and dispatched messages to key contacts. He calculated each move and considered each alliance.

The sun climbed higher, casting sharp shadows that mirrored the city's divisions. Étienne immersed himself in the currents of revolution, intent on navigating them to his advantage.

His detachment was complete. The man who had left the estate that morning was a shadow of his former self, replaced by one driven solely by ambition.

As evening approached, he stood by his apartment window, watching the city bustle below. The air vibrated with unrest, and vendors' cries mingled with heated debates in the streets.

"Let the revolution come," he murmured. "I am ready."

He turned away from the window, the fading light casting his silhouette against the wall—a figure poised on the brink of transformation.

Thus, on 2 September 1786, Étienne Corbeau embraced the path that would lead him deeper into the heart of the revolution, his gaze fixed firmly on the horizon where power beckoned like a distant beacon.

• • •

Leaves rustling underfoot, Étienne Corbeau navigated the bustling streets of Paris as the crisp autumn air of 18 October 1786 enveloped the city in a cool embrace. The town was alive with anticipation. Whispers of change carried on the wind like secrets waiting to be told. The twilight sky blazed with hues of gold and crimson, casting a warm glow over the cobblestone avenues leading to Madame de Montigny's salon.

Madame de Montigny's townhouse stood modestly amidst grander façades, yet it was here that the minds shaping the future of France gathered. Étienne adjusted his coat, ensuring he perfectly arranged the lace at his cuffs and ascended the steps. A liveried servant opened the door, the animated conversation murmuring into the night.

"Ah, *Monsieur* Corbeau!" Madame de Montigny greeted him with a gracious smile, her silver hair swept atop her head and her emerald earrings catching the light. "It's a pleasure to see you."

"*Madame,*" Étienne replied, bowing slightly. "The pleasure is mine. Your salons are renowned for their enlightening discourse."

"Flatterer," she teased lightly. "But I sense you have much to contribute this evening. Please, make yourself at home."

As she moved to welcome new arrivals, Étienne surveyed the room. Crystal chandeliers bathed the salon in a warm glow, illuminating clusters of guests deep in discussion. The scent of beeswax mingled with hints of perfume and the rich aroma of coffee.

He spotted Camille Desmoulins near a grand fireplace, his dark curls and expressive eyes unmistakable. Desmoulins gestured passionately as he spoke to a small group, his words eliciting nods and murmurs of agreement. Étienne made his way towards them, weaving through the crowd.

"—and if the monarchy continues to ignore the plight of the people," Desmoulins declared, "they will find the tides of revolution rising against them!"

"Stirring as always, Camille," Étienne interjected smoothly, a hint of a smile on his lips.

Desmoulins turned, his face lighting up. "Étienne! I was thinking you'd forsaken us for the tranquillity of the countryside."

"Hardly," Étienne replied. "Though I must admit, the city's pulse quickens daily."

"Indeed, it does." Desmoulins eyed him thoughtfully. "Join us. We're discussing the latest pamphlets circulating in the Faubourg Saint-Antoine."

"Happy to," Étienne said, accepting a glass of wine from a passing servant.

A young woman with keen blue eyes extended her hand. "Marie Dupont," she introduced herself. "An admirer of your writings, Monsieur Desmoulins, speaks highly of you."

"Étienne Corbeau," he replied, kissing her hand lightly. "An admirer? I fear Camille exaggerates my modest contributions."

"Nonsense," Desmoulins interjected. "Your insights into societal reforms are both sharp and necessary."

"Speaking of necessary," Étienne began, turning to the group, "have any of you noticed the emerging divisions within our movement?"

A gentleman with a neatly trimmed beard frowned. "Divisions?"

"Yes," Étienne continued. "Some advocate for moderate reform, seeking change within the existing structures. Others push for more radical actions, perhaps even the dissolution of the monarchy itself."

Desmoulins nodded vigorously. "It's true. The question is, which path will lead to true liberty?"

"Perhaps a synthesis of both approaches," Marie suggested. "Bold ideas tempered with strategic implementation."

"An astute observation," Étienne agreed. "But we must be cautious. Factions can weaken our cause if we're not united."

"Unity doesn't mean uniformity," Desmoulins argued. "We need diverse voices to challenge complacency."

"Of course," Étienne conceded. "Yet, without a shared vision, we risk fragmenting."

A thoughtful silence settled over the group. Étienne sipped his wine, gauging their reactions. Planting seeds required patience; he needed to stir thought without revealing his hand too soon.

Breaking the silence, Desmoulins clapped a hand on Étienne's shoulder. "You always provoke the most interesting discussions."

"Merely observations," Étienne demurred. "But tell me, Camille, how do you see the role of the press in all this?"

Desmoulins's eyes sparkled. "Ah, the power of the pen! It's our most potent weapon. Through words, we ignite minds and inspire action."

"Exactly," Étienne said. "Imagine if we could unify the message across all our publications. A coordinated effort to rally the people."

"An intriguing idea," Marie remarked. "But would that not stifle an individual expression?"

"Not at all," Étienne assured her. "It's about amplifying our collective voice while preserving unique perspectives."

Desmoulins rubbed his chin thoughtfully. "There's merit in that. A shared platform could strengthen our reach."

"Perhaps we could discuss this further," Étienne suggested. "Gather the key pamphleteers and journalists."

"I'll arrange it," Desmoulins agreed eagerly. "Together, we'll craft a narrative the monarchy cannot ignore."

As the conversation shifted to logistics, Étienne excused himself to circle the room. He needed to gauge the sentiments of others to see how far he could push the boundaries.

He approached a cluster of young radicals engaged in animated debate. "Gentlemen," he greeted them. "What stirs such passion this evening?"

A fiery-eyed man named Jacques turned to him. "The King's latest decree—he intends to increase taxes yet again!"

"An outrage," Étienne replied, his voice measured. "But perhaps an opportunity."

"How so?" another man demanded.

"The decree fuels discontent by demonstrating the Crown's disregard for its subjects," Étienne explained. "We can channel that into support for our cause."

Jacques frowned. "Words won't fill empty bellies."

"True," Étienne acknowledged. "But strategic actions might. What if we organised community aid, showcasing solidarity while undermining the monarchy's authority?"

The men exchanged glances. "It's a bold move," Jacques admitted.

"Boldness is required in times like these," Étienne said smoothly. "Consider it."

Leaving them to ponder, he moved on, his mind calculating. He left them to ponder and moved on, his mind calculating.

He spotted Olympe de Gouges standing alone near a window, gazing thoughtfully into the night. Approaching her, he inclined his head. "Madame de Gouges, your recent play was a triumph."

She turned to him, a hint of scepticism in her eyes. "Monsieur Corbeau, flattery is the currency of courtiers."

"Then consider it genuine appreciation," he replied. "Your advocacy for women's rights is both courageous and necessary."

She studied him for a moment. "Do you truly believe that, or are you merely echoing fashionable sentiments?"

"I assure you, my convictions are sincere," Étienne said. "Equality must extend to all, or it is merely a façade."

A faint smile touched her lips. "Perhaps there's hope for you yet."

"High praise," he said with a slight bow. "May I ask, how do you see the role of women in the revolution?"

"As equals," she stated firmly. "Participants, leaders, thinkers—not mere spectators."

"Then we must make sure that we listen to their voices," Étienne agreed. "United in purpose."

She raised an eyebrow. "Words again, *Monsieur.* Will you back them with action?"

He met her gaze steadily. "Count on it."

The salon buzzed with a subtle shift as the evening drew close. Étienne sensed his conversations had sown the desired seeds. Factions were forming, and ideas were fermenting—some more radical than others.

Outside, the chill night air was refreshing after the warmth of the salon. Étienne pulled his coat tighter as he walked, the streetlamps casting pools of golden light along his path. The muted sounds of the city accompanied racing thoughts.

He reflected on his interactions with Desmoulins. The journalist's influence was undeniable, his words reaching the masses in ways few others could. Aligning with him was strategic, but Étienne knew he must subtly guide that influence.

"Testing the waters," he thought. "And finding them receptive."

Reaching his lodging, Étienne climbed the narrow stairs to his modest apartment. Inside, he lit a candle, the flickering flame casting shadows on the walls. With a quill, he sat at his desk and started writing.

Through penning letters, he proposed meetings and suggested collaborations with critical individuals. He carefully chose his words, designing each phrase to inspire while revealing little of his true intent.

Pausing, he glanced at a miniature portrait of his family on the desk—Cécile, Henri, and Sophie smiling softly from the miniature canvas. A flicker of emotion stirred, but he pushed it aside. There would be time for such sentiments later.

For now, his focus was singular.

He sealed the letters and leaned back, his ambitions settling comfortably. The path ahead was uncertain, but the allure of power was a beacon he could not ignore.

Extinguishing the candle, Étienne stood by the window, gazing out over the rooftops of Paris. The city slept, unaware of the forces gathering beneath its surface.

"Let the factions form," he whispered. "I will be there to shape them."

As he turned away, the first light of dawn paled the eastern sky. A new day beckoned, and with it, new opportunities.

Étienne Corbeau was ready to seize them.

• • •

By 20 December 1786, the chill of winter had settled over Paris, a thin veil of frost glazing the cobblestones and etching delicate patterns upon the windowpanes of shuttered shops. Étienne Corbeau pulled his cloak tighter around his shoulders as he navigated the city's labyrinthine streets, his breath forming fleeting clouds in the frigid air. The sky hung low and leaden, promising snow that had yet to fall.

He moved with purpose, his eyes keen beneath the brim of his hat, observing the subtle shifts in the city's rhythm. The Seine flowed sluggishly, its surface disturbed only by the occasional barge breaking through thin layers of ice. Street vendors huddled beside makeshift braziers, their usual cries muted by the cold and the season's weight.

As Étienne walked along the Rue Saint-Honoré, he noted the clusters of men gathered outside cafés and taverns, their conversations hushed but intense. The air was thick with a palpable tension, a simmering unrest lurking beneath everyday life's veneer. Posters plastered on walls bore bold proclamations demanding justice and denouncing the excesses of the monarchy. The words *"Liberté"* and *"Égalité"* appeared increasingly frequently, scrawled in ink and chalk by unseen hands.

He paused near a group of labourers, their faces ruddy from the cold and hardship. They spoke in low tones, casting wary glances at passers-by.

"It's the bread prices again," one man muttered. "How can we feed our families when the cost keeps rising?"

"While the King and his cronies feast in Versailles," another spat, "we starve."

Étienne lingered just within earshot, feigning interest in a nearby shop window displaying a modest assortment of goods. His gaze drifted over the reflection of the men behind him.

"A change is coming," the first man said. "People won't stand for this much longer."

"Careful with your words," cautioned a third. "There are ears everywhere."

Étienne allowed himself a faint smile. The seeds of discontent were sprouting, nourished by the harsh winter and the relentless inequities of the time. He resumed his walk, turning onto a narrower street where the buildings leaned in as if conspiring.

He made his way to the Café de Foy, a bustling establishment despite the cold, known as a gathering place for intellectuals and agitators alike. Pushing open the heavy wooden door, a warm air scented with coffee and tobacco greeted him. The murmur of voices enveloped him, punctuated by the clink of porcelain cups and the occasional outburst of laughter.

"Ah, Monsieur Corbeau!" Madame Dupont, the proprietress, greeted him warmly. She was a stout woman with kind eyes and a knack for remembering her patrons' preferred drinks.

"*Madame*," Étienne replied with a slight bow. "A pleasure, as always."

"Your usual seat is free," she said, gesturing towards a corner table. "Shall I bring you a coffee?"

"*Merci,*" he responded, removing his gloves and tucking them into his coat pocket.

Settling into the chair, Étienne surveyed the room. Familiar faces dotted the crowd—students animatedly debating philosophy, tradesmen seeking respite from the cold, and the occasional nobleman attempting to blend inconspicuously into the milieu. His gaze settled on a figure seated alone, poring over a stack of papers with an intensity that seemed to shut out the surrounding hubbub—Maximilien Robespierre.

Étienne observed him for a moment. The young lawyer's attire was simple but immaculate, and his powdered wig was slightly askew, giving him an air of earnest dishevelment. His contemplative expression, eyes flickering across the page with unwavering focus, softened his sharp features.

"Your coffee, Monsieur," Madame Dupont interrupted his thoughts, placing the steaming cup before him. "*Merci beaucoup,*" he said, offering her a courteous smile.

He contemplated his approach. Infiltrating Robespierre's inner circle would require tact and subtlety. People knew the man for his principled stances and discerning judgement of character. Étienne would need to present himself as a genuine ally whose convictions aligned with the burgeoning revolutionary ideals.

Taking a sip of his coffee, he rose from his seat and approached Robespierre's table. As he drew near, he cleared his throat softly.

"Pardon me, Monsieur Robespierre," he began. "May I join you?"

Robespierre looked up, surprise flickering across his features before he composed himself. "Monsieur Corbeau, is it not?" he replied, recognising Étienne from previous assemblies.

"Indeed," Étienne confirmed. "I couldn't help but notice your dedication. It's admirable."

Robespierre gestured to the empty chair. "Please, sit. Dedication is required in times such as these."

Étienne took the seat, setting his cup down carefully. "I must agree. The state of our nation weighs heavily on many minds."

"More should feel as we do," Robespierre remarked, his gaze piercing yet earnest. "Change is imperative, but complacency hinders progress."

"Complacency and ignorance," Étienne added. "But perhaps we can awaken the people with the right guidance," Étienne said.

Robespierre studied him thoughtfully. "You speak with conviction. Tell me, what has led you to these conclusions?"

Étienne chose his words with care. "Observations, mostly. The disparity between the classes grows ever wider. The suffering of the many to uphold the luxuries of the few is unsustainable."

"A truth that some refuse to see," Robespierre said, a hint of bitterness in his tone.

"Wilful blindness," Étienne agreed. "But I believe we can illuminate these injustices through concerted effort."

Robespierre nodded slowly. "Your insights are refreshing. Have you considered taking a more active role in our cause?"

"I have," Étienne replied, allowing a note of earnestness to enter his voice. "I was hoping to discuss how I might contribute more directly."

"Excellent," Robespierre said, a rare smile touching his lips. "We are organising a meeting after the new year. A gathering of those committed to enacting genuine change. Your presence would be most welcome."

"I am honoured," Étienne said sincerely. "Please, keep me informed of the details."

"Of course," Robespierre affirmed. He hesitated briefly before continuing. "Forgive me, but I recall hearing that you come from a noble lineage?"

Étienne inclined his head. "That is correct. Though my family's fortunes have waned, I cannot in good conscience ignore the plight of those less fortunate."

Robespierre regarded him with a measured gaze. "It is uncommon for someone of your background to empathise so deeply with the common people."

"Perhaps it is because I have witnessed both sides," Étienne suggested. "I see the flaws within our current system, and I believe reform is not only necessary but inevitable."

"Wise words," Robespierre conceded. "We need more allies who understand the intricacies of the structures we aim to transform."

"Then consider me at your service," Étienne said, extending his hand.

Robespierre shook it firmly. "Together, we may steer France towards a more just future."

As they delved deeper into conversation, discussing philosophies and potential strategies, Étienne subtly guided the dialogue, probing for insights into Robespierre's plans and associates. He learned of upcoming pamphlets, rallies, and the influential figures who would be pivotal in the months ahead.

After some time, Robespierre glanced at the clock on the wall. "I must take my leave," he said, gathering his papers. "There is much to prepare."

"Allow me to accompany you," Étienne offered. "It's on my way."

"Very well," Robespierre agreed.

They stepped out into the biting cold, and the sky released a delicate snowfall. The streets glistened under the lantern light, and a calm serenity settled over the city.

"You mentioned earlier the importance of awakening the people," Robespierre said as they walked. "How would you propose we achieve this on a broader scale?"

Étienne considered his response. "Through a unified message disseminated across multiple platforms—print, speeches, and perhaps even art. Reaching people in ways that resonate personally."

"An ambitious undertaking," Robespierre mused. "But not without merit."

"I believe we underestimate the power of collective storytelling," Étienne continued. "If we can frame our cause within narratives people connect with, we can inspire action."

Robespierre glanced at him appreciatively. "Your perspectives are valuable. I look forward to exploring these ideas further."

They parted ways at a crossroads, with promises to meet again soon. As Robespierre disappeared into the swirling snow, Étienne felt a surge of triumph. They had completed the first step.

He turned down a side street, allowing the quiet of the evening to envelop him. The faint sounds of the city—a distant carriage, muffled laughter from a nearby tavern—created a backdrop to his thoughts.

Étienne knew that gaining Robespierre's trust was crucial. The man was principled, perhaps to a fault, and his influence among the revolutionaries was significant. By positioning himself as an indispensable ally, Étienne could steer the movement in ways that served his ambitions.

He wandered towards the Seine, the river's dark waters reflecting the glimmer of the few stars visible through the clouded sky. Leaning against the stone parapet of a bridge, he contemplated the path ahead.

He thought to himself, "People seldom give power." He thought, "One must take power."

His mind drifted to the others—Danton's charisma, Desmoulins's fiery rhetoric, Marat's relentless agitation. Each played a role and could be a stepping stone or an obstacle. Navigating these dynamics required finesse.

A voice interrupted his reverie. "Beautiful evening, is it not?"

Étienne turned to see a man standing nearby, cloaked and with a hat pulled low. His features were obscured, but his posture relaxed.

"Indeed," Étienne replied cautiously. "Though cold for idle musings."

The man chuckled softly. "True enough. But sometimes, the quiet moments offer the clearest insights."

"Perhaps," Étienne allowed. "Do we know one another?"

"Not yet," the stranger said, stepping closer. "But we share common interests."

Étienne's gaze sharpened. "Is that so?"

"Word travels swiftly in certain circles," the man continued. "Your name has come up more than once."

"And who, may I ask, are you?"

"An observer," he replied cryptically. "One who appreciates the value of discretion."

Étienne assessed him silently. "If you have something to say, I suggest you say it plainly."

The man nodded. "Very well. Some believe the revolution requires a… firmer hand. Individuals capable of making tough decisions for the greater good."

"And you think I am such an individual?"

"Possibly," the stranger said. "Consider this a friendly overture. Opportunities may present themselves soon."

Before Étienne could respond, the man tipped his hat and melted back into the shadows.

Étienne remained on the bridge, the encounter replaying in his mind. The web was more comprehensive than he had expected, with threads intersecting unexpectedly.

"Intriguing," he whispered. "More pieces to the puzzle."

He resumed his walk, a renewed determination propelling him forward. The city unfolded before him, a complex mixture of ambition, desperation, and possibility.

Returning to his apartment, Étienne lit a fire in the hearth, the warmth seeping into his bones. He sat at his desk, quill poised over a fresh sheet of parchment.

He wrote, sketching out a framework of alliances, potential leverage points, and contingency plans. Names filled the page—Robespierre, Danton, Desmoulins, Marat—all orbiting around his central aim.

"The first steps toward manipulation," he noted, the words stark against the parchment.

He paused, gazing into the dancing flames. Doubt flickered at the edges of his consciousness, but he dismissed it. The world was changing, and he intended to shape that change to his advantage.

As the night deepened, Étienne secured his notes in a hidden compartment. He extinguished the lamps, leaving only the glow of the fire to cast shadows across the room.

"Let the revolution come," he whispered into the darkness. "I will be ready."

Outside, the snow continued to fall, blanketing Paris in a silent shroud. But beneath the surface, the city stirred with the rumblings of upheaval, and Étienne Corbeau stood poised to seize whatever opportunities arose from the chaos.

CHAPTER TWO: (1789)

BASTILLE'S BREACH

The oppressive heat of 10 July 1789 hung heavily over Paris, turning the city's narrow streets into winding ovens. A few years had passed, and Étienne Corbeau stood at the edge of the Place de Grève, the sun casting sharp shadows across his angular features. Sweat beaded on his brow beneath the brim of his hat, but he remained motionless, eyes fixed on the gathering crowd. Merchants, labourers, and artisans mingled restlessly, their faces etched with anger and desperation.

The clamour of voices rose like a swelling tide, fragments of conversation reaching his ears.

"Did you hear? Necker has been dismissed!"

"More soldiers arrive each day. The King plots against us!"

"Our children starve while the aristocrats feast!"

Étienne allowed himself a subtle smile. The city's discontent had intensified since his last foray among the common folk. The dismissal of Jacques Necker, the popular finance minister, had ignited a spark that now threatened to become an inferno. Tension crackled in the air, ripe for exploitation.

He adjusted his coat's delicate but understated fabric and wove through the crowd. His movements were deliberate, his posture unassuming. To the untrained eye, he appeared just another concerned citizen caught in uncertainty.

A familiar voice called out amidst the din. "Étienne! Over here!"

He turned to see Camille Desmoulins perched atop a makeshift platform—a barrel overturned near the entrance of a tavern. With dark curls clinging to his damp forehead, Desmoulins' eyes shone with intensity.

"Citoyens!" Desmoulins shouted, waving a pamphlet above his head. "Will you stand idly by while tyranny tightens its grip?"

The crowd roared in response, a cacophony of agreement and anger.

Étienne moved closer, positioning himself at the front. Desmoulins caught his eye and gave a slight nod before continuing. "Necker's dismissal is a declaration of war against the people! We must arm ourselves, defend our rights!"

"To arms!" someone shouted, echoed by others until the chant filled the square.

Étienne joined in, his voice measured but firm. "To arms!"

Beside him, a burly man with soot-streaked cheeks turned and clasped his shoulder. "We march for justice, Monsieur!"

"Indeed," Étienne replied, meeting the man's gaze. "The time for action has come."

Desmoulins leapt down from his perch, pushing through the crowd to reach Étienne. "Can you feel it?" he exclaimed breathlessly. "The city awakens!"

"It's impossible to ignore," Étienne agreed. "Your words have a remarkable effect."

Desmoulins grinned. "Passion ignites passion. But we need more than words now."

"Agreed," Étienne said thoughtfully. "Have you considered our next steps?"

"We gather at the Palais-Royal this evening," Desmoulins said. "Danton and others will be there. Join us."

"I wouldn't miss it," Étienne replied.

Étienne, flanked by a cluster of excited supporters, lingered and gracefully whisked Desmoulins away. The man's influence among the masses was undeniable—a valuable asset in the tumult to come.

He felt a presence beside him. Turning, he found himself face to face with Jean-Paul Marat, the radical journalist known for his incendiary writings. Marat's piercing eyes studied him with keen interest.

"Monsieur Corbeau," Marat rasped, his voice roughened by years of impassioned oration. "You move comfortably among these people."

"I seek understanding," Étienne replied evenly. "One cannot grasp the nation's pulse from the confines of a parlour."

Marat's lips twisted into a sardonic smile. "Understanding or opportunity?"

Étienne met his gaze steadily. "Perhaps both. The lines blur in times like these."

"Indeed, they do," Marat acknowledged. "Be wary. The tides can turn swiftly."

"I appreciate the counsel," Étienne said. "Your writings have illuminated much that was obscured," Étienne expressed his appreciation for the counsel.

Marat inclined his head slightly. "Information is power. Use it wisely."

The journalist melted into the crowd, leaving Étienne to ponder the encounter. Marat was a figure to approach cautiously—his influence was substantial, but his suspicions ran deep.

As the crowd dispersed, carried by agitation towards new epicentres of unrest, Étienne navigated the winding streets towards the Tuileries. The air was thick with the mingled scents of unwashed bodies, roasting meat from street vendors, and the ever-present undertone of refuse. Snatches of conversation floated past him.

"They say the Bastille holds caches of weapons."

"Troops gather outside the city—mercenaries!"

"*Liberté!* We must fight for our *liberté!*"

Étienne's mind churned. The volatile environment presented a rare convergence of factors—mass discontent, weak leadership, and the rise of influential voices like Desmoulins and Marat. It was a crucible in which he could forge his path to power.

He recalled his recent discussions with Maximilien Robespierre. The man had unwavering principles, but his idealism could be influenced. If Étienne could insinuate himself deeper into Robespierre's confidence, he might steer the course of events from within.

Lost in thought, he nearly collided with a young woman hurrying in the opposite direction. Papers spilt from her grasp, fluttering to the ground.

"Pardonnez-moi," Étienne said, bending to help gather the scattered sheets.

"Thank you," Olympe de Gouges replied, her voice tinged with urgency. Her eyes were bright, framed by wisps of chestnut hair that escaped her bonnet.

He glanced at the papers—pamphlets emblazoned with bold headings calling for equality and the abolition of feudal privileges.

"Important work," he noted, handing them back.

She studied him for a moment. "Every hand helps in spreading the message."

Étienne regarded Olympe with a thoughtful expression. "Olympe, it's good to see you."

She smiled, her features softening. "Étienne, always a pleasure."

He raised an eyebrow. "Still writing those fiery pamphlets?"

"Among other things," she replied, her eyes gleaming with determination. "And you, *Monsieur* Corbeau? Do you lend your voice to the cause as passionately as before?"

"I strive to," Étienne admitted. "Though I fear I lack your eloquence."

"Then perhaps action is your forte," she suggested. "There is much to be done."

"Perhaps we might collaborate," he proposed. "Our goals seem aligned."

Olympe considered him for a moment, her smile fading into a more guarded expression. "Perhaps. But I must attend to other matters now."

"Of course," he nodded. "Until we meet again."

She offered a brief nod before slipping back into the bustling crowd, leaving Étienne with a renewed sense of purpose.

Étienne watched her go, the weight of their conversation lingering in his mind. The Revolution demanded both words and deeds, and aligning with Olympe could amplify their efforts to reshape society. He felt a surge of determination, knowing that their combined strengths could make a significant impact.

Arriving at the grand gardens of the Palais-Royal, he found the area teeming with people. People had erected makeshift stages, and speakers addressed clusters of citizens. The atmosphere was electric, charged with the possibility of imminent upheaval.

He spotted Georges Danton amidst a sea of faces. The man's towering stature and booming voice were unmistakable. Danton was rallying a group of men, and his rhetoric was fiery and direct.

"Will you be slaves in your land?" Danton bellowed. "Or will you rise and claim the freedom that is your birthright?"

The crowd roared in response.

Étienne edged closer, positioning himself within earshot but not directly engaging. He needed to observe to assess the dynamics at play.

Desmoulins appeared at Danton's side, his energy complementing the more prominent man's forceful presence. Together, they were a potent combination.

"Étienne!" Desmoulins called out upon noticing him. "Join us!"

He obliged, stepping forward. "An impressive gathering," he remarked.

"These are the men who will shape history," Danton declared.

"With guidance and purpose," Étienne added.

Danton eyed him appraisingly. "Purpose we have. Guidance we can always use more of."

"Then perhaps I can be of service," Étienne offered.

Desmoulins clapped him on the back. "I knew you were the right man to have here."

As the evening unfolded, Étienne engaged with the revolutionaries, carefully projecting earnest commitment while subtly steering conversations. He emphasised the need for strategic planning, the importance of unity, and the potential pitfalls of uncontrolled aggression.

Inwardly, he calculated his moves. The city was a tinderbox; all it needed was a spark. By aligning himself with key figures and feigning solidarity, he positioned himself to influence events.

As darkness settled, punctuated by the flicker of torches and the hum of restless voices, Étienne felt a surge of anticipation.

"10 July 1789," he thought. "The tensions ignite, and so does my opportunity."

He gazed out over the assembled masses, the faces of men and women alight with hope, anger, and determination. They sought a new order, a redefinition of their world—and he intended to shape it to his design.

• • •

The morning of 14 July 1789 dawned under a sky streaked with ominous clouds, the air thick with anticipation. Étienne Corbeau stood at the window of his modest apartment overlooking the Rue Saint-Antoine, the distant silhouette of the Bastille fortress etched against the horizon. The medieval prison loomed like a sentinel over Paris, its stone walls bearing witness to centuries of secrets and despair.

He sipped his coffee thoughtfully, observing the restless stirrings of the city below. Groups of men moved with purpose, their expressions grim and resolute. The news of the King's dismissal of Necker had spread like wildfire, igniting the volatile atmosphere. Rumours of royal troops poised to assault the populace fuelled a collective anxiety that teetered on the edge of the eruption.

After he set his cup down and put on his coat, Étienne made sure to securely tuck the small notebook he always carried into his pocket. He descended the narrow staircase and stepped into the street, the murmur of voices swelling around him. Vendors shouted half-hearted about their wares, but few purchased; the day held more pressing matters.

As he made his way towards the Bastille, the crowd thickened. Men armed with makeshift weapons—pikes fashioned from broom handles, swords rusted but sharp—pressed forward. Women and children followed, some carrying stones and others watching with wide eyes.

A familiar voice called out from the crowd. "Étienne! Over here!"

He turned to see Georges Danton pushing through the mass of bodies, his formidable stature and booming voice carving a path. Flush spread across Danton's face, and hunger blazed in his eyes.

"Georges," Étienne greeted him, clasping his outstretched hand. "It seems the entire city has converged here."

"And with good reason," Danton replied. "The Bastille is a symbol of tyranny. Its fall will herald a new era."

"Do you truly believe an assault will succeed?" Étienne inquired, his tone measured.

Danton grinned wolfishly and declared, "The people are united, and their anger is powerful. "

"Anger without strategy can be perilous," Étienne cautioned.

"Ever the pragmatist," Danton chuckled. "But sometimes, my friend, a spark is needed to ignite the flame."

Étienne nodded thoughtfully. "Perhaps you're right."

A surge of movement rippled through the crowd as shouts erupted from the front lines. Étienne craned his neck to see over the sea of heads. The gates of the Bastille remained closed, and the soldiers atop the battlements appeared as dark silhouettes against the grey sky.

"Look there," Danton pointed. "Delegates approach to negotiate."

Indeed, a small group had broken away, approaching the fortress under a hastily constructed white flag. Étienne recognised among them the Marquis de Lafayette, his posture erect, his uniform immaculate despite the chaos.

"Do you think the governor will capitulate?" Étienne asked.

Danton snorted. "De Launay is a stubborn fool. He underestimates the resolve of the people."

Gunfire suddenly cracked through the air, the sharp report silencing the murmurs. Screams followed as smoke curled from the ramparts.

"They're firing on us!" someone shouted.

Panic threatened to overtake the crowd, but Danton's voice boomed above the din. "Stand firm! Do not falter!"

Étienne felt the tide shift, fear transforming into rage. The crowd pressed forward with renewed vigour, the cacophony of voices rising to a fever pitch.

Beside him, a young man clutched a musket tightly, his hands trembling. "I didn't sign up for this," he muttered.

"Steady yourself," Étienne advised, placing a firm hand on the youth's shoulder. "Courage will see you through."

The ground beneath them seemed to vibrate as cannon fire erupted from the revolutionary side, the roar echoing off the stone walls. Étienne watched as the first breaches appeared, stones crumbling under the relentless assault.

"She's falling!" Danton exulted. "The Bastille is ours!"

Étienne allowed a thin smile. The spectacle unfolded before him like a grand theatre, each act bringing him closer to his aim. The fall of the Bastille would send shockwaves throughout France, destabilising the old order and creating a vacuum ripe for manipulation.

Amidst the chaos, he caught sight of Camille Desmoulins darting through the crowd, his green coat flaring behind him. Desmoulins's face was a mixture of exhilaration and grim determination.

"Étienne!" Desmoulins called out breathlessly as he reached them. "We need more men at the western gate. Can you rally support?"

"Consider it done," Étienne replied without hesitation.

He moved swiftly, his voice cutting through the tumult as he called upon those around him. "To the western gate! Follow me!"

A contingent of men fell in behind him, their expressions a blend of fear and fierce resolve. As they navigated the perimeter of the fortress, Étienne's mind raced. Every action and decision was a step further into the intricate dance of revolution. He positioned himself as a leader to solidify his standing among the insurgents.

Reaching the western gate, they found a knot of defenders holding the line. Étienne assessed the situation quickly. "We need to flank them," he directed. "Half of you circle to the left; the rest with me on the right."

They moved to obey, encouraged by his confidence. The clash that followed was brutal and swift. Étienne fought with calculated efficiency, his movements precise. Amidst the cries and the smoke, he felt a detached clarity—a sense of purpose sharpened by the immediacy of danger.

The defenders faltered, and a triumphant roar surged from the attackers as the gate gave way. Étienne stepped back, allowing others to surge forward—blood-stained the cobblestones, mingling with the grime of the city.

He surveyed the scene, noting the critical figures amidst the fray. Danton rallied groups to secure the fortress, his voice hoarse but unyielding. Desmoulins scribbled furiously in a notebook, capturing the moment for posterity. Marat observed from a distance, his eyes calculating.

A bell tolled in the distance, its sombre tones a counterpoint to the crowd's delight. The Bastille had fallen.

He knew that this victory would not quell the unrest, but amplify it. The monarchy would face the impact of turmoil, and the nobility would experience disturbance. In the ensuing crisis, opportunities would abound for those astute enough to seize them.

As the sun waned, casting long shadows over the ravaged fortress, Étienne passed through the jubilant masses. He encountered Olympe de Gouges, whose face flushed with emotion.

"Did you see?" she exclaimed. "The people have spoken!"

"An extraordinary day," he agreed.

"This is but the beginning," she declared. "In the new order, we guarantee the recognition of the rights of all," she stated.

"Indeed," Étienne said. "Your voice will be crucial in shaping what comes next."

She regarded him thoughtfully. "And yours as well, Monsieur Corbeau. Do not underestimate the power you wield."

He inclined his head. "I shall endeavour to use it wisely."

They parted ways, and Étienne continued towards the edge of the crowd. The surrounding euphoria was palpable, but he remained inwardly detached.

He found a quiet corner near a damaged carriage, its wheel shattered. Sitting upon it, he pulled out his notebook and jotted down observations. Names, actions, alliances—each detail could prove valuable.

"Étienne," a voice interrupted his thoughts.

He looked up to see Maximilien Robespierre standing before him, his expression solemn. "Maximilien," Étienne greeted him. "A momentous day."

"One that carries great responsibility," Robespierre replied. "The path ahead is fraught with challenges."

"All the more reason to proceed with care," Étienne said. "But also with conviction."

Robespierre nodded. "I have been observing you. Your influence among the people grows."

"I merely act where I am needed," Étienne demurred.

"Humility is a virtue," Robespierre noted. "But do not hide your light. We will need powerful leaders in the days to come."

"I am at the service of the cause," Étienne assured him.

"Good," Robespierre said. "We should speak further. There is much to discuss."

"Name the time and place," Étienne replied.

"I shall send word," Robespierre promised before moving on.

As darkness settled over Paris, punctuated by the glow of torches and the distant strains of song, Étienne stood and pocketed his notebook. The storming of the Bastille was not merely a historical event; it was a catalyst, a doorway to possibilities he had long expected.

He walked away from the fortress's remnants, blending into the tapestry of revolutionaries and citizens. His path was clear, his resolve unwavering.

"Chaos breeds opportunity," he thought. "And I am poised to harness it."

Thus, amidst the jubilation and the uncertainty, Étienne Corbeau stepped further into the labyrinth of revolution, his sights set firmly on the power within its depths.

• • •

The morning of 16 July 1789 broke with a calm serenity that belied the tumultuous events of days prior. Paris stirred cautiously under a pale sky, the air crisp with a hint of lingering smoke from scattered fires now extinguished. Étienne Corbeau navigated the maze of streets towards the Café Procope, his boots echoing softly against the cobblestones still damp from an early drizzle.

The café, renowned as a hub for intellectuals and revolutionaries alike, exuded an inviting warmth as he entered. A combination of the rich aroma of freshly brewed coffee and the scent of aged wood and parchment filled the air. Diners huddled around gleaming tables, their low conversations a mosaic of clandestine murmurs and impassioned discussions.

Étienne spotted Maximilien Robespierre seated near a window overlooking the bustling Rue de l'Ancienne Comédie. Sunlight filtered through the glass, casting delicate patterns upon the papers strewn across the table before him. Robespierre's attire was meticulously neat, his dark coat contrasting with his powdered wig and the crisp white of his cravat.

"Maximilien," Étienne greeted, approaching with a measured smile. "May I join you?"

Robespierre looked up, his sharp blue eyes reflecting a mix of surprise and friendship. "Étienne Corbeau. Please, have a seat."

Étienne settled into the chair opposite, noting the intensity etched upon Robespierre's features. "It seems the city is still catching its breath after the storming of the Bastille."

"An event that shall reverberate through history," Robespierre replied solemnly. "We can no longer ignore the people's voice," Robespierre declared.

"Indeed," Étienne agreed. "But with such monumental change comes the question: what path do we tread next?"

Robespierre sipped his coffee thoughtfully. "We must steer the revolution towards establishing true liberty and justice. The National Assembly must enact reforms that reflect the general will."

"A noble aspiration," Étienne remarked. "However, I wonder if the Assembly, composed largely of those clinging to remnants of the old order, is capable of such transformation."

Robespierre regarded him carefully. "You doubt their commitment?"

"I question their resolve," Étienne clarified. "Many speak of change, yet hesitate when faced with the sacrifices it entails."

Robespierre nodded slowly. "Your scepticism is not unfounded. Some would temper the revolution to preserve their interests."

"Precisely," Étienne said. "Which is why voices like yours are essential in guiding the movement."

A faint flush coloured Robespierre's cheeks. "I am but one among many."

"One whose principles inspire others," Étienne countered. "But principles alone may not suffice. One who inspires others with their principles," Étienne countered. "But principles alone may not suffice. We must consider practical measures to ensure we do not impede progress."

"What do you propose?" Robespierre asked, his gaze unwavering.

Étienne leaned forward slightly. "We should merge influence within the Assembly by aligning with those genuinely committed to radical reform. Apply pressure where necessary to marginalise obstructive elements."

"Such tactics tread a fine line," Robespierre cautioned. "We must avoid descending into the very tyranny we oppose."

"True," Étienne conceded. "Yet, allowing adversaries to sabotage our efforts poses a greater risk. Firm action now could prevent bloodshed later."

Tapping his fingers lightly against the table, Robespierre declared, "I strive to uphold justice above all. We base any measures we take on virtue."

"Of course," Étienne assured him. "But consider this: if the revolution falters because of hesitation, the people may lose faith, leading to chaos. A decisive approach could preserve the integrity of our cause."

Robespierre's eyes flickered with contemplation. "You make compelling points."

Before he could respond further, a figure approached their table. It was Jacques-Louis David, the renowned painter, his hands stained with traces of charcoal. "Gentlemen," David greeted, inclining his head. "I hope I'm not intruding."

"Not at all," Robespierre said. "Join us."

"I wanted to share sketches from yesterday's assembly," David explained, producing a portfolio. "Capturing the spirit of the revolution through art is my contribution."

He displayed many sketches capturing enthusiastic crowds, passionate speeches, and symbolic acts of togetherness.

"Remarkable," Étienne praised, examining the detailed strokes. "Your work conveys the emotion of the moment profoundly."

"Art speaks where words falter," David replied modestly. "It's imperative that we document these times accurately."

"Agreed," Robespierre affirmed. "The visual representation of our struggle can inspire and educate."

David shifted his attention to Étienne and said, "I don't believe we have formally met."

"Étienne Corbeau," he said, extending his hand. "An associate of Maximilien's."

"Jacques-Louis David," the painter responded, shaking his hand. "A pleasure."

As they delved into a discussion about the role of art in revolution, Étienne deftly steered the conversation back to strategy. "Jacques-Louis, your depictions could also rally support. Imagine disseminating engravings of these scenes among the populace."

"An excellent idea," David agreed. "Visual propaganda, in a sense."

"Precisely," Étienne said. "We must utilise every medium to fortify the movement."

Robespierre glanced between them. "While I appreciate the enthusiasm, we ensure such efforts remain truthful and ethical."

"Of course," Étienne assured him. "We intend to enlighten, not deceive."

David gathered his sketches. "I shall consider ways to reproduce these works for wider distribution. If you'll excuse me, I must return to my studio."

"Thank you for sharing your vision," Robespierre said warmly.

As David departed, Étienne seized the moment. "Maximilien, I sense some reluctance to embrace the measures fully. Perhaps it's time to expand our circle—to include those willing to act decisively."

Robespierre regarded him pensively. "Morality must guide change. I will not condone actions that compromise our ethical foundations."

"I understand," Étienne replied. "But remember, we should acknowledge that inaction can be just as damaging as misguided action. We are on a dangerous path and sometimes must make hard decisions."

"You speak as a pragmatist," Robespierre observed.

"I speak as someone who desires the success of our revolution," Étienne said earnestly. "And I believe you are the key to that success."

Robespierre sighed softly. "The weight of responsibility grows heavier each day."

"Allow me to help shoulder that burden," Étienne offered. "Together, we can navigate these challenges."

A moment of silence hung between them, the ambient chatter of the café fading into the background. Finally, Robespierre nodded. "Very well. I welcome your counsel."

Étienne allowed himself an inward smile. "Thank you. I shall endeavour to prove worthy of your trust."

They spent the next hour discussing plans for upcoming assemblies, mobilising support within various districts, and drafting proposals to present to the Assembly. Étienne carefully interwove his suggestions, subtly encouraging more assertive actions while appearing to prioritise Robespierre's ideals.

As they concluded their meeting, Robespierre rose. "I must attend to matters at the Assembly. Your insights have been most helpful."

"I'm glad to be of help," Étienne replied, standing as well. "Shall we reconvene in a few days?"

"Yes," Robespierre agreed. "I'll send word."

They parted ways outside the café, Robespierre heading towards the grandeur of the Palais Bourbon, while Étienne remained on the bustling street. The city thrummed with renewed energy, the air alive with the scent of possibility and the distant strains of a street musician's melody.

Étienne began wandering, his mind orchestrating the following movements in his intricate game. He had planted the seeds of influence within Robespierre's mind; now, patience and precision were required to cultivate them.

He found himself near the Seine, the river's steady flow mirroring his contemplative state. Leaning against the stone railing, he watched a barge drift lazily downstream, its solitary occupant silhouetted against the afternoon light.

"Étienne!" a voice called out.

He turned to see Camille Desmoulins approaching, his ever-present notebook tucked under one arm. "Camille," Étienne greeted. "Out gathering inspiration?"

"Always," Desmoulins laughed. "The city is a wellspring of stories these days."

"That it is," Étienne agreed.

Desmoulins joined him at the railing. "I heard you met with Robespierre earlier."

"Word travels fast," Étienne remarked.

"Newsworthy figures attract attention," Desmoulins teased. "How did it go?"

"Productive," Étienne said. "We're aligning our efforts to strengthen the revolution's direction."

"Excellent," Desmoulins said. "Maximilien is a man of unwavering principle, but sometimes he needs a nudge towards practicality."

"Precisely my aim," Étienne replied. "We must balance ideals with actionable plans."

Desmoulins tapped his notebook thoughtfully. "Perhaps we should collaborate on some pamphlets—articulate our vision to the masses."

"A splendid idea," Étienne said. "Communication is key."

"Then it's settled," Desmoulins declared. "We'll meet tomorrow to begin."

As Desmoulins departed with a jaunty wave, Étienne felt a surge of satisfaction. He was weaving himself deeper into the fabric of the revolution, positioning himself as an indispensable asset to its leading figures.

The sun cast long shadows as it dipped towards the horizon, gilding the city's rooftops with a golden hue. Étienne resumed his stroll, the weight of his ambitions lightened by the progress. "16 July 1789," he mused aloud. "The manipulator sets his pieces."

He knew the path ahead would require deft manoeuvring. The revolution was a living entity, unpredictable and volatile, but within its chaos lay the opportunity for ascent.

As twilight settled over Paris, Étienne returned to his apartment. He lit a candle, the flame illuminating the room with a warm glow. Seating himself at his desk, he began drafting letters and notes, his pen gliding smoothly across the paper.

Each word became a stride ahead, each plan woven into the complex fabric of his creation.

He reminded himself, through a whisper, that power is not given. "Take power," he whispered to himself.

With steadfast resolve, Étienne Corbeau embraced his role, the manipulator amidst the maelstrom, determined to shape the revolution—and his destiny—with calculated precision.

• • •

The midsummer heat weighed heavily upon Paris on 20 July 1789, the air thick with anticipation and the scent of change. Étienne Corbeau stood beneath the shade of a chestnut tree in the *Jardin des Tuileries*, observing the ebb and flow of people through the park's gravel paths. Clusters of citizens gathered in animated discussion, their voices a murmur of dissent and hope. As the revolution gained momentum, unity fractured.

"Factions are forming," Étienne muttered, a wry smile curling his lips. "Perfect."

He turned his gaze towards the sound of a familiar hearty laugh. Georges Danton emerged from a gathering, his imposing frame and ruddy complexion making him a beacon amidst the crowd. Danton's eyes gleamed with mischief and conviction, his deep voice carrying as he regaled those around him with tales of defiance.

"Georges," Étienne called out, approaching with measured strides.

Danton looked up, his expression brightening. "Étienne Corbeau! Just the man I wished to see." He extended a hand, his grip firm and warm.

"And why is that?" Étienne inquired, arching an eyebrow.

"Because you have a knack for seeing through the fog," Danton replied. "These are turbulent times and rational minds are in short supply."

Étienne chuckled softly. "Flattery will get you everywhere, my friend."

"Come, walk with me," Danton suggested, gesturing towards a less crowded path.

They strolled beneath the canopy of trees, the city's din fading slightly. "Tell me, Georges," Étienne began, "what do you make of the divisions emerging among our compatriots?"

Danton sighed, his pleasant demeanour tempered by concern. "It's inevitable, I suppose. When the old structures crumble, people scramble to shape the new order to their liking. The moderates wish for gentle reforms, the radicals for complete upheaval."

"And where do you position yourself?" Étienne probed.

"I am a man of the people," Danton declared. "I believe in swift action to dismantle tyranny, but with an eye towards stability. France must not descend into chaos."

"A delicate balance," Étienne mused. "One that requires careful navigation."

"Your voice is exactly what we need," Danton said, casting a sidelong glance. "You've a way of mediating between extremes."

Étienne inclined his head modestly. "I strive to understand all perspectives."

Danton halted, turning to face him fully. "Between you, me, and Maximilien, we could steer this revolution towards a future that benefits all."

"Maximilien Robespierre is a man of unyielding principles," Étienne noted. "His dedication is admirable, but sometimes inflexible."

"True," Danton agreed. "He often sees the world in stark contrasts—right and wrong, justice and injustice."

Étienne proposed that they could offer some nuances, alluding to a touch of irony in his voice.

Danton laughed heartily. "Indeed! Though I suspect he would balk at the notion."

They resumed walking; the conversation turning to the practicalities of rallying support. Étienne listened attentively as Danton outlined plans to engage the working-class districts, recognising the man's deep connection with the common people.

"You have a gift for inspiring others," Étienne remarked. "Your oratory moves hearts and minds."

Danton waved a dismissive hand. "A loud voice and a bit of theatrics, that's all."

"Don't underestimate your influence," Étienne cautioned. "In these times, leadership can emerge from the most unexpected places."

As they exited the garden onto a bustling street, they encountered a procession of women marching resolutely, banners aloft bearing slogans demanding bread and fair wages.

"Les femmes prennent position," Étienne observed.

"About time," Danton said appreciatively. "Their voices add weight to our cause."

Among the procession, Étienne spotted Olympe de Gouges, her eyes fierce, leading the chant. She caught his gaze and offered a brief nod of acknowledgement.

"Formidable woman," Danton commented. "She won't rest until equality extends to all."

"Another ally worth cultivating," Étienne noted.

Danton raised an eyebrow. "Ever the strategist, aren't you?"

Étienne smiled enigmatically. "Merely observant."

They parted ways shortly after, Danton heading towards the Cordeliers District to address a gathering, while Étienne made his way to a nearby café frequented by members of the Jacobin Club. The establishment buzzed with animated discourse, the air thick with the aroma of coffee and the undercurrents of ambition.

Maximilien Robespierre sat at a corner table, engrossed in writing. Étienne approached, his footsteps soft against the tiled floor.

"Mind if I join you?" he asked.

Robespierre looked up, momentarily startled. "Étienne, of course."

Taking a seat, Étienne glanced at the parchment. "Drafting your next speech?"

"Refining some proposals for the Assembly," Robespierre replied, setting down his quill. "The challenge lies in uniting our increasingly divergent factions."

"Unity seems a scarce commodity these days," Étienne remarked.

"Yet essential," Robespierre insisted. "Without it, the revolution risks collapse."

"Perhaps we need to embrace the diversity of thought," Étienne suggested. "Use it to strengthen our strategies rather than viewing it as an obstacle."

Robespierre considered this. "There's merit in that. However, certain elements push agendas that could lead us astray."

"You're referring to the more radical voices?"

"Precisely," Robespierre affirmed. "Their methods border on anarchy."

"Then perhaps we should engage them directly," Étienne proposed. "Understand their motivations, find common ground."

Robespierre sighed. "It's a daunting task."

"One we can handle," Étienne assured him. "Between your principles and Danton's charisma, we can bridge the gaps."

A flicker of hesitation crossed Robespierre's face. "Danton is… pragmatic, sometimes excessively so."

"Pragmatism has its place," Étienne countered gently. "As does idealism. Balance is key."

Robespierre offered a faint smile. "You always find the middle path."

"Merely seeking the best course forward," Étienne replied.

Their conversation continued, delving into plans for upcoming assemblies and the need to address the populace's immediate concerns—food shortages, unemployment, and the looming threat of foreign intervention.

As the afternoon waned, Robespierre excused himself to attend a committee meeting. Étienne remained, ordering a glass of wine and reflecting on the intricate web he was weaving. Balancing relationships with various leaders required finesse, but the rewards were substantial.

A slender man with piercing eyes and a sharp nose approached him. "Monsieur Corbeau?"

"Yes?"

"Jean-Paul Marat," the man introduced himself, extending a hand.

"Ah, the esteemed journalist," Étienne said, shaking his hand. "Your publications have stirred quite the response."

Marat's gaze was intense. "That is the intent. France must awaken to the realities that plague her."

"Agreed," Étienne concurred. "How can I assist you?"

"I've heard of your connections with both Robespierre and Danton," Marat said bluntly. "I seek to understand where you stand amidst the emerging factions."

Étienne met his stare evenly. "I stand with the revolution."

"A diplomatic answer," Marat remarked dryly.

"An honest one," Étienne insisted. "My goal is to facilitate collaboration among our leaders."

Marat folded his arms. "Be cautious. Aligning with too many sides can lead to mistrust."

"To achieve our goal—a just and fair France," Étienne emphasised the importance of maintaining transparency.

Marat studied him for a moment before nodding. "Very well. Perhaps we shall speak again."

"Until then," Étienne said, watching as Marat departed.

The encounter left him pensive. Marat's warning was clear, but Étienne was confident in his ability to navigate the complexities. He orchestrated his alliances with careful consideration, each one serving a purpose in his overarching plan.

As evening settled over Paris, casting long shadows and igniting the sky with hues of amber and rose, Étienne stepped out onto the street. The city's pulse thrummed beneath his feet, a living entity teetering on the edge of transformation.

He made his way along the Seine; the river reflecting the twilight glow. Thoughts of his estranged family flickered briefly in his mind—Cécile, Henri, and Sophie—but he brushed them aside. Personal ties were a distraction he could ill afford.

Approaching the Pont Neuf, he encountered a group of Sans-culottes engaged in a heated debate. One of them recognised him.

"Monsieur Corbeau! What news from the Assembly?"

"Progress is being made," Étienne assured them. "But your voices must continue to be heard."

"Too many promises, not enough action," a man grumbled.

"Change takes time," Étienne reasoned. "But we are working tirelessly on your behalf."

They regarded him with a mix of scepticism and hope. "We'll hold you to that," another said.

"I would expect nothing less," Étienne replied with a reassuring smile.

Continuing on, he reflected on the encounter. The people's trust was fragile, easily swayed by whispers and unmet expectations. He needed to ensure that their support remained steadfast.

As he reached his lodgings, the first stars pierced the velvet sky. Étienne paused at the door, casting a last glance at the city enveloped in the night.

"Balancing on a knife's edge," he thought. "But balance is where I thrive."

Entering the quiet solitude of his apartment, he lit a candle and seated himself at his desk. Maps, letters, and notes sprawled before him—a testament to his meticulous planning.

He picked up his quill and wrote, his script fluid and precise. Letters to allies, proposals for initiatives, and reflections on the day's events flowed onto the parchment.

"Factions may form," he wrote, "but within division lies opportunity."

He sealed the documents, his course set. Étienne Corbeau was a man adept at walking the fine line between conflicting interests, his influence growing with each calculated move.

The revolution's path was uncertain, fraught with peril and possibility. But amidst the chaos, he would forge his destiny, a master of shadows, navigating the tumultuous tides of change.

• • •

The oppressive heat of late July bore down upon Paris on 28 July 1789, the city's narrow streets radiating warmth like the walls of an oven. Étienne Corbeau made his way through the labyrinthine alleys of the Marais district. The clamour of market vendors and the scent of overripe fruit mingled with the pervasive undercurrent of tension gripping the capital. He adjusted his cravat, feeling the sting of sweat at his collar, and quickened his pace towards the modest townhouse where Maximilien Robespierre lived.

Upon arrival, Robespierre's sister, Charlotte, a woman of quiet grace and discerning eyes, greeted him. "*Monsieur* Corbeau," she acknowledged with a slight nod. "My brother is expecting you. He's in the study."

"*Merci, Mademoiselle Robespierre,*" Étienne replied, offering a courteous bow.

He ascended the creaking staircase, each step accompanied by the city's distant sounds—horse hooves clattering on cobblestones, muffled conversations, the occasional outburst of distant laughter. Reaching the study, he found the door ajar. Robespierre sat at a cluttered desk, quill in hand, surrounded by stacks of pamphlets and legal texts. The room was dim, lit only by the glow of an oil lamp that cast elongated shadows upon the walls.

"Maximilien," Étienne greeted softly.

Robespierre looked up, his eyes momentarily reflecting surprise before settling into a weary smile. "Étienne. Please, come in."

Étienne closed the door behind him and took a seat opposite his host. "You seem fatigued, my friend."

Robespierre sighed, setting down his quill. "The weight of responsibility grows heavier by the day. The Assembly is rife with indecision. Those who cling to outdated notions stymy progress."

"You're referring to the moderates," Étienne surmised.

"Precisely," Robespierre confirmed. "They speak of change but fear the steps necessary to achieve it."

Étienne leaned forward, his gaze intent. "Perhaps it's time to reconsider our approach."

Robespierre regarded him cautiously. "What do you suggest?"

"Trust is a fragile thing," Étienne began. "Especially when placed in those whose convictions waver. The moderates may hinder our efforts more than help them."

Robespierre frowned slightly. "I believe in the power of dialogue, in persuading others through reason."

"An admirable stance," Étienne acknowledged. "But reason falls on deaf ears when self-interest is at play. The aristocracy and their sympathisers within the Assembly will not relinquish power willingly."

Robespierre's jaw tightened. "We cannot abandon our principles, Étienne. To do so would make us no better than the tyrants we oppose."

"Agreed," Étienne said, his tone measured. "But there is a distinction between compromising principles and adopting a firmer stance. Consider the events of the past weeks—the storming of the Bastille, the uprisings in the provinces. The people demand action."

Robespierre stood, moving to the window where the sun cast a harsh light upon the streets below. "I am acutely aware of their demands."

Étienne joined him by the window. "Then perhaps we accept that more decisive measures are necessary. The moderates hesitate, their loyalties divided. Can we afford such uncertainty?"

Robespierre remained silent for a moment, his gaze distant. "What are you proposing?"

"That we surround ourselves with those unwavering in their commitment to true reform," Étienne replied. "Those willing to make hard choices for the greater good."

Robespierre turned to face him. "You speak of embracing extremism."

"I speak of embracing resolve," Étienne corrected gently. "Intent defines the line between firmness and extremism. Our intent is just."

Robespierre's eyes searched his, a flicker of doubt shadowed by contemplation. "I fear where such a path may lead."

"Fear is natural," Étienne conceded. "But inaction borne of fear can be more perilous than bold action guided by conviction."

Robespierre returned to his desk, absently straightening a stack of papers. "I've received reports of increasing unrest. Violence against nobles, properties seized. It's escalating beyond control."

"Which is why we must guide the tide rather than allow it to sweep us away," Étienne urged. "The moderates would have us restrain the people's fervour, but suppressing it could lead to greater chaos."

Robespierre rubbed his temples. "I wish for a revolution that upholds virtue and justice, not one mired in bloodshed."

"As do I," Étienne assured him. "But we recognise that the old order will not crumble without resistance. If we falter, the opportunity for meaningful change may slip through our fingers."

A knock at the door interrupted them. Charlotte peeked in, her expression apologetic. "Maximilien, a courier has arrived with urgent correspondence."

"Thank you, Charlotte," he said, taking the sealed letter she offered.

As Robespierre broke the seal and read, his brow furrowed. "It's from the Assembly. They've postponed the vote on the Declaration of the Rights of Man."

Étienne's eyes narrowed. "Postponed? On whose insistence?"

Tersely, Robespierre responded to the claim by ensuring that delegates knew that more deliberation was needed—stalling tactics.

Étienne placed a hand on his friend's shoulder. "You see? They undermine progress at every turn."

Robespierre's grip on the letter tightened. "This cannot continue."

"Then let us act," Étienne pressed. "We must rally those who share our vision and push forward despite opposition."

Robespierre met his gaze, a steely resolve hardening his features. "Perhaps you're right. Perhaps firmer action is required."

Étienne allowed a subtle smile. "I'm glad you see the necessity."

Robespierre began pacing. "We should convene a meeting with our closest allies. Danton, Desmoulins, others we can trust."

"An excellent idea," Étienne agreed. "Together, we can strategise a path forward."

Robespierre paused. "But we must be cautious. I will not condone unnecessary violence."

"Of course," Étienne said smoothly. "We ensure our actions are measured, and our intentions are pure."

Robespierre nodded, the tension in his posture easing slightly. "Very well. I'll arrange for us to meet tomorrow evening."

"I'll be there," Étienne affirmed.

As he prepared to leave, Charlotte reappeared. "Will you stay for supper, Monsieur Corbeau?"

"Thank you, Mademoiselle, but I have other matters to attend to," he replied politely.

Robespierre extended his hand. "Thank you for your counsel, Étienne. Your perspective is invaluable."

"Anytime," Étienne said, shaking his hand firmly. "We are in this together."

Descending the staircase, Étienne felt a surge of satisfaction. The seeds of doubt he'd planted were taking root. Steering Robespierre towards a more radical stance would destabilise the moderates and create opportunities for Étienne to assert more significant influence.

Stepping out into the sweltering afternoon, he approached the Seine. The river's sluggish flow mirrored the heavy atmosphere of the city. Along the banks, clusters of citizens gathered, exchanging rumours and grievances. The whispers of discontent had grown into open discussions of rebellion.

He spotted Camille Desmoulins seated at an outdoor café, feverishly scribbling in his ever-present notebook. Catching Étienne's eye, Desmoulins waved him over.

"Étienne! Sit, sit," he beckoned. "I've just penned what I believe may be my most compelling piece yet."

"Always the passionate scribe," Étienne remarked, taking a seat. "What's the subject this time?"

Desmoulins's eyes sparkled. "A call to arms against those in the Assembly who hinder our progress. The people must know who obstructs their path to liberty."

"A bold move," Étienne commented. "But necessary."

"Precisely," Desmoulins agreed. "We have tolerated indecision, too long."

"Maximilien shares your frustration," Étienne informed him. "We've just discussed taking more assertive actions."

Desmoulins raised an eyebrow. "Robespierre advocating for assertiveness? That's a shift."

"He recognises the urgency," Étienne said. "We plan to meet with our trusted circle tomorrow to chart a course forward."

"Count me in," Desmoulins declared. "It's time we take the reins."

As they conversed, Étienne subtly guided the dialogue, reinforcing that bolder strategies were acceptable and imperative. Desmoulins, ever the firebrand, readily embraced the ideas.

Leaving the café, Étienne wove through the bustling streets, his mind orchestrating the next movements in his intricate plan. He knew pushing Robespierre towards extremism would sew discord among the revolutionaries, allowing him to manipulate the chaos to his advantage.

While passing by the Palais-Royal, he noticed passionate debates among groups of Sans-culottes, their voices filled with anger and despair. The city's energy surged as the potential for change hung in the air.

"28 July 1789," he mused quietly. "A pivotal moment in the shaping of France—and my ascent."

He thought briefly of his family, wondering if they were aware of the monumental shifts occurring. But such musings were fleeting; his focus remained steadfast on his objectives.

As dusk settled, casting long shadows across the façades of buildings, Étienne returned to his apartment. The familiar surroundings offered a brief respite from the day's machinations. He lit a single candle, its flame illuminating the scattered papers and maps that cluttered his desk.

He began drafting letters to key figures, carefully choosing his words to incite action without revealing his manipulations. Each missive was a thread, weaving a web that tightened around his unsuspecting associates.

Pausing, he gazed out the window at the city enveloped in twilight. The distant sounds of Paris at night—laughter, arguments, the clatter of carriage wheels—blended into a symphony of unrest.

"Trust is a fragile thing," he reflected. "Easily swayed, easily shattered."

He knew that his path was treacherous, but the allure of power overshadowed any reservations. The revolution was a crucible, and he intended to rise from its flames, reborn.

Extinguishing the candle, Étienne settled into the darkness, a faint smile lingering on his lips.

"Let the moderates falter," he whispered. "Their hesitation will be their undoing—and my opportunity."

Thus, on that sultry July evening, Étienne Corbeau solidified his role as both confidant and manipulator, steering the course of the revolution—and those within it—towards a destiny he aimed to control.

• • •

Summer lingered over Paris on 5 August 1789, casting a haze that blurred the edges of the city's narrow streets and grand boulevards alike. Étienne navigated the bustling Rue Saint-Honoré with purpose, the cacophony of market vendors and clatter of carriage wheels fading into the background of his thoughts. Clad in a modest yet well-tailored suit, he exuded an air of understated authority that parted crowds just enough to ease his passage.

He clutched a leather-bound portfolio beneath his arm, its contents the culmination of weeks of discreet inquiries and carefully cultivated whispers. He carefully recorded the names of Royalist sympathisers, hidden amidst the ranks of the National Assembly and beyond, within—the ammunition for his next move.

Reaching the discreet entrance of a modest townhouse, Étienne rapped lightly on the weathered wooden door. It creaked open to reveal Maximilien Robespierre, his austere features softened momentarily by a hint of a smile.

"Étienne," Robespierre greeted, stepping aside to allow him entry. "Your message mentioned urgent matters."

"Indeed," Étienne replied, his tone measured. "I believe I have information that will be of significant interest."

They settled in the dimly lit parlour, the scent of parchment and ink mingling with that of freshly brewed coffee. Robespierre's sister, Charlotte, appeared briefly to offer refreshments before withdrawing, her presence a quiet constant in the background.

Étienne placed the portfolio on the table between them, unfastening the clasp with deliberate care. "Over the past weeks, I've been conducting investigations into certain members of the Assembly."

Robespierre leaned forward, his eyes narrowing. "What have you discovered?"

"Royalist sympathisers," Étienne stated plainly. "Individuals who, under the guise of moderation, seek to undermine our efforts and restore the old order."

Robespierre's jaw tightened. "Do you have proof?"

"Names, correspondences, accounts of clandestine meetings," Étienne confirmed, sliding a sheaf of documents towards him. "They conspire to sow discord, to fracture the unity we've fought to build."

Robespierre examined the papers, his expression darkening as he absorbed the implications. "This is… troubling."

"More than troubling," Étienne pressed. "It's a direct threat to the revolution."

Robespierre looked up, a flicker of uncertainty in his gaze. "We must proceed carefully. Accusations of this nature require irrefutable evidence."

"Which is why I've corroborated these findings," Étienne replied smoothly. "Testimonies from reliable sources, witnesses willing to come forward if necessary."

Robespierre stood, pacing the length of the room. "If we act on this, it could lead to significant repercussions."

"Allowing these traitors to continue their machinations would be far worse," Étienne countered. "We cannot afford hesitation."

Robespierre paused by the window, the muffled sounds of the city seeping through the glass. "What do you propose?"

"Expose them," Étienne said firmly. "Bring their duplicity to light before the Assembly. Demand their expulsion and prosecution."

Robespierre turned to face him. "Such actions could deepen divisions, incite conflict."

Étienne met his gaze unflinchingly. "A necessary risk. Unity built on false foundations will crumble at the slightest pressure. Better to address the rot now than allow it to fester."

Robespierre considered this, the weight of leadership pressing visibly upon his shoulders. "Very well," he conceded. "I will review this evidence thoroughly. If it holds, we shall proceed."

Étienne allowed a subtle smile. "I knew you would see the necessity."

As they delved into the specifics, Étienne guided the conversation with calculated precision, steering Robespierre towards decisive action. Every agreement, every nod of assent, propelled him towards achieving his own ambitions.

Leaving the townhouse, Étienne felt a surge of satisfaction. The obstacles posed by the moderates were on the verge of being dismantled, their influence waning under the scrutiny he had orchestrated. The path to greater power lay before him, yet impatience gnawed at the edges of his composure.

Making his way to the Palais-Royal, he discovered the gardens teeming with afternoon liveliness. Étienne made a beeline for Georges Danton, who stood out among a group of passionate followers.

"Danton," he called out.

The imposing man turned, a broad grin spreading across his face. "Étienne! Join us. We were just discussing the latest decrees."

"In a moment," Étienne replied. "I have matters to discuss with you privately."

Danton's expression shifted to one of curiosity. "Very well." He excused himself from the group, leading Étienne to a quieter corner beneath the shade of a chestnut tree.

"What presses you so urgently?" Danton inquired.

"I've just come from a meeting with Robespierre," Étienne began. "We've uncovered Royalist sympathisers within the Assembly."

Danton's eyes widened. "Is that so? I can't say I'm entirely surprised."

"Indeed," Étienne agreed. "But more concerning is Robespierre's hesitance. He worries about the repercussions of acting against them."

Danton huffed. "Maximilien is a man of principles, sometimes to a fault."

"Which is why I believe we must be prepared to take matters into our own hands if necessary," Étienne suggested.

Danton eyed him shrewdly. "And what exactly do you have in mind?"

"Should Robespierre falter, we must be ready to rally the people ourselves," Étienne said. "To ensure that justice is served, and the revolution remains on course."

A slow smile spread across Danton's face. "I admire your initiative. Perhaps it's time for stronger voices to lead the charge."

"Precisely," Étienne affirmed. "Will you stand with me?"

Danton clapped a hand on his shoulder. "You can count on it."

As they parted ways, Étienne's impatience simmered just beneath the surface. The incremental steps towards power were no longer sufficient; he craved direct influence, the ability to shape events without the need to navigate others' hesitations.

The sight of Olympe de Gouges interrupted his thoughts, addressing a small crowd, her eloquent words carrying on the warm breeze.

"*Liberté* and *égalité* must extend to all citizens, regardless of gender!" she proclaimed, passion lighting her eyes.

Étienne listened, acknowledging the sway she held over her audience. An alliance with her could bolster his position further, yet he recognised the need for caution. Her ideals, while aligned with the revolution, might clash with his own objectives.

She caught his eye, offering a nod of recognition. "Monsieur Corbeau," she called out. "Care to join the discourse?"

"Another time, perhaps," he replied with a courteous smile. "I applaud your dedication."

Her gaze lingered, a hint of scepticism clear. "The revolution requires action from all fronts."

"Indeed, it does," Étienne agreed before continuing on his way.

As evening settled over Paris, casting the sky in hues of amber and crimson, Étienne returned to his apartment. The familiar surroundings did little to quell the restlessness that churned within him.

Seating himself at his desk, he unfurled a map of the city, marking locations of strategic importance—the assembly hall, the homes of key figures, gathering places of the Sans-culottes. The network he had woven was intricate, yet he yearned to tighten the threads.

A knock at the door drew his attention. He opened it to reveal a young courier, breathless and wide-eyed.

"Monsieur Corbeau?" the boy stammered.

"Yes?"

"A message for you, sir." He handed over a folded note before scurrying away.

Étienne unfolded the parchment, scanning the brief contents. A summons from Jean-Paul Marat, requesting a meeting at midnight.

"Interesting," Étienne murmured.

Marat, with his radical views and influence through his publication, *L'Ami du peuple*, could prove a valuable ally—or a formidable adversary. The invitation was unexpected, but not unwelcome.

As the hour approached, Étienne made his way to the designated location—a modest abode tucked away in a narrow alley off Rue Saint-Jacques. The interior was sparse, illuminated by the flicker of candlelight that cast elongated shadows upon the walls.

Marat greeted him with a curt nod. "Corbeau. Thank you for coming."

"Your message piqued my interest," Étienne replied. "What can I do for you?"

Marat's gaze was intense, his features drawn and sharp. "Word has reached me for your actions regarding the moderates. You move decisively."

"I act in the best interests of the revolution," Étienne said evenly.

"Do you?" Marat challenged. "Or do you pursue your own agenda?"

Étienne met his stare unflinchingly. "The two are not mutually exclusive."

Marat leaned forward. "Be cautious, Corbeau. Ambition can blind even the most astute minds."

"Is that a warning?" Étienne inquired a hint of amusement in his tone.

"An observation," Marat replied. "We may share common enemies, but our methods differ."

"Perhaps," Étienne conceded. "But our goals align—for now."

Marat regarded him silently before extending a hand. "Then let us ensure that the revolution does not falter."

Étienne shook his hand firmly. "Agreed."

Leaving the meeting, Étienne felt the weight of scrutiny upon him. Marat's suspicions were palpable, yet they mattered little in the grand scheme. His impatience for direct power surged anew, driving him to hasten his plans.

He resolved to press Robespierre further, to dismantle any remaining barriers to his ascent. The time for subtlety was waning; decisive action beckoned.

Returning home, he penned a letter to Robespierre, urging immediate action against the Royalist sympathisers. He emphasised the urgency, the necessity of swift justice to preserve the revolution's integrity.

Sealing the letter, he felt a sense of finality. The die was cast.

As he prepared for rest, Étienne gazed out over the city, the moon casting a pale glow upon the rooftops. The distant sounds of Paris at night drifted through the open window—a lullaby of unrest.

"Power awaits," he whispered into the darkness. "And no one will keep me from it," he whispered into the darkness.

Thus, with ambition burning brightly, Étienne Corbeau edged ever closer to the precipice of authority, his impatience a catalyst that threatened to ignite both his triumph and his undoing.

• • •

As 10 August 1789 arrived, the atmosphere was charged with a stifling tension, relieving the oppressive heat of summer. Paris seemed to hold its breath, the air thick with anticipation and the acrid scent of smoke lingering from distant fires. Étienne Corbeau stood atop the steps of a boarded-up shop in the Rue Saint-Antoine, his gaze sweeping over the throngs of people that surged like a restless tide through the narrow streets.

Men brandished makeshift weapons—clubs, knives, rusted swords—while women clutched their children close, eyes wide with fear and defiance. The Sans-culottes moved with purpose, their red caps bobbing amidst the crowd as they shouted slogans of liberty and justice. Overhead, the sky hung low and grey as if weighed down by the gravity of the day's events.

A sudden commotion erupted near the Place de la Bastille, drawing Étienne's attention. He watched as a contingent of Royalist soldiers clashed with the masses, the sharp retort of musket fire cutting through the din. Bodies fell, cries of pain and fury intertwining in a grotesque symphony.

Étienne observed the scene with a detached calm, his expression unreadable. The violence unfolding before him was neither shocking nor distressing; it was a necessary progression, a catalyst propelling the revolution forward. Each life lost was a stepping stone towards the upheaval he sought to navigate and control.

"Étienne!" a voice called out amidst the turmoil.

He turned to see Camille Desmoulins pushing through the crowd, his face flushed, eyes bright with excitement and dread. "Have you seen what's happening?"

"It is impossible to miss it," Étienne replied with a dry tone. The city is filled with passionate excitement.

Desmoulins reached his side, huffing. "The people have stormed the Hôtel de Ville. They're arming themselves with whatever they can find."

"Desperate times breed desperate actions," Étienne remarked.

Desmoulins searched his face. "You don't seem moved by any of this."

Étienne met his gaze steadily. "Emotions cloud judgement. We need rational minds now more than ever."

Before Desmoulins could respond, a surge in the crowd forced them closer together. The air was thick with the scent of sweat and fear, the press of bodies almost suffocating.

"We should find Danton," Desmoulins suggested. "He'll know how to channel this… energy."

"Very well," Étienne agreed.

They navigated the chaotic streets, sidestepping skirmishes and dodging debris. A discordant melody of shouts, gunfire had replaced the city's usual rhythm, and the ominous tolling of church bells.

As they approached the Cordeliers District, they found Georges Danton standing atop a makeshift platform—a toppled cart—addressing a crowd with his characteristic zeal.

"Citoyens!" Danton's voice boomed over the din. "The time casts off the shackles of oppression! We must stand united against those who would see us subjugated!"

The crowd roared in response, fists raised skyward.

Desmoulins leaned towards Étienne. "He's magnificent, isn't he?"

"He's effective," Étienne conceded.

Danton caught sight of them and gestured for them to join him. "Étienne! Camille! Come, lend your voices to the cause!"

Desmoulins eagerly climbed onto the platform, but Étienne hesitated. He preferred the role of observer, the puppeteer, rather than the performer.

"Perhaps another time," Étienne said, offering a faint smile.

In spite of the situation, Danton casually shrugged and turned his focus back to the crowd. Desmoulins sparked the enthusiasm of the people through his speech.

Étienne slipped away, blending into the sea of faces. He walked with deliberate ease, unperturbed by the chaos that enveloped him. The violence was escalating, but to him, it was merely a means to an end—a necessary upheaval that would strip away the old order and create a vacuum he intended to fill.

Turning onto a quieter street, he nearly collided with Maximilien Robespierre, who was striding purposefully in the opposite direction. Robespierre's face showed concern and his usually composed demeanour strained.

"Étienne!" Robespierre exclaimed. "I've been looking for you."

"Maximilien," Étienne replied. "What brings you into the midst of this turmoil?"

Robespierre glanced around at the surrounding unrest. "I could ask you the same."

"I'm merely observing the unfolding events," Étienne said.

"Observing?" Robespierre repeated, a note of disbelief in his voice. "People are dying in the streets! We must act to quell this violence."

Étienne raised an eyebrow. "Quell it? This is the very uprising we've been fostering."

"Not like this," Robespierre insisted. "Violence without purpose leads only to anarchy. We must guide the people towards constructive action, not senseless bloodshed."

Étienne's gaze hardened slightly. "Change is seldom bloodless, Maximilien. You cannot expect to dismantle centuries of tyranny without casualties."

Robespierre shook his head. "There must be another way. We cannot sacrifice our humanity for the sake of expedience."

A distant explosion punctuated his words, followed by a chorus of screams. Robespierre flinched, his eyes reflecting a deepening despair.

"Your idealism is admirable but impractical," Étienne remarked coolly. "The revolution has its own momentum now."

Robespierre studied him intently. "I wonder sometimes where your true loyalties lie, Étienne."

"With the revolution," Étienne replied without hesitation.

"And what of the people?" Robespierre pressed. "Do you not care about their suffering?"

Étienne's expression remained impassive. "Their suffering is a consequence of the oppression we've vowed to eliminate. Short-term pain for long-term gain."

Robespierre's shoulders sagged slightly. "I fear we are losing our way."

"Perhaps you are," Étienne said pointedly. "But I see clarity amidst the chaos."

Before Robespierre could respond, a group of National Guardsmen marched past, their presence causing both men to step aside. The guards' faces were grim, their uniforms stained with dust and blood.

"I must return to the Assembly," Robespierre announced. "We need to address this madness before it consumes us all."

"Do as you must," Étienne replied.

Robespierre hesitated. "Be careful, Étienne. The path you're on is perilous."

"I could say the same to you," Étienne countered.

With a final, weary glance, Robespierre hurried away, disappearing into the labyrinth of streets.

Étienne watched him go, a subtle sense of detachment settling over him. The widening chasm between his own pragmatic indifference and Robespierre's moral anguish was becoming increasingly apparent. Where Robespierre saw tragedy, Étienne saw opportunity.

He resumed his stroll, eventually arriving at a quiet square where Olympe de Gouges was tending to the wounded. With her sleeves rolled up, she tended to the wounded, binding a young man's injured arm with her blood-stained hands.

"Olympe," Étienne greeted.

She looked up, surprise flickering across her features, before giving way to a stern expression. "Étienne. Are you here to help?"

"In my way," he replied.

She narrowed her eyes. "And what way is that? Standing by while the city tears itself apart?"

He gestured vaguely. "This is the natural progression of revolution."

"Natural?" she echoed incredulously. "There's nothing natural about this carnage. People are dying needlessly."

"Change demands sacrifice," he said evenly.

Olympe stood, wiping her hands on a rag. "You're as cold as the stones beneath our feet. Do you feel nothing for these people?"

"I feel ambition," Étienne answered. "A desire to see France reborn."

"At what cost?" she challenged.

"Whatever cost is necessary," he stated.

She shook her head, disappointment etched in her eyes. "I pity you, Étienne. For all your intelligence, you've lost sight of your humanity."

He shrugged. "Emotions are a hindrance."

"Then you're no better than the tyrants we oppose," she declared before turning away to assist another wounded citizen.

Étienne watched her for a moment before departing. Her words did little to stir him; empathy was a luxury he had long since discarded.

As night fell, the city remained restless. Fires burned unchecked, casting an eerie glow against the darkened sky. The sounds of conflict echoed through the streets, a relentless reminder of the turmoil that gripped Paris.

Étienne returned to his apartment, the quiet solitude a stark contrast to the chaos outside. He lit a single candle, its flame flickering unsteadily as he settled at his desk.

Unfolding a map of Paris, he marked areas of significant unrest, noting the movements of various factions. The pattern was clear: the old order was crumbling, and in its place, a new hierarchy was emerging—one he intended to ascend.

A faint knock interrupted his thoughts. He opened the door to find a young messenger, eyes wide with fear.

"Monsieur Corbeau?" the boy stammered.

"Oui?"

"A letter for you, sir." The boy handed over a sealed envelope before scurrying away.

Étienne broke the seal, scanning the brief missive. It was from Jean-Paul Marat requesting an urgent meeting.

He sighed, folding the letter carefully. Marat's increasingly erratic behaviour made him both a valuable ally and a potential liability. The meeting could prove helpful.

Glancing out the window, Étienne observed the city enveloped in darkness, punctuated by the glow of distant fires. The revolution was devouring itself, and he stood poised to seize control amidst the chaos.

"10 August 1789," Étienne mused aloud. "A day of reckoning."

He felt no remorse, no hesitation—only an icy determination to see his plans through. The violence was a means to an end, a necessary upheaval to dismantle the structures that had oppressed him and so many others.

But beneath his calculated exterior, a subtle shift was occurring. The disconnect between himself and those who clung to moral ideals—Robespierre, Olympe, even Desmoulins—was widening. Their concerns for humanity, for the sanctity of life, were obstacles he no longer had patience for.

Extinguishing the candle, Étienne embraced the darkness. The path ahead was fraught with peril, but he was resolute.

"Let the streets run red," he whispered. "I will forge my destiny from the ashes."

In the silence that followed, the distant sounds of a city in turmoil served as a haunting backdrop to his unwavering ambition. Étienne Corbeau had become a man apart, his detachment complete, his purpose singular.

• • •

Étienne Corbeau navigated the labyrinthine streets of the Marais district on 14 August 1789, the cobblestones radiating the day's warmth beneath his boots. The scent of smoke and sweat lingered in the air, mingling with the distant echoes of unrest that had become the city's constant backdrop.

He approached a nondescript townhouse nestled between a shuttered bakery and an abandoned atelier. The façade was unremarkable, its weathered stone blending seamlessly into the row of buildings. Despite its modest exterior, it housed the hub of a revolutionary movement.

Étienne rapped a coded sequence on the oak door—three quick knocks followed by two slow ones. A sliver of light appeared as a peephole slid open, and a pair of cautious eyes assessed him.

"Le Corbeau cherche son nid," Étienne uttered softly.

"Entrez," came the whispered reply.

The door creaked open just enough for him to slip inside. Flickering candles dimly lit the interior, their flames casting elongated shadows that danced along the walls. He descended a narrow staircase into a cellar transformed into a clandestine meeting chamber. The atmosphere was thick with anticipation and the muted hum of hushed conversations.

Around a large oak table sat the key architects of the revolution: Maximilien Robespierre, his eyes intense behind wire-framed spectacles; Georges Danton, his imposing figure commanding attention even in silence; Camille Desmoulins, his quill poised over a notebook; and Jean-Paul Marat, his gaze piercing from beneath a furrowed brow.

"Ah, Étienne," Robespierre acknowledged upon entering, "we were wondering if you had been delayed."

"Apologies," Étienne replied smoothly, taking his place at the table. "The streets are restless tonight."

Danton grunted. "When are they not? The people are hungry for change—and bread."

A faint smile tugged at Étienne's lips. "Both are in short supply, it seems."

Marat leaned forward, his voice edged with impatience. "We haven't convened here to jest. Time is of the essence."

"Quite right," Robespierre agreed. "The monarchy grows bolder in its defiance. Reports show that Louis XVI has summoned additional troops to Versailles."

Desmoulins scribbled furiously. "A show of force to intimidate us, no doubt."

"Or a prelude to something more sinister," Étienne interjected. "We cannot dismiss the possibility of a crackdown."

By striking the table with a fist, Danton caused the candles to flicker and declared, "Then we must strike first to show that the will of the people cannot be silenced."

Robespierre raised a hand. "Patience, Georges. Rash actions could undermine our position."

Marat's eyes flashed. "Patience is a luxury we can ill afford. The blood spilt in the streets cries out for justice."

Étienne observed the interplay with measured interest. The fissures in their united front were widening—a circumstance he intended to exploit. Clearing his throat, he addressed the assembly.

"*Mes amis,* perhaps there is a path that balances decisive action with strategic prudence."

All eyes turned to him.

"Go on," Robespierre prompted.

Étienne chose his words carefully. "The monarchy underestimates our resolve. If we can secure key positions within Paris—arsenals, guard posts, communication centres—we can neutralise their ability to retaliate swiftly."

Danton nodded thoughtfully. "A pre-emptive move."

"Precisely," Étienne affirmed. "We need not storm Versailles outright. Instead, we tighten our hold on the city, forcing the King into a position where negotiation becomes his only viable option."

Robespierre tapped his chin. "It's a calculated risk."

"One worth taking," Marat insisted. "The people are ready. They merely await our command."

Desmoulins looked up from his notes. "We could disseminate pamphlets to rally support, outline our intentions to avoid misunderstandings."

Étienne seized the moment. "We can reach out to sympathetic members of the National Guard. Their allegiance could tip the scales in our favour without excessive bloodshed."

Robespierre's gaze lingered on Étienne. "You seem well-versed in matters of strategy."

"I've made it my business to understand the dynamics at play," Étienne replied modestly. "Our strength lies not just in numbers but in coordination."

Danton let out a hearty laugh. "I like this plan. It's bold, yet cunning."

Marat's expression softened ever so slightly. "For once, we agree."

Robespierre exhaled slowly. "Very well. Let's formalise our objectives."

They spent the next hour detailing their strategy, assigning roles, and identifying key targets. Étienne ensured his suggestions aligned with his own ambitions, subtly guiding decisions to merge his influence.

As the meeting drew to a close, Robespierre pulled Étienne aside. "You've shown remarkable insight tonight."

"Thank you, Maximilien," Étienne replied. "I merely wish to see our cause succeed."

Robespierre studied him intently. "I've had my reservations about certain methods, but perhaps a firmer hand is necessary."

Étienne measured his tone as he said, "Sometimes, we have to make hard choices for the greater good."

Robespierre nodded slowly. "I trust your judgement. Let's proceed with caution and conviction."

They rejoined the others, who were dispersing with renewed purpose. Danton clapped Étienne on the back. "You may be a quiet one, but you have the mind of a general."

"High praise," Étienne responded with a slight bow. "I hope to live up to it."

Marat approached his earlier scepticism abated. "Perhaps there's more to you than meets the eye, Corbeau."

"One strives to be of service," Étienne replied.

Marat's lips curled into a faint smirk. "We'll see."

Emerging from the townhouse, Étienne inhaled the cool night air, starkly contrasting the oppressive atmosphere within. The city stretched out before him, its flickering lights resembling a constellation of possibilities.

Desmoulins caught up to him. "Walk with me?"

"Of course."

They strolled along the Seine, the river's dark surface reflecting the moonlight. Silence settled between them, comfortable yet expectant.

"Your proposal was well-received," Desmoulins remarked eventually.

"I'm pleased it resonated," Étienne replied.

Desmoulins hesitated before speaking again. "Do you ever worry about where this path may lead us?"

Étienne considered the question. "Uncertainty is inevitable in times of significant change. But I believe the end justifies the means."

Desmoulins sighed. "I admire your confidence. Sometimes, I wonder if we're merely trading one form of tyranny for another."

"Revolutions are seldom clean affairs," Étienne observed. "But without upheaval, progress stalls."

They paused on a bridge overlooking the water. Desmoulins gazed into the distance. "I suppose you're right. It's just… the cost weighs on me."

Étienne placed a hand on his shoulder. "Stay resolute, Camille. Doubt is natural, but it mustn't hinder us."

Desmoulins offered a wan smile and said, "Thank you, Étienne. I appreciate your counsel."

"Anytime," Étienne assured him.

Parting ways, Étienne made his way back to his lodgings. The streets were quieter now, the earlier unrest subdued, if only temporarily. As he climbed the stairs to his apartment, he felt a palpable shift within himself—a recognition that he was no longer merely a participant but a driving force in the unfolding events.

After lighting a candle, he settled at his desk, the flickering glow casting long shadows across scattered papers and maps. He drafted letters to various contacts, meticulously coordinating the next steps.

A soft knock interrupted his concentration. Puzzled, he opened the door to find Olympe de Gouges standing there, her expression inscrutable.

"Olympe," he greeted, surprised. "What brings you here at this hour?"

She stepped inside without invitation. "I needed to speak with you."

"By all means," he said, closing the door behind her.

She turned to face him, eyes searching. "I've heard whispers of your plans—of decisive actions that may plunge the city into deeper chaos."

Étienne raised an eyebrow. "Information travels swiftly."

"Indeed," she replied sharply. "I came to implore you to consider the ramifications of your actions. Innocent lives hang in the balance."

He sighed. "Change requires sacrifice. You know this."

"Don't patronise me," she snapped. "I'm well aware of the stakes, but there must be a line we do not cross."

He met her gaze evenly. "And who determines the placement of that line?"

"Conscience," she said firmly. "Morality."

"Abstract concepts in the face of tangible oppression," he countered. "We cannot afford hesitation."

She shook her head. "I fear you are losing yourself, Étienne."

"Perhaps I'm finding my true purpose," he retorted.

A tense silence settled between them.

"Very well," she said finally. "I won't keep you. Just remember that history will judge us not only by our victories, but by the means we employed."

She turned to leave.

"Olympe," he called after her.

She paused but did not look back.

"Take care," he whispered.

Without another word, she exited, leaving him alone once more.

Étienne returned to his desk, her words echoing faintly in his mind. Dismissing the flicker of doubt, he refocused on his plans. The die was cast, and he was determined to see it through.

As the first light of dawn crept over the horizon, Étienne stood by the window, watching the city stir awake. The path ahead was fraught with uncertainty, but he embraced it with a steely resolve.

"14 August 1789," he murmured to himself as if the narrator of his story, "The road to power lies before me."

He felt a surge of anticipation, a sense of purpose that eclipsed any lingering hesitation. He did not fear the coming chaos but harnessed it as a force that would propel him to the heights he sought.

Turning away from the window, he extinguished the candle, plunging the room into semi-darkness. Étienne Corbeau was ready to step fully into the role he had meticulously crafted—a leader poised to shape the destiny of a nation, whatever the cost.

CHAPTER THREE: (1790)
STRATEGIST'S GAMBIT

On 5 February 1790, the chill of winter lingered in the air, casting a pale light over Paris as the sun struggled to pierce the overcast sky. Étienne Corbeau stood at the grand entrance of the Manège, the converted riding school that now housed the National Assembly. The building loomed before him, its stone façade bearing the weight of a nation in flux. He adjusted the lapels of his charcoal-grey coat, brushing away an errant speck of dust, and stepped inside.

The hall buzzed with the enthusiasm of vigorous debate. Delegates milled about, their voices a cacophony of ideals and convictions clashing in the charged atmosphere. The scent of ink and parchment mingled with damp wool and tobacco smoke's faint aroma. Chandeliers overhead cast a warm glow, illuminating the faces of men determined to shape the future of France.

Étienne navigated through the crowd with practised ease, his keen eyes observing the clusters of moderates and radicals forming like opposing tides. He spotted familiar faces—Maximilien Robespierre deep in conversation with Louis de Saint-Just, Georges Danton gesturing animatedly to a group of deputies, and Camille Desmoulins scribbling notes at a furious pace.

He approached Robespierre, whose austere countenance betrayed a hint of weariness. "Maximilien," Étienne greeted, inclining his head slightly.

"Étienne," Robespierre replied, offering a tight smile. "Have you been following the debates?"

"Indeed," Étienne affirmed. "Though I must admit, the call for a constitutional monarchy grows tiresome."

Robespierre sighed softly. "Many believe it to be a necessary compromise—a means to stabilise the nation without descending into anarchy."

Étienne arched an eyebrow. "And what do you believe?"

Robespierre hesitated. "I believe in the sovereignty of the people, but I also fear the consequences of precipitous action."

Before Étienne could respond, the Speaker's gavel echoed through the chamber, calling the assembly to order. Delegates moved to their seats, the murmur of conversation subsiding into a tense silence.

The Marquis de Lafayette ascended the podium, his uniform immaculate, medals gleaming under the chandelier's light. His voice carried with the authority of one accustomed to command. "*Messieurs,* the question before us is whether to adopt a constitutional monarchy that preserves the throne while instituting reforms to ensure liberty and justice for all citizens."

An applause coursed through the moderate faction while murmurs of dissent arose from the radicals.

Étienne felt a surge of frustration tightening his chest. He leaned towards Robespierre. "They seek to placate the masses with half-measures."

"Patience," Robespierre whispered. "Let us hear them out."

Lafayette continued, "The King has expressed a willingness to cooperate. By retaining the monarchy, we maintain stability and avoid the chaos resulting from its abolition."

Danton rose from his seat. "Stability at the cost of true freedom is a compromise too great! We cannot trust the promises of a king who has consistently acted against the interests of his people."

A chorus of agreement echoed from the radical benches.

Étienne watched as the debate intensified, his frustration mounting. The moderates clung to the notion of a benevolent monarchy, blind to the duplicity he knew lurked beneath the surface. He recalled the intelligence he had gathered—secret correspondences between the King and foreign powers, whispers of plots to quash the revolution.

As the arguments volleyed back and forth, Étienne's gaze settled on the figures of the moderate leaders—men like Antoine Barnave and the Comte de Mirabeau—whose eloquence masked their reluctance to sever ties with the old order. He resolved then to undermine their influence.

The session adjourned for a brief recess. Delegates spilt into the adjoining corridors, voices overlapping in a heated discussion. Étienne seized the opportunity to approach Danton.

"Georges," he called, catching up to the larger man.

Danton turned, his eyes alight with anger. "Can you believe their audacity? Clinging to the monarchy as if it's some sacred institution."

"Precisely why we must act," Étienne urged. "The moderates sway too many with their rhetoric. We need to expose the King's true intentions."

Danton stroked his chin thoughtfully. "And how do you propose we do that?"

Étienne lowered his voice. "I've come across documents that suggest the King is seeking help from Austria and Prussia. Proof of his betrayal could turn the tide against the monarchy."

Danton's brows knit together. "If such evidence exists, we must bring it to light."

"Agreed," Étienne affirmed. "But we must proceed carefully. The moderates will attempt to discredit us."

"Let them try," Danton scoffed. "The truth will speak for itself."

They rejoined the assembly as the session resumed. Étienne watched as Mirabeau took the floor, his commanding presence drawing the attention of all.

"Messieurs," Mirabeau began, his voice resonant, "we stand at a crossroads. The monarchy, reformed and restrained by a constitution, can serve as a unifying symbol for our nation. To discard it entirely is to invite instability and external threats."

Applause erupted from the moderate faction.

Étienne exchanged a glance with Robespierre, whose expression remained impassive but whose eyes betrayed a flicker of concern.

Unable to contain himself any longer, Étienne stood. *"Monsieur* Mirabeau, may I pose a question?"

Mirabeau turned his gaze upon him. "The floor recognises *Monsieur* Corbeau."

Étienne stepped forward. "You speak of unity and stability, yet how can we trust a monarch who has consistently undermined our efforts? Is it not naïve to believe that mere words and parchment can bind a king who views himself as divinely appointed?"

A murmur of agreement swept through the radicals.

Mirabeau's smile was thin. "Trust is built by cooperating and making mutual concessions. Extremism only serves to fracture our cause."

"Extremism?" Étienne retorted. "I call it vigilance. The people demand accurate representation, not the illusion of it."

The Speaker interjected, "Gentlemen, please direct your comments to the assembly."

Étienne held Mirabeau's gaze a moment longer before returning to his seat.

As the session wore on, the moderates held sway, their calls for compromise resonating with a significant portion of the assembly.

After adjournment, Étienne convened with Robespierre, Danton, and Desmoulins in a quiet alcove.

"We're losing ground," Desmoulins lamented. "The moderates' appeal to reason placates those who fear upheaval."

"Then we must shift the narrative," Étienne declared. "Expose the monarchy's duplicity and the moderates' complicity."

Robespierre frowned. "I caution against unfounded accusations. We must maintain our integrity."

Étienne suppressed a sigh. "Maximilien, I respect your principles, but we cannot afford to play by the rules when our opponents do not."

Danton nodded in agreement. "Étienne has a point. If we can provide evidence of the King's betrayal, it could galvanise support for our cause."

Robespierre considered this. "Very well. But we ensure that any actions we take are justifiable."

"Leave it to me," Étienne assured them. "I will buy the proof."

Later that evening, Étienne retreated to his lodgings, a modest apartment overlooking the Seine. The river's dark waters reflected the city's glimmering lights, a tapestry of shadows and flickering flames. He settled at his desk, spreading out a collection of documents he had gathered through carefully cultivated connections.

Among them were letters hinting at the King's correspondence with foreign monarchs, coded messages that, if deciphered, could reveal plans to suppress the revolution. Étienne's lips curled into a satisfied smile. With these, he could tilt the balance in favour of the radicals.

A soft knock at his door pulled him from his thoughts. He opened it to find Olympe de Gouges standing there, her expression a mix of concern and determination.

"Olympe," he greeted, surprised. "What brings you here at this hour?"

"I've heard whispers you intend to escalate tensions within the Assembly," she replied, stepping inside without waiting for an invitation.

He closed the door behind her. "Whispers travel quickly."

She faced him, eyes sharp. "Is it true?"

"I aim to reveal the truth," he said evasively.

"At what cost?" she pressed. "You're treading a dangerous path, Étienne. Undermining the moderates could fracture the revolution."

He met her gaze. "The revolution has already fractured. The moderates hinder progress by clinging to outdated institutions."

"Not everyone shares your appetite for radical change," she cautioned. "We must consider the will of the people."

He arched an eyebrow. "I am considering the will of the people—the ones who suffer while the Assembly debates semantics."

She sighed. "Just promise me you won't resort to underhanded tactics."

He offered a thin smile. "I promise to do what is necessary."

She searched his face for a moment before nodding reluctantly. "Very well. But remember, history judges not only our actions but our motives."

As she departed, Étienne returned to his desk, her words lingering in his mind. He dismissed them with a shake of his head. Motives were secondary to outcomes.

The following day, armed with the incriminating documents, Étienne presented his findings to Danton and Desmoulins.

"This is exactly what we need," Danton declared, his eyes gleaming. "With this, we can expose the King's treachery."

Desmoulins added, "I'll draught pamphlets immediately, disseminate the information to the public."

"Wait," Étienne interjected. "We must be strategic. Release the information in stages, building momentum. Overwhelm the moderates before they can mount a defence."

Danton clapped him on the back. "You're a cunning one, Étienne."

Robespierre joined them, his expression guarded. "Are we certain this is the right course?"

"It's the only course," Étienne asserted. "The time for half-measures is over."

Robespierre glanced at the documents. "Then let us proceed, but we must remain vigilant against falsehoods."

"Agreed," Étienne replied a glint of triumph in his eyes.

As they parted ways, Étienne felt a surge of satisfaction. The seeds he had sown were taking root. The moderates would discredit themselves, further undermining the monarchy and solidifying his influence within the revolutionary ranks.

Walking along the Seine, he allowed himself a rare moment of reflection. The path ahead was fraught with uncertainty, but he relished the challenge. The revolution was not merely a movement but an opportunity, a crucible in which he could forge his destiny.

As dusk settled over Paris, casting long shadows across the cityscape, Étienne turned his steps homeward. The debates would continue, but he was confident that soon, the scales would tip irrevocably in favour of radical change.

He would be at the forefront, guiding the course of history with a steady hand and unwavering resolve.

• • •

The winter chill had not yet loosened its grip on Paris by 10 February 1790. A pale sun hung low in the sky, casting long shadows over the cobbled streets, dusted with a thin layer of frost. Étienne Corbeau navigated the maze of alleys of the Île de la Cité, his breath forming fleeting clouds that dissipated into the crisp air. Clutching a leather-bound portfolio beneath his arm, he made his way towards the modest apartment of Maximilien Robespierre.

Arriving at a narrow building tucked discreetly between a bookshop and a tailor's, Étienne rapped softly on the weathered wooden door. It creaked open to reveal Robespierre himself, his sharp features softened by the flickering candlelight from within.

"Étienne," Robespierre greeted, a hint of surprise colouring his tone. "I was not expecting you."

"Apologies for the intrusion, Maximilien," Étienne replied with a courteous nod. "But I believe we have much to discuss."

Robespierre stepped aside, allowing him entry. The apartment was sparse but orderly, shelves lined with legal tomes and philosophical treatises. A small hearth crackled softly, offering a welcome reprieve from the cold.

"Please, have a seat," Robespierre gestured towards a modest table adorned with scattered papers and an unfinished letter.

"Thank you," Étienne said, settling into a wooden chair. "I trust you are well?"

"As well as one can be amidst the current turmoil," Robespierre sighed, taking the seat opposite. "The debates in the Assembly grow more contentious by the day."

"Indeed," Étienne agreed, his gaze steady. "Which is precisely why I wished to speak with you."

Robespierre regarded him curiously. "Go on."

Étienne placed the portfolio on the table, his fingers tracing its worn edges. "I've been observing the increasing influence of the moderates—their reluctance to embrace the reforms."

Robespierre's eyes flickered with a mix of weariness and contemplation. "They believe in gradual change, in preserving certain institutions for stability."

"Stability at the expense of progress," Étienne countered. "Their hesitance undermines the very foundation of the revolution."

Robespierre leaned back, his expression pensive. "I cannot deny that their caution frustrates me. Yet, we must consider the broader implications. A divided assembly weakens our position."

"Precisely why we must merge our efforts," Étienne pressed. "The moderates are an anchor, dragging us into complacency. We need decisive action."

Robespierre's gaze drifted to the window, where the faint glow of streetlamps pierced the encroaching dusk. "I fear that severing ties could lead to further fragmentation."

Étienne leaned forward, his voice low and measured. "Maximilien, the people look to us for leadership. They hunger for change—for justice. We cannot afford to be shackled by those who lack the conviction to see it through."

Robespierre met his eyes, a flicker of uncertainty shadowing his resolute façade. "What do you propose?"

"Distance yourself from the moderates," Étienne urged. "Align with those who share your vision without compromise. Your influence is substantial; others will follow your lead."

A heavy silence settled between them, punctuated only by the soft crackling of the fire.

Robespierre exhaled slowly. "I have always sought to bridge divides, to find common ground."

"And where has that led us?" Étienne challenged gently. "Endless debates, diluted resolutions, and a monarchy that still holds sway over our destiny."

Robespierre's jaw tightened. "You speak passionately, but we must temper emotion with reason."

"Reason dictates we cannot progress while burdened by indecision," Étienne replied. "You are a beacon for many, Maximilien. But a beacon must shine unimpeded."

Robespierre stood, pacing the length of the room. "I have dedicated myself to the principles of liberty and equality. To abandon dialogue feels… contrary to those ideals."

Étienne watched him intently. "Sometimes, we must make hard choices to preserve our principles."

Robespierre paused, his gaze distant. "I cannot help but question whether such a course leads us down a perilous path."

"Every path worth taking is fraught with challenges," Étienne said softly. "But consider the alternative—a revolution stalled, its potential squandered."

Robespierre turned to face him. "You are persuasive, Étienne. But I must be certain that this is the right course."

Étienne rose, placing a reassuring hand on his friend's shoulder. "Allow me to assist you. Together, we can navigate these uncertainties."

Robespierre offered a faint smile. "Your counsel is invaluable. I admit, the weight of leadership can be… isolating."

"Then let me share the burden," Étienne replied, suggesting creating a strategy and identifying committed allies.

"Very well," Robespierre conceded. "Let us proceed with caution."

"Of course," Étienne agreed, a glimmer of satisfaction in his eyes. "We shall move forward thoughtfully."

They spent the next hour discussing potential allies and outlining steps to strengthen their position within the Assembly. Étienne deftly guided the conversation, subtly reinforcing that the moderates were hindrances rather than partners.

As the evening wore on, Robespierre seemed to regain his usual composure. "I appreciate your dedication, Étienne. It's reassuring to have someone so steadfast by my side."

"Always," Étienne affirmed, confirming his dedication to achieving our goals as they align.

Robespierre escorted him to the door. "We shall reconvene soon to refine our plans."

"Until then," Étienne said, stepping out into the chilly night.

The streets were quiet, the usual bustle subdued under the cloak of darkness. Étienne pulled his coat tighter, a faint smile playing on his lips as he walked away from Robespierre's residence. He was positioning himself as an indispensable advisor, a calculated move that had yielded the desired results.

Turning a corner, he nearly collided with Jacques-Louis David, the renowned painter hurrying in the opposite direction.

"Monsieur Corbeau!" David exclaimed, steadying himself. "My apologies."

"No harm done," Étienne replied smoothly. "A pleasure to see you, Jacques-Louis. Out for a late stroll?"

"Hardly," David chuckled. "I've been attending a salon at Madame de Staël's. The discussions were invigorating, but time slipped away from me."

"Madame de Staël hosts the most enlightening gatherings," Étienne remarked. "Perhaps I'll attend the next one."

"You would be most welcome," David assured him. "Your insights would add much to the discourse."

"I shall consider it," Étienne said. "Safe travels."

"And to you," David replied before continuing on his way.

Étienne resumed his walk, contemplating the broader mosaic of connections and influences at play. Madame de Staël's salons were fertile ground for shaping opinions among the intellectual elite. Perhaps it was time to extend his reach further into those circles.

As he approached the Seine, the moon cast a silvery sheen over the river's surface. The gentle water lapping against the embankment provided a soothing counterpoint to his swirling thoughts.

A figure emerged from the shadows—a slender man with a pointed chin and piercing eyes. Jean-Paul Marat.

"Étienne," Marat greeted, his voice barely above a whisper.

"Jean-Paul," Étienne replied, unfazed. "Out late this evening."

"I could say the same of you," Marat observed. "Conspiring under the cover of darkness?"

"Merely engaging in necessary discussions," Étienne said evenly.

Marat's gaze narrowed. "With Robespierre, no doubt."

"Your information network is impressive," Étienne remarked dryly.

"I make it my business to stay informed," Marat retorted. "Be cautious, Étienne. Robespierre is not as malleable as you might hope."

Étienne countered. "He is a man of principle who understands the need for decisive action."

Marat scoffed. "Principles are luxuries we can ill afford. The time for words is over. We must act."

"And we shall," Étienne assured him. "But actions without strategy are futile."

Marat studied him for a moment. "Just remember, the revolution does not wait for those who hesitate."

"Wise words," Étienne conceded. "I trust we are on the same side."

"For now," Marat replied cryptically before slipping back into the shadows.

Étienne watched him disappear, a faint unease stirring within. Marat was unpredictable—a wildcard whose allegiance could shift without warning. This was a reminder that his path was fraught with potential pitfalls.

Reaching his apartment, Étienne ascended the narrow staircase, the creak of each step echoing in the silence. He entered his quarters, lighting a lamp that cast a warm glow over the spartan furnishings.

He sat at his desk, quill in hand, and began drafting letters to critical figures—carefully worded missives that would sow seeds of doubt among the moderates and bolster support among the radicals. His pen moved swiftly, ink flowing like the currents of the Seine, shaping narratives to his design.

Pausing, he gazed out the window at the city sprawled beneath the night sky. The silhouettes of rooftops and spires formed a jagged horizon against the backdrop of stars.

He felt a surge of determination. Manipulating Robespierre's doubts was a crucial step. The moderates' grip would weaken, and the influential leader would lean towards a more radical stance.

Yet, amidst his calculated manoeuvres, a sliver of introspection pierced his thoughts. Olympe's earlier caution echoed faintly—a reminder of the moral complexities entwined with his ambitions.

He dismissed the sentiment with a shake of his head. The stakes were too high for hesitation.

Extinguishing the lamp, Étienne settled into the darkness, his resolve unwavering. The wheels were in motion, and he was at the helm.

As sleep eluded him, he contemplated the days ahead—a tapestry of possibilities woven with threads of intrigue and influence. He would navigate them with precision, ever closer to realising his vision.

The revolution was a crucible, and he intended to emerge forged anew, unburdened by the constraints of the past.

• • •

The chill of early spring lingered in the air on 15 March 1790 as Étienne Corbeau made his way through the bustling streets of Paris. The city was awakening from winter's grasp, yet the atmosphere remained tense. Street vendors hawked their wares amidst the din of horse-drawn carriages and the chatter of citizens debating the latest developments from the National Assembly.

Étienne adjusted his coat, the fine wool shielding him from the brisk breeze that swept along the Rue Saint-Honoré. His eyes scanned the crowd, noting the clusters of Sans-culottes discussing the price of bread and the murmurings of discontent that simmered beneath the surface. The revolution was gaining momentum, but so were the factions within it.

He arrived at the Café Procope, its façade unassuming but its interior abuzz with political discourse. Pushing open the heavy wooden door, the familiar aroma of roasted coffee beans and the hum of animated conversation greeted him. Candles flickered on tables scattered throughout the establishment, casting a warm glow.

Spotting Camille Desmoulins hunched over a pile of pamphlets, Étienne weaved through the maze of chairs to join him. "Camille," he greeted, his voice cutting through the din.

Desmoulins looked up, a smile spreading across his boyish features. "Étienne! Sit, please. Have you seen the latest declarations?"

Étienne settled into the chair opposite him. "Not yet. Anything of interest?"

"Always," Desmoulins replied, his eyes alight with enthusiasm. "The tide is turning in our favour. The people grow weary of half-measures."

"Indeed," Étienne mused, though his thoughts were elsewhere.

Before he could delve further, a booming voice resonated from the corner of the café. "Ah, if it isn't, Monsieur Corbeau gracing us with his presence!"

Étienne turned to see Georges Danton approaching, his towering frame and commanding presence drawing the attention of nearby patrons. Danton's eyes sparkled with a mix of delight and challenge. "I was thinking you'd forgotten your old comrades."

"Danton," Étienne acknowledged with a measured nod. "I see you're keeping the spirits high."

"Someone must," Danton quipped, pulling up a chair without invitation. "The Assembly debates drag on endlessly, and the people grow restless."

Desmoulins interjected, "We were discussing the need for more decisive action."

"Were you now?" Danton's gaze flickered between them. "And what does our esteemed strategist propose?"

Étienne met his gaze evenly. "I believe it's time we push for more radical reforms. The monarchy remains a thorn in our side, and the moderates lack the resolve to address it."

Danton leaned back, a hint of a smirk playing on his lips. "Radical reforms? Or perhaps you mean radical control?"

"What's that supposed to mean?" Étienne's tone sharpened.

"Only that you've been quite eager to steer the revolution according to your designs," Danton remarked casually. "Some might say too eager."

Desmoulins shifted uncomfortably. "We're all working towards the same goal, are we not?"

"Are we?" Danton's eyes bore into Étienne's. "I've heard whispers, my friend. Whispers that you seek to undermine those who stand in your way."

Étienne's jaw tightened. "Whispers are the currency of cowards. If you have something to say, speak plainly."

"Very well," Danton said, his voice dropping to a lower register. "Your machinations have not gone unnoticed. You sow discord among our allies and manipulate opinions to suit your agenda. I wonder where your true loyalties lie."

Desmoulins glanced between them, his expression one of alarm. "Gentlemen, this is neither the time nor the place—"

Étienne cut him off. "My loyalties are to the revolution and France. Can you say the same, Danton?"

Danton's smirk vanished. "Careful, Étienne. Accusations can be dangerous."

"As an unchecked ambition," Étienne retorted.

The tension between them was palpable, drawing the gaze of others nearby. A hush fell over the immediate vicinity, the surrounding conversations fading into murmurs.

At that moment, Maximilien Robespierre entered the café, his keen eyes immediately assessing the situation. Sensing the charged atmosphere, he approached swiftly. "What is the meaning of this?" he demanded quietly.

Danton broke the stare with Étienne, turning to Robespierre. "A simple disagreement, nothing more."

Étienne rose from his seat. "Perhaps it's best we continue this discussion elsewhere."

"Perhaps," Danton agreed, though his tone suggested the matter was far from settled.

Robespierre placed a calming hand on Danton's arm. "We cannot afford internal strife. The revolution requires unity."

"Tell that to those who undermine it from within," Danton replied, casting a last glance at Étienne before moving away.

Desmoulins exhaled heavily. "That escalated quickly."

Étienne remained standing, his gaze fixed on Danton's retreating figure. "He oversteps," he muttered.

Robespierre regarded him thoughtfully. "Georges is passionate, but his influence among the people is significant. We must tread carefully."

"His popularity blinds him," Étienne replied. "He believes himself untouchable."

"Perhaps a private conversation would be more productive," Robespierre suggested.

Étienne nodded curtly. "Agreed. I have no desire for public spectacles."

"Good," Robespierre said. "We shall arrange a meeting."

As Robespierre departed to speak with Danton, Desmoulins touched Étienne's arm. "What was that about?"

Étienne's expression hardened. "Danton sees me as a threat to his prominence. He cannot fathom that others may have ideas worth considering."

"He's brash, yes, but his heart is in the right place," Desmoulins offered.

"Is it?" Étienne countered. "Or is he simply another obstacle?"

Desmoulins frowned. "You speak as though we're enemies."

Étienne sighed, softening his tone. "Forgive me, Camille. Tensions are high, and perhaps I've let my frustrations get the better of me."

"I understand," Desmoulins said gently. "But we must remain united."

"Of course," Étienne agreed, though his mind already contemplated possibilities. Danton's influence was indeed a problem—one that needed addressing.

Leaving the café, Étienne stepped out into the fading light of day. The streets were alive with activity, but he felt disconnected from the surrounding bustle. As he walked, he contemplated his next move.

Perhaps we could subtly undermine Danton without drawing undue attention by spreading rumours and raising questions about his motives—nothing overt but enough to sow seeds of doubt among his supporters.

Lost in thought, Étienne nearly walked past Olympe de Gouges, who was emerging from a print shop laden with pamphlets.

"Étienne!" she called out, her eyes bright with surprise.

He paused. "Olympe. Good evening."

She approached him, adjusting the stack of papers in her arms. "You seem preoccupied."

"Just the usual," he replied lightly. "The revolution waits for no one."

"True enough," she agreed. "But one must take care not to lose oneself."

He offered a small smile. "Wise advice."

She studied him for a moment. "I heard about the exchange at the café. Word travels fast."

"Does it now?" Étienne said, his expression unreadable.

"Be cautious, Étienne," she urged. "Division within our ranks only serves those who oppose us."

"Danton and I had a disagreement, nothing more."

"Perhaps," she allowed. "But he's a valuable ally."

"Allies can become liabilities," Étienne remarked before he could stop himself.

Her eyes narrowed slightly. "Take care that ambition does not cloud your judgement."

He met her gaze. "Ambition drives progress."

"At what cost?" she challenged softly.

He sighed. "You misunderstand me."

"Do I?" she asked, her tone gentle but firm. "Just remember, the revolution is bigger than any of us."

"I'll keep that in mind," he said, his voice betraying nothing.

"Good." She offered a warm smile. "Take care, Étienne."

As she walked away, Étienne felt something akin to regret. But he pushed it aside. There was too much at stake to be swayed by sentiment.

Returning to his apartment, he sat at his desk, quill in hand. He began drafting letters to critical individuals—subtle missives that would plant doubts about Danton's commitment and motives. He knew it was a calculated risk, but one he deemed necessary. "15 March 1790," he wrote at the top of a page. "Today marks the beginning of a necessary shift."

He paused, the silence of the room pressing in around him. For a fleeting moment, he considered the path he was embarking upon. But the moment passed, and his resolve hardened.

Danton's popularity threatened Étienne's ambitions and the revolution's potential for genuine change. If others could not see that, he would have to show them.

As the candle burned low, Étienne worked late into the night, orchestrating the next move in his intricate game. The pieces were in place; it was time to set them in motion.

•••

The early morning of 22 April 1790 brought a brisk breeze that rustled through the budding leaves along the Boulevard du Temple. Étienne Corbeau stood beneath the archway of an unassuming building, his eyes fixed on the crowds moving through the Parisian streets. The city pulsed with restless energy, the undercurrents of revolution stirring the hearts of radicals and moderates alike.

He pulled his coat tighter against the chill, the fabric whispering against the leather-bound journal beneath his arm. Today, he had arranged a meeting that could tip the balance in his favour—a gathering of the most sincere radicals, those whose passion for change burned brightest. Among them was Louis de Saint-Just, a young deputy whose eloquence and intensity had caught Étienne's attention.

As the bells of a distant church chimed the hour, Étienne made his way inside, ascending a narrow staircase to a private salon adorned with ornate yet fading tapestries. The room was dimly lit by a chandelier whose candles cast a warm glow over the faces of those assembled. Saint-Just stood near the fireplace, his sharp features softened by the flickering light. His eyes, however, held a steely determination that belied his youthful appearance.

"Étienne," Saint-Just greeted him with a curt nod. "We were wondering if you would join us."

"I wouldn't miss it," Étienne replied smoothly, offering a thin smile. "The matters at hand are too pressing."

Around them, murmurs of agreement rippled through the group. Jean-Paul Marat sat at a heavy wooden table, his quill scratching furiously across parchment as he penned his latest diatribe for *L'Ami du peuple*. Nearby, a cluster of Sans-culottes listened intently, their rough-hewn attire contrasting with the polished boots of the bourgeois radicals.

Saint-Just gestured towards an empty chair. "Please share your thoughts."

Étienne took his seat, allowing a moment of silence to draw their attention fully. "We stand at a crossroads," he began, his voice measured. "The moderates in the Assembly grow complacent, their vision clouded by a desire to placate the monarchy."

Marat looked up from his writing, his eyes narrowing. "They are cowards, the lot of them."

"Perhaps," Étienne conceded. "But we should not underestimate their influence," Étienne conceded. "To steer the revolution towards genuine change, we must unite our efforts."

A Sans-culotte with a weathered face and a fiery gaze leaned forward. "And how do you propose we do that, Monsieur Corbeau?"

Étienne's steady gaze by presenting a unified front. "We must channel our shared enthusiasm to fight for the reforms the people are calling for—ending the monarchy, redistributing land, and achieving true *egalité*."

Saint-Just's lips curved into a faint smile. "Spoken like a man who understands the heart of the revolution."

"Flattery aside," Marat interjected, "actions speak louder than words. The moderates talk of change but fear the very essence of it."

"Precisely," Étienne agreed. "Which is why we need to influence the discourse within the Assembly. Our voices must be the ones that resonate, drowning out the timid whispers of compromise."

Saint-Just regarded him thoughtfully. "You suggest a strategic alliance?"

"Yes," Étienne affirmed. "One that leverages our strengths. Your oratory skills, Louis, are unparalleled. And Marat's writings reach the masses in ways few others can."

Marat huffed though a glint of pride flickered in his eyes. "At least someone appreciates my efforts."

A murmur of assent swept through the room. The radicals were eager, their passions stoked by the prospect of tangible action.

"However," Étienne continued, "We must also be cautious. The moderates may be hesitant, but they have their merits. If we approach them correctly, we may sway some of them to our cause."

Saint-Just arched an eyebrow. "You propose we collaborate with those who lack conviction?"

"Not collaborate," Étienne corrected gently. "Influence. Guide them towards the inevitable conclusions that we have already reached."

Marat's expression darkened. "I have little patience for those who waver."

"And yet," Étienne countered, "alienating them could hinder our progress. We must be tacticians and idealists."

Saint-Just nodded slowly. "There's wisdom in your words. We cannot afford to create enemies within our own ranks."

A young woman with sharp features and piercing eyes spoke up. "And what of the people? They grow impatient with the lack of progress."

Étienne turned his attention to her. "*Mademoiselle,* the people's impatience is both our weapon and our responsibility. We must channel it constructively, lest it erupts uncontrollably."

She tilted her head. "You speak like one who walks the line between worlds."

"Perhaps I do," he admitted. "But it's a line that allows me to see the broader picture."

Saint-Just glanced around the room. "Very well. I propose we formalise this alliance. Together, we'll draught a manifesto that outlines our demands unequivocally."

Marat tapped his quill against the table. "I'll ensure it reaches every corner of Paris."

Étienne inclined his head. "Excellent. I can facilitate introductions to certain moderates who may be receptive. They could prove valuable in swaying votes within the Assembly."

Saint-Just extended his hand. "To the revolution, then."

Étienne grasped it. "To the revolution."

As the meeting dispersed, Étienne lingered by the window, gazing out at the cityscape bathed in the golden hues of late afternoon. The voices behind him faded into the background as he contemplated the path ahead.

"You're quite the strategist," came a voice at his side.

He turned to find Olympe de Gouges observing him, her expression inscrutable. "Olympe," he acknowledged. "I wasn't aware you were here."

"I have a knack for blending into the background," she replied wryly. "Unlike you, who seems to prefer centre stage."

He offered a faint smile. "I merely do what needs to be done."

She studied him for a moment. "Be careful, Étienne. Balancing between radicals and moderates is a precarious act."

"I'm well aware," he assured her. "But it's necessary."

"Is it?" she challenged. "Or is it simply a means to advance your ambitions?"

He met her gaze unflinchingly. "Can it not be both?"

She sighed softly. "Just remember that the revolution is not a game. People's lives hang in the balance."

"Trust me," he said quietly, "I haven't forgotten."

She searched his face before nodding subtly. "Very well. Take care."

As she walked away, Étienne felt a pang of something—was it doubt? He dismissed the notion. There was no room for hesitation.

Leaving the salon, he stepped out onto the bustling street. The sounds of Paris enveloped him—the clatter of carriage wheels, the distant strains of a violin, the murmur of countless conversations weaving together in an intricate tapestry.

He made his way towards the Tuileries Garden, where clusters of citizens gathered to discuss the latest news. He approached, spotting a familiar figure seated on a bench beneath a chestnut tree.

"Maximilien," Étienne greeted.

Robespierre looked up from the book in his lap, surprise flickering across his features. "Étienne. This is an unexpected meeting."

"Is it?" Étienne took a seat beside him. "Paris is small when one walks its streets enough."

Robespierre closed his book, marking his place with a ribbon. "How did your gathering go?"

"Productive," Étienne replied. "The radicals are eager to take decisive action."

Robespierre regarded him carefully. "And you align yourself with them fully now?"

"I align myself with progress," Étienne said. "The moderates stagnate, Maximilien. They fear the very change they profess to support."

Robespierre sighed. "Principle, not merely speed, must guide change."

"Agreed," Étienne allowed. "But principle without action is merely philosophy."

A faint smile tugged at Robespierre's lips. "Ever the pragmatist."

"Someone has to be," Étienne retorted lightly.

Robespierre's gaze drifted to the canopy of leaves overhead. "The intensity of the radicals concerns me, as it may lead to extremism."

"Which is why it's crucial to have voices like yours involved," Étienne urged. "To temper passion with wisdom."

Robespierre glanced at him. "And you believe you can bridge that gap?"

"I believe I can facilitate understanding," Étienne said. "But I need your support."

A moment of silence stretched between them.

"Very well," Robespierre conceded. "I will attend the next meeting."

Étienne inclined his head. "Your presence would be invaluable."

As they parted ways, Étienne felt satisfied. He had pulled Robespierre closer to the radicals, furthering his agenda of consolidating influence.

That evening, he attended a salon hosted by Madame de Staël. The air was thick with the scent of jasmine and intellectual discourse. Parisian society's crème de la crème mingled, their conversations blending art, politics, and philosophy.

Madame de Staël approached him, her eyes bright beneath an elaborate hairstyle. "Monsieur Corbeau, I've heard much about your recent endeavours."

"All favourable, I hope," he replied with a charming smile.

"Intriguing," she countered. "You seem to be at the heart of many developments."

"I prefer to think of myself as a humble participant," he demurred.

She laughed lightly. "Humility suits you, though I suspect it's only part of the story."

"Perhaps," he conceded. "But tell me, what is the mood among your guests tonight?"

She gestured gracefully towards the assembled crowd. "Mixed, as always. There is excitement, apprehension, hope."

"All fertile ground for progress," Étienne observed.

"Indeed," she agreed. "Just be cautious not to create discord where unity is needed," she cautioned, agreeing.

"Sound advice," he acknowledged.

As the evening progressed, Étienne navigated the salon easily, engaging in conversations that allowed him to gauge and subtly influence opinions. He noted potential allies, assessed sceptics and planted seeds of thought that might bear fruit later.

Returning home in the quiet hours, he reflected on the day's events. Mastering the art of balancing the radicals' zeal and the moderates' prudence was a challenge he felt assured in conquering.

22 April 1790, he wrote in his journal. *The pieces align ever more closely. Influence grows, and with it, opportunity.*

He paused, the quill hovering over the page. A flicker of doubt surfaced—Olympe's words echoing faintly. Shaking his head, he dismissed the thought. There was no place for hesitation.

Extinguishing the candle, he gazed out the window at the city bathed in moonlight. The revolution churned like the currents of the Seine, and he was determined to steer it towards the future he envisioned.

With a resolute heart, Étienne Corbeau embraced his chosen path, ever mindful of the balance he maintained between passion and pragmatism, between radical and moderate. The game was advancing, and he intended to hold all the cards.

•••

The morning of 15 May 1790 dawned with a sullen, overcast sky, the clouds hanging low over Paris as if mirroring the mood of its inhabitants. Étienne Corbeau stood at the window of his modest apartment overlooking the Rue Saint-Honoré, watching the city stir to life. The distant clatter of hooves on cobblestones and the murmur of vendors setting up their stalls reached his ears, a familiar symphony of the waking metropolis.

He sipped his coffee thoughtfully, his gaze distant. Today, he had met Maximilien Robespierre at a quiet café near the *Jardin des Tuileries.* Word had reached him that Robespierre was wrestling with doubts about the revolution's trajectory—a vulnerability that Étienne intended to exploit.

Dressing with care, he donned a tailored coat of deep burgundy, its brass buttons twinkling in the muted light. He adjusted his cravat, ensuring that every fold was precise. Appearance, he knew, could be as persuasive as words.

By mid-morning, Étienne arrived at Café des Fleurs, a quaint establishment tucked away from the bustling thoroughfares. The scent of freshly baked bread and the subtle aroma of roasted coffee beans greeted him as he entered. When he entered Café des Fleurs, he found Robespierre seated at a corner table, with a stiff posture and a cup of untouched tea before him.

"Maximilien," Étienne greeted warmly, approaching the table. "I hope I haven't kept you waiting."

Robespierre looked up, a faint smile flickering across his pale features. "Not at all, Étienne. I fear my thoughts have been poor company this morning."

Étienne took the seat opposite him, signalling to the proprietor for a coffee. "You seem troubled. Is everything all right?"

Robespierre sighed, his fingers tracing the rim of his teacup. "I find myself at odds, conflicted about the path we tread. The revolution surges forward, yet I wonder if we are losing sight of our principles."

Étienne leaned in slightly. "What brings about these doubts?"

"Violence escalates in the streets," Robespierre replied, his eyes reflecting a deep weariness. "The people grow restless, and factions within the Assembly pull us in divergent directions. I fear we risk becoming the very thing we sought to overthrow."

Étienne studied him carefully. "Change is seldom without turmoil. You know that as well as anyone."

"True," Robespierre conceded. "I wonder if our methods are consistent with the values of liberty and justice that we passionately proclaim."

Their drinks arrived, and Étienne took a moment to savour the rich aroma of his coffee before speaking. "Maximilien, your dedication to principle is admirable. It's what sets you apart. But perhaps you're being too harsh on yourself and the revolution."

Robespierre looked at him intently. "Explain."

Étienne chose his words with care. "Consider the enormity of what we're attempting. Overturning centuries of entrenched monarchy, restructuring society—these are monumental tasks. Resistance and conflict are inevitable."

Robespierre nodded slowly. "I accept that. Yet, I cannot shake the feeling that we are teetering on the edge of a precipice."

"Then perhaps," Étienne suggested gently, "we need to take firmer control. Guide the revolution more decisively to prevent it from veering off course."

"Firmer control?" Robespierre echoed. "You mean embracing more extreme measures?"

Étienne met his gaze steadily. "Not extremism for its own sake. But decisive action is to safeguard the revolution's integrity. We cannot allow indecision or half-measures to undermine all we've worked for."

Robespierre sighed again. "I worry about the cost. The lives disrupted, the potential for abuse of power."

"Power, in the right hands, can steer us towards our goals," Étienne asserted. "Think of it not as wielding power over others, but as a responsibility to lead."

Robespierre was silent for a moment, his expression contemplative. "Perhaps you're right. Perhaps I've been too cautious."

"Your caution stems from your integrity," Étienne acknowledged. "But sometimes, the times demand boldness."

Robespierre took a sip of his now-cold tea, grimacing slightly at the taste. "I've always believed that virtue must guide our actions."

"And it should," Étienne agreed. "But virtue without strength is vulnerable. We must be prepared to defend our ideals with conviction."

A subtle shift occurred in Robespierre's demeanour—a straightening of the shoulders, a renewed focus in his eyes. "You've given me much to consider."

"That's all I ask," Étienne said with a reassuring smile. "We stand on the cusp of significant change. Together, we can ensure it's the change we envision."

Robespierre offered a faint smile in return. "Your counsel is invaluable, Étienne. I appreciate your friendship."

"As I appreciate yours," Étienne replied.

They settled into more casual conversation, discussing the latest debates in the Assembly and the ever-present issue of the monarchy's influence. Étienne continued subtly reinforcing his points, guiding Robespierre's thoughts towards a more assertive stance.

As they parted ways outside the café, the sun had broken through the clouds, casting a pale light over the city.

"Perhaps the weather reflects a change in fortunes," Robespierre remarked, glancing upward.

"Let us hope so," Étienne said. "I'll be in touch soon. There is much work to be done."

"Indeed," Robespierre agreed. "Until then."

Watching Robespierre walk away, Étienne allowed himself a moment of satisfaction. His words had found their mark, nudging Robespierre towards the path he desired.

Turning to make his way back through the *Jardin des Tuileries*, Camille Desmoulins, who appeared slightly out of breath, intercepted Étienne.

"Étienne! I've been looking for you," Camille exclaimed.

"Camille, always a pleasure. What urgent matter brings you here?"

Desmoulins fell into step beside him. "Have you heard about the latest proposal from the moderates? They're pushing for a constitutional monarchy with significant powers kept by the King."

Étienne's expression darkened. "I was not aware. It seems they grow bolder in their foolishness."

"Exactly," Desmoulins agreed. "We need to rally opposition. Robespierre's support would be invaluable."

Étienne nodded thoughtfully. "I just spoke with him. He's beginning to see the necessity of a firmer approach."

"That's encouraging," Desmoulins said. "Perhaps we should convene a meeting of like-minded deputies."

"A wise idea," Étienne concurred. "I'll make the arrangements."

As they walked, they passed a group of Sans-culottes gathered around a street performer. The atmosphere was lively, yet an undercurrent of tension was palpable.

"Have you noticed the growing unrest?" Desmoulins asked quietly.

"It's difficult to miss," Étienne replied. "All the more reason for us to provide clear direction."

"Agreed. The people need leadership."

They parted ways at a crossroads, with Étienne promising to contact him soon.

Continuing alone, Étienne contemplated the shifting dynamics. His influence over Robespierre was strengthening, and with it, his ability to shape the revolution's course. Yet he remained cautious. Others might seek to sway Robespierre differently.

As he approached the Louvre, he encountered Olympe de Gouges, carrying a stack of pamphlets.

"Étienne," she greeted him with a warm smile. "It's been a while."

"Olympe, always a delight," he responded. "Spreading the word, as usual?"

"Indeed," she said, adjusting the papers in her arms. "And you? Plotting the revolution's next move?"

He chuckled softly. "Something like that."

Her gaze turned serious. "I've heard rumours that tensions within the Assembly are escalating. Some speak of more extreme measures."

"Rumours often exaggerate," Étienne replied evasively.

"Perhaps, but there's often a kernel of truth," she countered. "I worry that the revolution is veering towards unnecessary violence."

"Change is rarely peaceful," he said. "But my aim is to guide events towards a positive outcome."

She studied him for a moment. "Just be careful, Étienne. The line between leadership and manipulation is thin."

He met her eyes. "I appreciate your concern. I assure you, my intentions are honourable."

"Very well," she said, though her expression remained thoughtful. "Take care."

"And you," he replied.

Continuing on his way, Étienne dismissed her cautions. He was certain of his path.

Later that afternoon, he arrived at the National Assembly, the grand hall buzzing with activity. Deputies clustered in groups, their discussions animated. Étienne sought Louis de Saint-Just, finding him engaged in a heated debate with a moderate deputy.

"Louis," Étienne interrupted smoothly. "A moment, if you please."

Saint-Just turned to him, his sharp features relaxing slightly. "Étienne, of course."

They stepped aside. "I've just spoken with Robespierre," Étienne informed him. "He's beginning to understand the need for more decisive action."

"That's encouraging news," Saint-Just said. "The moderates grow more obstinate by the day."

"Indeed. We need to present a united front," Étienne said. "I suggest we organise a gathering to formalise our strategy."

"Agreed," Saint-Just replied. "I'll reach out to our allies."

As they spoke, Étienne noticed Georges Danton across the hall, his booming laugh carrying over the din. Their eyes met briefly, and Étienne detected a hint of suspicion in Danton's gaze.

"Be mindful of Danton," Saint-Just remarked quietly. "He watches everyone."

"I'm aware," Étienne said. "But we have nothing to fear."

Saint-Just nodded. "Very well. I'll see you this evening."

As the day wore on, Étienne immersed himself in the Assembly's machinations, deftly navigating conversations and alliances. His influence was growing, and threads of connection were weaving ever tighter around key figures.

By nightfall, he returned to his apartment, weary but satisfied. Settling at his desk, he penned letters to various contacts, solidifying plans for the days ahead.

"15 May 1790," he wrote in his journal. "Robespierre's doubts have opened the door. Control slips further into my grasp."

He paused, considering the weight of his actions. Yet his conviction overshadowed any lingering hesitation as he paused, considering the weight of his actions. The revolution needed direction, and he was prepared to provide it.

Extinguishing the candle, Étienne gazed out into the darkness. The city sprawled before him, its myriad lights flickering like stars fallen to earth.

"To shape the future," he whispered. "That is the path I've chosen."

With that, he turned away, resolute in his purpose. The days ahead would demand much of him, but he was ready to meet the challenge.

The revolution marched on, and Étienne Corbeau intended to lead the way.

• • •

The heat of early summer settled over Paris on 10 June 1790, casting a hazy glow upon the city's bustling streets. Étienne Corbeau strolled along the Rue de Rivoli, his polished boots clicking softly against the cobblestones. The scent of blooming jasmine mingled with the distant aroma of fresh bread from a nearby boulangerie. Yet, beneath the veneer of a city in bloom, tensions simmered within the National Assembly.

Étienne adjusted his waistcoat, a finely tailored garment of deep emerald, as he approached a discreet entrance to a renowned salon.

Madame de Staël's gatherings were the epicentre of intellectual discourse; tonight, they would serve his purpose well. He slipped inside, the murmur of conversation and the clinking of crystal glasses enveloping him.

The salon was awash with the elite of Parisian society—philosophers, politicians, artists—all engaged in animated discussions. Chandeliers cast a warm glow over gilded mirrors and opulent tapestries depicting scenes of pastoral tranquillity, a stark contrast to the undercurrents of political unrest.

Spotting Jacques-Louis David, the eminent painter, Étienne approached him. David stood near a grand piano, his intense gaze fixed upon a heated debate between the two deputies.

"Jacques-Louis," Étienne greeted with a subtle nod.

"Étienne," David replied, offering a faint smile. "Have you come to observe the spectacle?"

"Indeed," Étienne said lightly. "One can always rely on Madame de Staël's salons for spirited entertainment."

David chuckled softly. "Tonight's topic seems to be the virtues of a constitutional monarchy versus a republic."

"Ah, a debate as old as the revolution itself," Étienne remarked. "And where do you stand?"

David's eyes narrowed thoughtfully. "I find myself increasingly disillusioned with those who cling to the remnants of the old order."

Étienne glanced across the room, where the Marquis de Lafayette conversed earnestly with a group of moderates. His impeccable uniform and measured gestures exuded confidence. Nearby, Honoré Gabriel Riqueti, the Comte de Mirabeau, held court, his commanding presence drawing admirers and critics alike.

"Lafayette and Mirabeau," Étienne mused, his tone laced with subtle disdain. "Men who speak of change yet fear its true implications."

David followed his gaze. "They wield significant influence within the Assembly."

"Perhaps too much," Étienne said softly. "Their moderation hampers progress."

David inquired curiously if he believed they could be swayed.

Étienne offered a cryptic smile. "All men have their weaknesses."

Excusing himself, Étienne moved gracefully through the crowd, his path deliberately crossing that of Madame de Staël. She was a vision of elegance, her auburn hair artfully arranged, her eyes bright with intellect.

"Madame," he greeted, kissing her gloved hand. "Your salon is as enchanting as ever."

"Étienne," she replied warmly. "You flatter me. I trust you are finding the evening enlightening?"

"Most certainly," he assured her. "The diversity of thought here is unparalleled."

She leaned in slightly. "Tell me, what are your thoughts on our esteemed Marquis's latest propositions?"

He adopted a thoughtful expression. "While Lafayette's intentions may be noble, I fear his ties to the monarchy cloud his judgement."

Madame de Staël raised an eyebrow. "An interesting perspective."

"One shared by many," Étienne added conspiratorially. "There are whispers that his loyalties may not lie entirely with the people."

She tilted her head. "Whispers can be dangerous, Étienne."

He met her gaze. "Only when they carry truth."

She regarded him for a moment before nodding subtly. "I see. Enjoy the rest of your evening."

As she moved away, Étienne allowed himself a satisfied smile. Someone had planted the seed.

Later, he conversed with a group of young deputies, eager and impressionable.

"Mirabeau's debts are a matter of public record," Étienne remarked casually. "One wonders how they might influence his positions within the Assembly."

A deputy named Lucien leaned in. "Are you suggesting that someone has compromised him?"

Étienne shrugged delicately. "I merely observe that financial pressures can sway even the most steadfast individuals."

Another deputy, Henri, frowned. "If true, this could undermine his credibility."

Étienne placed a reassuring hand on Henri's shoulder. "It is our duty to ensure that those beyond reproach lead the revolution."

The murmurs of agreement that followed told him his words had found their mark.

As the evening waned, Étienne stepped onto the balcony overlooking the Seine. The river glistened under the moonlight, the gentle ripple of water providing a momentary respite from the intrigues within.

"Finding solace in solitude?" a familiar voice asked.

He turned to see Olympe de Gouges approaching, her expression blending curiosity and concern.

"Olympe," he acknowledged. "The air inside grew stifling."

She joined him at the balustrade. "I couldn't help but notice your conversations tonight. You seem intent on casting shadows over certain individuals."

He raised an eyebrow. "I merely share information. What others choose to do with it is their prerogative."

She sighed softly. "Étienne, spreading rumours serves no one but those who wish to see us divided."

"Perhaps the truth is divisive," he countered.

"Or perhaps it's being manipulated," she retorted. "Lafayette and Mirabeau have their faults but have also contributed significantly to our cause."

"Have they?" Étienne's tone grew sharper. "Or have they sought to temper the revolution to maintain their own standing?"

She studied him intently. "What is your endgame, Étienne? Do you wish to see the revolution succeed, or simply to see your rivals fall?"

He met her gaze, unflinching. "Sometimes, the two are the same."

She shook her head. "Be careful, my friend. In seeking to undermine others, you may find the ground crumbling beneath your own feet."

"Thank you for your concern," he said coolly. "But I assure you, I am quite steady."

She looked as though she might say more but thought better of it. "Good night, Étienne."

"Good night, Olympe."

After she departed, Étienne lingered a moment longer, his mind already plotting his next moves.

The following day, 11 June 1790, the National Assembly was abuzz with speculation. Rumours of Mirabeau's alleged dealings with the court and whispers questioning Lafayette's commitment to the revolutionary cause spread like wildfire.

Étienne sat in the gallery, observing the unease ripple through the deputies. Camille Desmoulins approached, his brow furrowed.

"Have you heard the latest?" Camille asked, sliding into the seat beside him.

"I've heard many things," Étienne replied enigmatically. "To which are you referring?"

"Mirabeau is under scrutiny for supposedly negotiating with the Royalists," Camille said in a hushed tone. "And there are claims that Lafayette seeks to suppress the people's voice."

Étienne feigned surprise. "Troubling, if true."

Camille eyed him sceptically. "You wouldn't know anything about the origins of these rumours?"

"Me?" Étienne placed a hand over his heart. "I am but a humble observer."

Camille sighed. "Étienne, these allegations could fracture the Assembly."

"Perhaps it's time we confront uncomfortable truths," Étienne suggested. "Our movement cannot afford to be led astray."

Before Camille could respond, Georges Danton's voice boomed across the chamber as he addressed the Assembly.

"Honourable deputies," Danton declared, "certain individuals may not hold the revolution's best interests at heart. We must investigate these claims thoroughly."

Étienne watched with concealed satisfaction as tension escalated. Mirabeau rose to defend himself, his eloquence doing little to quell the doubts sown among his peers. Scepticism greeted Lafayette's attempts to restore order.

Maximilien Robespierre observed the proceedings with a grave expression. Catching Étienne's eye, he gestured for him to join him outside the chamber.

Once in the corridor, Robespierre spoke quietly. "This discord is alarming. Do you know anything about it?"

Étienne met his gaze evenly. "I've heard the rumours, as have we all. If there is merit to them, we must act accordingly."

Robespierre studied him. "I hope you're not involved in spreading unverified claims."

"Maximilien," Étienne said evenly, "my only concern is the integrity of the revolution."

Robespierre nodded slowly. "Very well. But we must tread carefully. Baseless accusations could lead to chaos."

"Agreed," Étienne replied, though inwardly he revelled in the unfolding turmoil.

Over the next few days, the Assembly became a battlefield of ideologies and personal vendettas. The moderates found themselves on the defensive, and their proposals met with increasing hostility. Étienne continued to fan the flames subtly, his influence growing among the radicals who sought decisive action.

Jean-Paul Marat approached him after a contentious session. "Your handiwork is clear," Marat remarked, a hint of admiration in his tone.

"I strive only to expose the truth," Étienne said modestly.

Marat's eyes gleamed. "With the moderates weakened, we can push forward with our agenda."

"Precisely," Étienne agreed. "The path is clearing."

As the weeks progressed, Mirabeau's health faltered under the strain, and Lafayette's reputation suffered irreparable damage among the revolutionaries. Étienne watched with satisfaction as his rivals stumbled, their influence waning.

The key radical leaders convened a secret meeting on 25 June 1790. Étienne, Robespierre, Danton, Saint-Just, and Marat convened in a dimly lit chamber beneath a tavern.

"The time seizes the initiative," Étienne declared. "With the moderates discredited, we can drive the revolution towards its rightful conclusion."

Robespierre nodded thoughtfully. "We ensure our actions serve the people's interests."

"Of course," Étienne agreed smoothly. "But we cannot allow hesitation to undermine us."

Danton grinned. "I must admit, Étienne, your tactics have been effective."

Marat leaned forward. "We should capitalise on this momentum."

Saint-Just added, "Agreed. We must purge the Assembly of those who hinder progress."

Étienne felt a surge of triumph. "Then we all share a common purpose."

As the meeting adjourned, Robespierre pulled Étienne aside. "I trust we shall maintain transparency among ourselves."

"Naturally," Étienne replied. "Our strength lies in our unity."

Robespierre's gaze lingered. "See that it does."

Walking home through the maze of streets, Étienne reflected on the events he had set in motion. The revolution was speeding up, and his position strengthened with each passing day.

Yet, in the shadows, unseen eyes watched. Olympe de Gouges observed him from a distance, concern etched upon her face. She resolved to confront him once more, hoping to appeal to whatever remnants of conscience he might possess.

But for Étienne Corbeau, the path was clear. The downfall of his rivals was a necessary sacrifice on the altar of progress. He embraced the chaos, confident in his ability to navigate its treacherous currents.

The Seine flowed steadily beside him, its dark waters reflecting the glimmer of lanterns. Paris slept uneasily, unaware of the machinations that would shape its destiny.

Étienne smiled to himself, the satisfaction of his schemes unfolding, warming him against the night's chill. The revolution was his to mould, and he intended to leave an indelible mark upon history.

• • •

The heavy air of 1 July 1790 hung over Paris like a damp cloak, the summer heat pressing down upon the city and its restless inhabitants. Étienne Corbeau navigated the labyrinthine streets with a purposeful stride, his mind a tumult of ambition and simmering frustration. The whispers of his recent machinations had rippled through the National Assembly, yet recognition eluded him. Others basked in the limelight, while he remained a shadowy orchestrator behind the scenes.

He arrived at the discreet entrance of a townhouse in the Rue Saint-Honoré, the appointed venue for a gathering of Maximilien Robespierre's inner circle. A stern-faced attendant nodded in silent acknowledgement as Étienne slipped inside, the murmur of voices guiding him towards a spacious salon illuminated by the warm glow of candlelight.

Robespierre stood near the marble fireplace, his austere features softened by the flickering flames. Beside him, Louis de Saint-Just listened intently, his sharp eyes reflecting a fiery intensity. Georges Danton dominated the centre of the room, his booming laughter and broad gestures commanding attention. Camille Desmoulins hovered at the periphery, scribbling notes with a quill that seemed an extension of his own restless energy. Jean-Paul Marat leaned against a bookcase, his gaze piercing beneath a furrowed brow.

"Étienne," Robespierre greeted him with a slight incline of his head. "I'm pleased you could join us."

"Thank you for the invitation," Étienne replied smoothly, suppressing the irritation that gnawed at him. He moved to pour himself a glass of wine, the rich aroma of the vintage offering a momentary distraction.

Danton clapped a hand on his shoulder. "Our resident strategist arrives! We've been debating the latest proposals from the Assembly. Care to share your insights?"

Étienne forced a smile. "Always eager to contribute."

As the group settled into discussion, Étienne listened as Danton and Desmoulins regaled the others with tales of their public engagements, the crowds they had stirred, and the accolades they had received. Even Marat's incendiary pamphlets garnered nods of approval. Étienne felt a surge of resentment. His efforts helped advance their cause, yet his name remained unspoken.

Robespierre cleared his throat. "We must contemplate our next steps. The moderates grow weaker, but the monarchy still holds sway. Public sentiment is volatile."

"Precisely why we need to maintain our presence among the people," Danton asserted. "They look to us for leadership."

Saint-Just interjected, "Principle must guide our actions. The purity of the revolution is paramount."

Étienne seized the moment. "Visibility is indeed important, but so is strategic planning. We should focus on consolidating our influence within the Assembly to enact lasting change."

Danton glanced at him. "Theory is well and good, Étienne, but it's the orators who inspire action."

A ripple of laughter passed through the group. Étienne's smile tightened. "Without a solid foundation, inspiration falters. My efforts have laid the groundwork for our recent successes."

Marat eyed him shrewdly. "True enough. Yet, perhaps it's time you stepped into the light. The people respond to those they can see and hear."

Robespierre nodded thoughtfully. "Marat raises a valid point. Your insights are valuable, Étienne. Perhaps you should address the Assembly directly."

Étienne inclined his head. "I would welcome the opportunity."

Desmoulins grinned. "Then it's settled. We'll arrange for you to speak at the next session."

As the conversation shifted, Étienne felt a flicker of satisfaction, yet the realisation that he still relied on others tempered it to grant him a platform. He yearned for a more prominent role that recognised his contributions and allowed him to shape events openly.

The gathering continued late into the evening, the air thick with the scent of wax and the rich tones of heated debate. When the attendees dispersed, Étienne lingered, approaching Robespierre as he sorted through a stack of papers.

"Maximilien," he began carefully, "I appreciate your support earlier."

Robespierre glanced up. "You've earned it. Your strategies have been instrumental."

"Thank you," Étienne said, choosing his words with care. "I wonder if we might discuss ways to further our objectives more aggressively."

Robespierre's gaze sharpened. "What do you have in mind?"

Étienne lowered his voice. "The time for cautious measures is waning. We must consider actions that will decisively undermine the monarchy and those who support it."

Robespierre regarded him steadily. "We must not compromise our principles. Unnecessary violence or tyranny must not taint the revolution."

"Of course," Étienne agreed smoothly. "But targeted actions could hasten our progress. We cannot allow hesitation to stall us."

Robespierre sighed softly. "I understand your eagerness, but we must proceed judiciously. The eyes of the world are upon us."

Étienne forced a smile. "Naturally. I merely wished to offer my help in any capacity you deem appropriate."

"I acknowledge your dedication," Robespierre replied, his tone polite but firm. "We shall speak further."

Recognising the dismissal, Étienne took his leave, frustration simmering beneath his composed exterior. Stepping out into the night, he inhaled the cool air, his mind racing. If Robespierre hesitated to embrace more decisive measures, perhaps it was time to pursue alternative avenues.

As he made his way along the dimly lit streets, a voice called out from a nearby alleyway. "Monsieur Corbeau!"

He turned to see a figure emerge from the shadows—Antoine, a Sans-culotte with whom he had cultivated a discreet alliance.

"Antoine," Étienne acknowledged. "What brings you out at this hour?"

Antoine glanced around before approaching. "There is unrest brewing in the Faubourg Saint-Antoine. The people grow impatient."

"Understandable," Étienne said thoughtfully. "Perhaps it's time to harness that impatience."

Antoine's eyes gleamed. "What do you propose?"

Étienne considered his response. "Gather your associates. We need to organise demonstrations that will compel the Assembly to act."

"Direct action," Antoine murmured appreciatively. "It would send a powerful message."

"Precisely," Étienne affirmed. Étienne affirmed, "We can channel it effectively with the right guidance."

Antoine nodded eagerly. "I'll make the arrangements."

As they parted ways, Étienne felt a surge of determination. If the established leaders hesitated, he would forge his own path. Applying the pressure to speed up the revolution, he could elevate his status by gaining the support of the Sans-culottes.

Étienne went to Jean-Paul Marat's print shop on the following day, 2 July 1790. The scent of ink and parchment permeated the cramped space, stacks of freshly printed pamphlets teetering precariously on the wooden tables.

"Étienne," Marat greeted him without looking up from his work. "What brings you here?"

"I have information that may interest you," Étienne replied, producing a folded paper from his coat.

Marat set down his quill, curiosity piqued. "Go on."

Étienne unfolded the document. "Details of the King's continued correspondence with foreign monarchs. Proof of his intent to undermine the revolution."

Marat's eyes flickered with intensity. "Where did you get this?"

"I have my sources," Étienne said evasively. "The people deserve to know the truth."

Marat's grip tightened on the paper. "Indeed, they do. This could ignite the enthusiasm we need."

"Exactly," Étienne agreed. "If you publish this in *L'Ami du peuple*, it would reach a vast audience."

Marat nodded slowly. "Consider it done."

As he left the print shop, Étienne allowed himself a rare smile. The pieces were aligning. With the Sans-culottes mobilised and Marat's inflammatory writings circulating, the pressure on the Assembly would intensify.

He spent the afternoon meeting discreetly with various contacts—organisers, agitators, sympathetic deputies—all the while weaving a web designed to elevate his profile and force the revolution towards a more radical course.

That evening, he attended a performance at the *Théâtre de la République*. The opulent surroundings and the melodious strains of the orchestra provided a stark contrast to the turmoil he was inciting. Spotting Olympe de Gouges in the audience, he approached her during the intermission.

"Étienne," she greeted him with a cautious smile. "A pleasure to see you."

"And you, Olympe," he replied. "Are you enjoying the performance?"

"It's a welcome respite from the day's tensions," she admitted. "Though I suspect you rarely allow yourself such indulgences."

He chuckled softly. "Even I must unwind occasionally."

She regarded him thoughtfully. "I've heard whispers of renewed unrest in the city. Do you know anything about it?"

He met her gaze evenly. "The people are restless. It's only natural."

"Natural, perhaps, but also dangerous," she cautioned. "We must strive to guide them constructively."

"Agreed," he said smoothly. "I'm doing what I can to ensure I hear their voices," he said.

She sighed softly. "Just be careful, Étienne. The line between leadership and exploitation is thin."

"Your concern is touching," he replied with a hint of sarcasm. "I have the revolution's best interests at heart."

She appeared to have more to say, but the chime signalling the end of intermission interrupted her.

"Until next time," she said, her expression unreadable.

"Indeed," he replied.

As the performance resumed, Étienne found his thoughts drifting. Olympe's words lingered, but he dismissed them as the product of misplaced idealism. He had no time for such distractions.

In the days that followed, the streets of Paris became a hive of activity. Demonstrations erupted, fuelled by Marat's publications and orchestrated by Étienne's network. The Assembly found itself besieged by demands for swift action against the monarchy.

Robespierre sought him out amidst the chaos. "Étienne, what is happening? The city teeters on the brink."

"Change is upon us," Étienne replied. "We must seize this moment."

Robespierre's eyes searched his. "Did you have a hand in this?"

"I merely provided the means for the people to express their will," Étienne said evasively.

Robespierre frowned. "This is reckless. We risk inciting violence that could consume us all."

"Bold action is required," Étienne insisted. "You said it yourself—we cannot compromise our ideals."

Robespierre shook his head. "This is not what I intended."

"Perhaps not," Étienne retorted. "But it's necessary."

As Robespierre walked away, Étienne felt a pang of irritation. If the so-called leaders lacked the resolve to act decisively, he would proceed without them.

By mid-July, his efforts bore fruit. His name circulated among the revolutionaries, his role in mobilising the masses earning him both admiration and scrutiny.

"Étienne Corbeau," they whispered. "A man to watch."

Satisfied but not content, Étienne continued to push forward, his ambitions stoked by the taste of recognition. He knew the path ahead was fraught with danger, but the allure of power outweighed any reservations.

As the sun set over Paris, casting the city in hues of gold and crimson, Étienne stood atop the steps of the Palais-Royal, surveying the throngs below. The crowd's murmur was a symphony to his ears—the heartbeat of a revolution poised on the edge of transformation.

He smiled to himself, a sense of destiny settling upon his shoulders. The game was far from over, but he held the pieces firmly in his grasp.

The future awaited, and Étienne Corbeau intended to claim it.

• • •

The oppressive heat of 25 July 1790 bore down upon Paris, the sun's relentless glare reflecting off the cobblestones and casting sharp shadows along the narrow streets. Étienne Corbeau navigated the bustling thoroughfares with a purposeful stride, his mind awash with schemes and the scent of revolution thick in the air. The city was a tinderbox, and he held the match.

He approached the modest residence of Maximilien Robespierre, a three-storey building nestled amidst a row of similar façades on the Rue Saint-Denis. A few potted plants wilted under the summer sun on the wrought-iron balcony, and partially drawn shutters were used to ward off the heat. Étienne rapped the brass knocker against the weathered oak door, the sound echoing in the quiet afternoon.

Moments later, the door creaked open to reveal Robespierre himself. His crisp white cravat and neat waistcoat belied the weariness etched upon his face. His eyes widened slightly at the sight of his visitor.

"Étienne," Robespierre greeted him with a hint of surprise. "I wasn't expecting you."

"Apologies for the unannounced visit," Étienne replied smoothly. "But I have matters of urgency to discuss."

Robespierre stepped aside, gesturing for him to enter. "By all means. Come in out of this oppressive heat."

The interior was modest yet orderly, with shelves lined with books on law, philosophy, and the rights of man. A faint scent of parchment and ink lingered in the air. They settled in a small sitting room where a ceiling fan stirred the warm air lazily.

"Can I offer you something to drink?" Robespierre inquired.

Étienne wiped a bead of sweat from his brow and replied, "I would appreciate a glass of water."

As Robespierre fetched the water, Étienne surveyed the room. Papers—draughts of speeches, notes on legislation, correspondence with fellow deputies—were strewn across the table. The weight of leadership was evident in the clutter.

Robespierre returned, handing him a glass. "Now, what brings you here with such urgency?"

Étienne sipped the water before speaking. "Maximilien, I've been monitoring the situation closely. The monarchy grows increasingly bold in its attempts to undermine the revolution. The King's recent vetoes of key legislation are a blatant affront to the will of the people."

Robespierre sighed, his gaze distant. "I am aware. It is a matter of grave concern."

"Then we must act decisively," Étienne pressed. "We can no longer afford half-measures. The time adopts a harsher stance against the monarchy."

Robespierre regarded him thoughtfully. "What are you proposing?"

Étienne leaned forward, his voice low and insistent. "We must mobilise the National Assembly to pass measures that strip the King of his remaining powers." Étienne leaned forward, speaking in a low and insistent voice, and emphasised the need to mobilise the National Assembly. He clarified that uncompromising resistance would be the response to any further attempts to subvert the revolution.

Robespierre shook his head slightly. "Such actions could plunge us into chaos. We risk alienating moderates and provoking a violent backlash."

Étienne countered. "The people are ready. They grow weary of the King's duplicity. By showing strength, we unify our supporters and dissuade our enemies."

Robespierre's eyes narrowed. "I fear that escalating tensions could lead to unnecessary bloodshed. We must find a balance between firmness and restraint."

Étienne suppressed a flicker of impatience. "Maximilien, I respect your commitment to principle. But principles alone will not safeguard the revolution. We need to be pragmatic."

Robespierre stood, pacing slowly across the room. "Pragmatism must not come at the expense of justice. If we become tyrants in the name of liberty, we betray everything we stand for."

Étienne rose as well, his tone measured yet insistent. "And if we hesitate, we risk losing everything we've fought for. The King conspires with foreign powers. Every day we delay strengthens his position."

Robespierre paused by the window, gazing out at the street below where children played amidst the shadows. "I cannot in good conscience endorse measures that could lead to widespread violence."

Étienne moved to stand beside him. "Sometimes, sacrifice is necessary. The storm is approaching, whether we will do it. Better to face it on our terms."

Robespierre turned to face him, a flicker of sorrow in his eyes. "You are passionate, Étienne. But I must consider the broader implications."

Sensing an opening, Étienne softened his tone. "Then at least consider proposing stricter measures to monitor the monarchy's activities. Increased transparency, limitations on their ability to interfere with the Assembly."

Robespierre sighed. "That is a more tenable position. I will bring it before the Committee."

"Thank you," Étienne said, masking his disappointment. "It's a step in the right direction."

As they returned to the sitting area, the tension eased slightly. Robespierre poured himself a glass of water, his expression contemplative.

"How are you finding your increased involvement with the Assembly?" he asked.

Étienne smiled wryly. "Challenging, but necessary. There are those who still underestimate the severity of our situation."

Robespierre nodded. "True. We must remain vigilant."

They discussed the nuances of upcoming legislation, the challenges of rallying support among disparate factions. Yet, beneath the surface, Étienne's mind churned. Robespierre's reluctance to embrace a more aggressive stance was a hindrance. They would need to employ alternative methods if they couldn't persuade him.

As he prepared to take his leave, Étienne clasped Robespierre's hand. "I appreciate your time and your counsel."

"Likewise," Robespierre replied. "Let us hope that wisdom guides our actions in the days ahead."

Stepping back into the sweltering streets, Étienne made his way towards the Seine, the river's sluggish flow mirroring his own thoughts. He found a shaded bench beneath a cluster of plane trees and sat, watching as a barge drifted lazily downstream.

"Maximilien's hesitation will be our undoing," a voice muttered nearby.

Étienne turned to see Jean-Paul Marat approaching, his features gaunt but eyes alight with enthusiasm.

"Marat," Étienne greeted him. "A coincidence to find you here."

"Perhaps," Marat replied, settling beside him. Marat settled beside him and replied, "Or perhaps our minds are troubled, and we both strongly inclined towards the same places."

Étienne arched an eyebrow. "What troubles you today?"

Marat scoffed lightly. "Just like always, it's the same. The complacency of our so-called leaders. The King's machinations continue unchecked, and the people suffer."

"I share your concerns," Étienne admitted. "I've just come from a meeting with Robespierre. He remains cautious."

Marat sneered. "Caution is a luxury we cannot afford. We must act."

"I agree," Étienne said, choosing his words carefully. "But we need to rally the people for support."

Marat's gaze sharpened. "They are ready. They simply need direction."

"Then perhaps it's time we provide it," Étienne suggested.

Marat studied him for a moment. "What do you propose?"

"An assembly," Étienne replied. "A gathering of the Sans-culottes and other patriots. We can present the evidence of the King's betrayal, stoke the fires of revolution."

Marat nodded slowly. "With the right rhetoric, we can ignite a movement that cannot be ignored."

"Precisely," Étienne affirmed. "Will you lend your voice?"

"Gladly," Marat declared. "I will draught a call to arms in *L'Ami du peuple.*"

"Excellent," Étienne said, a sense of momentum building. "Together, we can set the wheels in motion."

As they parted ways, Étienne felt a surge of anticipation. Marat's influence among the masses allowed him to orchestrate the instability he sought. The approaching storm would not be a mere metaphor—it would be a force he could harness.

Over the next few days, the city buzzed with unrest. Pamphlets circulated, denouncing the monarchy and calling for immediate action. In taverns and public squares, people gathered for meetings, raising their voices in unison against perceived tyranny.

On 28 July 1790, Étienne stood before a crowd gathered at the Champ de Mars. The late afternoon sun cast long shadows as he ascended a makeshift platform. Faces turned towards him—expectant, hungry for guidance.

"Citoyens!" he began, his voice carrying over the murmurs. "We stand at a crossroads. The promises of the revolution remain unfulfilled, stifled by those who cling to power."

A rumble of agreement rippled through the assembly.

"The King, who swore to uphold the constitution, conspires against us," Étienne continued. "Shall we remain silent while our freedoms are threatened?"

"Non!" the crowd roared.

"Then we must act," he declared. "We must demand accountability, assert our sovereignty. The time for patience is over!"

Cheers and shouts filled the air, the fervour palpable. Étienne felt a thrill course through him. This was power—the ability to move the masses with words, to shape the course of history.

As he stepped down, Marat clasped his shoulder. "Well spoken. The people are stirred."

"Let us hope they remain so," Étienne replied, though inwardly he knew.

That evening, he received a summons to meet with Georges Danton and Camille Desmoulins at a café near the Palais-Royal. The atmosphere inside was tense, conversations hushed.

"Danton, Camille," Étienne greeted them as he took a seat.

Danton leaned forward, his expression serious. "Word reaches us you're inciting the populace."

Étienne met his gaze evenly. "I am giving voice to their frustrations."

Desmoulins frowned. "Robespierre is concerned that this could escalate beyond our control."

"Perhaps that is necessary," Étienne retorted. "We have not been assertive enough," Étienne retorted.

Danton shook his head. "There's a fine line between revolution and chaos. We cannot afford to lose the support of moderates."

"Moderates, who would see us bound by compromise?" Étienne scoffed. "They hinder progress."

"Careful, Étienne," Danton warned. "Your ambition is apparent, but reckless actions could endanger us all."

Étienne's eyes flashed. "I act for the good of the revolution."

Desmoulins placed a placating hand on Danton's arm. "We all want what's best. Perhaps we should reconvene with Robespierre to discuss our strategies."

"Very well," Étienne said coolly. "But know that the tide is turning, with or without your approval."

As he departed, irritation gnawed at him. Caution blinded them, unable to seize the opportunities before them. If they would not support his efforts, he would proceed alone.

Returning to his apartment, Étienne found Olympe de Gouges waiting at his door, her expression a mix of concern and determination.

"Olympe," he greeted her with surprise. "What brings you here at this hour?"

"We need to talk," she insisted.

He unlocked the door, gesturing for her to enter. "Very well."

Inside, she wasted no time. "I've heard about your speeches, the unrest you're fostering. This path leads to bloodshed."

Étienne closed the door, his patience wearing thin. "Change is not without cost."

"But at what price?" she implored. "You risk tearing the fabric of our society apart."

He met her gaze, unwavering. "A new society must emerge from the ashes of the old."

She shook her head. "This is not the way. There are better means to achieve our goals."

"Your idealism is admirable, but naïve," he replied dismissively. "The monarchy will not yield willingly."

"Neither will you, it seems," she retorted. "Be careful, Étienne. In seeking to destroy your enemies, you may become like them."

"Thank you for your concern," he said curtly. "But I have determined my course," he declared resolutely.

She regarded him sadly. "I hope you find the wisdom to see the consequences of your actions before it's too late."

As she left, Étienne felt a momentary pang of doubt. But he brushed it aside. The die was cast.

Standing by the window, he gazed out over the city, the lights flickering like stars fallen to earth. The murmur of distant voices drifted upwards—a city on the brink. "25 July 1790," he whispered to himself. "The storm approaches."

He contemplated the instability he had sown, the forces he had set in motion. It was a delicate balance—one misstep could lead to disaster. But if he succeeded, the rewards would be unparalleled.

Étienne allowed himself a rare moment of introspection. Was this truly for the revolution, or for his own ascent? The lines had blurred, ambition entwined with ideology.

A faint smile curved his lips. Perhaps it did not matter. In the end, he would shape the destiny of France, carving his name into the annals of history.

"The storm comes," he murmured. "And I shall stand at its eye."

As the night enveloped the city, Étienne Corbeau embraced the chaos he had cultivated, ready to seize whatever power the tempest might bring.

CHAPTER FOUR: (1791)
THE KING'S BETRAYAL

The dawn of 21 June 1791 broke with a heavy stillness over Paris, a silence that felt unnatural in a city accustomed to the clamour of revolution. Étienne Corbeau stood on the balcony of his modest apartment overlooking the Rue Saint-Honoré, the cool morning air brushing against his face. He sipped his coffee thoughtfully, his gaze fixed on the horizon, where the spires of Notre Dame pierced the pale sky.

A sudden commotion erupted below, shattering the quiet. A messenger on horseback galloped down the cobblestone street, his urgent shouts echoing off the stone façades.

"*Le roi est parti!* The King has fled!"

Étienne's eyes sharpened. He set his cup down with deliberate care, the porcelain clinking softly against the saucer. The King's flight? A slow smile spread across his lips—as a predator sensing opportunity.

He descended the narrow staircase to the street, joining the gathering crowd. Faces reflected a mix of disbelief, fear, and burgeoning anger. Whispers surged through the masses like wildfire.

"Did you hear? The royal family has escaped!"

"Traitors! They've abandoned us!"

Étienne moved among them, his dark coat billowing like a shadow. He caught sight of Camille Desmoulins, his friend and sometimes rival, standing near a fountain, his expression a portrait of stunned betrayal.

"Camille," Étienne called out, approaching him. "Is it true?"

Desmoulins turned, his eyes wide. "Étienne! The King—he's gone. Fled in the night like a thief!"

Étienne placed a reassuring hand on his shoulder. "This could be the catalyst we need."

Camille frowned. "Catalyst? The people are frightened. This could plunge us into chaos."

"Or galvanise us," Étienne countered. "The King's betrayal exposes the monarchy's true colours. We must seize this moment to push for decisive action."

Before Desmoulins could respond, a familiar voice rang out. "Étienne! Camille!"

They turned to see Georges Danton striding towards them, his formidable presence parting the crowd. "Have you heard the news?"

"Yes," Étienne replied. "We were just discussing the implications."

Danton's eyes blazed with intensity. "We must convene the Assembly immediately. The people will demand answers."

"Agreed," Étienne said. "But we must also guide their response. Fear can be a powerful tool if wielded correctly."

Desmoulins glanced between them, hesitation flickering across his face. "We should proceed with caution. The situation is volatile."

Étienne met his gaze steadily. "Caution has its place, but hesitation now could cost us dearly."

Danton nodded. "Étienne is right. We must act swiftly."

As they moved towards the Tuileries, the seat of the National Assembly, Étienne's mind raced. The King's flight was a gift—a means to eliminate the remaining moderates who still clung to the hope of reconciliation with the monarchy. This allowed him to push the revolution towards the radical change he envisioned.

Upon reaching the Assembly, they found it already in turmoil. Deputies shouted over one another, the air thick with accusation and panic. Maximilien Robespierre stood at the centre, attempting to restore order.

"*Messieurs,* please!" Robespierre's voice cut through the cacophony. "We must address this with reason, not hysteria."

Étienne approached the dais. "Maximilien, the King's actions speak louder than any words. He has abandoned his people. We cannot ignore this treachery."

Robespierre's gaze met his, a hint of sadness in his eyes. "I am well aware, Étienne. But we must contemplate our next steps. Rash decisions could have dire consequences."

"Rash?" Étienne echoed, allowing a note of incredulity to colour his tone. "The time for half-measures is over. The monarchy has shown its true face. We must declare a republic."

A murmur of agreement rippled through a fraction of the deputies. Others exchanged uneasy glances.

Pierre Vergniaud, a leading moderate, stepped forward. "We cannot make such a drastic decision in the heat of the moment. We must investigate and confirm the facts."

Étienne fixed him with an icy stare. "The facts are simple. The King has fled. What more proof do you require of his betrayal?"

Vergniaud bristled. "We must not let emotion cloud our judgement."

"Emotion?" Étienne's voice rose. "It is not emotion but justice that demands we act!"

Robespierre intervened. "Gentlemen, please. Let us form a committee to determine the details and propose a course of action."

Étienne saw the hesitation in Robespierre's demeanour—the lingering desire to preserve unity. He leaned in, lowering his voice. "Maximilien, every moment we delay, the monarchy gains strength. The people will not forgive inaction."

Robespierre sighed softly. "I understand your urgency, but we must maintain legitimacy in the eyes of the nation."

"Legitimacy comes from decisive leadership," Étienne pressed. "We solidify the revolution."

Robespierre hesitated, then nodded reluctantly. "Very well. We shall draught a proclamation condemning the King's flight and convene an emergency session."

As the Assembly moved into action, Étienne stepped back, satisfaction coursing through him. Yet, he knew this was only the beginning.

Later that afternoon, he sought Jean-Paul Marat at his printing press. The constant clatter of machinery and the sharp scent of ink filled the cramped space. Marat looked up from his work, his eyes feverish.

"Étienne," Marat greeted him briefly. "I assume you're here about the King's escape."

"Indeed," Étienne replied. "We must incite the populace. Your writings can ignite the spark we need."

Marat's lips curled into a grim smile. "I've already begun. The people will know of the monarchy's treason."

"Emphasise the danger," Étienne urged. "Make them understand that only by eradicating the remnants of the old regime can we secure our future."

Marat nodded, his quill scratching furiously across the parchment. "Fear is a powerful motivator."

"Exactly," Étienne affirmed. "And fear can drive them to support the radical changes we propose."

As he left the print shop, Étienne felt the weight of his manoeuvrings settle into place. The moderates were on the defensive, their calls for restraint increasingly drowned out by the clamour for retribution.

That evening, he attended a gathering at the salon of Madame de Staël. The atmosphere was tense, conversations hushed. Olympe de Gouges approached him, concern etched upon her face.

"Étienne, I feared I might find you here," she said softly.

He raised an eyebrow. "And why is that?"

"Because I know how you intend to use this crisis," she replied. "You're pushing us towards extremism."

He met her gaze unflinchingly. "I am pushing us towards necessary action."

"At what cost?" she challenged. "Innocent lives? Are these the very ideals we fought for?"

He replied, asserting that the cost of inaction is greater. "The monarchy's betrayal cannot go unanswered."

She shook her head. "You're blinded by ambition."

"Perhaps," he conceded. "But ambition achieves results."

Olympe sighed. "Be careful, Étienne. In destroying your enemies, you may destroy yourself."

He offered a thin smile. "I appreciate your concern, but I know what must be done."

Turning away, he engaged with a group of deputies, steering the conversation towards the need for decisive measures. He calculated his words, designing each one to sow doubt in the moderates and embolden the radicals.

As the night wore on, whispers circulated of plans to suspend the King and call for new elections. Étienne moved through the room like a conductor, orchestrating the symphony of unrest.

By the next morning, Paris was a city transformed. Posters plastered the walls, denouncing the King as a traitor. Crowds gathered in the streets, their voices raised in anger. The tension was palpable, a storm on the brink of breaking.

Étienne stood atop the steps of the Hôtel de Ville, addressing a sea of faces.

"*Citoyens!* The time has come to cast off the shackles of tyranny once and for all. Will we allow the betrayal of the monarchy to go unanswered?"

"*Non!*" the crowd roared.

"Then let us unite," he urged. "Let us show the world that the people of France will not be mocked or oppressed," he urged. "Together, we can forge a new destiny!"

The cheers swelled, and a fiery spirit surged through the city. Étienne felt a surge of triumph. The revolution was speeding up, driven by the very chaos he had helped unleash.

Amidst the throng, he caught sight of Robespierre watching him, a mixture of admiration and unease in his expression. Étienne descended the steps to join him.

"You've stirred them well," Robespierre remarked.

"It's necessary," Étienne replied. "We must maintain this momentum."

Robespierre nodded slowly. "But we also ensure it does not spiral out of control."

"Control is an illusion," Étienne said quietly. "We can only ride the wave and guide it as best we can."

Robespierre's eyes searched his. Robespierre looked into his eyes as he said, "I hope you are not misplaced in your confidence."

"Trust me, Maximilien," Étienne assured him. "I have the revolution's best interests at heart."

As they parted ways, Étienne felt a shadow of doubt flicker within him. But he dismissed it. They determined the path.

Returning to his apartment, he penned letters to critical allies, outlining plans to push for the abolition of the monarchy. Each quill stroke was a step further down a path from which there was no return.

21 June 1791, he wrote. *The day the monarchy sealed its fate—and we seized our destiny.*

He sealed the letters and summoned a courier. As he handed over the messages, he gazed at the city—a tapestry of light and shadow, hope and despair.

Étienne knew that the days ahead would be fraught with peril, but he prepared himself. The royal betrayal was more than an event; it was an opportunity—a catalyst to reshape France according to his vision.

He stood at the window long into the night, the distant sounds of unrest a lullaby to his restless spirit. The moon cast a pale glow over the rooftops, and he felt a kinship with its solitary vigil.

"The revolution needs a guiding hand," he murmured. "And I will be that hand."

As sleep finally claimed him in the early hours, Étienne dreamed not of peace but of the storm he had helped conjure—a tempest that would sweep away the old and usher in the new.

• • •

The morning sun of 22 June 1791 filtered through the gauzy curtains of Maximilien Robespierre's modest study, casting elongated shadows across stacks of parchment and well-worn volumes of Rousseau and Montesquieu. The air was thick with the scent of ink and the lingering aroma of coffee, a testament to the sleepless night gripping the city following the King's attempted flight.

Étienne Corbeau stood at the threshold, his dark attire a stark contrast to the warm hues of the room. He rapped his knuckles lightly against the open doorframe. "Maximilien?"

Robespierre looked up from his desk, his eyes rimmed with fatigue yet alight with a fervent intensity. "Étienne," he acknowledged, gesturing for him to enter. "I had a feeling you might visit today."

"I couldn't stay away," Étienne replied, stepping inside. "Not after last night's revelations."

Robespierre leaned back in his chair, his fingers interlaced. "The King's betrayal weighs heavily upon us all."

"Indeed," Étienne agreed, his gaze sweeping over the cluttered desk. "But it also presents us with a clear path forward."

Robespierre raised an eyebrow. "A path fraught with peril. The Assembly is divided; the moderates call for patience and investigation."

Étienne scoffed softly. "Patience? The King has shown his true colours. To hesitate now is to invite further treachery."

Robespierre sighed, rubbing his temples. "I understand your frustration, but we must act judiciously. Rash decisions could fracture the revolution."

Étienne moved closer, his voice lowering. "Maximilien, the people look to us for leadership. They feel betrayed and abandoned. We must channel their anger into decisive action."

Robespierre regarded him thoughtfully. "What would you have me do?"

"Condemn the monarchy unequivocally," Étienne urged. "Stand before the Assembly and declare that the King's actions are unforgivable. Advocate for the immediate suspension of his powers."

Robespierre hesitated. "Such a stance could alienate the moderates and provoke civil unrest."

"Or it could unite the revolutionaries under a common cause," Étienne countered. "Your voice carries weight, Maximilien. The people trust you to uphold justice."

Robespierre rose from his chair, pacing slowly beside the window. "Justice," he murmured. "It is justice that I seek, but not vengeance."

Étienne watched him intently. "Justice demands accountability. If the King can flout the constitution without consequence, what message does that send?"

Robespierre paused, his gaze fixed on the bustling street below where citizens moved with an anxious energy. "You make a compelling argument."

"Consider Jean-Jacques Rousseau's words," Étienne pressed. "When the social contract is broken, the people may choose new leaders."

Robespierre turned to face him. "You believe the social contract has been irreparably damaged?"

"Can there be any doubt?" Étienne replied. "The King attempted to flee, abandoning his sacred duty. He has renounced his role in our society."

A silence stretched between them, the weight of the moment palpable. Finally, Robespierre nodded slowly. "Perhaps you are right. Perhaps this is the time to take a firmer stand."

Étienne allowed a faint smile. "Your conviction will inspire others. We cannot afford to let this opportunity slip away."

Robespierre returned to his desk, picking up a quill. "I will draught a speech for the Assembly. But I will not advocate for violence, Étienne."

"Of course not," Étienne agreed smoothly. "We seek justice, not bloodshed."

As Robespierre wrote, Étienne moved to the bookshelf, running his fingers along the spines of the volumes. "You know," he mused, "history will remember those who stood firm in the face of adversity."

Robespierre glanced up. "And those who succumbed to extremism."

"Extremism is a matter of perspective," Étienne replied. "To some, even the idea of revolution was once extreme."

Robespierre considered this. "True. But we ensure our actions align with our principles."

"Principles are our guiding light," Étienne affirmed. "And sometimes, they require us to make hard choices."

Robespierre set down his quill, his expression resolute. "I will address the Assembly this afternoon. Will you stand with me?"

"It would be my honour," Étienne said, inclining his head.

Leaving Robespierre's study, Étienne felt a surge of satisfaction. He had sown the seeds of conviction in a man whose influence could tip the balance. Now, he needed to ensure that the Assembly was primed to receive the message.

He made his way through the winding streets to the Palais-Royal, where he found Camille Desmoulins amid an animated discussion with a group of young deputies.

"Étienne!" Camille called out, waving him over. "We've been debating the implications of the King's flight."

"An event that changes everything," Étienne remarked, joining the circle.

One deputy, a sharp-eyed man named Philippe, frowned. "But what can we do? The moderates caution restraint."

"Restraint?" Étienne echoed, feigning incredulity. "The time for restraint has passed. We must hold the King accountable."

Camille nodded vigorously. "Étienne is right. We cannot let this betrayal go unanswered."

Philippe looked uncertain. "But without the support of the entire assembly, our actions could backfire."

"Maximilien Robespierre will address the Assembly this afternoon," Étienne informed them. "He intends to condemn the monarchy's actions. With his leadership, we can rally the support."

The deputies exchanged glances. Another, a tall woman named Sophie, spoke up. "If Robespierre takes such a stance, others will follow."

"Precisely," Étienne said. "We must prepare ourselves to back him unequivocally."

Camille clapped a hand on Philippe's shoulder. "This is our moment, *mon ami*. We must seize it."

As the group dispersed to spread the word, Étienne pulled Camille aside and said, "We need to ensure that sympathetic citizens fill the gallery. Their presence will put pressure on the deputies."

Camille grinned. "Leave it to me. The people will be there."

"Excellent," Étienne replied. "And Camille, emphasise the need for unity. The moderates must feel the tide turning against them."

"Understood," Camille said, his eyes gleaming with purpose.

With arrangements underway, Étienne headed towards the Tuileries Garden, seeking a moment of reflection. The manicured lawns and orderly rows of trees provided a stark contrast to the turmoil gripping the nation.

He settled on a bench beneath a chestnut tree, the dappled sunlight casting patterns at his feet. While lost in thought, the sudden appearance of Olympe de Gouges startled him as she sat beside him.

"Étienne," she greeted, her tone cautious.

"Olympe," he responded, masking his surprise. "Out for a stroll?"

"Seeking solace, perhaps," she admitted. "These are troubling times."

"Indeed," he agreed. "But times that call for decisive action."

She studied him. "I hear Robespierre plans to condemn the King in the Assembly."

"He does," Étienne confirmed. "A necessary step."

She sighed. "I worry such measures will lead us down a path of no return."

Étienne met her gaze. "Sometimes, we must clear away the old to build anew."

"But must it be done with such fervour?" she questioned. "What of moderation? Of finding a peaceful resolution?"

He shook his head. "Peaceful resolutions require willing participants. The King has shown he is not one."

She looked away, her expression troubled. "I fear for what lies ahead."

"As do I," he admitted, surprising himself with the candour. "But fear cannot paralyse us."

She rose, smoothing her skirts. "Just promise me one thing, Étienne."

"What's that?"

"Remember the humanity in those you oppose? Do not let zeal blind you to compassion."

He inclined his head. "I will keep that in mind."

As she walked away, Étienne pondered her words. Compassion seemed a luxury in the face of such betrayal. Yet, a small voice within him acknowledged the weight of her caution.

The afternoon sun climbed higher as he went to the National Assembly. The crowds of citizens who filled the galleries amplified the hall's grandeur, their murmurs creating a low hum of anticipation.

Robespierre stood at the podium, his posture upright, a sheaf of papers in his hand. As the room settled into silence, he spoke.

"*Citoyens,* we find ourselves at a pivotal moment in our nation's history. Yesterday's events have shaken the very foundations of our fledgling republic."

Étienne watched intently as Robespierre's words flowed, each measured yet laden with conviction.

"The King, entrusted with the sacred duty of upholding the constitution, has sought to abandon his post and his people. We cannot dismiss or excuse this act. It is a betrayal of the highest order."

A ripple of assent moved through the assembly.

"Therefore," Robespierre continued, "I propose we suspend the King's powers and start proceedings to determine the monarchy's future within our society."

Étienne noted the strategic phrasing—firm yet leaving room for deliberation.

Pierre Vergniaud rose in opposition. "We must not act in haste. The stability of our nation depends on careful consideration."

Before Robespierre could respond, Étienne stood. "M. Vergniaud, how much more consideration do we need? The King's intentions are obvious. To delay is to endanger the revolution."

The assembly erupted into debate, voices overlapping in a cacophony of dissent and support.

Robespierre raised his hand, calling for order. "Let us not descend into chaos. We must vote on the matter at hand."

The vote proceeded, tensions high. When they announced the results, they passed the motion to suspend the King by a narrow margin.

A sense of triumph surged within Étienne. The scales were tipping.

As the session adjourned, Robespierre approached him. "Your intervention was timely."

"I merely spoke the truth," Étienne replied.

Robespierre gave a faint smile. "We have set a course. Let us hope it leads to justice."

"Justice will prevail if we remain steadfast," Étienne affirmed.

Leaving the Assembly, Jacques-Louis David, the renowned painter, approached Étienne.

"Monsieur Corbeau," David greeted him. "Your words today were inspiring."

"Thank you," Étienne said. "Art and revolution often walk hand in hand, do they not?"

David nodded. "I seek to capture the spirit of these times. Perhaps we could collaborate."

Étienne replied, "I would be honoured."

As they parted ways, Étienne felt the threads of influence weaving ever tighter. His role was expanding beyond the shadows, his voice gaining resonance.

That evening, he returned to his apartment, the weight of the day's events settling upon him. He lit a candle and sat at his desk, the flickering light casting long shadows.

22 June 1791,

Today, we took a decisive step towards true liberty. Yet, the path ahead is steep, and allies waver. I must remain vigilant.

He paused, considering the moral complexities that Olympe had alluded to. But ambition and conviction overrode hesitation.

Extinguishing the candle, he gazed out the window at the city bathed in moonlight. The distant sounds of Paris at night—a mix of laughter, song, and the occasional shout—reached his ears.

"The revolution is alive," he whispered. "And I will shape its destiny."

As sleep eluded him, Étienne contemplated the strategies required to steer the revolution towards the future he envisioned. The King's flight had provided the impetus; now, it was up to him to ensure that the momentum was not lost.

He resolved to press forward with unwavering determination, even as the shadows lengthened and the stakes grew higher.

• • •

The heat of 25 June 1791 weighed heavily upon Paris; as Étienne Corbeau made his way through the cobblestone streets of the Faubourg Saint-Antoine, his intense gaze mirrored the passion of the revolutionary spirit that filled the air. The scent of freshly baked bread mingled with the acrid smoke from countless chimneys, creating a heady aroma that seemed to fuel his resolve.

He navigated through clusters of Sans-culottes, their voices rising in heated debate outside crowded taverns and cafés. Snatches of conversation reached his ears—discussions of the King's betrayal, whispers of retribution, and, to his irritation, calls for moderation. Étienne's jaw tightened. The moderates, with their pleas for leniency, threatened to undermine the revolution's momentum. It was time to act.

Crossing into the shadowed alleys near the Place de la Bastille, he made his way to a discreet meeting place—a dimly lit back room of Le Serpent Rouge, a tavern known to harbour radical thinkers. Pushing open the heavy wooden door, the indistinct murmur of voices and the flickering glow of candlelight greeted him, reflecting off smoke-stained walls.

"Étienne," a gravelly voice called out. Jean-Paul Marat emerged from the gloom, his intense gaze fixed upon him. "We've been waiting."

"Apologies for the delay," Étienne replied smoothly, removing his hat and glancing around the room. The assembly included important members of the radical faction: Marat, whose passion was barely contained; Louis de Saint-Just, the dynamic and young orator; and several influential Sans-culotte leaders whose loyalty Étienne had diligently nurtured.

"Time is of the essence," Saint-Just remarked, his piercing blue eyes alight with determination. "The moderates grow bolder in their attempts to placate the monarchy."

"Which is precisely why we must act decisively," Étienne asserted, taking a seat at the rough-hewn table. "Their calls for leniency are a poison that threatens to weaken our cause."

Marat leaned forward, his hands clasped tightly. "What do you propose?"

Étienne allowed a brief smile to curve his lips. "We must expose them for what they are—sympathisers of the old regime, wolves in sheep's clothing. If we can sow doubt about their loyalties, we can diminish their influence."

A Sans-culotte leader named Antoine grunted in agreement. "Rumours easily swayed the people, especially when they confirm their suspicions."

"Precisely," Étienne said. "We can circulate pamphlets, anonymous, of course, that highlight their connections to the aristocracy. Suggest that their wealth comes from royal patronage, that their reluctance to act against the King stems from personal interest."

Saint-Just frowned slightly. "We must be cautious. Unfounded accusations could backfire."

"Who said they were unfounded?" Étienne countered, a glint in his eye. "I've gained information that suggests Vergniaud and his cohorts have been meeting secretly with royal emissaries."

Marat's expression darkened. "If that's true, then they are traitors."

Étienne spread his hands. "Whether it's true is irrelevant. Perception is reality in these times. We need only plant the seed."

A murmur of assent rippled through the group. Marat nodded decisively. "I'll publish an exposé in *L'Ami du peuple*. The people trust my word."

"Excellent," Étienne replied. "And Antoine, ensure that these rumours reach the ears of the Sans-culottes. Let them know the moderates cannot be trusted."

Antoine smirked. "Consider it done."

Saint-Just remained contemplative. "I still have reservations about resorting to deceit."

Étienne fixed him with a steady gaze. "Sometimes, Louis, the ends justify the means. Our priority must be the preservation of the revolution."

Saint-Just hesitated, then sighed. "Very well."

As the meeting concluded, Étienne felt a surge of satisfaction. The plan was in motion. Soon, the moderates would find themselves besieged by doubt and suspicion, their influence waning as the radicals gained ascendancy.

Leaving the tavern, he emerged into the fading light of evening. The streets were alive with activity; vendors called out their wares, children darted between pedestrians, and groups of labourers shared coarse laughter over mugs of ale. Yet an undercurrent of tension was palpable—a city poised on the edge of transformation.

Making his way towards the Seine, Étienne crossed paths with Olympe de Gouges near the Pont Neuf. She wore a simple yet elegant dress, her intelligent eyes reflecting concern as she recognised him.

"Étienne," she greeted him cautiously. "A moment, if you please."

He inclined his head. "Madame de Gouges. How may I assist you?"

She fell into step beside him. "I've heard unsettling rumours you intend to discredit the moderates through dubious means."

He arched an eyebrow. "Is it dubious to reveal the truth?"

"Is it the truth?" she challenged. "Or are you manipulating facts to serve your own agenda?"

He met her gaze unflinchingly. "The moderates threaten the revolution with their indecision. They lack the courage to do what is necessary."

She sighed. "But at what cost, Étienne? Spreading falsehoods undermines the very principles we fight for."

"Principles mean little if the revolution fails," he retorted. "I do what must be done."

Olympe shook her head sadly. "Be careful not to become the very thing you despise."

He offered a thin smile. "I appreciate your concern, but my conscience is clear."

"Is it?" she asked softly. "I wonder."

Without waiting for a response, she turned and walked away, disappearing into the throng of pedestrians. Étienne watched her go, a flicker of irritation disrupting his composure. Her naiveté was a liability he could ill afford to indulge.

Continuing, he arrived at a bustling café near the Palais-Royal, where Camille Desmoulins and Georges Danton were engaged in animated conversation over glasses of wine.

"Étienne!" Danton boomed, his rugged features breaking into a grin. "Join us!"

"Gladly," Étienne replied, pulling up a chair. "I trust you're both well."

"As well as one can be in these turbulent times," Desmoulins remarked, pushing his spectacles up the bridge of his nose. "Word is spreading of unrest among the moderates."

Étienne feigned surprise. "Oh? What have you heard?"

Danton chuckled. "Rumours that some of them have been consorting with Royalists. Marat's latest pamphlet is quite the scandal."

"Troubling, if true," Étienne said, sipping his wine.

Desmoulins studied him shrewdly. "You wouldn't know anything about that, would you?"

Étienne met his gaze evenly. "I may have heard whispers. We must remain vigilant."

"Indeed," Danton agreed. "If the moderates are compromised, we must take action," Danton agreed and affirmed.

Desmoulins frowned slightly. "But we should verify these claims before taking drastic measures."

Étienne leaned forward. "Can we afford to wait? The King's escape attempt has already emboldened our enemies. Any hesitation could be fatal."

Danton nodded firmly. "Étienne has a point. We must protect the revolution at all costs."

Desmoulins sighed. "Very well. But we must proceed carefully."

"Of course," Étienne assured him, masking his satisfaction. "Caution is always wise."

As the evening wore on, they discussed strategies to strengthen their position within the Assembly. Étienne subtly steered the conversation, ensuring his ideas took root in their plans.

When he parted ways with Danton and Desmoulins, the moon hung high above Paris, casting a silvery glow over the city. Étienne returned to his apartment; the streets were quieter now but still humming with the energy of a populace on the brink of change.

The following morning, 26 June 1791, the impact of his efforts became apparent. Marat's pamphlet circulated rapidly; its inflammatory accusations against the moderates causing an uproar. Citizens gathered in public squares, debating heatedly, their trust in the moderates eroding.

Tensions were palpable at the National Assembly. Pierre Vergniaud stood at the podium, his usually composed demeanour strained.

"These allegations are baseless!" Vergniaud declared, his voice echoing through the chamber. "I have never betrayed the revolution!"

Murmurs of scepticism rippled among the deputies. Étienne observed from his seat, a faint smile playing at the corners of his mouth.

Maximilien Robespierre rose calmly. "Monsieur Vergniaud, we cannot ignore the seriousness of these claims. Perhaps we should investigate to clear your name,"

Vergniaud's eyes flashed with indignation. "An investigation? This is an affront!"

"Transparency serves us all," Robespierre replied evenly.

Étienne watched as the moderates squirmed under the scrutiny, their unity fracturing. The radicals, emboldened, pressed for stricter measures against any perceived traitors.

Later, in the corridors outside the chamber, Robespierre approached Étienne. "This discord troubles me."

"Necessary growing pains," Étienne responded. "We must root out any elements that could weaken us."

Robespierre sighed. "I only hope we do not sacrifice justice in positing purity."

"We cannot compromise," Étienne stated, emphasising the intertwining of justice and purity. "We cannot allow ourselves to be compromised."

Robespierre regarded him thoughtfully. "Your conviction is admirable. But we must tread carefully."

"Agreed," Étienne said, though inwardly he dismissed the caution.

Over the next few days, the moderates' influence waned significantly. Several resigned under the pressure, while others shifted their positions to align more closely with the radicals. Étienne's standing within the movement solidified his role as a strategist and instigator acknowledged, albeit quietly.

Madame de Staël organised a gathering at her home on the evening of 30 June 1791. The opulent salon bustled with the elite of revolutionary society—politicians, writers, artists—all engaged in fervent discussion.

Jacques-Louis David approached Étienne, a glass of champagne in hand. "You've certainly stirred the pot, *mon ami.*"

Étienne smiled. "Change requires a bit of agitation."

David chuckled. "True enough. I'm considering a new painting—a depiction of the revolution's guardians. Perhaps you'd sit for it?"

"I would be honoured," Étienne replied. "Immortalising these times is crucial."

As David moved on, Olympe de Gouges appeared at his side once more. "I see your influence has grown."

"It seems so," he acknowledged.

She studied him with a mix of concern and resignation. "I fear where this path leads."

"To a stronger revolution," he asserted.

"Or to tyranny under a different name," she countered softly.

Étienne's gaze hardened slightly. "I seek freedom for our people."

"Just ensure that in seeking freedom, you do not become an oppressor."

He inclined his head. "Your counsel is noted."

She sighed, turning away to join another conversation.

As the night progressed, Étienne mingled effortlessly, gauging opinions, reinforcing alliances, and subtly guiding the discourse. The seeds he had sown were bearing fruit, and the path to his vision of the revolution was becoming clearer.

Returning home in the early hours, he felt a rare contentment. The city was quiet, the chaos momentarily subdued. Standing at his window, he gazed out over the rooftops, the first light of dawn hinting at the horizon.

"25 June 1791," he murmured to himself. "A day of progress."

He knew challenges lay ahead, but his position was stronger than ever. The moderates were silenced, their voices drowned out by the rising tide of radicalism he had helped unleash.

Étienne Corbeau allowed himself a small smile. The revolution was advancing according to his design, and he stood poised to shape the future of France.

As he extinguished the lamp and settled into bed, his thoughts were already turning to the next move in his intricate game—a game where the stakes were nothing less than the soul of a nation.

• • •

On 29 June 1791, the air hung over Paris like a shroud, thick with the scent of impending change. Étienne Corbeau navigated the labyrinthine streets of the Marais district, his boots echoing softly against the cobblestones. The city was filled with restless energy as rumours of the King's betrayal spread throughout, stirring up strong emotions among the people.

He arrived at a discreet entrance tucked between two shuttered shops—a modest door marked only by a faded brass knocker in the shape of a lion's head. Étienne glanced over his shoulder, ensuring he hadn't been followed, before rapping three times in quick succession. The door creaked open, and a young man with sharp features and wary eyes beckoned him inside.

"You're expected," the man murmured.

Étienne stepped into the dimly lit corridor, the scent of burning tallow candles mingling with the earthy aroma of aged wood. He descended a narrow staircase that led to a subterranean chamber—a sanctuary for the most ardent revolutionaries. The room buzzed with hushed conversations, the faces of those gathered illuminated by the flickering light.

At the centre stood Louis de Saint-Just, his piercing blue eyes and austere demeanour commanding attention. Dressed in a simple black coat, he radiated an intensity that belied his youth. Jean-Paul Marat hovered nearby, his gaunt visage and feverish gaze adding to the charged atmosphere. A circle of Sans-culottes leaders and radical deputies completed the assembly.

"Étienne," Saint-Just greeted him with a curt nod. "We were wondering if our cautious colleagues detained you."

Étienne offered a wry smile. "I left them entangled in debates over procedure. Time is not a luxury we possess."

Marat's eyes gleamed. "Agreed. The King's attempted escape has unveiled his true intentions. We must respond decisively."

"Precisely why I've called for this gathering," Saint-Just declared, his voice cutting through the murmurs. "The moderates falter, clinging to outdated notions of reconciliation. It falls upon us to steer the revolution forward."

Étienne stepped forward. "The King's betrayal is a clarion call. We can no longer afford half-measures. The people demand action, and we must be the instruments of their will."

A Sans-culotte leader named Lucien, his rough hands gripping the brim of his cap, spoke up. "What would you have us do? The masses are restless, but they need direction."

Saint-Just's gaze swept over the assembly. "We propose a march— a demonstration of unity and resolve. We will gather at the Champ de Mars and present a petition demanding the abdication of the King and the establishment of a republic."

Marat interjected, his voice low and earnest. "And should the authorities resist, we must be prepared to meet force with force."

A murmur rippled through the room, a mixture of agreement and apprehension. Étienne sensed the hesitation and seized the moment.

"*Citoyens,*" he began, his tone measured yet impassioned, "we stand at a crossroads. The monarchy has revealed itself as an enemy of the people. If we do not act now, we risk losing everything we've fought for. Our cause is just, and history favours the bold."

Lucien's eyes narrowed. "But what of the National Guard? Lafayette's men may oppose us."

Étienne's lips curled into a slight smile. "Lafayette's allegiance wavers. His attempts to straddle both worlds leave him vulnerable. If we present a united front, even he will think twice before opposing the will of the people."

Saint-Just nodded. "Our strength lies in our conviction. Those who lack the courage to embrace genuine change must not deter us."

Another deputy, a woman named Émilie Duval, with fiery red hair and an unyielding gaze, stepped forward. "I've heard whispers that the

Assembly seeks to placate the King, offering concessions for empty promises. We cannot let this happen."

"Exactly," Étienne affirmed. "We must pressure the Assembly to act under the people's demands."

Marat clenched his fists. "Then it's settled. We mobilise immediately. I'll publish a call to arms in *L'Ami du peuple*. The citizens will rally to our cause."

As plans solidified, Étienne felt a surge of exhilaration. The room brimmed with determination; the radicals unified in purpose. The King's betrayal had ignited a fire that he intended to stoke into an inferno.

After the meeting adjourned, Étienne walked alongside Saint-Just through the winding streets. The waning sunlight cast long shadows, the city's architecture a patchwork of grandeur and decay.

"You handled the assembly well," Saint-Just remarked, his tone contemplative. "Your words carry weight."

Étienne glanced at him. "As do yours. Together, we make a formidable force."

Saint-Just's expression remained impassive. "Do you ever question the path we're on?"

"Do you?" Étienne countered.

A moment of silence passed before Saint-Just spoke again. "I believe in the revolution with every fibre of my being. But I wonder if the others possess the same resolve."

Étienne considered this. "Conviction is tested in times of crisis. Those who waver will fall away, leaving only the truly committed."

Saint-Just nodded slowly. "We must be prepared for what lies ahead. The road will not be easy."

"Nothing worth achieving ever is," Étienne replied.

They parted ways near the Place de la Révolution, the site already echoing with the footsteps of history yet to be written. Étienne watched Saint-Just disappear into the crowd, his figure melding with the throng of citizens who moved with a newfound urgency.

As dusk settled, Étienne made his way to a small café frequented by the intellectual elite. Inside, he spotted Olympe de Gouges seated alone at a corner table, her gaze distant as she sipped a glass of wine. Against his better judgement, he approached her.

"Olympe," he greeted softly.

She looked up, surprise flickering across her features before giving way to guarded politeness. "Étienne."

"May I join you?"

She hesitated briefly before gesturing to the empty seat. "If you wish."

He sat down, ordering a coffee from the waiter, who hovered nearby. "You seem lost in thought."

"I could say the same of you," she replied, her eyes probing. "Word spreads quickly in Paris. There's talk of a mass demonstration."

Étienne inclined his head. "The people are taking a stand."

"And you are among those leading them."

"Is that a concern?" he asked lightly.

She sighed. "I worry that passion unchecked can lead to destruction. Unnecessary violence must not taint the ideals of the revolution."

"Unnecessary?" Étienne echoed. "The monarchy's betrayal warrants a powerful response. To hesitate is to show weakness."

"Force solely measures strength," she countered. "There is power in restraint, in diplomacy."

He leaned forward. "Diplomacy has failed us. The King attempted to flee, abandoning his duty. How can we negotiate with someone who disregards the very foundation of our society?"

Her gaze softened slightly. "I understand your frustration, but I fear the path you're on may lead to a loss of humanity."

Étienne studied her for a moment. "Humanity is often a casualty of progress."

She shook her head. "It doesn't have to be."

Before he could respond, the waiter returned with his coffee. They sat in silence for a few moments, the ambient noise of the café filling the space between them.

Finally, Olympe spoke again. "Promise me you'll consider the ramifications of your actions."

He took a sip of his coffee. "I assure you, I calculate every action I take carefully."

"That's what concerns me," she said softly.

He met her gaze, a hint of defiance in his eyes. "Then perhaps we must disagree."

She offered a faint smile. "Perhaps."

They parted amicably, yet Étienne couldn't shake the lingering unease her words stirred. Dismissing it as a momentary lapse, he refocused his thoughts on the tasks ahead.

That night, he convened a smaller meeting with key organisers to complete plans for the march. The atmosphere was electric, the air thick with anticipation.

"Security measures are in place," Lucien reported. "Our men strategically positioned to deter any interference," Lucien reported.

"Good," Étienne replied. "We cannot afford disruptions."

Émilie stepped forward. "I've coordinated with sympathetic members of the National Guard. Some will turn a blind eye."

"Excellent work," Étienne acknowledged.

As the meeting progressed, he felt a growing confidence. The pieces were aligning, each element contributing to the overarching strategy he had meticulously crafted.

By the early hours of the morning, they had set the plans. Étienne stepped outside, the cool night air a welcome relief. The city was quiet, a deceptive calm before the storm.

He made his way to the banks of the Seine, the water glistening under the pale light of the moon. Standing on a stone bridge, he gazed over the river, his reflection distorted by the gentle ripples.

"29 June 1791," he murmured to himself. "A day that will herald a new chapter."

The weight of his actions settled upon him—not as a burden, but as a mantle of purpose. The radical shift he championed was not merely a response to the King's betrayal but a necessary evolution of the revolution.

He considered Robespierre, whose careful strategy now appeared insufficient. Danton and Desmoulins both possess charisma that must be coupled with decisive action, while Saint-Just, a like-minded individual, exhibited a determination that mirrored theirs.

As dawn approached, Étienne returned to his apartment. He sat at his desk, quill in hand, and began drafting a manifesto—a declaration of intent that would accompany the petition at the march. His words flowed with clarity and conviction, each pen stroke reinforcing his commitment to the cause.

"Let everyone know," he wrote, "that the people of France will no longer tolerate the chains of a corrupt monarchy. We stand united, resolute in our pursuit of liberty, equality, and fraternity."

He paused, gazing at the flickering flame of the candle beside him. The shadows it cast danced across the parchment, intertwining with the inked letters.

Extinguishing the candle, he allowed himself a moment of reflection. The path ahead was fraught with danger, but the tide of radical sentiment buoyed him. He was no longer a mere participant in the revolution; he was shaping its very course.

As he lay down to rest, the distant sounds of the city beginning to stir, Étienne felt a profound sense of purpose. The King's betrayal had not weakened the revolution—it had forged it anew, stronger and more determined than ever.

"Tomorrow," he thought, "we take the next step."

Sleep claimed him swiftly. His dreams were filled not with doubt or fear but with visions of a France reborn—a nation reshaped by his hand, where the ideals of the revolution reigned supreme.

• • •

Étienne Corbeau stood at the window of his modest apartment overlooking the Rue Saint-Honoré on 10 July 1791, the distant clamour of the city filtering through the open shutters. The faint aroma of baking bread, yet it could not distract him from the papers spread across his desk—pamphlets freshly printed, ink still glistening.

He picked one up, the coarse paper rough against his fingers. Bold letters screamed from the page: *"Le Roi Traître*—The King's Betrayal! *"* Beneath, a crude illustration depicted Louis XVI as a serpent coiled around the throat of Marianne, the symbol of liberty. Étienne's lips curled into a satisfied smile. The artwork was sensationalist, inflammatory language—a perfect concoction to inflame the masses.

A knock at the door interrupted his thoughts. He set the pamphlet down and crossed the room, opening the door to reveal Antoine, a burly Sans-culotte with a scar tracing his jawline.

"Ah, Antoine," Étienne greeted him. "Come in."

Antoine stepped inside, wiping sweat from his brow with a grubby handkerchief. "The men are ready," he announced. "At nightfall we will distribute the pamphlets."

"Excellent," Étienne replied, closing the door behind him. "Ensure they reach every quartier—from the Faubourg Saint-Antoine to the Marais. I want no corner of Paris untouched by our message."

Antoine nodded. "Consider it done. The people are restless. This will stir them further."

"Good," Étienne affirmed. "The time for complacency is over. We must ignite the spark that will consume the remnants of tyranny."

Antoine hesitated, his gaze flickering briefly. "Some say the tensions are already high. That pushing further could lead to bloodshed."

Étienne met his eyes steadily. "Change is seldom wrought without sacrifice. The King's treachery demands a response. Or do you suggest we wait for him to tighten the noose around our necks?"

Antoine shook his head. "*Non, Monsieur.* I merely relay what I've heard."

"I appreciate your loyalty," Étienne said, his tone softening slightly.

"But remember, fear is the weapon of our oppressors. We must not succumb to it."

"Understood," Antoine replied. "I'll see to the distribution."

As Antoine departed, Étienne returned to his desk, his mind already strategising the next move. The pamphlets were merely the first wave. He had orchestrated a network of agitators—speakers who would fan out across the city, stirring discontent in taverns, marketplaces, and public squares.

He donned his coat and hat, the dark fabrics absorbing the midday heat as he ventured onto the bustling streets. The city thrummed with life; vendors hawked their wares, children darted between pedestrians, and conversations buzzed with the latest rumours.

Étienne made his way to a small café near the Palais-Royal, a known gathering place for political radicals. Inside, the air was thick with smoke and animated discourse. He spotted Camille Desmoulins at a corner table, scribbling furiously in a notebook.

"Camille," Étienne greeted him, sliding into the seat opposite.

Desmoulins looked up, pushing his spectacles up the bridge of his nose. "Étienne! I've just finished an article for *Les Révolutions de France et de Brabant.* Exposing the duplicity of the monarchists."

"Timely," Étienne remarked. "I've taken steps to ensure the public is well-informed of the King's betrayal."

Desmoulins raised an eyebrow. "I've heard whispers of pamphlets circulating. Your handiwork, I presume?"

Étienne smiled enigmatically. "Merely facilitating the truth."

"Careful, *mon ami,*" Desmoulins cautioned. "The line between enlightenment and incitement is thin."

"The people deserve to know the depths of the King's treachery," Étienne countered. "Only then can they act accordingly."

Desmoulins sighed, leaning back in his chair. "I fear we may steer towards chaos."

"Chaos precedes order," Étienne replied calmly. "A necessary upheaval to purge the old and make way for the new."

Before Desmoulins could respond, a commotion outside drew their attention. A crowd had gathered, voices raised in anger as a man stood atop a cart, waving one of Étienne's pamphlets.

"See here!" the man shouted. "The King conspires against us! Will we stand idle while he sells us to foreign powers?"

The crowd roared in disapproval, fists shaking in the air.

Desmoulins glanced at Étienne. "You've certainly struck a chord."

"Precisely the intention," Étienne said, his gaze fixed on the scene. "The people's anger is a powerful force."

Desmoulins frowned. "And one that can be unpredictable."

Étienne turned back to him. "Only if left unguided. We must channel it towards purposeful action."

Desmoulins shook his head. "Just ensure it doesn't consume us all."

"Trust me," Étienne assured him. "I have matters well in hand."

Leaving the café, Étienne wove through the throng, absorbing the charged atmosphere. He headed towards the Seine, the river's cool breeze offering respite from the heat. As he crossed the Pont Neuf, he encountered Jacques-Louis David sketching the skyline, his keen artist's eye capturing the city's turmoil.

"Monsieur David," Étienne greeted him.

David looked up, a smudge of charcoal on his cheek. "Étienne. The city is alive with unrest. An artist's paradise, if somewhat perilous."

"Indeed," Étienne agreed. "These are moments that will shape history."

David studied him thoughtfully. "And you seem determined to be at the centre."

Étienne smiled faintly. "One must seize opportunity when it arises."

David nodded. "I've heard of the pamphlets. Bold move."

"Boldness is required in times like these," Étienne replied. "Perhaps you'll capture the spirit of the revolution in your next piece."

"Perhaps," David mused. "Assuming there is a revolution left to capture."

Étienne arched an eyebrow. "Do you doubt our cause?"

"Not the cause," David clarified. "But the methods. Be careful, Étienne. The flames you fan may burn beyond control."

"I appreciate your concern," Étienne said evenly. "But progress demands risk."

They parted ways, and Étienne continued along the riverbank until he reached a secluded spot beneath a willow tree. There, he found Olympe de Gouges seated on a bench, a notebook in her lap.

"Olympe," he called softly.

She looked up, surprise mingled with wariness. "Étienne. What brings you here?"

"A moment of reflection," he answered, taking a seat beside her. "And you?"

"Writing," she said simply. "A new play, though inspiration is scarce amidst the chaos."

"Chaos can be a muse," he suggested.

"Or a distraction," she countered.

They sat in silence for a moment, the gentle rustling of leaves masking the distant sounds of the city.

"I've heard about the pamphlets," Olympe said finally. "You're stirring the pot vigorously."

Étienne replied, "We must know the truth."

"Truth?" she echoed. "Or propaganda?"

He met her gaze. "The King's actions are indefensible. The people have a right to be angry."

"Anger is understandable," she conceded. "But inciting unrest— where does it end?"

"With the dismantling of tyranny," he stated firmly.

She sighed. "I fear you're using the masses to further your own ambitions."

"Ambition drives change," he retorted. "Without it, feudal chains would still shackle us."

"But at what cost?" she pressed. "The lives of innocents? The very fabric of our society?"

"We must tear down society before we can rebuild it," he insisted. "You, of all people, should understand the need for transformation."

She looked away, her expression pained. "I advocate for equality, for justice. Not for manipulation and bloodshed."

Étienne stood, a hint of irritation creeping into his voice. "Sometimes, we must make sacrifices,"

She gazed up at him. "Just be certain that the sacrifices are worth it."

He paused, a flicker of uncertainty crossing his features before he masked it. "They will be."

Turning on his heel, he left her beneath the willow, her figure a solitary silhouette against the setting sun's backdrop.

As night fell, Étienne returned to his apartment. From his window, he observed the city transforming under the cloak of darkness. In the distance, fires flickered - not from destruction, but from gatherings where people read his pamphlets aloud, fuelling the enthusiasm he had so carefully cultivated.

A knock at his door drew him away from the window. Opening it, he found Louis de Saint-Just standing there, his expression grave.

"Louis," Étienne greeted him. "What news?"

"Your pamphlets have had the desired effect," Saint-Just reported. "The people are mobilising. But so is the National Guard."

Étienne's eyes narrowed. "Lafayette's doing, no doubt."

"Indeed," Saint-Just confirmed. "We must be prepared for confrontation."

"Let them come," Étienne declared. "Our cause is just."

Saint-Just hesitated. "Some among us question the path we're on."

Étienne fixed him with a steely gaze. "Do you?"

Saint-Just met his gaze unflinchingly. "I believe in the revolution. But I also believe in strategy. We must not act recklessly."

Étienne nodded slowly. "Agreed. We must channel the people's anger effectively. We convene at the Cordeliers Club tomorrow to plan our next move."

"Very well," Saint-Just said. "I'll inform the others."

As Saint-Just departed, Étienne closed the door, his mind racing. Doubt was a contagion he could ill afford among his ranks.

He sat at his desk, quill in hand, and began drafting a speech—a rallying cry to be delivered at the upcoming assembly. His words flowed with calculated precision, designed to inflame passions and solidify loyalty.

Citoyens,

We stand on the precipice of a new dawn. The chains of oppression are cracking. It is our duty, our destiny, to shatter them completely.

He paused and dipped the quill into the inkwell, the dark liquid swirling like the depths of his ambition.

The monarchy has betrayed us. Will we allow their treachery to go unpunished? Non! We shall rise as one, a force unstoppable, to claim the freedom that is rightfully ours.

Setting the quill down, he read over his words, a sense of satisfaction settling over him. The masses were a tool—a means to an end. With their support, he could reshape France according to his vision.

As the first light of dawn crept over the horizon, Étienne extinguished the lamp and leaned back in his chair. The city stirred below, unaware of the forces at play, the threads he wove binding them to his purpose.

He allowed himself a rare moment of introspection. Was he driven solely by the cause or by the allure of power? The line had blurred, and ambition and ideology were entwined like lovers in a clandestine embrace.

But doubts were a luxury he could not indulge. He determined the path and would follow it until the end.

Rising, he moved to the window. The dawn cast a golden hue over Paris. The bells of a distant church tolled, their echoes resonating through the streets.

"The revolution marches on," he whispered. "And I shall lead the charge."

As the city awakened, Étienne Corbeau stood poised at the cusp of destiny, the weight of his actions both a burden and a beacon.

The masses stirred, their voices rising—a symphony of dissent that he had composed, each note a testament to his influence.

As the new day unfolded, he embraced the chaos with unwavering resolve, the architect of a future only he could envision.

• • •

The morning of 16 July 1791 dawned heavily with a humid haze that clung to the streets of Paris, shrouding the city in a veil of anticipation. Étienne Corbeau stood at the edge of the Place de la Révolution, watching workers erected a platform adorned with tricolour banners. The growing buzz of the crowd gathering overshadowed the distant murmur of the Seine for Maximilien Robespierre's much-anticipated public address.

Étienne adjusted the cuffs of his dark coat, his mind a labyrinth of calculations. He had spent the past days carefully orchestrating this moment, guiding Robespierre towards a narrative that would stoke the fires of revolution into an unquenchable blaze. The King's attempted flight had provided the perfect pretext, and now it was time to solidify their radical course.

As the sun climbed higher, casting a golden hue over the assembled masses, Étienne navigated through the crowd towards the backstage area where Robespierre was reviewing his speech. The scent of freshly baked bread from nearby vendors mingled with the sharp tang of sweat and anticipation.

"Maximilien," Étienne called softly as he approached, careful not to startle the pensive orator.

Robespierre looked up from his notes, his pale eyes reflecting a mixture of determination and fatigue. "Étienne," he acknowledged. "The crowd is larger than I expected."

"Indeed," Étienne agreed. "The people are hungry for guidance. Your words today will shape the course of the revolution."

Robespierre sighed, folding the parchment in his hands. "I've rewritten this speech countless times. I worry my words may incite more unrest than unity."

Étienne placed a reassuring hand on his shoulder. "Sometimes, unrest is necessary to awaken those who slumber in complacency. We must not react to the King's betrayal with meekness."

Robespierre frowned slightly. "I wish to appeal to reason, not merely to passion. The revolution must not descend into blind fury."

"Reason and passion are not mutually exclusive," Étienne countered. "But we must acknowledge the depth of the betrayal. The people feel wounded, abandoned by a monarch who swore to protect them."

Robespierre's gaze drifted over the crowd. "What would you have me say?"

"Speak to their hearts," Étienne urged. "Remind them of the ideals we fight for, but do not deny the truth. The King has forsaken his duty. We must take decisive action to safeguard our future."

Robespierre nodded slowly. "Perhaps you are right. The time for equivocation has passed."

Étienne offered a faint smile. "Trust in your convictions. They have guided you this far."

As Robespierre returned to his notes, Étienne felt a pang of something akin to guilt tug at the edges of his conscience. He dismissed it swiftly. This was no time for hesitation.

A voice called out from behind them. "Robespierre, they're ready for you."

Turning, they saw Camille Desmoulins approaching, his ever-present notebook tucked under his arm. His youthful face bore an uncharacteristic seriousness.

"Camille," Robespierre greeted him. "Is everything in order?"

"As much as it can be," Desmoulins replied. His gaze flickered to Étienne. "The atmosphere is tense."

"All the more reason to address them promptly," Étienne interjected.

Robespierre took a deep breath. "Very well."

He approached the platform, with Étienne and Camille following close behind. The crowd's murmurs hushed as Robespierre ascended the steps, his slender figure silhouetted against the clear sky.

"*Citoyens* of Paris," he began, his voice carrying over the sea of upturned faces. "We gather here today at a moment of profound significance."

Étienne watched intently; every word weighed against the script he had so carefully influenced.

"The events of recent weeks have tested the very fabric of our nation," Robespierre continued. "Our King, whom we entrusted with the sacred duty of upholding the Constitution, has attempted to abandon us in our hour of need."

A ripple of discontent swept through the crowd.

"But we must not let this betrayal shatter our resolve," he urged. "Rather, let it strengthen our commitment to liberty, equality, and fraternity."

Étienne noted the measured tone, the careful balance between condemnation and inspiration.

Robespierre pressed on. "Denouncing the actions of one man is not enough. We must look within ourselves and ask: what kind of nation do we wish to build? One that clings to the vestiges of a failed monarchy or boldly steps into a new era of true democracy?"

The crowd responded with cheers and applause.

"Let us not be swayed by those who preach moderation in the face of injustice," Robespierre declared, his voice rising. "The time for decisive action is upon us. We must take the reins of our destiny and forge a republic that reflects the people's will."

Étienne felt a surge of satisfaction. The speech was unfolding as he had envisioned.

As Robespierre concluded, the crowd erupted into chants of *"Vive la Révolution!"* The hunger was palpable, a living entity that thrummed in the air.

Descending from the platform, Robespierre was met with a barrage of questions from fellow deputies and journalists. Étienne manoeuvred through the crowd to reach him.

"An excellent address," Étienne commended. "You captured the essence of the moment."

Robespierre gave a modest nod. "I only hope it serves to unite rather than divide."

Before Étienne could respond, Georges Danton approached, his broad frame cutting an imposing figure.

"Well spoken, Maximilien," Danton boomed. "You've certainly stirred the pot."

"Let us hope it brews something palatable," Robespierre replied wryly.

Danton clapped him on the back. "With the tide turning, we must be prepared for what's coming."

Étienne interjected, "Indeed. We should convene a meeting to discuss our next steps."

"Agreed," Danton said. "This evening at the Jacobin Club?"

Robespierre assented. "I'll be there."

As Danton moved away to address the press, Robespierre turned to Étienne. "Walk with me."

They weaved through the dispersing crowd, the cacophony fading into a backdrop of distant noise.

"Étienne," Robespierre began quietly, "do you ever question our path?"

Étienne glanced at him, measuring his response. "In what sense?"

"This push towards radical action," Robespierre elaborated. "I fear we may unleash forces we cannot control."

Étienne considered this. "Change is seldom without turbulence. But without bold steps, we risk stagnation."

Robespierre sighed. "I understand the necessity, yet I cannot shake the feeling that we are teetering on the edge of a precipice."

"Your caution is admirable," Étienne acknowledged. "But we must not let fear dictate our actions."

They walked silently for a moment, the weight of unspoken thoughts hanging between them.

Finally, Robespierre spoke. "I value your counsel, Étienne. You have a way of clarifying the murkiness of these times."

Étienne felt that pang again—a subtle tug at his conscience. "We all seek to navigate the same storm," he whispered.

Robespierre offered a faint smile. "Perhaps together, we can find safe harbour."

They parted ways at a crossroads, Robespierre heading towards his lodgings. Étienne watching him go. The doubt gnawed at him more persistently now. Was he merely guiding events or manipulating them to his own ends?

He shook off the thought. The revolution demanded sacrifice, and personal qualms were a small price for the greater good.

Making his way towards the Seine, he encountered Olympe de Gouges seated at an outdoor café, her attention fixed on a newspaper.

"Étienne," she called out upon seeing him. "Join me?"

He hesitated briefly before acquiescing. "Good afternoon, Olympe."

She regarded him with a keen eye. "I attended Robespierre's speech. Stirring, though I detected your influence."

He raised an eyebrow. "Is that so?"

"Your fingerprints are all over the call for radical action," she observed. "Are you certain this is the path we should tread?"

Étienne sighed. "The situation leaves us little choice."

She leaned forward. "Or perhaps you've orchestrated it to appear that way."

He bristled slightly. "You give me too much credit."

"Do I?" she challenged. "I've seen how you operate, nudging others towards your desired outcome."

Étienne met her gaze evenly. "I act in the revolution's interest."

"Or in the interest of your ambition?" she pressed.

A flicker of irritation crossed his features. "Must the two be mutually exclusive?"

She sat back, a hint of sadness in her eyes. "Be careful, Étienne. The line between visionary and manipulator is thin."

He stood abruptly. "Thank you for your concern, but I know what I'm doing."

As he walked away, her parting words lingered. The weight of his manipulations pressed upon him more heavily than before.

The Jacobin Club buzzed with a charged atmosphere that evening. Discussions ranged from proposed legislation to rumours of counter-revolutionary plots.

Étienne observed from the periphery as Robespierre and other leaders debated strategies. Despite the day's successes, an undercurrent of tension pervaded the room.

Louis de Saint-Just approached him quietly. "You seem distant tonight."

"Merely reflective," Étienne replied.

"Robespierre's speech has set things in motion," Saint-Just noted. "But not all are pleased."

Étienne glanced around. "Dissent is inevitable."

"True," Saint-Just agreed. "We must remain vigilant."

Étienne nodded, but his thoughts were elsewhere. The cumulative effect of his manoeuvres was becoming apparent, and for the first time, he contemplated the repercussions.

As the meeting adjourned, he lingered behind, the empty hall echoing with the ghosts of impassioned discourse.

"16 July 1791," he whispered to himself. "A day of triumph—or the beginning of unforeseen consequences?"

He exited into the cool night air, the streets quiet save for the distant sounds of merriment from taverns. The stars overhead seemed indifferent to the struggles below.

Returning to his apartment, he sat at his desk, staring at a blank sheet of parchment. The words that usually flowed so readily eluded him.

He considered writing to his sister in the countryside, seeking solace in familial connection. But what could he say? That he helped to steer a nation towards an uncertain fate?

The weight of his manipulations settled upon him like a mantle—both empowering and burdensome.

He extinguished the lamp and moved to the window, gazing out over the city he sought to reshape.

"Is this the price of progress?" he mused. "To bear the weight of choices that may damn or deliver?"

Sleep was a long time coming, his mind a tumult of ambition, doubt, and the inexorable march of events he had set into motion.

As dawn approached, Étienne resolved to press on. The revolution waited for no one, and neither could he afford to falter.

But the shadows of his actions lingered, whispering questions he dared not fully confront.

• • •

Étienne Corbeau stood at the window of his modest apartment overlooking the Rue du Faubourg Saint-Honoré on 20 July 1791, his gaze fixed on the bustling street below. The scent of baked bread mingled with the distant clamour of merchants hawking their wares, yet the familiar cacophony offered little solace.

He turned away, the weight of his thoughts pressing heavily upon him. Spread across his desk were newspapers and pamphlets, some praising the revolutionary passion, others cautioning against the tide of radicalism that threatened to engulf them all. Among them lay a letter bearing the seal of his family—a stark reminder of the noble lineage he had long sought to distance himself from.

"Le sang ne peut pas être effacé," he muttered to himself. Blood cannot be erased.

Despite his sincere efforts to align with the revolutionaries, Étienne knew that his aristocratic heritage remained an indelible mark. It barred him from taking the public role he so desperately craved, forcing him to operate from the shadows, manipulating events like a puppeteer hidden behind the curtain.

A sharp rap at the door pulled him from his reverie. He crossed the room and opened it to reveal Louis de Saint-Just, his expression as inscrutable as ever. Dressed in austere black, Saint-Just carried an air of solemn intensity that belied his youth.

"Louis," Étienne greeted him, stepping aside. "I wasn't expecting you."

Saint-Just entered without ceremony. "Urgent matters require discussion," he stated plainly.

"Of course," Étienne replied, closing the door. "What troubles you?"

Saint-Just cast a glance at the scattered papers. "The Assembly convenes this afternoon to debate the fate of the monarchy. The moderates are rallying support to preserve the King's position, albeit with diminished powers."

Étienne's jaw tightened. "Fools clinging to a rotting vestige," he spat. "They endanger the revolution with their cowardice."

"Agreed," Saint-Just said. "But their influence grows. We must counteract their efforts decisively."

Étienne moved to the desk, sifting through the documents. "I've been gathering information on several key moderates—evidence of their collusion with Royalists."

Saint-Just arched an eyebrow. "Substantial evidence?"

Étienne met his gaze. "Substantial enough to sow doubt. We can expose their duplicity, turn the tide of opinion against them."

A flicker of concern crossed Saint-Just's features. "We tread a dangerous path, Étienne. Fabricated accusations could backfire."

"It's a risk we must take," Étienne insisted. "The revolution cannot afford to be undermined from within."

Saint-Just considered this, then gave a curt nod. "Very well. I will present this information discreetly to those who can act upon it."

"Excellent," Étienne replied. "Time is of the essence."

As Saint-Just prepared to leave, he paused. "You should attend the Assembly."

Étienne sighed. "You know my presence there raises questions. My name still carries… implications."

"Your insights are valuable," Saint-Just countered. "We need every advantage."

Étienne managed a tight smile. "Perhaps when the shadows no longer serve me."

After Saint-Just departed, Étienne felt the familiar frustration gnawing at him. His noble background, once a shield of privilege, had become a chain tethering him to anonymity. While others stood before the crowds, stirring hearts with rousing speeches, he remained behind the scenes, his contributions unacknowledged.

He recalled the fiery orations of Georges Danton, whose booming voice could sway even the most reluctant listener, and the eloquence of Camille Desmoulins, whose pen wielded the power of a thousand swords. Étienne longed to stand among them, to have his voice heard, his presence felt.

But the spectre of his lineage loomed large. In a revolution that vilified the aristocracy, revealing his true identity could be tantamount to a death sentence. The increasing radicalism he had helped foment now threatened to consume him.

A soft knock interrupted his thoughts once more. Surprised, he opened the door to find Olympe de Gouges, her eyes searching his face.

"Olympe," he greeted her, masking his surprise. "This is an unexpected pleasure."

"May I come in?" she asked quietly.

"Of course."

She entered, her gaze drifting over the cluttered room. "You're hard to find these days," she remarked.

"I've been busy," he replied evasively. "What brings you here?"

She turned to face him. "I wanted to warn you."

"Warn me?"

"There's talk among the Jacobins," she said. "Whispers about a nobleman influencing radical elements from the shadows."

Étienne's heart skipped a beat, but he maintained a façade of calm. "Rumours are the currency of the paranoid."

"Perhaps," she conceded. "But these rumours carry weight. If they believe you to be… well, you could be in danger."

He forced a light laugh. "And who would suspect me? A humble citizen devoted to the cause."

She stepped closer, her voice softening. "Étienne, I've known you long enough to see the burdens you carry. You must be careful."

He met her eyes, the usual defiance tempered by gratitude. "Your concern is touching, but unnecessary."

She sighed. "Always so guarded."

"Self-preservation demands it," he replied.

They stood in silence for a moment, the unspoken words hanging heavily between them.

"Very well," she said finally. "Just promise me you'll consider your position carefully."

"I will," he assured her.

As she left, Étienne felt a pang of regret. Olympe's warnings echoed the unease that had been creeping into his thoughts. The revolution was a beast he had helped unleash, but one that might not distinguish friend from foe.

Determined to regain his focus, he gathered the incriminating documents and set out towards the Tuileries, where the Assembly would soon convene. The streets were alive with a tense energy, citizens clustering in animated discussions, their faces a mosaic of hope and fear.

Approaching a side entrance reserved for officials, Étienne slipped inside the grand building. The corridors bustled with deputies and aides, the air thick with the scent of ink and heated debate. He spotted Jean-Paul Marat emerging from a chamber, his gaze sharp beneath his furrowed brow.

"Marat," Étienne called softly.

Marat turned, his expression softening slightly. "Ah, Étienne. What brings you here?"

"I have information that may prove useful," he said, lowering his voice. "Proof of moderate deputies engaging in clandestine meetings with Royalist agents."

Marat's eyes gleamed. "Interesting. This could be the leverage we need."

"Precisely, but handling it delicately is necessary," Étienne affirmed. "We cannot afford missteps."

Marat scoffed. "Delicacy is a luxury. The truth must be exposed."

"Agreed, but timing is crucial," Étienne cautioned. "Release the information too soon, and they'll have time to counter. Wait too long, and their influence may solidify."

Marat considered this. "Very well. I'll prepare an article for *L'Ami du peuple*, to be published at the opportune moment."

"Excellent," Étienne replied. "Keep me informed."

As Marat moved away, Étienne lingered in the shadows of the corridor, observing the flow of individuals entering the Assembly chamber. His frustration mounted. Here he was, orchestrating pivotal actions, yet unable to actively take part openly in the debates that would shape the future of the nation.

A familiar figure caught his eye—Maximilien Robespierre, his countenance thoughtful as he engaged in conversation with a fellow deputy. Étienne contemplated approaching him, but hesitated. Their last discussion had left him with a sense of unease, the weight of his manipulations pressing more heavily upon him.

Instead, he retreated from the building, the stifling air inside giving way to a merciful breeze outdoors. He wandered aimlessly, his mind a tumult of conflicting emotions.

Passing by the banks of the Seine, he watched the river's steady flow. The water reflected the hues of the setting sun, a kaleidoscope of gold and crimson. He thought of Rousseau's writings on the natural state of man, the search for freedom and self-determination.

"Have I strayed too far from the path?" he wondered aloud.

"Étienne?" a voice called from behind.

He turned to see Camille Desmoulins approaching, his usual vivacity tempered by concern.

"Camille," Étienne acknowledged. "What brings you here?"

"I could ask you the same," Desmoulins replied. "You seemed troubled."

Étienne offered a faint smile. "Merely contemplating the state of affairs."

Desmoulins joined him at the water's edge. "These are trying times. The Assembly is in turmoil."

"I've heard," Étienne said. "The moderates persist in their folly."

Desmoulins sighed. "Not all of them are blind to reason. Some may yet be swayed."

"Optimism suits you," Étienne remarked dryly.

"Perhaps," Desmoulins conceded. "But we must avoid tearing ourselves apart from within."

Étienne glanced at him. "Do you doubt our course?"

"I question the methods," Desmoulins admitted. "Rumours and accusations can be dangerous tools."

"Tools that achieve results," Étienne countered.

"At what cost?" Desmoulins pressed. "We risk becoming the very thing we oppose."

Étienne felt a flicker of irritation. "Necessity dictates our actions. The revolution cannot be gentle."

Desmoulins studied him for a moment. "Just be wary, Étienne. The line between justice and vengeance is easily blurred."

Before he could respond, Desmoulins clapped him on the shoulder. "Take care, *mon ami.*"

As Desmoulins walked away, Étienne was left alone with his thoughts. The warnings from Olympe and now Desmoulins echoed in his mind, stirring a disquiet he struggled to suppress.

Night descended, the city's lights flickering to life like stars fallen to earth. Étienne made his way back to his apartment, the shadows lengthening around him.

Upon entering, he lit a single candle, its flame casting a warm glow over the cluttered room. He sat at his desk, pulling out a fresh sheet of parchment.

20 July 1791,

The revolution advances, yet the path grows treacherous. Allies waver, and enemies close in from all sides. My heritage binds me to the periphery, even as my actions shape the core.

Am I a catalyst for change, or a pawn in a larger game? The danger mounts, but retreat is not an option. I must press on, for the sake of the cause—and perhaps, for my redemption.

Setting the quill aside, he leaned back, the weight of his position settling upon him like a mantle. The danger was real, and his frustration palpable. Yet, he could not abandon his course.

A faint knock startled him. Rising cautiously, he opened the door to reveal a messenger—a young boy, eyes wide with urgency.

"Monsieur Corbeau?" the boy asked.

"Oui?"

"A letter for you," the boy said, handing over a sealed envelope.

Étienne took it, recognising the seal of the Jacobin Club. *"Merci"*

The boy nodded and dashed away.

Closing the door, Étienne broke the seal and unfolded the letter. It was a summons to an emergency meeting—news of significant developments required immediate attention.

He folded the letter thoughtfully. The game was speeding up, and his role, though concealed, remained pivotal.

Extinguishing the candle, he steeled himself. The night was young, and the revolution waited for no man.

As he stepped back into the Parisian night, the distant echoes of voices and the faint strains of a violin drifted through the air. The city pulsed with life and possibility, danger and hope intertwined.

Étienne Corbeau pulled his coat tighter against the evening chill. The path ahead was uncertain, but he would navigate it as he always had—in the shadows, his eyes fixed on the horizon as he made his way to another meeting.

• • •

27 July 1791, Étienne Corbeau stood on the balcony of his modest apartment overlooking the Rue Saint-Honoré, his sharp eyes surveying the restless crowd below. The scent of warm bread mingled with the acrid smell of smoke from distant fires—a city teetering on the edge of chaos.

Étienne's thoughts churned as he contemplated his next move. The revolution had gained momentum, but the moderates still clung to their waning influence, threatening to undermine the radical changes he envisioned. He knew that to solidify his position, he needed to become indispensable to the revolution's leadership.

A knock at the door pulled him from his reverie. He turned to see Louis de Saint-Just entering, his youthful face etched with intensity.

"Étienne," Saint-Just greeted him, closing the door behind him. "We must speak."

"Louis," Étienne replied, gesturing for him to sit. "What news do you bring?"

Saint-Just took a seat, his gaze unwavering. "The Assembly remains divided. The moderates grow bold, proposing measures to limit the revolution's progress."

Étienne's expression hardened. "They are blind to the needs of the people. Their reluctance hinders us."

"Precisely why we must act swiftly," Saint-Just asserted. "Robespierre hesitates, caught between caution and conviction."

Étienne leaned forward, his voice low. "Then we must guide him towards the path."

Saint-Just studied him. "And how do you propose we do that?"

"By illuminating the urgency of our cause," Étienne replied. "We must make him see that only through decisive, radical policies can we secure the revolution's future."

Saint-Just nodded thoughtfully. "He respects your counsel. Perhaps a direct conversation is in order."

"Agreed," Étienne said, rising from his chair. "I will speak with him tonight."

As evening descended, Étienne made his way to Robespierre's residence on the Rue Saint-Denis. The streets were alive with murmurs of dissent and impatience, the city's pulse quickening with each passing hour. The glow of lanterns cast long shadows, illuminating the faces of citizens hungry for change.

Reaching the modest building, Étienne rapped lightly on the door. An attendant admitted him, and he was led to Robespierre's study—a cluttered room lined with books and papers, the air thick with the scent of ink and candle wax.

"Étienne," Robespierre greeted him warmly, looking up from a stack of documents. His eyes bore the weight of sleepless nights and the burden of leadership. "To what do I owe this visit?"

"Maximilien," Étienne began, taking a seat across from him. "I come with concerns about the direction of the revolution."

Robespierre sighed, setting his quill aside. "You are not alone in your worries. The path ahead is fraught with challenges."

"Indeed," Étienne agreed. "The moderates' influence persists, and their reluctance endangers our progress. We must adopt more decisive measures."

Robespierre regarded him carefully. "What measures do you suggest?"

Étienne met his gaze. "We need policies that address the root of dissent—policies that show our commitment to the people's will. Land reforms, price controls, and the dismantling of remaining aristocratic privileges."

Robespierre leaned back, his fingers steepled. "Such actions could provoke a backlash from those who still hold power."

"Only if we hesitate," Étienne countered. "If we move swiftly, we can outpace opposition. The people are with us—they crave bold leadership."

Robespierre's eyes flickered with contemplation. "I fear the repercussions of extreme actions."

"Maximilien," Étienne said earnestly, "history does not favour the timid. We stand at a pivotal moment. To secure the revolution, we must be unyielding."

A silence settled between them, the distant sounds of the city filtering through the open window—a chorus of voices demanding change.

Finally, Robespierre spoke. "You make compelling arguments. Perhaps I have been too cautious."

Étienne seized the opportunity. "Your integrity and dedication inspire many, but now is the time to translate conviction into action."

Robespierre nodded slowly. "Very well. I will bring these proposals before the Committee of Public Safety."

A satisfied smile touched Étienne's lips. "Together, we can steer the revolution towards its rightful course."

As they discussed the specifics, Étienne felt a surge of triumph. By influencing Robespierre, he inched closer to becoming indispensable—a linchpin in the machinery of revolution.

Leaving Robespierre's residence, Étienne stepped into the balmy night. The city stretched before him like a living entity, its heart beating in time with his own ambitions. He wandered aimlessly, his mind strategising the next moves to solidify his standing.

Turning a corner, he nearly collided with Jacques-Louis David, the renowned painter, who carried a sketchbook under his arm.

"Étienne!" David exclaimed, steadying himself. "Out enjoying the night air?"

"Jacques," Étienne replied, regaining his composure. "Lost in thought, I'm afraid."

David chuckled. "A common ailment these days. Inspiration strikes at odd moments."

"Indeed," Étienne agreed. "Working on a new piece?"

"Yes—a depiction of the revolutionary spirit," David said enthusiastically. "I seek to capture the essence of our times."

"A noble endeavour," Étienne remarked. "The arts play a crucial role in shaping public sentiment."

"Precisely," David affirmed. "Perhaps you could offer some insights. Your perspective is… unique."

Étienne considered this. "I would be honoured to contribute."

They strolled together, discussing themes and symbols that might encapsulate the revolution's spirit. Étienne found the conversation refreshing—a temporary respite from the constant manoeuvring.

As they parted ways, Étienne felt a rare sense of camaraderie. Yet, the moment was fleeting—the weight of his ambitions pressed upon him once more.

Making his way to a dimly lit café tucked away on a quiet street, he entered to find Jean-Paul Marat hunched over a table, scribbling furiously. The flickering candle cast sharp shadows across Marat's intense features.

"Jean-Paul," Étienne greeted him, taking a seat opposite.

Marat glanced up, his eyes gleaming. "Étienne. I've just penned an article exposing the latest treacheries of the moderates."

"Excellent," Étienne replied. "Their influence must be eradicated."

Marat tapped his quill against the parchment. "Public support is vital. We must ensure the people understand the necessity of our actions."

"Agreed," Étienne said. "I've spoken with Robespierre. He's amenable to more assertive policies."

Marat's eyebrows rose. "Is that so? You've swayed him?"

"He's seen reason," Étienne stated. "But we must present a united front."

Marat leaned forward. "There's talk of unrest in the provinces. Peasants rising against landlords. It's the perfect storm—we can harness this energy."

"Then we should coordinate efforts," Étienne suggested. "Align our messages to amplify the impact."

Marat nodded approvingly. "You're proving to be quite the strategist."

Étienne offered a modest smile. "I serve the revolution as best I can."

As they delved into plans, Étienne felt the threads of his influence weaving tighter. Each alliance, each conversation, brought him closer to the heart of power.

Leaving the café, the night had deepened. The streets were quieter now, the earlier fervour subdued but simmering beneath the surface.

He turned towards his apartment but hesitated. A familiar figure stood under a streetlamp—Olympe de Gouges, her expression unreadable.

"Olympe," he called softly, approaching her. "Out at this hour?"

She met his gaze evenly. "I could ask you the same."

"Meetings," he replied vaguely. "The revolution keeps us all busy."

She studied him for a moment. "Word spreads quickly in Paris. They say Robespierre is adopting more extreme positions."

"Leadership requires adaptation," Étienne responded.

"And influence," she added pointedly. "Yours, perhaps?"

He shrugged lightly. "I offer counsel where I can."

Olympe's eyes searched his. "Be cautious, Étienne. Power is a seductive force. It can consume even the most well-intentioned."

He felt a flicker of irritation. "I am well aware of the responsibilities it entails."

She sighed softly. "I worry about you. For all of us."

"Your concern is noted," he said curtly. "But unnecessary."

A tense silence settled between them.

"Very well," she said finally. "Good night, Étienne."

"Good night," he replied, watching as she walked away, her figure dissolving into the shadows.

Returning home, Étienne settled at his desk, the flicker of the candle casting a warm glow over his features. He pulled out a fresh sheet of paper and began drafting a letter to Saint-Just, outlining strategies to further marginalise the moderates.

As he wrote, a gnawing awareness crept in—the recognition of the turmoil he was helping to foment. The revolution was a temper, and he stood at its eye, both conductor and participant.

27 July 1791,

The die is cast. With each passing day, the stakes rise, and my involvement deepens. I must remain vigilant, for the path ahead is treacherous.

Yet, to hesitate now would be to invite failure. I have chosen my course and will see it through, regardless of the cost.

Setting the quill aside, Étienne leaned back, his gaze drifting to the window. Outside, the city slept fitfully, its dreams haunted by the spectres of uncertainty and desire.

He extinguished the candle, plunging the room into darkness. In the quiet, he confronted the weight of his actions—the manipulations, the alliances forged and broken, the relentless pursuit of an ideal that seemed both noble and perilous.

Étienne lay awake long into the night, the boundaries between ambition and necessity blurring. The revolution demanded sacrifice, and he had given much. But at what point did the cost outweigh the gain?

As dawn's first light seeped into the sky, he rose, resolve hardening within him. The looming turmoil was both a challenge and an opportunity. To become indispensable, he would need to navigate the coming storms with deftness and conviction.

"Let the tempest rage," he whispered to himself. "I will not be swept aside."

With renewed determination, Étienne prepared to face the day—a key player in a grand tableau, fully aware of the perils but unwilling to yield.

CHAPTER FIVE: (1792)
BLOODIED PATHS

Étienne Corbeau stood in the shadowed recess of a narrow alleyway off the Rue Saint-Antoine, watching as the sun cast long, golden rays over the cobblestone streets. The distant tolling of church bells on 2 September 1792 mingled with the murmur of anxious voices—a city on the brink of upheaval.

He adjusted the brim of his tricolour cockade hat, a subtle symbol of his revolutionary allegiance, and stepped into the bustling thoroughfare. The air was thick with the scent of uncollected refuse and the underlying fear that had gripped the populace. Whispers of foreign invasion and internal betrayal rippled through the crowds like a contagion.

As Étienne navigated the throng, he caught sight of a familiar figure— Jean-Paul Marat—emerging from a dimly lit print shop. A fiery intensity illuminated Marat's gaunt features, his eyes darting with restless energy.

"Jean-Paul," Étienne called out, weaving through the masses to reach him.

Marat turned sharply, his expression softening marginally upon recognition. "Étienne. I trust you bring news."

"Indeed," Étienne replied, lowering his voice conspiratorially. "The Prussian forces draw nearer by the hour. There's talk that the Duke of Brunswick's manifesto has incited panic among the deputies."

Marat scoffed, his lips curling into a sneer. "Let them panic. Perhaps now they'll realise the folly of their complacency."

Étienne leaned closer. "But there's more. I've heard whispers that the imprisoned Royalists plan to aid the invaders from within. A coordinated assault to reclaim the city."

Marat's eyes narrowed. "If that's true, we cannot afford inaction. The enemy within is as dangerous as the one at our gates."

"Precisely," Étienne agreed. "We must alert the people, rally them to defend the revolution."

Marat nodded slowly, a grim determination settling over his features. "I'll publish an urgent appeal in *L'Ami du peuple*. The citizens must realise the imminent threat."

"Time is of the essence," Étienne urged. "Every moment we delay increases the risk."

Standing on Étienne's shoulder, Marat commended, "Your vigilance serves us well, *mon ami*. Let's work together to expose the enemies of liberty."

As Marat disappeared into the print shop, Étienne allowed himself a fleeting smile. Someone had planted the seeds of fear. He moved swiftly through the maze of streets, his destination clear—the Cordeliers Club, where Georges Danton frequented.

The club was bustling with activity, filled with smoke and the passionate conversations of revolutionaries. Étienne spotted Danton at a table near the back, his robust frame commanding attention even in repose. Beside him sat Camille Desmoulins, his quick eyes observing the room with a journalist's keen interest.

"Étienne!" Danton boomed as he approached. "Join us. We were just discussing the latest developments."

"Georges, Camille," Étienne greeted them, taking a seat. "The situation grows more dire by the hour."

Desmoulins leaned in, his expression eager. "What news do you bring?"

Étienne adopted a grave tone, saying, "There's credible information suggesting that the Royalist prisoners intend to stage an uprising in tandem with the Prussian advance. If they succeed, they could extinguish the revolution overnight."

Danton's brow furrowed. "We cannot allow this," Danton said with a furrowed brow. "We must take preventative measures."

"Agreed," Étienne replied. "But we need the support of the people. They must understand the gravity of the threat."

Desmoulins tapped his fingers thoughtfully on the table. "A mass mobilisation, perhaps? We could organise a citizen's militia to guard the prisons."

"An excellent notion," Étienne affirmed. "But we must also consider more… definitive actions."

Danton's gaze sharpened. "What are you suggesting?"

Étienne met his eyes steadily. "The elimination of the threat entirely. If the prisoners are no longer alive, they cannot aid our enemies."

A heavy silence settled over the table. Desmoulins shifted uncomfortably. "That's a drastic step."

"Drastic but necessary," Étienne insisted. "The lives of thousands hang in the balance. Are we willing to gamble the revolution on moral hesitation?"

Danton stroked his chin thoughtfully. "There will be those who oppose such measures."

"Then we must persuade them," Étienne countered. "For the greater good."

Before they could continue, a commotion erupted near the entrance. Citizens flooded into the club, their voices raised in alarm.

"The Prussians have taken Verdun!" someone shouted. "They're but a day's march from Paris!"

Panic rippled through the room. Danton stood abruptly, his voice cutting through the chaos. "Silence!"

The room quieted, all eyes turning to him.

"We cannot succumb to fear," Danton declared. "Now is the time for action. We must defend our city, our revolution!"

Étienne seized the moment. "Georges is right! But to do so, we must first secure Paris from internal threats. The Royalist prisoners plot against us even as we speak."

Murmurs of agreement spread among the crowd.

A man stepped forward—Antoine, a leader among the Sans-culottes. His weathered face bore the scars of hard labour, his eyes fiercely determined. "What would you have us do?"

"Guard the prisons," Étienne urged. "Ensure that no traitors escape to join the enemy."

"Better yet," another voice interjected, "we should rid ourselves of them entirely!"

A chorus of assent rose, the atmosphere growing increasingly volatile.

Desmoulins glanced at Étienne, a hint of unease in his gaze. "Are we truly considering this?"

Étienne placed a steadying hand on his shoulder. "We must be resolute. Hesitation could cost us everything."

Danton raised his fist. "To the prisons, then! For the revolution!"

The crowd surged towards the exit, a tide of righteous indignation sweeping them along. Étienne watched as they poured into the streets, the distant peal of alarm bells echoing through the city.

Desmoulins lingered beside him. "This could spiral beyond our control."

"Perhaps," Étienne conceded. "But better that than the alternative."

Desmoulins shook his head. "I hope you're right."

As they parted ways, Étienne felt the weight of his actions settle upon him—a mix of exhilaration and foreboding. He had set events in motion, but their outcome remained uncertain.

He navigated the chaotic streets, the city alight with the enthusiasm he had helped ignite. Fires burned in the distance, and the cries of the masses formed a dissonant symphony. He encountered Olympe de Gouges near the Hôtel de Ville, her expression etched with concern.

"Étienne!" she called out, weaving through the crowd to reach him. "What's happening?"

He met her gaze coolly. "The people are taking the action."

She searched his face. "Rumours abound of massacres at the prisons. Tell me it's not true."

He looked away. "Desperate times demand desperate measures."

"How can you justify this?" she implored. "It's madness!"

"It's survival," he retorted. "Would you prefer the Prussians march unopposed into Paris? That the Royalists reclaim their tyranny?"

She grasped his arm. "At what cost, Étienne? Our humanity?"

He pulled free. "Humanity is a luxury we cannot afford."

She stared at him, a mixture of sorrow and disbelief. "You've become a stranger to me."

"Then perhaps you never truly knew me," he replied, turning away.

As he walked into the night, her words lingered like a spectre. Doubt flickered at the edges of his resolve, but he pushed it aside. The revolution required sacrifices—moral ambiguities were a necessary burden.

He found himself at the Place de la Bastille, now a symbol of liberation. The once-imposing fortress lay in ruins, a testament to the people's power. Yet, the atmosphere was far from triumphant. Groups of citizens huddled together, their whispers carrying tales of bloodshed and retribution.

Étienne approached a cluster of Sans-culottes, their faces hardened by determination.

"Is it done?" he inquired.

One man, his hands stained crimson, nodded grimly. "We have dealt with the traitors," the man with crimson-stained hands nodded grimly.

"Good," Étienne replied, though an icy knot formed in his stomach.

Another man eyed him suspiciously. "And who are you to give orders?"

Étienne met his gaze unflinchingly. "A patriot, like you. One who seeks to safeguard our revolution."

The man grunted, satisfied, and turned back to his comrades.

As dawn approached, Étienne retreated to his apartment, exhaustion weighing upon him. He slumped into a chair, the echoes of the night's events replaying in his mind.

He reached for a quill and parchment, his hand trembling ever so slightly as he wrote.

> *We have purged the threat within, but the cost weighs heavily.*
> *Fear has proven a potent weapon, but one that cuts both ways.*
> *I must remain steadfast. The revolution depends upon unwavering conviction.*

He set the quill down, rubbing his temples. The line between manipulation and necessity had blurred, leaving him in a moral fog. But retreat was not an option.

A faint knock at the door startled him. Rising cautiously, he opened it to find Louis de Saint-Just, his expression inscrutable.

"Louis," Étienne greeted him. "You're out late."

"Or early," Saint-Just replied. "May I come in?"

"Of course."

Saint-Just entered, glancing around the modest room. "I've heard reports of the massacres."

Étienne nodded. "Unfortunate but necessary."

"Perhaps," Saint-Just mused. "But such actions can have unintended consequences."

"Étienne asserted, "We must harness fear. It's a tool to be wielded."

"True," Saint-Just conceded. "But a tool that can turn on its master."

Étienne studied him. "Do you question our methods?"

"I question everything," Saint-Just replied. "It's the only way to ensure we're on the correct path."

"Then you'll understand the importance of decisiveness."

Saint-Just met his gaze. "Just ensure that in seeking to control fear, you do not become enslaved by it."

With that, he turned and left, leaving Étienne alone once more.

As the first light of dawn filtered through the window, Étienne contemplated his chosen path. The fear of Royalist retribution had been a catalyst, but the repercussions were yet to unfold.

He steeled himself. There was no turning back. He would navigate the turmoil he had helped unleash, his sights set firmly on the goal—a revolution secured and his place within it irrevocably established.

• • •

Étienne Corbeau navigated the labyrinthine streets towards the modest townhouse where Maximilien Robespierre had summoned an urgent meeting on 3 September 1792. The distant peal of alarm bells echoed through the alleys, mingling with the murmur of fearful voices—a symphony of unease that set his nerves on edge.

Reaching the door, Étienne rapped lightly. It swung open to reveal Georges Danton, his imposing frame filling the doorway. His brow glistened with sweat, and concern filled his usually cheerful eyes.

"Étienne," Danton greeted him gruffly. "You're the last to arrive."

"Apologies," Étienne replied, stepping inside. "The streets are restless tonight."

"Aren't they always?" Danton muttered, closing the door behind them.

They entered a dimly lit parlour where Maximilien Robespierre sat at a cluttered table, papers strewn about like fallen leaves. Jean-Paul Marat paced near the window, his sharp features cast in shadow.

"Étienne," Robespierre acknowledged with a slight nod. "We have much to discuss."

"Indeed," Étienne agreed, taking a seat opposite Robespierre. "The situation grows more precarious by the hour."

Marat ceased his pacing, turning to face the group. "The Prussians inch closer to our borders, and the Austrian threat looms large. Yet our greatest danger lies within—the traitors festering in our midst."

Danton crossed his arms. "The prisons are overflowing with Royalists and conspirators. If the enemy reaches Paris, who knows what chaos they could unleash from inside those walls?"

Robespierre steepled his fingers, his gaze distant. "We must ensure the security of the nation, but we must tread carefully. The rule of law must prevail, even in times such as these."

Étienne leaned forward, his voice measured. "Maximilien, your dedication to justice is admirable. Yet, the law is only as strong as those who uphold it. Desperate times may require… extraordinary measures."

Marat's eyes flickered with interest. "What are you suggesting, Étienne?"

He chose his words with care. "Merely that the people are frightened. Fear can drive them to act independently if they believe we are not protecting them adequately."

Danton raised an eyebrow. "Are you implying we should sanction vigilantism?"

"Not at all," Étienne replied smoothly. "But we cannot control every action of a passionate populace. Perhaps if certain information were to become widespread—rumours of an imminent prison break orchestrated by the Royalists—it could galvanise the citizens to safeguard their own revolution."

Robespierre frowned. "Spreading unverified rumours could incite panic."

"True," Étienne conceded. "But consider the alternative: inaction leading to catastrophe. The people trust us to lead, but they also possess the will to act when necessary."

Marat stroked his chin thoughtfully. "There's merit in allowing the people to express their revolutionary fervour."

Danton uncrossed his arms, his expression contemplative. "We must be cautious. Unchecked violence could undermine everything we've worked for."

Étienne met Danton's gaze. "Georges, you once said that audacity is the key to success. This moment requires us to be bold, to trust in the strength and righteousness of the people."

Robespierre sighed heavily. "I fear the consequences of unleashing forces we cannot control. We must find a balance between security and justice."

"Then perhaps," Étienne suggested, "we focus on ensuring the people are well-informed of our threats. Allow them to draw their own conclusions."

Marat's eyes gleamed. "I can prepare an article for *L'Ami du peuple*, highlighting the dangers posed by the prisoners and the situation's urgency."

Robespierre hesitated. "Jean-Paul, ensure that you stick to the facts. We cannot afford to spread misinformation."

"Of course," Marat replied, though a hint of a smirk betrayed his true intentions.

Danton placed a hand on Robespierre's shoulder. "Maximilien, we must trust in the revolution's spirit. The people have risen before; they will rise again to defend what is theirs."

Robespierre rubbed his temples. "Very well. But we must remain vigilant. The line between defence and atrocity is thin."

Étienne sensed an opportunity to solidify his influence. "Perhaps we could organise patrols to monitor the prisons—volunteers from among the citizens. It would give them a sense of agency and allow us to maintain some oversight."

Danton nodded approvingly. "A practical solution. I'll see that the National Guard coordinates with these patrols."

"Excellent," Étienne said, a subtle satisfaction settling within him.

Robespierre rose from his seat, signalling an end to the meeting. "Let us proceed with caution. The future of the revolution depends upon our wisdom."

As they filed out of the parlour, Étienne lingered momentarily. "Maximilien," he began, "I appreciate your commitment to justice. It is a beacon in these dark times."

Robespierre offered a weary smile. "And I appreciate your counsel, Étienne. We all serve the revolution in our ways."

Stepping into the cool night air, Étienne felt a surge of vindication. He had planted the seeds. He made his way through the dimly lit streets, the sounds of distant shouts and the occasional crash hinting at the unrest simmering beneath the surface.

Turning a corner, he nearly collided with Camille Desmoulins, who appeared flustered, his spectacles askew.

"Camille," Étienne exclaimed, steadying him. "In a hurry?"

Desmoulins adjusted his glasses, his eyes wide. "Étienne! I've just come from the Assembly. The atmosphere is volatile—everyone's on edge."

"Understandable," Étienne replied. "These are uncertain times."

Desmoulins searched his face. "There's talk that something is brewing among the populace. Rumours of plans to storm the prisons."

Étienne feigned surprise. "Is that so? The people are resourceful when they feel threatened."

Desmoulins frowned. "I can't help but feel that someone's fanning the flames."

"Perhaps," Étienne said lightly. "But can you blame them? Action feels necessary with the Prussians advancing and traitors in our midst."

"Action, yes. But violence?" Desmoulins shook his head. "We risk losing our moral high ground."

Étienne placed a reassuring hand on his shoulder. "Sometimes, we must make hard choices for the greater good," Étienne said.

Desmoulins sighed. "I suppose you're right. I just hope we don't become what we despise."

"Trust in the revolution, Camille. It will guide us."

They parted ways, and Étienne continued towards his apartment. As he approached, he noticed a figure seated on the steps—a woman, her posture rigid yet graceful. Olympe de Gouges.

"Olympe," he greeted her cautiously. "To what do I owe this visit?"

She stood, her eyes reflecting a steely resolve. "We need to talk."

"Very well," he replied, unlocking the door and gesturing for her to enter.

Inside, she wasted no time. "I've heard disturbing reports." She immediately addressed the issue, saying, "I've heard disturbing reports. The prisons may experience violence because of the agitation and fear among the people."

Étienne maintained a neutral expression. "Emotions are running high."

She narrowed her eyes. "Don't play coy with me. I know you have a hand in this."

He met her gaze evenly. "I advocate for the security of the revolution."

"At any cost?" she challenged. "You're manipulating fear, serving your own ends."

"That's a harsh accusation," he retorted.

"But is it untrue?" she pressed. "You speak of the greater good, but ambition clouds your judgement."

He clenched his jaw. "You underestimate the gravity of our situation. Drastic times call for decisive actions."

She shook her head. "There's a difference between decisiveness and recklessness. Innocent lives are at stake."

"Innocence is a luxury we can ill afford," he snapped.

A tense silence settled between them.

"I came here hoping to appeal to your conscience," she said softly. "Perhaps I was mistaken."

"Perhaps you were," he replied coldly.

She moved towards the door, pausing briefly. "Be careful, Étienne. The path you're on leads to a dark place."

"Good night, Olympe," he said, opening the door for her.

After she left, Étienne felt a pang of something resembling regret, quickly smothered by his resolve. He could not afford to waver now.

He sat at his desk, the flicker of a solitary candle casting elongated shadows across the room. Reaching for a sheet of parchment, he began drafting a notice—a call to vigilance, carefully worded to stir the hearts of the citizens without overtly inciting violence.

"Citoyens,

The hour is upon us. Our enemies press in from all sides, and treachery lurks within our walls. It falls upon each of us to defend the sanctity of our revolution. Remain alert, remain resolute.

He would distribute it anonymously, allowing the message to spread organically. The people would feel empowered and compelled to act—not by his hand directly but by the collective will he had helped shape.

As the night wore on, Étienne gazed out his window at the city below. Fires dotted the landscape, beacons of unrest and determination. He wondered, fleetingly, if he had set forces beyond his control in motion.

"3 September 1792," he murmured. "The storm gathers, and I stand at its eye."

Sleep eluded him, his mind a maelstrom of plans and possibilities. The revolution was a living entity, unpredictable and consuming. Yet, he believed himself capable of steering it—or at least surviving its tempests.

Dawn approached, a pale light creeping over the horizon. Étienne rose, fatigue tugging at his limbs but purpose driving him forward. There was much to be done, and the day promised to be consequential.

He donned his coat and hat and stepped out into the awakening city. The air was thick with anticipation, the silence before the deluge. As he walked towards the heart of Paris, he felt a strange mix of exhilaration and trepidation.

His path was fraught with peril, but he embraced it. For in the crucible of revolution, he sought not only the transformation of a nation but the forging of his destiny.

• • •

The morning of 4 September 1792 dawned with a crimson hue as if the sky foresaw the coming bloodshed. Étienne Corbeau stood upon the steps of the Hôtel de Ville, surveying the restless crowd that swelled in the square below. The air was thick with tension, and the usual scents of Paris—fresh bread and damp cobblestones—were overpowered by the acrid smell of fear and enthusiasm.

Men and women milled about, their faces a mosaic of anger and anxiety. Whispers rippled through the masses: tales of foreign armies marching towards the city, of traitors plotting within their midst. Étienne felt a surge of grim satisfaction. The seeds he had sown were bearing fruit.

He descended the steps, merging into the crowd. Nearby, they erected a makeshift platform where Georges Danton addressed the assembly with zeal.

"*Citoyens!*" Danton's voice boomed his broad shoulders and fiery gaze commanding attention. "The enemy approaches our gates, and still treachery haunts us from within! Will we stand idle while unseen hands strangle our revolution?"

A roar of dissent answered him, fists raised in solidarity.

Étienne edged closer, noting the enthusiasm that danced in the eyes of those around him. The crowd's energy was palpable, a living entity that pulsed and writhed, hungry for direction.

From the corner of his eye, he spotted Camille Desmoulins pushing through the masses, his face pale beneath his dark curls. Catching sight of Étienne, he made his way over.

"Étienne," Desmoulins greeted him, breathless. "This is getting out of hand."

Étienne arched an eyebrow. "Is it? The people are merely expressing their rightful anger."

Desmoulins glanced around nervously. "Rumours are spiralling. They're saying prisoners are to be executed without trial. This isn't justice—it's anarchy."

"Justice takes many forms," Étienne replied coolly. "Perhaps swift action is what's needed to secure our future."

Desmoulins shook his head. "I fear we've unleashed something we cannot control."

"Fear is a tool," Étienne countered. "One we can wield to our advantage."

Before Desmoulins could respond, a commotion erupted near the entrance to the Abbaye Prison. A group of Sans-culottes, identifiable by their trousers and red caps, had gathered, brandishing makeshift weapons—pikes, clubs, and rusted swords.

"Death to the traitors!" a voice cried out, igniting a chorus of angry shouts.

Étienne watched as the mob surged forward, slamming against the prison gates. Guards stationed outside hesitated, their loyalties torn between duty and self-preservation. Within moments, the crowd breached the gates and poured inside like a flood breaking through a dam.

Desmoulins grabbed Étienne's arm. "We have to stop this!"

Étienne pulled free. "And how do you propose we do that? Stand before the tide and command it to retreat?"

"This isn't what the revolution stands for!" Desmoulins insisted, desperation tinging his voice.

Étienne's gaze hardened. "Perhaps it's exactly what it needs."

Turning away, he moved towards the prison entrance, curiosity and a darker intrigue drawing him in. Inside, the stone corridors echoed with the cacophony of chaos—shouts, screams, the clang of metal against stone.

He ascended a narrow staircase to an overlooking balcony, granting him a grim vantage point of the unfolding scene below. The guards forcefully pulled prisoners from their cells, their faces filled with terror. Some pleaded for mercy; others stood silent, resigned to their fate.

A makeshift tribunal had formed—a parody of justice. Names were called, accusations hurled, and sentences pronounced in mere moments. The verdict was invariably the same.

Étienne felt a cold detachment settle over him. This was the manifestation of the fear and anger he had helped cultivate. It was a necessary purge, he told himself—a cleansing fire to burn away the rot of betrayal.

Yet, as the executions continued, a nagging unease gnawed at the edges of his conscience. The violence was indiscriminate. Among the condemned were aristocrats, priests, servants, women, and even children.

Below, a young priest stood before the mob, his hands bound. "I have served the people my entire life," he implored. "I am no enemy."

"All priests are traitors!" someone shouted, and the crowd echoed the sentiment.

They cut down the priest without further deliberation, and his body collapsed amidst the jeers. Étienne's jaw tightened. The scene repeated itself throughout the prison—and likely in others across the city.

A voice broke through his thoughts. "Is this what you wanted?"

He turned to see Olympe de Gouges standing behind him, her eyes ablaze with fury and sorrow. How had she found him here?

"Olympe," he began, but she cut him off.

"Don't," she snapped. "I warned you. This blood is on your hands."

He bristled. "I am not responsible for the actions of the masses."

"Aren't you?" she retorted. "You've manipulated them, stoked their fears. And now, innocent people are dying."

"Innocence is subjective," he replied defensively. "We are at war—both from without and within."

She stepped closer, her voice low but fierce. "This isn't war; it's murder. And deep down, you know it."

Étienne felt a flicker of doubt but quashed it. "We must sacrifice for the greater good."

She searched his face. "At what point does the greater good become a mere justification for atrocity?"

He had no answer. Instead, he turned his gaze back to the grim tableau below. The mob showed no signs of relenting. Blood slicked the stone floors, and the air was thick with the metallic scent of death.

Olympe laid a hand on his arm. "It's not too late to stop this."

He pulled away. "And do what? Preach moderation to an unhearing crowd? The tide has turned."

She shook her head sadly. "Then we've lost more than lives today. We've lost our humanity."

Without another word, she left, her footsteps echoing down the corridor.

Étienne remained, a hollow feeling settling in his chest. The satisfaction he had expected felt tainted, overshadowed by a growing realisation that the violence was spiralling beyond any intent or control.

Descending the staircase, he exited the prison into a city transformed. Similar scenes played out elsewhere—La Force, the Conciergerie—all engulfed in the same frenzy.

He went through the streets, the mob's cries fading into a haunting backdrop. Near the Place de la Bastille, he encountered Maximilien Robespierre, his face ashen.

"Étienne," Robespierre called out, approaching him. "I've been searching for you."

"Maximilien," Étienne acknowledged, noting the strain in the other man's eyes.

"This… this massacre," Robespierre said, his voice wavering. "It's an abomination."

Étienne regarded him carefully. "The people act out of fear and anger. Emotions we've all felt."

Robespierre shook his head. "But this indiscriminate killing—it's a stain on the revolution."

"Perhaps," Étienne conceded. "But can we afford to denounce them openly? Risk alienating those who have supported us?"

Robespierre sighed heavily. "We walk a dangerous path. If we lose our moral compass, we risk becoming the very tyrants we overthrew."

Étienne felt a flicker of irritation. "Moralising will not save us from the guillotine if the Prussians take the city."

"Nor will this bloodshed," Robespierre countered. "We must restore order."

"Then lead the way," Étienne challenged softly. "If you believe it possible."

Robespierre met his gaze, a mixture of determination and despair. "I intend to try."

As Robespierre departed, Étienne stood alone amidst the turmoil. An unsettling awareness of the unleashed beast overshadowed the satisfaction he had felt earlier—a beast that did not discriminate between friend and foe.

He continued walking, the streets a labyrinth of chaos. Fires burned unchecked, and the wails of the bereaved pierced the night air. He passed groups of Sans-culottes celebrating their grim victories, their faces smeared with grime and blood.

He paused at the banks of the Seine. The river flowed undisturbed, starkly contrasting the turmoil engulfing the city. The moon cast a silvery sheen upon the water, its serene beauty mocking the day's horrors.

He pondered whether history would harshly judge him or if his actions would fade into the broader strokes of revolution and war.

Footsteps approached from behind. Turning, he saw Louis de Saint-Just, his expression unreadable.

"Louis," Étienne greeted him. "Out surveying the aftermath?"

Saint-Just nodded. "It's worse than we imagined."

Étienne gestured towards the city. "The people have taken matters into their own hands."

"With some encouragement," Saint-Just noted pointedly.

Étienne met his gaze. "You disapprove?"

"I understand the necessity of strength," Saint-Just replied. "But uncontrolled violence serves no one."

"Perhaps it's a lesson we needed," Étienne mused. "A reminder of the forces at play."

Saint-Just studied him. "Be careful, Étienne. Those who unleash the storm often find themselves consumed by it."

"Are you warning me?"

"Merely observing," Saint-Just said quietly. "The revolution is greater than any of us."

With that, he turned and walked away, leaving Étienne to his thoughts.

As the first light of dawn crept over the horizon, Étienne felt an unfamiliar weight settle upon him. The chaos he had helped insight was no longer a tool he could wield but a force unto itself—unpredictable and potentially perilous.

He wondered if he had overstepped - if the manipulation of fear had birthed a monster beyond control.

Yet, even amidst the doubt, a part of him clung to the belief that such turmoil was necessary—that a stronger France would emerge from the ashes of this destruction.

Turning away from the river, he made his way back into the heart of the city, resolved to face whatever consequences awaited.

The die was cast, and there was no turning back.

•••

The morning sun of 6 September 1792 cast a pale, hesitant light over Paris, uncertain whether to illuminate the horrors that had unfolded in the preceding days. Étienne Corbeau stood by the window of his modest apartment, gazing out at the city that roiled beneath a veneer of uneasy calm. The distant cries had subsided, but an undercurrent of tension still thrummed through the cobblestone streets.

He turned away from the window, the shadows of his thoughts as heavy as the smoke that lingered in the air. A knock at the door interrupted his reverie. Crossing the sparsely furnished room, he opened it to reveal Camille Desmoulins, his face drawn and eyes haunted.

"Camille," Étienne greeted him with a faint smile. "To what do I owe this visit so *tôt?*"

Desmoulins pushed past him into the room, his movements abrupt. "We need to talk, Étienne."

Closing the door, Étienne regarded his old friend with curiosity and caution. "Very well. Shall I offer you some coffee?"

"Non," Desmoulins replied tersely, pacing the room's length. "I cannot sit idly by while this—this madness consumes us."

Étienne arched an eyebrow. "Madness? I assume you're referring to the recent events."

Desmoulins stopped pacing and faced him. "You know precisely what I mean. The massacres. The butchery in the prisons. Innocent blood spilt in the name of *liberté.* How can you stand there so composed?"

Étienne sighed, clasping his hands behind his back. "Camille, the times demand tough choices. We are at war, both within and without. The enemy is at our doorstep, and traitors lurk among us."

"Traitors?" Desmoulins's voice rose. "Do you truly believe that every soul slaughtered in those prisons was a threat? Women, children, the clergy— since when did they become our enemies?"

Étienne's gaze hardened. "Since they aligned themselves with forces seeking to destroy the revolution. Do not be naïve. Mercy is a luxury we cannot afford."

Desmoulins shook his head, his curls tumbling over his forehead. "This is not the revolution we dreamed of. We fought for justice, for the rights of man—not for this orgy of violence."

"You forget the cost of inaction," Étienne retorted. "Had we hesitated, the Prussians might have already marched through our streets, reinstating the monarchy and extinguishing the flame we've ignited."

"At what price, Étienne? Our souls?" Desmoulins's eyes glistened with unshed tears. "I cannot reconcile this brutality with the ideals we once shared."

Étienne stepped closer, his voice lowering. "Sometimes, we must sacrifice for the greater good," Étienne said, stepping closer and lowering his voice. "History will judge us not by the means, but by the ends we achieve."

"Spare me your justifications," Desmoulins snapped. "You've become as cold and unfeeling as the aristocrats we overthrew."

A flicker of anger crossed Étienne's face. "Mind your words, Camille. Do not forget that we stand on the same side."

"Do we?" Desmoulins challenged. "I look at you now and see a stranger—a man consumed by ambition, willing to tread over corpses to climb higher."

Étienne's jaw tightened. "If you cannot stomach what must be done, perhaps you have lost sight of our cause."

Desmoulins laughed bitterly. "Our cause? Or yours? Tell me, Étienne, when did the revolution become a vehicle for your ascent?"

"Careful," Étienne warned, his eyes narrowing. "Accusations such as that can have consequences."

Desmoulins met his gaze unflinchingly. "Is that a threat?"

"An observation," Étienne replied coolly. "Paris is not safe for those who sow discord."

"Then perhaps it is time I spoke out," Desmoulins declared. "The people deserve to know the truth—that men like you manipulate their fears for your own ends."

Étienne took a step back, a calculated calm settling over him. "You would not dare."

"Watch me," Desmoulins said, turning towards the door.

"Camille," Étienne called after him, a note of urgency creeping into his voice. "consider your next move. The times are volatile. Rash actions could lead to unintended consequences—for you and those you care about."

Desmoulins paused his hand on the doorknob. "Is that concern I hear?"

"A warning," Étienne replied. "We have seen what happens to those who stand in the way of progress."

Desmoulins looked over his shoulder, his expression a mixture of sorrow and resolve. "If this is progress, then perhaps it's time someone stood in its way."

Without another word, he exited, the door closing with a decisive click.

Étienne stood alone in the silence, the weight of the confrontation settling upon him. He moved to the window once more, watching Desmoulins disappear into the throng of Parisians going about their day, oblivious to the turmoil that raged within the hearts of their leaders.

A knock sounded again, startling him. He opened the door to find Louis de Saint-Just, his visage as mysterious as ever.

"Louis," Étienne greeted, gesturing for him to enter. "What brings you here?"

"I heard you and Desmoulins had words," Saint-Just stated, bypassing pleasantries.

"Information spreads quickly," Étienne dryly commented.

"He's a passionate man," Saint-Just continued. "But passion without direction can be dangerous."

Étienne nodded. "He cannot see the necessity of our actions."

"Perhaps," Saint-Just mused. "Or perhaps he sees what we choose to ignore."

Étienne studied him. "Do you share his reservations?"

Saint-Just met his gaze. "I believe in the revolution above all else. But we must be cautious not to lose ourselves."

"Meaning?"

"Meaning that the line between justice and tyranny is perilously thin," Saint-Just replied. "We must ensure we do not cross it."

Étienne sighed, running a hand through his dark hair. "I grow weary of these moral quandaries. We face existential threats, yet some among us quibble over ethics."

"Ethics define the revolution," Saint-Just countered. "Without them, we are no better than the oppressors we oppose."

"Fine words," Étienne said with a hint of sarcasm. "But words do not win wars."

Saint-Just regarded him thoughtfully. "Alienating allies like Desmoulins could prove detrimental."

"Are you suggesting I placate him?"

"I'm suggesting you consider the value of unity," Saint-Just replied. "Divisions within our ranks only serve our enemies."

Étienne waved a hand dismissively. "Camille is emotional but ultimately harmless. His conscience will not deter the course we've set."

"Do not underestimate the power of a voice raised in opposition," Saint-Just warned.

"Noted," Étienne said curtly. "Was there anything else?"

Saint-Just inclined his head. "No. I merely wished to offer counsel."

Étienne acknowledged the appreciation for the counsel, though his tone suggested otherwise.

As Saint-Just departed, Étienne felt a simmering frustration. The doubts expressed by Desmoulins and echoed subtly by Saint-Just gnawed at him. Were they all becoming too soft, too hesitant to do what was necessary?

He resolved to press on, convinced of the righteousness of his path. The revolution required strength and decisiveness, not hand-wringing over collateral damage.

Later that afternoon, Étienne ventured to a café near the Palais-Royal, seeking the company of those who shared his convictions. He found Jean-Paul Marat hunched over a table, scribbling furiously in a notebook.

"Jean-Paul," Étienne greeted, taking a seat opposite him.

Marat looked up, his eyes gleaming with feverish intensity. "Étienne. Have you seen the latest reports? Near Valmy, the French forces successfully repelled the Prussian forces."

"Encouraging news," Étienne acknowledged. "Perhaps our actions have fortified the nation's resolve."

"Indeed," Marat agreed. "But we must remain vigilant. Traitors still lurk among us."

"Agreed," Étienne said. "Which is why I believe we should push for more stringent measures."

Marat leaned in. "I'm listening."

"Surveillance of suspected Royalists, tighter controls on the press, public trials to root out dissent," Étienne listed. "We cannot afford complacency."

Marat nodded approvingly. "I shall advocate for these in my next publication."

"Excellent," Étienne replied. "We need to maintain momentum."

As they discussed strategies, Étienne felt a reaffirmation of purpose. Here was someone who understood the stakes, who did not flinch from hard truths.

Yet, later that evening, as he returned to his apartment, the shadows seemed longer, the silence heavier. He lit a candle and sat at his desk, intending to document the day's events.

6 September 1792,

Camille confronted me today, his conscience pricked by the actions we've taken. His sentimentality blinds him to the larger picture.

He paused, tapping the quill against the parchment.

Am I wrong to dismiss his concerns? No. The revolution demands sacrifice, and I will make it—even if others falter.

Setting the quill aside, Étienne leaned back, gazing into the flickering flame. Despite his confidence, a small voice whispered doubts—a voice he was determined to silence.

He extinguished the candle and retired for the night, relentless in his course yet unable to escape the lingering echoes of his friend's parting words.

As sleep eluded him, Étienne stared into the darkness, contemplating the widening chasm between himself and those who once stood beside him.

The path he had chosen was a solitary one, fraught with peril and moral compromise. But he clung to Niccolò Machiavelli's belief that the ends would justify the means—that history would absolve him.

Outside, the city of Paris slept fitfully, unaware of the silent battles waged within the hearts of its revolutionaries.

And Étienne Corbeau, ever the pragmatist, steeled himself for the challenges yet to come, convinced that doubt was a luxury he could ill afford.

• • •

Étienne Corbeau stood on the steps of the Palais-Royal, his gaze fixed upon the restless crowd that ebbed and flowed like a turbulent sea before him. On 7 September 1792, the echoes of the September Massacres still reverberated through the city, a grim reminder of the volatile forces he had helped unleash.

He adjusted his tricolour cockade, the symbolic red, white, and blue ribbon pinned to his hat, and descended into the crowd. The surrounding faces were a mosaic of exhaustion and defiance, eyes darting with suspicion and mouths set in grim lines. Whispers of further purges and retribution threaded through the conversations, an undercurrent of tension that threatened to erupt at any moment.

As Étienne navigated the crowd, he caught sight of Georges Danton emerging from a nearby café. Danton's broad shoulders and towering stature made him an imposing figure, yet there was weariness in his step, a heaviness that belied his usual exuberance. His dark eyes scanned the crowd with a distant detachment, and a deep furrow between his brows now marred his once jovial expression.

"Georges," Étienne called out, weaving his way towards him.

Danton turned, a flicker of recognition crossing his face. "Ah, Étienne," he replied, his voice lacking its customary warmth. "These are trying times, are they not?"

"Indeed," Étienne agreed, falling into step beside him. "The city is ablaze with rumours and unrest. One would expect our leaders to address the situation."

Danton sighed heavily. "The people are grieving, angry. Perhaps it's best to allow them space to process."

Étienne studied him closely and said, "Grieving requires guidance. Silence may lead to misunderstanding, or even worse, complicity."

Danton paused, his gaze fixed on a group of Sans-culottes chanting nearby. "And what would you have me say? That the massacres were justified? That the blood of innocents is a necessary sacrifice?"

Étienne arched an eyebrow. "Innocents? Traitors lurked within our very walls. The actions may have been harsh, but they were essential to safeguard the revolution."

Danton rubbed his temples. "I cannot condone such violence. We cannot condone such violence."

"Your reluctance to speak only fuels the uncertainty," Étienne pressed. "Leadership demands decisiveness, especially in tumultuous times."

Danton's eyes flashed with irritation. "Careful, Étienne. You tread dangerously close to insubordination."

Étienne held his gaze. "I merely point out that perceiving hesitation as weakness is common. The people look to you for direction."

Danton's shoulders slumped ever so slightly. "Perhaps you're right. But I cannot in good conscience endorse what has transpired."

"Then perhaps others will step forward to fill the void," Étienne remarked, his tone measured.

Danton's expression hardened. "Is that a threat?"

"A simple observation," Étienne replied smoothly. "The revolution cannot afford vacillation."

Before Danton could respond, a familiar voice called out. "Étienne! Georges!"

Turning, they saw Maximilien Robespierre approaching. The shadows cast by his powdered wig stressed his pale complexion and sharp features. His intense and unwavering eyes flickered between the two men.

"Maximilien," Danton greeted him with a nod. "We were just discussing the recent… events."

Robespierre's gaze settled on Étienne. "And what are your thoughts, Monsieur Corbeau?"

Étienne inclined his head. "Strong measures were necessary to protect the revolution from internal threats."

Robespierre's lips pressed into a thin line. "The massacres have cast a dark stain upon our cause. The unchecked violence undermines the very principles we stand for."

"Principles are meaningless if the revolution fails," Étienne countered. "We must be pragmatic."

Danton glanced between them. "There must be a balance. We cannot sacrifice our humanity for the sake of expedience."

Robespierre sighed. "We must tread carefully. The eyes of the nation are upon us."

Étienne noted the caution in Robespierre's words, reflecting his growing isolation. The unity that once bound them was fraying, threads unravelling under conflicting ideologies.

"Perhaps a public address would quell the unrest," Étienne suggested. "Reassure the citizens that their leaders remain steadfast."

Robespierre considered this. "A measured response could be beneficial."

Danton nodded reluctantly. "Very well. We can convene at the Convention tomorrow."

As they parted ways, Étienne felt a coldness settle within him. Danton's unwillingness to condemn the violence presented both an opportunity and a liability. Étienne saw an opportunity to advance his own position by leveraging Danton's silence, yet it also highlighted the fractures within their ranks.

Walking along the banks of the Seine, Étienne contemplated the shifting landscape of power. The river flowed steadily, its surface reflecting the hues of the setting sun—a stark contrast to the turmoil that churned within him. He recalled the enthusiasm with which he had embraced the revolution, the conviction that their actions would forge a better future. Yet now, doubts whispered at the edges of his mind.

"Étienne!"

He turned to see Olympe de Gouges hurrying towards him; her skirts gathered in one hand to avoid the muddy streets. Concern clouded her eyes, which were usually bright with determination.

"Olympe," he greeted her, offering a slight bow. "You seem troubled."

She stopped before him, catching her breath. "I've been searching for you. There's talk that the Convention plans to address the massacres."

"Indeed," Étienne confirmed. "A necessary step to restore order."

She studied him intently. "And what role have you played in all this?"

He met her gaze without flinching. "I advocate for protecting the revolution. Measures taken were harsh but indispensable."

"At what cost?" she challenged. "You've distanced yourself from those who once stood by you. Even Danton hesitates to align with your methods."

Étienne's expression hardened. "Danton's hesitation reveals his weakness. Others will rise to the occasion if he cannot lead effectively."

"You're isolating yourself, Étienne," she warned softly. "Power without allies is precarious."

He turned away, gazing out over the river. "Perhaps solitude is the price of conviction."

She placed a hand on his arm. "It doesn't have to be. There's still time to reconcile, to find a path that doesn't forsake our humanity."

He shrugged off her touch. "Idealism is a luxury we can no longer afford."

A shadow crossed her face. "Then I fear for what you've become."

Without another word, she departed, leaving Étienne alone with his thoughts. The weight of her words pressed upon him, yet he dismissed them as sentimental folly.

As night descended, he made his way to a dimly lit tavern frequented by the Sans-culottes. The air was thick with the scent of stale ale and unwashed bodies, voices rising in boisterous camaraderie. Étienne sought Antoine, a fervent supporter of the radical cause, finding him at a corner table surrounded by a group of rough-looking men.

"Antoine," Étienne greeted him, taking a seat.

"Ah, Monsieur Corbeau," Antoine replied with a toothy grin. "What brings you to our humble establishment?"

"I come seeking your perspective," Étienne began. "How do the people view the recent events?"

Antoine spat on the floor. "The people are restless, eager for change. Some think the massacres went too far; others believe they didn't go far enough."

"And what do you think?" Étienne probed.

Antoine leaned forward, his eyes gleaming. "I think we need leaders with the courage to do what's necessary without flinching at the sight of blood."

Étienne smiled subtly. "Then perhaps you and I share common ground."

Antoine chuckled. "Perhaps we do. The word is, Danton's gone soft. Maybe it's time for fresh voices to rise."

"An interesting notion," Étienne mused. "One worth exploring."

They discussed plans late into the night, Étienne carefully sowing seeds of support among those who might prove helpful. Yet even as he manoeuvred, a sense of isolation gnawed at him. The alliances he forged were transactional, lacking the camaraderie he once shared with the likes of Desmoulins and Danton.

Returning to his apartment in the early hours, Étienne sat at his desk, the flickering candle casting long shadows across the room. He retrieved a piece of parchment and wrote.

7 September 1792,

The tides are shifting. Danton's reluctance to embrace the measures reveals his faltering resolve. His silence is both a weakness and an opportunity—one I intend to exploit. Yet, in the quiet moments, I find myself increasingly isolated, a solitary figure navigating treacherous waters.

He paused, the quill hovering over the page. Doubt threatened to surface, but he pushed it aside, his resolve hardening.

The revolution demands sacrifice. Personal attachments cannot hinder progress. If I must stand alone to ensure its success, so be it.

Setting the quill down, he extinguished the candle and gazed out the window at the city shrouded in darkness. The distant sounds of Paris at night drifted up—a horse's hooves on cobblestone, a muffled laugh, the melancholic strains of a violin.

Étienne closed his eyes, the weight of his choices settling upon him. The path ahead was fraught with uncertainty, but he remained convinced of his purpose. Isolation was a small price to pay for the realisation of his vision.

As dawn approached, he resolved to move forward with renewed determination, undeterred by the growing chasm between himself and those who questioned his methods.

For in the crucible of revolution, only the resolute would prevail.

• • •

The morning of 9 September 1792 dawned with an eerie stillness as if Paris held its breath in the storm's wake. Étienne Corbeau stepped out onto the cobblestone streets, the air heavy with the metallic scent of blood mingled with the smoke of dying fires. The sky was a sullen grey, clouds hanging low as though burdened by the atrocities they had witnessed.

He pulled his coat tighter against the chill that seeped into his bones, though the day was unseasonably warm. The echoes of distant cries and the clatter of cartwheels reached his ears, muffled as if from another world. Around him, the city stirred—not with the bustling energy of life but with the sluggish movements of a populace numbed by recent horrors.

As Étienne walked, his boots splashed in puddles tinted red, remnants of the violence that had swept through Paris like a plague. The September Massacres had left an indelible mark on the city, and the stench of death lingered in every alleyway. He passed the once-grand façade of the Abbaye Prison, its gates battered and doors ajar. A guard stood nearby, his uniform dishevelled and eyes vacant, staring into nothingness.

"9 September 1792," Étienne murmured to himself, noting the date as if etching it into the annals of his memory. Each step took him deeper into the heart of the devastation he had helped orchestrate, though he now questioned the cost.

Turning onto the Rue Saint-Antoine, he encountered scenes that unsettled even his hardened disposition. He encountered shuttered shops and boarded-up or shattered windows. A woman knelt beside a fallen man, her hands stained as she clutched his lifeless form. She looked up as Étienne passed, her eyes hollow. He averted his gaze, the weight of her despair pressing upon him like a physical burden.

He made his way towards the Place de la Bastille, where the ruins of the old fortress stood as a stark reminder of the revolution's genesis. There, he found Jean-Paul Marat addressing a small crowd, his voice hoarse but unwavering.

"*Citoyens!* We must remain vigilant! We have not yet conquered the enemies of the revolution!" Marat's fervour was undiminished, his eyes blazing with conviction.

Étienne paused at the edge of the gathering, observing. The listeners' faces were gaunt, shadows etched beneath their eyes. Some nodded in agreement, while others stared blankly, their spirits drained.

Marat caught sight of Étienne and signalled him over. "Étienne! Join us. We appreciate your valuable insights."

He approached reluctantly. "Jean-Paul, the people are weary. Perhaps they need respite more than rousing."

Marat frowned. "Respite breeds complacency. We cannot allow our guard to falter."

Étienne glanced at the crowd. "Fear has served its purpose. But uncontrolled violence threatens to consume us all."

"Uncontrolled?" Marat scoffed. "It is a necessary purge."

"A purge without end becomes a slaughter," Étienne retorted quietly.

Marat's eyes narrowed. "Have you lost your resolve?"

Étienne met his gaze steadily. "I question only the means, not the end."

Before Marat could respond, a commotion erupted nearby. A group of Sans-culottes dragged a man into the square, his clothes torn and face bloodied.

"He's a traitor!" one shouted. "We found Royalist letters on him!"

The crowd's murmur grew ominous. Marat seized the opportunity. "You see? The rot runs deep! Justice must be swift!"

Étienne felt a knot tighten in his stomach. The man's pleas were pitiful, his cries for mercy falling on deaf ears. Without trial or deliberation, they descended upon him. Étienne turned away as the brutality unfolded, a bitter taste rising in his throat.

He moved swiftly from the square, the sounds of violence fading behind him. His footsteps led him to the Seine, the river's calm surface a stark contrast to the chaos elsewhere. Leaning on the stone parapet, he stared into the water, his reflection distorted by the gentle ripples.

"Is this what we have become?" he whispered. The question lingered, unanswered.

"Étienne."

He looked up to see Maximilien Robespierre approaching, his expression sombre. Dressed immaculately as always, Robespierre seemed untouched by the grime that clung to the rest of the city.

"Maximilien," Étienne acknowledged. "Out for a stroll?"

Robespierre joined him at the railing. "I could ask you the same. These are troubling times."

"Indeed." Étienne hesitated before continuing. "Do you ever question where this path is leading us?"

Robespierre sighed softly. "More often than you might think. But doubt is a luxury we cannot indulge."

"Is it doubt," Étienne mused, "or conscience?"

"A fine distinction," Robespierre replied. "The revolution requires sacrifice."

Étienne glanced at him. "At what cost? The streets run red, and the people grow desensitised to death."

Robespierre's gaze hardened. "The enemies of liberty are relentless. We must be equally so."

"Unbridled violence could be our undoing," Étienne cautioned. "We risk alienating the very citizens we aim to liberate."

"Then perhaps it falls to us to guide them," Robespierre suggested. "To channel their anger constructively."

Étienne nodded slowly. "Perhaps."

Robespierre placed a hand on his shoulder. "Your influence is significant, Étienne. Use it wisely."

As Robespierre departed, Étienne remained by the river, lost in thought. He had helped to fuel the fear and rage that now gripped Paris, but the repercussions were spiralling beyond his control. The revolution was devouring itself, and he stood at the maelstrom's centre.

A familiar voice interrupted his reverie. "Contemplating the state of your soul, Monsieur Corbeau?"

Turning, he saw Olympe de Gouges approaching, her eyes sharp beneath the brim of her bonnet.

"Olympe," he greeted her. "Ever the incisive observer."

She joined him at the parapet. "I wander the streets, seeking signs of hope amidst the ruins. It's a futile endeavour."

"Hope is scarce these days," Étienne admitted.

She studied him. "Even you seem affected. Has the bloodshed finally stirred something within you?"

He met her gaze. "I am not devoid of feeling, despite what you might think."

"Then why persist on this path?" she pressed. "You can influence change for the better."

"It's not that simple," he replied. "The revolution demands certain actions."

"That's a convenient excuse," she retorted. "At some point, you must take responsibility for the consequences of your choices."

Étienne looked away. "And what would you have me do?"

"Use your voice to temper the madness," she urged. "Advocate for justice, not vengeance."

He considered her words. "I fear it may be too late."

"It's never too late," she insisted. "Unless we concede defeat."

He sighed. "I'll consider it."

"See that you do," she said softly. "Before we lose what's left of our humanity."

As she walked away, Étienne felt a flicker of something—perhaps regret or a yearning for the ideals they once shared. The enormity of the revolution's descent into chaos weighed upon him, but his ambitions remained a stubborn flame within.

Determined to reconcile his goals with the reality before him, he sought Louis de Saint-Just, knowing the young deputy often frequented a nearby café. He found him seated alone, pouring over a stack of documents.

"Louis," Étienne greeted, taking a seat opposite.

Saint-Just glanced up. "Étienne. News?"

"Observations," he corrected. "Paris teeters on the brink. We must address the uncontrolled violence."

Saint-Just regarded him thoughtfully. "You've reconsidered."

"A change of strategy," Étienne clarified. "Excessive brutality undermines our cause."

"True," Saint-Just agreed. "But reining it in may prove challenging."

"Not impossible," Étienne countered. "We need to redirect the people's energy towards constructive efforts."

Saint-Just nodded. "Education, mobilisation for the war effort, rebuilding infrastructure."

"Exactly," Étienne affirmed. "We can strengthen the revolution without sacrificing our principles."

"Robespierre shares these sentiments," Saint-Just revealed. "Perhaps together we can implement measures to restore order."

"Time is of the essence," Étienne urged. "Every day we delay risks further decay."

Saint-Just offered a rare smile. "It's good to see your pragmatism tempered with wisdom."

Étienne accepted the compliment with a slight inclination of his head. "We must adapt to survive."

As they parted ways, Étienne felt a renewed sense of purpose. The streets of Paris remained stained and scarred, but perhaps there was a way to navigate the revolution towards a more sustainable path.

Walking back towards his apartment, he passed by the Théâtre-Français, its doors closed and posters peeling. Memories of past performances flickered in his mind—moments when art and culture had united people more effectively than any speech or decree.

An idea took root. Perhaps rekindling the spirit of unity through shared experiences could help heal the fractured city. He resolved to speak with Jacques-Louis David, the renowned painter and influential figure in the arts.

Reaching his apartment, Étienne settled at his desk. The events of the day had left an indelible impression on him. Retrieving his journal, he wrote.

9 September 1792,

The aftermath of the massacres lays bare the fragility of our revolution. The brutality I once deemed necessary now reveals itself as a double-edged sword. I stand amidst the ruins of my making, questioning whether ambition has blinded me to the cost.

He paused, the nib of his quill hovering over the parchment.

Yet, I cannot abandon my aspirations. If I can steer the revolution back from the precipice, perhaps redemption is possible—not just for myself, but for France.

Setting aside the journal, Étienne gazed out the window as dusk settled over Paris. The city breathed in slow, laboured rhythms, its heartbeat uneven but persistent. There was still time to make a difference, to shape the course of events towards a more just and fair outcome.

He rose, determination hardening his resolve. The path ahead would be fraught with challenges, but he was no stranger to adversity. If the revolution were to endure, it would require not only the zeal of its people but the guidance of those willing to balance ambition with conscience.

And Étienne Corbeau was prepared to be that guiding force, whatever the cost.

• • •

September 11, 1792, the heat enveloped Paris like a fever, exacerbating the simmering unrest beneath the city's surface. Étienne Corbeau stood at the edge of the Place de la Révolution, the air thick with the scent of unwashed bodies and the faint metallic tang of blood that seemed ever-present these days. The distant tolling of church bells marked the hour; their solemn echoes were a stark contrast to the chaotic heartbeat of the capital.

He adjusted the cuffs of his frayed coat, eyes scanning the crowds of citizens milling about with a restless energy. Whispers of conspiracy and betrayal flitted through the crowd like spectres, each rumour more insidious than the last. The September Massacres had left an indelible stain on the soul of Paris, and the paranoia they had birthed showed no signs of abating.

A familiar voice called out from behind him. "Étienne, I've been searching for you."

Turning, he found Maximilien Robespierre approaching. His visage was paler than usual, and his eyes were shadowed with fatigue. Dressed impeccably despite the heat, Robespierre exuded an air of controlled intensity, his gaze sharp beneath the brim of his hat.

"Maximilien," Étienne greeted him with a slight bow. "You look as though sleep has been a scarce commodity."

Robespierre offered a wan smile. "Sleep eludes those burdened with the weight of a nation in turmoil."

They began walking side by side along the cobblestone streets, the din of the city enveloping them. Street vendors shouted half-heartedly about their wares while clusters of Sans-culottes huddled in hushed conversations.

"I've been reflecting on the recent events," Robespierre began, his tone measured. "The violence that has gripped our city—it's spiralling beyond control."

Étienne glanced at him, noting the tension etched into his features. "Unpleasant, perhaps, but necessary. The enemies of the revolution are cunning, embedded deep within our society."

Robespierre sighed. "I fear we've unleashed forces we cannot contain. The rule of law must prevail, or we risk descending into anarchy."

"Anarchy?" Étienne scoffed gently. "Surely you exaggerate. The people's actions, though extreme, are driven by a desire to protect the revolution."

They paused near a fountain, the water flowing sluggishly and its surface marred by debris. Robespierre ran a hand over his face as if attempting to wipe away his weariness.

"I've received reports," he whispered. "Innocents executed without trial, families torn apart. This is not justice."

Étienne placed a reassuring hand on his shoulder. "Maximilien, you cannot allow sentiment to cloud your judgement. The path to a new France is fraught with hardship."

Robespierre met his gaze, a flicker of doubt in his eyes. "At what cost, Étienne? How many must perish before we deem the revolution secure?"

"As many as necessary," Étienne replied firmly. "Consider the alternative—a return to tyranny, the erasure of all we've fought for."

They resumed walking, their conversation heavy. Étienne sensed an opportunity to steer Robespierre's concerns toward a more helpful course.

"Have you considered," he began carefully, "that the genuine threat lies not in the people's actions but those who manipulate them from the shadows?"

Robespierre arched an eyebrow. "What are you implying?"

"There are those," Étienne continued, "who spread dissent, who fan the flames of paranoia for their own ends. Counter-revolutionaries masquerading as patriots."

Robespierre frowned. "Do you have evidence of this?"

"Whispers, rumours," Étienne admitted. "But where there's smoke, there's often fire. We must be vigilant."

They reached a narrow street where the buildings leaned towards each other like conspirators. A group of children darted past, their laughter incongruous against the backdrop of tension.

Robespierre's expression hardened. "If what you say is true, we cannot stand idle. The Committee of Public Safety must act decisively."

"Exactly," Étienne agreed, suppressing a smile. "By tightening our measures, we can root out these elements before they cause irreparable harm."

Robespierre nodded slowly. "Perhaps you're right. But we ensure our actions are just, that we do not become the very thing we despise."

"Of course," Étienne said smoothly. "Justice tempered with resolve."

They parted ways shortly after, Robespierre heading towards the National Convention while Étienne lingered, watching him disappear into the crowd. He felt a pang of unease—a rare intrusion upon his calculated demeanour. The forces he had set in motion were growing more volatile, and even he wondered if control was slipping from his grasp.

"Étienne!"

He turned to see Camille Desmoulins approaching, his face flushed, eyes bright with agitation. Dressed in his usual dishevelled attire, Desmoulins exuded an endearing and exasperating frenetic energy.

"Camille," Étienne greeted him cautiously. "You seem perturbed."

Desmoulins halted before him, catching his breath. "I just left a meeting with Danton. There's talk of imposing stricter measures—surveillance, arrests without cause. This is madness!"

Étienne raised an eyebrow. "Madness? Or prudence in dangerous times?"

"Don't play coy," Desmoulins snapped. "I know you've been whispering in Robespierre's ear. You're pushing us towards a precipice."

Étienne regarded him coolly. "I advocate for protecting the revolution. Surely you, of all people, understand the stakes."

Desmoulins shook his head vehemently. "Not at the expense of our principles. No matter how well-intentioned, Liberty cannot flourish under the shadow of tyranny."

"Well-intentioned tyranny," Étienne mused. "An interesting paradox."

"Don't twist my words," Desmoulins retorted. "We must find a balance before it's too late."

Étienne's gaze hardened. "Balance is a luxury we can ill afford. The enemies of the revolution are many and cunning. Hesitation is tantamount to surrender."

Desmoulins searched his face, a mixture of frustration and sorrow in his eyes. "You've changed, Étienne. Or perhaps I never truly knew you."

"Perhaps not," Étienne replied tersely. "Now, if you'll excuse me, I have matters to attend to."

He left Desmoulins standing amidst the throng, the crowd's din swallowing any further protests. A gnawing doubt nibbled at the edges of his confidence as he walked away. The isolation he had cultivated as a shield now felt like a cage.

Seeking respite, he went to a quiet courtyard tucked away behind the Église Saint-Eustache. The air was more relaxed here, and the city's noise dulled to a distant hum. He sat on a stone bench beneath a withered tree, the leaves of which clung stubbornly despite the season.

"Étienne."

He looked up to see Olympe de Gouges approaching, her expression unreadable. Draped in a simple gown, she carried herself with a grace that belied the surrounding turmoil.

"Olympe," he acknowledged weary resignation in his voice. "Here to lecture me further?"

She sat beside him without invitation. "No lectures today. Merely an observation."

"Very well," he sighed. "Proceed."

She studied him for a moment before speaking. "You seem… troubled."

He barked a humourless laugh. "An astute observation indeed."

"You've always been adept at navigating the treacherous waters of politics," she continued. "But I wonder if you've considered the personal cost."

He frowned. "Personal cost is irrelevant in the face of greater objectives."

"Is it?" she challenged gently. "Isolation can erode even the strongest of wills."

He glanced at her, irritation flickering across his features. "I don't have the luxury of indulging in self-pity."

"It's not pity I offer, but perspective," she said softly. "The forces you've helped unleash are growing beyond control. Even Robespierre senses it."

Étienne's gaze drifted to the sky, where dark clouds gathered ominously. "What would you have me do? Renounce my beliefs? Stand aside while others falter?"

"I would have you consider the possibility that strength lies not in unyielding ambition but in adaptability."

He shook his head. "Adaptability is merely a euphemism for compromise."

"Sometimes, compromise is necessary for survival."

He stood abruptly. "I tire of these philosophical musings. If you have a concrete suggestion, speak it plainly."

She rose to face him. "Very well. Use your influence to temper the paranoia to prevent further descent into chaos. Advocate for reason over fear."

He regarded her for a long moment, the tension between them palpable. "I'll consider it."

"That's all I ask," she replied, a hint of relief in her voice.

As she departed, Étienne felt the weight of her words settle upon him. The path he tread was becoming increasingly precarious, the line between orchestrator and victim blurring. The very paranoia he had sown now threatened to ensnare him as well.

He meandered through the streets, the day's light fading into a bruised twilight. Lanterns flickered to life, casting pools of dim illumination that did little to dispel the encroaching darkness. He passed shuttered shops and boarded windows, the city huddling in on itself.

"Étienne Corbeau," a voice hissed from an alleyway.

He halted, peering into the shadows. A figure emerged—a gaunt man with hollow cheeks and eyes that gleamed unnaturally.

"Do I know you?" Étienne asked warily.

"Not yet," the man replied, a sinister smile curling his lips. "But we share common interests."

"I'm not in the habit of conversing with strangers."

"Then consider me a friend you haven't met," the man retorted. "Word has it you're seeking to root out enemies of the revolution."

Étienne narrowed his eyes. "Information of that nature is valuable. What's your price?"

The man chuckled darkly. "Oh, I seek no coin. Merely the satisfaction of seeing justice served."

"Very well," Étienne said cautiously. "What do you offer?"

"Names," the man whispered. "Addresses. Plans whispered in secret gatherings."

Étienne hesitated. The man's eagerness was unsettling, but the information could prove helpful. "Provide proof, and we can discuss further."

"Meet me here tomorrow night," the man said, retreating into the shadows. "Come alone."

As the figure vanished, Étienne felt a chill creep along his spine. The paranoia that gripped the city was manifesting in unexpected ways, drawing out the desperate and the dangerous.

He resumed his walk, thoughts churning. The line between ally and adversary was becoming increasingly blurred, and trust was a scarce commodity. Even Robespierre's steadfast demeanour showed cracks, his concern over the violence threatening to undermine their shared objectives.

Reaching his apartment, Étienne settled at his desk by candlelight. He retrieved a quill and parchment, intent on capturing his thoughts before sleep claimed him.

11 September 1792,

The tides of paranoia swell, threatening to engulf all that we have built. Robespierre wavers, his conscience a hindrance to the course. I must steer him towards resolve lest we falter at this critical juncture.

Yet, I find myself uneasily aware of the forces I've set in motion. The faces of those who question me—Desmoulins, Olympe, even shadows in the alleyways—linger in my mind. Control slips like sand through my fingers.

I cannot afford to doubt. The revolution demands unwavering commitment. I will navigate these treacherous waters, or they will consume me.

He set down the quill, the scratch of metal against parchment echoing in the silence. Extinguishing the candle, he gazed out the window at the city cloaked in darkness.

"Let the paranoia grow," he whispered to himself. "I will harness it, bend it to my will."

Yet, as he lay down to rest, sleep eluded him. The weight of his choices pressed heavily upon his chest, each breath a reminder of the precarious balance he struggled to maintain.

The revolution marched onward, relentless. And Étienne Corbeau, the architect of ambition, stood at the crossroads of destiny and downfall, uncertain which path would claim him.

• • •

The early morning mist of 15 September 1792 clung to Paris like a shroud, muffling the city's usual cacophony into a muted hum. Étienne Corbeau stood on the balcony of his modest apartment overlooking the Rue Saint-Honoré, his gaze fixed upon the maze of streets below. The cobblestones glistened with residual dampness, reflecting the pale light of a sun that seemed reluctant to rise fully, as if hesitant to cast its gaze upon the aftermath of recent events.

He sipped a lukewarm cup of coffee, the bitterness matching the taste of his thoughts. The September Massacres had ceased, leaving an uneasy silence weighing the populace heavily. Whispers of fear and uncertainty threaded through the air, entwined with the faint scent of smoke that lingered from extinguished fires.

Étienne turned away from the railing, retreating into the dim interior of his room. Papers cluttered his desk—pamphlets, speeches, and hastily scribbled notes—evidence of the relentless enthusiasm that had consumed him recently. He settled into a worn chair, the wood creaking beneath him, and picked up a pamphlet bearing the bold title *Le Peuple en Colère.* The rhetoric within mirrored his impassioned calls for vigilance against foreign and domestic enemies.

Yet now, in the quiet of this morning, a dissonance echoed within him. Triumph wrestled with apprehension, each vying for dominance in the labyrinth of his mind.

A knock at the door interrupted his reverie. Setting the pamphlet aside, he rose to answer it. The door swung open to reveal Louis de Saint-Just, his youthful features betraying a weariness that belied his age.

"Louis," Étienne greeted him with a faint smile. "To what do I owe this visit, *si tôt?*"

Saint-Just entered without waiting for an invitation, his gaze sweeping the room before settling on Étienne. "We need to talk."

"Very well." Étienne closed the door behind him. "Coffee?"

"Non, merci." Saint-Just remained standing, his posture rigid. "The Convention is in turmoil. Factions are forming, and alliances are shifting. The Girondins grow increasingly bold in their opposition."

Étienne arched an eyebrow. "And what of Robespierre?"

"Maximilien is steadfast but troubled," Saint-Just replied. "He senses the instability, fears the revolution may veer off course."

Étienne gestured for him to sit, but Saint-Just remained rooted. "We've always known that change breeds chaos," Étienne said. "It's a necessary crucible."

Saint-Just's eyes narrowed. "But at what cost? The massacres have sown seeds of doubt, even among our supporters."

Étienne leaned against the edge of the desk. "Doubt is the luxury of those who lack conviction."

"Or the wisdom of those who foresee disaster," Saint-Just countered. "The revolution devours its own, Étienne. We must be cautious lest we become its next victims."

A flicker of irritation crossed Étienne's face. "We've come too far to falter now. The old order teeters on the brink of oblivion. We must ensure it topples."

Saint-Just regarded him thoughtfully. "Just be certain that in toppling it, we do not collapse the very foundations we seek to build upon."

Before Étienne could respond, another knock resounded. He opened the door to find Olympe de Gouges standing there, her expression a blend of determination and concern.

"Olympe," he said, surprised. "You're becoming quite the early visitor."

She offered a curt nod. "May I come in?"

"Of course." He stepped aside, allowing her to enter. "Louis and I were just discussing the current state of affairs."

"I imagine so," she replied, glancing at Saint-Just. "The streets are rife with rumours. People speak of betrayal, of plots within the Convention itself."

Saint-Just crossed his arms. "Idle gossip, most likely."

"Perhaps," she conceded. "But dangerous. The people are weary, Étienne. They crave stability."

Étienne sighed. "We cannot achieve stability without first dismantling the remnants of tyranny," Étienne stated.

"At the expense of justice?" Olympe challenged. "We've sacrificed much already. How many more must suffer before you deem the price paid in full?"

He met her gaze evenly. "As many as necessary to secure the revolution's success."

Saint-Just shifted uncomfortably. "We must restore confidence to unify our efforts."

Olympe nodded. "Agreed. Which is why I propose organising a public forum—a gathering where we can hear voices from all sides. Transparency may ease some of the growing mistrust."

Étienne considered her suggestion. "A romantic notion, but one fraught with risk. It could provide a platform for dissenters to undermine our progress."

"Or an opportunity to address grievances and prevent further fragmentation," she countered.

Saint-Just glanced at Étienne. "It may be worth considering. Controlling the narrative is essential."

Étienne rubbed his temples, the weight of recent events pressing upon him. "Very well. Arrange your forum. But be mindful—it must not devolve into a spectacle that weakens our position."

Relief flickered across Olympe's face. "Thank you, Étienne. I believe it's a step in the right direction."

She departed soon after, leaving the two men alone once more.

"You surprise me," Saint-Just remarked. "I didn't expect you to agree."

Étienne shrugged. "Perhaps a semblance of openness will placate the masses, at least temporarily."

Saint-Just gave a curt nod. "I must return to the Convention. Will you join me?"

"In a while," Étienne replied. "I need to collect my thoughts."

After Saint-Just left, Étienne sank back into his chair. The room felt suffocating, the air thick with unspoken fears. He reached for a journal, its pages filled with observations and strategies penned in his precise hand.

15 September 1792,

The revolution teeters on the edge of an abyss of its own making. The forces I've helped unleash threaten to consume our enemies and ourselves. Triumph mingles with trepidation as I contemplate the path ahead.

He paused, tapping the quill against the inkwell.

Is this the inevitable course of revolutions? To spiral into chaos before emerging anew? Or have we strayed irreparably from our ideals?

A sudden noise from the street below drew his attention. Peering out the window, he saw a group of Sans-culottes marching past, their voices raised in a discordant chant. Banners fluttered above them, emblazoned with slogans calling for unity and vengeance in equal measure.

Étienne watched them disappear around a corner, a knot tightening in his stomach. The hunger he had once found invigorating now seemed ominous, a beast no longer under his command.

He dressed swiftly and made his way towards the Convention. The city's pulse quickened around him—hawkers peddling broadsheets, clusters of citizens engaged in heated debates, soldiers moving with purposeful strides. Yet beneath the surface buzz lay a palpable tension, like the charged air before a storm.

Entering the grand hall of the Convention, he found it abuzz with activity. Deputies huddled in whispered conversations, their faces etched with concern. Robespierre stood at the front, addressing a small gathering with animated gestures.

"We cannot allow internal divisions to weaken our resolve," Robespierre declared, his voice carrying across the chamber.

Étienne approached as the group dispersed. "Maximilien," he greeted.

Robespierre turned to him, a shadow of a smile on his lips. "Étienne. I trust you've heard the latest developments."

"Only fragments," Étienne admitted. "Tensions seem higher than ever."

"Indeed," Robespierre sighed. "The Girondins push for moderation, accusing us of authoritarianism."

"Perhaps it's time to assert our stance more firmly," Étienne suggested. "Decisive action could quell their dissent."

Robespierre shook his head. "Force may only deepen the rift. We must reconcile to present a united front against external threats."

"Reconciliation risks diluting our objectives." Étienne felt a flicker of frustration. "People may see compromise as weakness."

"Or wisdom," Robespierre countered. "A leader must know when to wield the sword and when to extend the olive branch."

Before Étienne could reply, Georges Danton strode over, commanding attention. "Gentlemen," he boomed. "I hear talk of unity. A fine notion, though perhaps overdue."

"Danton," Étienne acknowledged coolly.

"We must act swiftly," Danton continued. "The people grow restless, and the Prussian threat looms ever larger."

Robespierre nodded. "Agreed. We propose measures to strengthen our defences and address economic strains."

"And what of the internal strife?" Étienne pressed. "The Girondins sow discord at every turn."

Danton eyed him thoughtfully. "Perhaps it's time we set aside petty differences. The revolution cannot afford to devour itself."

Étienne bristled at the implication. "Petty differences? They undermine our very foundation."

"Enough," Robespierre interjected. "We must focus on solutions, not exacerbate conflicts."

An uneasy silence settled between them. Étienne felt the walls closing in—the alliances he had relied upon now seemed fragile, his influence waning amid the shifting tides.

Excusing himself, he left the Convention, the air outside a welcome relief despite its stifling warmth. He wandered, thoughts churning. The revolution he had so fiercely championed was transforming into something unrecognisable, its ideals warped by fear and ambition—his own included.

Crossing a bridge over the Seine, he watched the water flow beneath him, its surface disturbed by eddies and unseen currents—a metaphor for the undercurrents pulling at the fabric of the nation, threatening to rend it asunder.

"Étienne."

He turned to find Camille Desmoulins standing nearby, his expression guarded.

"Camille," Étienne greeted, a hint of surprise colouring his tone. "Out for a stroll?"

"I've been looking for you," Desmoulins replied. "We need to talk."

Étienne inclined his head. "By all means."

Desmoulins approached, leaning against the railing beside him. "I've heard whispers that your position within the Jacobins is… precarious."

Étienne arched an eyebrow. "Whispers travel swiftly in these times. What is it you're implying?"

"that alliances shift," Desmoulins said. "I know we've had our differences, but perhaps it's time to reconsider our approaches."

"Reconsider?" Étienne echoed. "Are you proposing a truce?"

"Of sorts," Desmoulins admitted. "We share a common goal—the betterment of France. Our methods may differ, but division only serves our enemies."

Étienne studied him, weighing the sincerity in his eyes. "And what do you suggest?"

"Collaboration," Desmoulins offered. "Pooling our resources to steer the revolution back on course."

A part of Étienne recoiled at conceding ground, yet another recognised the pragmatism in Desmoulins's proposal. "Very well. I'm open to discussion."

Desmoulins extended a hand. "To new beginnings, then."

Étienne clasped it, a tentative alliance forged. "To new beginnings."

As they parted ways, Étienne felt a glimmer of hope tempered by caution. The revolution was a temper, unpredictable and unforgiving. Survival required adaptability, perhaps even humility—a bitter pill for one so accustomed to control.

Returning to his apartment as dusk settled, he lit a candle against the encroaching darkness. Sitting at his desk, he penned a last entry for the day.

15 September 1792,

The aftermath of our actions weighs heavily. The realisation taints triumph that the revolution threatens to consume itself— and us along with it. I stand at a crossroads, uncertain whether to press forward with unyielding resolve or adapt to the shifting landscape.

Alliances fray and reform. Trust is a scarce commodity. Yet, amid the instability, to recalibrate, to ensure that the sacrifices made have not been in vain.

My survival—and perhaps that of the revolution itself— depends on my current choices. The path is unclear, but retreat is not an option.

Extinguishing the candle, Étienne gazed out into the night. The city's silhouette was a jagged line against the starless sky, a testament to its resilience and fragility.

He resolved to face whatever came next with caution and determination. The revolution was far from over, and he was determined to remain steadfast.

The future hung in the balance, and Étienne Corbeau intended to tip the scales.

CHAPTER SIX: (1793)
CAPET'S VERDICT

The chill of 5 January 1793 seeped through the stones of Paris, a biting cold that wrapped itself around the city like a shroud. Étienne Corbeau stood within the crowded chamber of the National Convention, the air thick with the murmur of voices and the faint scent of damp wool. The grand hall, adorned with republican banners and the tricolour flag, was a hive of restless energy as deputies shuffled to their seats, faces etched with anticipation and apprehension.

Étienne's dark eyes scanned the assembly, noting the clusters of Girondins huddled together, their whispers betraying their unease. The Montagnards, his own faction, sat resolute, their gazes fixed upon the empty chair at the centre of the dais—a throne stripped of its opulence, awaiting the man who had once been king.

"5 January 1793," Étienne mused quietly to himself, the date a milestone he had long expected. The trial of Louis Capet, formerly Louis XVI, was about to begin in earnest, and he intended to ensure its conclusion aligned with his vision for France.

Beside him, Jean-Paul Marat leaned in, his gaunt features illuminated by the flickering candlelight. "The Girondins waver," Marat muttered, his voice a rasp. "They speak of clemency, of exile. Fools."

Étienne's lip curled in disdain. "They lack the conviction to sever the ties to our sordid past. In this case, mercy is a poison that will corrupt the revolution from within."

Marat nodded approvingly. "We must make an example of the tyrant. Anything less is a betrayal to the people."

The crowd hummed as Maximilien Robespierre ascended the podium. His powdered wig framed a face marked by intensity and steadfast determination. He surveyed the assembly before speaking, his voice measured yet carrying the weight of authority.

"Citoyens," Robespierre began, "today we undertake a grave duty. The eyes of France, of all of Europe, are upon us. Let us proceed with the solemnity and justice befitting our republic."

Étienne oversaw Robespierre, noting the subtle tension in his posture. While they shared common goals, Étienne was acutely aware of the differences in their methods. Robespierre's adherence to virtue sometimes bordered on naivety in Étienne's estimation.

The doors at the rear of the chamber swung open, and a hush fell as armed guards escorted Louis Capet into the chamber. They replaced his once-regal attire with plain clothing, and exhaustion had etched lines on his pallid face. Yet, there was a dignity in his bearing that irked Étienne—a remnant of arrogance, perhaps, or an obliviousness to his own irrelevance.

Georges Danton leaned over from a nearby seat, his robust frame and ruddy complexion contrasting with the sombre atmosphere. "He looks diminished," Danton remarked, a hint of pity in his tone.

"Diminished but unrepentant," Étienne replied tersely. "He still believes himself ordained by God, above the laws of men."

Danton sighed. "Perhaps. But is there no merit in showing leniency? Exile him, remove the symbol without creating a martyr."

Étienne fixed Danton with a steely gaze. "Exile leaves the door ajar for his return, for counter-revolutionary forces to rally behind him. *Non,* we must extinguish any embers that could reignite the flames of monarchy."

Danton held his gaze for a moment before looking away. "You are resolute as ever, Étienne."

The proceedings began with the charges against Louis Capet read aloud—treason, conspiracy against the liberty of the nation, and the blood of patriots on his hands. As evidence was presented, Étienne observed the reactions of the deputies, keeping track of those who seemed swayed by the arguments for conviction and those who hesitated.

Camille Desmoulins stood to speak, his usually animated expression subdued. *"Citoyens,"* while the crimes of Louis Capet are undeniable, we must consider the ramifications of our judgement. Let us not act in haste, lest we sow the seeds of further discord."

Étienne felt a surge of irritation. Desmoulins, ever the idealist, failed to grasp the necessity of decisive action. He leaned over to Marat. "We cannot allow such sentimentality to infect the proceedings."

Marat sneered. "His manner of speaking is reminiscent of a man whose confidence has been worn down, like a blunted quill."

"Perhaps," Étienne agreed, a plan forming in his mind. If he could undermine the moderates' influence, the path to the desired verdict would be clearer.

As the session adjourned for a brief recess, Étienne went through the crowd towards a group of undecided deputies. Adopting a congenial expression, he approached Pierre Vergniaud, a prominent Girondin known for his eloquence.

"Monsieur Vergniaud," Étienne greeted him with a slight bow. "A moment of your time?"

Vergniaud regarded him cautiously. "Monsieur Corbeau. What can I do for you?"

"I wish to discuss the trial," Étienne began smoothly. "Surely you see the peril in allowing Louis to live."

Vergniaud sighed. "I see the complexity of the situation. Executing him may provoke greater unrest, perhaps even invite foreign intervention."

"Foreign intervention is inevitable," Étienne countered. "Our enemies will not rest until they see the revolution crushed. Our enemies will perceive showing mercy to the king as weakness."

"The blade solely measured strength," Vergniaud replied. "Wisdom must guide our actions."

Étienne's eyes hardened. "Wisdom without action is impotence. Consider the sacrifices already made—the lives lost for the promise of *liberté, égalité, fraternité*. Will you dishonour them by faltering now?"

Vergniaud shifted uncomfortably. "I will consider your words."

"See that you do," Étienne said, allowing a hint of steel to edge his tone. "France's future hangs in the balance."

He withdrew, leaving Vergniaud to his thoughts, and caught sight of Olympe de Gouges observing him from across the room. Her intelligent and unflinching eyes met his with a mixture of curiosity and concern.

"Étienne," she called softly as she approached. "You are quite the agitator today."

He offered a thin smile. "Merely ensuring that justice is served."

"Justice," she echoed. "Is that what you seek? Or is it vengeance?"

He bristled at the implication. "The two are not mutually exclusive in this case."

She tilted her head. "Be wary of the path you tread, as it is easy to cross the line between righteousness and tyranny."

"You assume much," he retorted. "I act in the republic's interest."

"And yet, you dismiss any perspective that does not align with your own," she observed. "A dangerous trait in times such as these."

Before he could respond, the bell signalled the resumption of the session. She gave him a lingering look before turning away, leaving Étienne with a simmering mix of annoyance and introspection.

Returning to his seat, he noted the murmurs spreading through the assembly. News had arrived that the Austrian and Prussian forces were regrouping, bolstering the fears of those advocating for a harsher stance against internal threats.

Robespierre took the floor once more, his voice carrying a genuine conviction. "*Citoyens,* we must not let our resolve waver. The fate of the revolution depends upon our ability to act decisively. Let us not forget the suffering endured to reach this moment."

The room erupted in applause, but Étienne noticed the hesitant clapping of certain deputies—their uncertainty a chink in the armour he needed to mend. He resolved to intensify his efforts, manipulate the undercurrents of fear and patriotism, and secure the desired outcome.

As the day's proceedings drew close, Étienne lingered in the hall, observing as the deputies dispersed in clusters. The weight of the day's events pressed upon him, a blend of satisfaction at the progress made and frustration at the remaining obstacles.

"5 January 1793," he whispered to himself. "The beginning of the end of Louis Capet."

As he exited the Convention, the biting wind of the Parisian winter greeted him. Pulling his coat tighter, he made his way through the streets, the gas lamps casting pools of dim light that flickered in the gusts. The city seemed to hold its breath, the usual bustle subdued as citizens awaited the trial's outcome.

Passing a group of Sans-culottes gathered around a makeshift bonfire, he caught snippets of their conversation—speculation about the king's fate, tales of hardship, expressions of hope mingled with despair. Illuminated by the flames, their faces bore the lines of toil and the scars of struggle.

"Death to the tyrant!" one shouted, raising a clenched fist.

Others echoed the sentiment, and Étienne felt a surge of vindication. The people's will aligned with his own, a force he could harness to counter the moderates' influence.

Reaching his apartment, he ascended the narrow staircase to his quarters. The familiar surroundings offered little comfort—the sparse furnishings and stacks of documents a testament to his singular focus. He sat at his desk, dipping his quill into ink, and penned letters to critical allies, outlining strategies to sway the undecided deputies.

"Time is of the essence," he wrote. "We must present a united front to ensure the king's execution, solidifying the revolution's foundation and deterring our enemies."

As the ink dried, Étienne leaned back, the flicker of the candle casting elongated shadows across the room. Doubts gnawed at the edges of his consciousness—echoes of Olympe's caution and his peers' uneasy glances. Yet he dismissed them, steeling himself with the conviction that his path was justified.

"The trial is but theatre," he mused aloud. "A performance where the script must lead to a singular conclusion."

He extinguished the candle and moved to the window, gazing at the city enveloped in darkness. The silhouettes of rooftops stretched into the distance, a jagged horizon against the starless sky.

"France must be reborn," he whispered. "And I will be one of its architects."

As sleep eluded him that night, Étienne contemplated the days ahead. The king's execution was not merely an act of retribution but a catalyst—a means to propel the revolution forward and eliminate any remnants of the old regime that threatened its progress.

In the silence of his room, he resolved to intensify his efforts and manipulate the political theatre to his advantage. He was unwilling to consider failure as an option, especially when the stakes had never been higher.

Étienne Corbeau, with his ambition and resolve unshaken amidst the tumult of a nation on the brink of transformation, was prepared to meet the new challenges the dawn would bring head-on.

• • •

The frigid air of 8 January 1793 settled over Paris like a relentless spectre, the Seine's waters sluggish under a thin layer of ice. Étienne Corbeau strode purposefully along the Rue de Rivoli, his breath forming ephemeral clouds that dissipated into the morning gloom. The city was a hive of whispers and rumours; citizens huddled in doorways discussing the ongoing trial of Louis Capet. The tension was palpable, a taut string ready to snap.

"8 January 1793," Étienne murmured to himself, the date etched into his mind as a crucial juncture. Today, he intended to tip the scales irrevocably towards the king's execution. The moderates' murmurs of exile and clemency threatened to undermine everything he had worked for.

He arrived at the Café Procope, a renowned gathering place for revolutionaries. Pushing open the heavy wooden door, a fug of pipe smoke and the low hum of urgent conversation greeted him. Scanning the room, he spotted Jacques-Louis David seated at a corner table, sketching furiously into a notebook.

"David," Étienne greeted him, sliding into the opposite chair.

The painter looked up, his intense gaze softened by recognition. "Étienne. You seem… driven today."

"These are critical times," Étienne replied. "I trust you're capturing the essence of our revolution?"

David tapped his charcoal against the page thoughtfully. "I'm attempting to. The trial has everyone on edge."

"Precisely why we must ensure the right outcome," Étienne said, lowering his voice. "The Girondins grow bold, spreading their poison of leniency. It's unacceptable."

David raised an eyebrow. "You have a plan, I presume?"

"I do," Étienne affirmed. "But I'll need your support. Your influence among the artists and pamphleteers is invaluable."

David leaned in. "Tell me more."

"I intend to discredit those advocating for the king's exile," Étienne explained. "We must expose their weakness, their lack of commitment to the revolution."

David considered this. "And you wish for me to...?"

"Use your art," Étienne urged. "Depict the dangers of half-measures. Show the people that mercy towards the king is a betrayal of our ideals."

A slow smile spread across David's face. "I believe I can craft something suitably persuasive."

"Excellent," Étienne said, rising. "Time is of the essence."

Leaving the café, Étienne approached the Tuileries Palace, now repurposed as a governmental hub. The corridors buzzed with activity, deputies and officials scurrying like ants in a disturbed nest. He sought Jean-Paul Marat, finding him hunched over a desk piled high with papers.

"Marat," Étienne greeted him.

Marat looked up, his eyes red-rimmed and feverish. "Étienne. Have you news?"

"Not yet," Étienne replied. "But I have a list."

He produced a folded parchment and slid it across the desk. Marat unfolded it, scanning the names with a growing smirk.

"These are the deputies wavering in their resolve," Étienne explained. "We need to ensure they vote for execution."

Marat nodded. "Agreed. And how do you propose we... persuade them?"

Étienne's gaze hardened. "By any means necessary."

Marat leaned back, a glint in his eye. "I have associates who can apply pressure."

"discreet," Étienne cautioned. "We cannot afford scandal."

"Naturally," Marat agreed. "Consider it done."

As he left Marat's office, Étienne felt a surge of grim satisfaction. The pieces were moving into place. However, he knew that some required more personal attention.

He headed towards the residence of Pierre Vergniaud, the influential Girondin deputy whose eloquence swayed many. The house was modest but well-kept, a testament to Vergniaud's understated taste. Étienne knocked sharply on the door.

After a moment, Vergniaud himself answered, surprise flickering across his features. "Monsieur Corbeau. This is unexpected."

"May I come in?" Étienne asked.

Vergniaud hesitated before stepping aside. "Very well."

The interior was warm, and a fire was crackling in the hearth. Étienne declined an offer of refreshment and got straight to the point.

"Pierre, we need to talk about the vote," he began.

Vergniaud sighed. "I suspected as much."

"You hold significant sway among the undecided," Étienne pressed. "Your call for clemency is ill-advised."

Vergniaud met his gaze evenly. "I believe executing the king will only escalate tensions. Exile is a more prudent course."

"Prudence is a veil of cowardice," Étienne retorted sharply. "Do you lack the courage to see justice served?"

Vergniaud's eyes flashed with anger. "Mind your tone, Corbeau. I act in what I believe to be the nation's best interest."

Étienne stepped closer. "I wonder how the public would react if they knew of your… correspondence with certain Royalist elements."

Vergniaud paled slightly. "What are you insinuating?"

"Merely that rumours can be dangerous," Étienne said smoothly. "But perhaps we can avoid any unfortunate misunderstandings."

"Are you threatening me?" Vergniaud asked, incredulous.

"Not at all," Étienne replied. "I offer you a chance to reaffirm your commitment to the revolution."

Vergniaud stared at him, the weight of the unspoken threat heavy in the air. Finally, he spoke, his voice tight. "Very well. You have made your point."

"Excellent," Étienne said, his tone brightening. "I knew you would see reason."

Leaving Vergniaud's residence, Étienne allowed himself a satisfied smile. Another obstacle was removed.

As dusk approached, he navigated the labyrinthine streets towards Camille Desmoulins's modest abode. The journalist had been increasingly vocal in his opposition to the execution, a stance Étienne could no longer tolerate.

He found Desmoulins in his study, surrounded by stacks of pamphlets and newspapers. The smell of ink and paper hung heavily in the air.

"Étienne," Desmoulins greeted him cautiously. "To what do I owe this visit?"

"We need to discuss your recent articles," Étienne said bluntly.

Desmoulins frowned. "I see. You censor me?"

"To advise you," Étienne corrected. "Your calls for leniency undermine the revolution."

"I'm advocating for justice," Desmoulins insisted. "There's a difference between justice and revenge."

"Spare me the semantics," Étienne snapped. "Your words sow doubt among the people."

Desmoulins stood, anger flashing in his eyes. "Intimidation will not silence me."

Étienne stepped forward, lowering his voice. "Think of your wife, Lucile. Your child. These are dangerous times."

Desmoulins recoiled slightly. "Is that a threat?"

"A reminder," Étienne said coldly. "That actions have consequences."

Desmoulins clenched his fists. "You've changed, Étienne. Or perhaps this is who you always were."

"Believe what you will," Étienne replied. "But heed my warning. Cease your opposition."

Without waiting for a response, he turned on his heel and left.

The confrontation left a bitter taste in his mouth, but Étienne pushed it aside. Personal relationships were secondary to the cause. Étienne would also sweep away former allies if they became obstacles.

Night had fallen when he reached his final destination—a discreet meeting with Antoine, a leader among the Sans-culottes. They met in a shadowed alcove beneath a dilapidated archway.

"Antoine," Étienne greeted him.

"Citizen Corbeau," Antoine replied. "What do you require?"

"I need the people's voice to be heard," Étienne said. "Demonstrations demanding the king's execution. Visible, vocal support."

Antoine grinned. "Easily arranged. The men are eager for action."

"Good," Étienne said. "And ensure that any counter-protests are… discouraged."

"Consider it done," Antoine assured him.

As he made his way home, Étienne felt the weight of his actions settle upon him. He had crossed lines, manipulated, threatened—all in the revolution's name. Yet, a nagging doubt gnawed at the edges of his conscience.

He sat by the window; the city spread out in a tapestry of flickering lights and shadows. He thought of Olympe's warnings, of Desmoulins's accusation.

"Have I become the tyrant I seek to destroy?" he whispered into the silence.

Shaking off the thought, he reminded himself of the stakes. The future of France depended on decisive action, and personal sacrifices were necessary.

"8 January 1793," he noted mentally. "A day of reckoning."

He penned a brief letter to Robespierre, urging him to take a firmer stance against the moderates. Folding it carefully, he sealed it with wax and set it aside for delivery.

As he prepared for bed, Étienne caught his reflection in a tarnished mirror. The man staring back seemed older, his eyes harder.

"Power demands a price," he murmured. "And I will pay it."

Extinguishing the lamp, he lay in darkness, the echoes of the day's encounters replaying in his mind. Sleep came fitfully, haunted by visions of guillotines and the faces of those he had alienated.

Dawn would bring the next phase of his plan, but for now, Étienne Corbeau grappled with the solitude his ambition had wrought, even as he steeled himself for the battles yet to come.

• • •

The dawn of 15 January 1793 broke cold and unyielding, a pale sun casting feeble light upon the frost-laden streets of Paris. Étienne Corbeau stood outside the National Convention, his breath forming ghostly vapours in the frigid air. The city was calm as if holding its breath for the spectacle about to unfold.

He adjusted his scarf, the coarse wool scratching against his skin, and went inside. The grand hall was already teeming with deputies, their voices an indistinct murmur that echoed off the vaulted ceilings. The atmosphere was thick with anticipation and something darker—an undercurrent of dread, perhaps, or the weight of history pressing upon them all.

He settled into his chair, the wood worn smooth by the countless occupants before him. Around him, familiar faces wore expressions ranging from grim determination to uneasy trepidation. Maximilien Robespierre sat poised and composed, his eyes fixed straight ahead. Georges Danton leaned back, arms crossed, his brow furrowed in contemplation. Jean-Paul Marat scribbled furiously in a notebook, his quill scratching like a restless insect.

The doors at the rear of the chamber swung open, and a hush fell as the guards escorted Louis Capet inside. The former king's appearance was a shadow of his former self—his once-robust frame now gaunt, his regal attire replaced with plain, ill-fitting garments. Yet, his demeanour remained a vestige of dignity, a stubborn remnant of a man who had once believed himself ordained by divine right.

Étienne observed him with detached indifference. The murmurs of the assembly faded into a distant hum as he studied the deposed monarch. There was no pity in his gaze, no flicker of empathy—only a cold appraisal of a man who had become an obstacle to the revolution's progress.

Louis Capet took his place before the assembly, his chains clinking softly—a stark reminder of his fallen status. The president of the Convention called for silence, and the room obeyed, the weight of the moment settling upon them all.

The king spoke, his voice steady but laced with desperation. "*Citoyens,* I stand before you not as a king but as a man accused. I ask only for justice, guided by your established laws."

Étienne felt a flicker of annoyance. "Justice?" he thought. "He dares invoke justice now?"

Louis continued, recounting his actions and defending his decisions as necessary measures taken for the good of France. He spoke of his love for his people and his desire for their prosperity.

Across the aisle, Camille Desmoulins leaned forward, his eyes intent, perhaps searching for sincerity in the king's words. Étienne dismissed it as naïveté. Desmoulins had always been prone to sentimentality—a weakness in times that demanded resolve.

As the king's plea wore on, Étienne's mind drifted. He recalled the countless lives lost—the men and women who had perished fighting for *liberté* and *égalité,* the blood-stained Paris's cobblestones, the cries of the hungry and oppressed. What were the words of one man weighed against the suffering of an entire nation?

"He's wasting our time," Marat hissed beside him, snapping Étienne back to the present.

"Indeed," Étienne replied quietly. "But let him speak. It changes nothing."

Louis concluded his defence, his eyes scanning the faces of the deputies as if seeking a glimmer of compassion. Étienne met his gaze briefly, his own eyes unyielding. The king's shoulders sagged ever so slightly, a man resigned to the fate that awaited him.

With the floor opened for deliberation by the president, deputies engaged in arguments, their voices filling the room. The Girondins advocated for clemency, exile perhaps, citing the potential backlash from foreign powers. The Montagnards, including Étienne, pressed for execution, insisting it was the only way to solidify the revolution's legitimacy.

Maximilien Robespierre addressed the audience, emphasising that they should consider the question before them as one of guilt and as one they had established beyond doubt. "It is a question of necessity. To ensure the survival of the republic, we must act decisively."

Applause rippled through the chamber, though pockets of dissent remained. Étienne noted the furrowed brows of sure deputies, the sidelong glances exchanged. Doubt lingered, and he felt a surge of impatience.

He rose from his seat, the assembly quieting as he prepared to speak. "*Citoyens*," he began, his voice measured yet firm. "We have heard the king's plea. We have witnessed his attempt to cloak his treachery in the guise of benevolence. But let us not forget the tyranny under which we suffered, the oppression that drove us to rise against the chains of monarchy."

He paused, allowing his words to settle. "Exile is a temporary solution. A weed plucked at the stem will grow back stronger. We must pull it out by the roots."

Murmurs of agreement spread among the Montagnards. Étienne continued, his gaze sweeping the assembly. "Do not let misplaced compassion undo all that we have fought for. The revolution demands justice, and justice demands that Louis Capet pays the ultimate price."

As he resumed his seat, he caught sight of Olympe de Gouges watching him from the gallery above. Her expression was inscrutable, a mix of sorrow and disapproval. He felt a pang of something—regret, perhaps?—but dismissed it. Emotions were a hindrance he could ill afford.

The debate stretched on, hours bleeding into one another as the winter light outside waned. Étienne listened with half an ear as others spoke, his thoughts consumed by the outcome he had laboured to secure. The arguments blurred, the voices melding into a cacophony that grated against his patience.

"How much longer must we endure this farce?" he muttered under his breath.

Danton, seated nearby, glanced over. "The process must be thorough," he said quietly. "For history's sake."

"History favours the bold," Étienne retorted. "Not the hesitant."

Danton sighed. "There is merit in due diligence."

Étienne refrained from rolling his eyes. Danton's pragmatism bordered on complacency in his view. The man possessed charisma, yes, but lacked the ruthlessness.

As the session wore on, fatigue settled over the assembly. The president called for a recess, and the deputies dispersed. Étienne remained seated, unwilling to engage in the idle chatter that ensued.

Marat approached, his ever-present notebook tucked under one arm. "We need to ensure the vote swings our way," he said in a low voice.

"I've done what I can," Étienne replied, "I have swayed those who can be."

Marat's eyes flickered with something akin to admiration. "Your methods are effective if… direct."

"Desperate times," Étienne said with a faint shrug.

Marat nodded. "I have a list of those still undecided. Perhaps a few pointed articles might tip the scales."

"By all means," Étienne agreed. "Let them feel the weight of public opinion."

Marat departed, and Étienne finally rose, stretching stiff limbs. He approached the exit, weaving through clusters of deputies deep in conversation. Snatches of dialogue reached his ears—concerns over foreign intervention and fears of civil unrest.

Outside, the air was sharp, the sky awash with the purples and blues of twilight. He drew in a deep breath, the cold searing his lungs. The city extended ahead of him, a mosaic of shadows and twinkling lights.

"Étienne."

He turned to see Olympe approaching, her cloak wrapped tightly around her slender frame. "Madame de Gouges," he acknowledged.

"You spoke passionately today," she remarked.

"Passion is required to stir men to action," he replied.

She regarded him with a steady gaze. "But at what cost? Do you not fear the precedent set by executing a king?"

"I fear inaction far more," he said, meeting her eyes.

"Even if it means forsaking humanity?"

"Humanity?" He allowed a bitter laugh. "Was it humane when the people starved while the king feasted? When did they use the blade to silence voices of dissent?"

"Matthew 26:52—All who draw the sword will die by the sword," she said softly.

"Spare me the platitudes," he retorted. "We stand on the precipice of a new era. Sentimentality has no place here."

She shook her head, sadness etching lines across her face. "I worry about you, Étienne. You've lost touch with what made this revolution worth fighting for."

He felt a flicker of irritation. "And I worry that your idealism blinds you to reality."

"Perhaps," she conceded. "But I would rather cling to my ideals than become consumed by vengeance."

Before he could respond, she turned and disappeared into the gathering dusk.

Étienne stood there momentarily, her words echoing uncomfortably in his mind. Shaking off the unease, he set off towards his lodgings. The streets were quieter now, and the chill was driving most indoors. A lone violin played somewhere in the distance, the melancholy notes drifting through the air like forlorn spirits.

Reaching his apartment, he entered and closed the door firmly behind him. The familiar surroundings offered little solace. He lit a candle, the small flame casting elongated shadows that danced across the walls.

He considered pouring a glass of wine but decided against it. Clarity was essential. The final vote loomed, and he needed to remain focused.

Yet, as the night wore on, he found sleep elusive. Images flitted through his mind—the king's weary face, Olympe's piercing gaze, the disquieting sense that perhaps, in his relentless pursuit, he had severed more than ties to the monarchy.

"Emotions are a weakness," he told himself firmly. "Regret is a luxury I cannot afford."

And yet, the gnawing emptiness persisted, a hollow space where conviction had once filled him. He rose abruptly, pacing the room like a caged animal. The shadows seemed to mock him, stretching and contorting with each flicker of the candle.

Finally, he sat back down, pressing his fingers to his temples. "Impatience will serve no purpose," he scolded himself. "The outcome is inevitable."

But was it? Doubt crept in, unbidden and unwelcome. Had he underestimated the resolve of the moderates? Had his manipulations been sufficient?

He forced himself to breathe deeply, to push aside the uncertainty. "I have done all that is necessary."

As the first light of dawn seeped through the gaps in the curtains, Étienne felt a semblance of calm return. The die was cast, and France soon witnessed the culmination of its struggle.

"Tomorrow," he whispered. "Tomorrow, a new chapter begins."

Rising, he extinguished the candle and prepared to face the day. The revolution waited for no man, and neither would he.

● ● ●

The winter morning of 18 January 1793 unfurled under a leaden sky, the clouds hanging low over Paris as if burdened by the weight of the decision that lay before the nation. Étienne Corbeau stood at the window of his modest apartment, gazing out at the thin layer of frost that clung to the cobblestones below. A tense hush enveloped the streets, muting the city's usual din as though the very air awaited the verdict.

"18 January 1793," Étienne whispered to himself, his breath fogging the glass. Today was the day he had meticulously orchestrated—a culmination of weeks spent navigating the treacherous currents of revolutionary politics. The trial of Louis Capet teetered on a knife's edge, and he intended to ensure it tipped irrevocably towards death.

Donning his coat and tricolour cockade, he stepped into the biting cold. The chill gnawed at his cheeks, but he welcomed it—it sharpened his focus. While heading towards the National Convention, he noticed that apprehension was etched on the faces of the people he passed. Market stalls stood unattended, and clusters of Sans-culottes huddled around smouldering braziers, their conversations hushed.

Inside the grand hall of the Convention, the atmosphere was electric. Deputies filled the benches, their voices an inaudible murmur that swelled and receded like the tide. Étienne moved through the crowd with purpose, his gaze fixed ahead. He spotted Maximilien Robespierre standing alone, his posture rigid, eyes distant.

"Maximilien," Étienne greeted him, affecting a warmth he did not feel.

Robespierre turned, his sharp features softening slightly. "Étienne. These are grave times."

"Indeed," Étienne agreed. "The responsibility upon us is immense. The future of the Republic hinges on our unity."

Robespierre nodded thoughtfully. "The decision we make today will reverberate through history. We must act with both justice and prudence."

Étienne leaned in, lowering his voice. "Justice demands that we set a definitive precedent. Mercy towards the king could embolden our enemies, both within and beyond our borders."

Robespierre's eyes searched Étienne's face. "I fear the consequences of execution—how it may fracture the nation further."

"Consider the alternative," Étienne pressed. "Allowing Louis to live risks him becoming a rallying point for counter-revolutionaries. Exile is a temporary solution at best."

Robespierre sighed, the weight of his conscience clear. "You may be right. Yet, I cannot help but feel the gravity of sentencing a man to death."

Étienne placed a firm hand on his shoulder. "Maximilien, your dedication to the Republic is unparalleled. Trust in your convictions. The people look to us for decisive action."

Before Robespierre could respond, Georges Danton approached, his robust frame and commanding presence cutting through the tension. "Gentlemen," he boomed, attempting a jovial tone that fell flat. "I see we're deep in contemplation."

"Danton," Étienne acknowledged. "We were discussing the importance of solidarity in today's vote."

Danton's gaze flickered between them. "Solidarity, yes. But we must also heed the voice of reason. The execution of the king is not a matter to be taken lightly."

Étienne sensed an opportunity. "Of course not. But surely you agree that the security of the Republic must come first."

Danton stroked his chin thoughtfully. "I have my reservations. There's merit in considering all repercussions."

"Repercussions that could be far worse if we hesitate," Étienne countered. "The people demand justice. To deny them could incite unrest."

Robespierre interjected gently. "Georges, the tide of opinion favours execution. Perhaps it is the course."

Danton looked at him with surprise. "You too, Maximilien?"

Robespierre's expression was sombre as he declared, "I have deliberated extensively. We must safeguard the Republic."

Étienne suppressed a smile. His subtle manipulations were bearing fruit. "We must present a united front," he reiterated. "For the good of France."

Danton hesitated before conceding with a reluctant nod. "Very well. I will lend my support."

As Danton moved away, Étienne turned back to Robespierre. "We align," Étienne said, as he turned back to Robespierre.

Robespierre regarded him quietly. "Perhaps. Yet, I cannot shake the unease that shadows this decision."

"Such feelings are natural," Étienne assured him. "But history will judge us by the strength of our resolve."

They took their seats as the session was called to order. The president of the Convention stood at the podium, his voice ringing out over the assembly. "*Citoyens*, we convene today to render the Assembly's position on Louis Capet. Each deputy shall cast their vote openly, in the name of transparency and accountability."

A hush fell as the roll call began. One by one, deputies rose to declare their positions. The hall was tense, the air thick with the gravity of the moment.

"Philippe Égalité," the clerk called.

A stir rippled through the crowd as the Duke of Orléans, a cousin of the king, stood. His face was pale but determined. "Death," he pronounced firmly.

Étienne noted the murmurs of surprise and approval. Even the king's own blood condemned him—a powerful statement that would sway the undecided.

As the votes continued, Étienne's attention shifted to those deputies he had identified as wavering. He watched intently as Pierre Vergniaud rose. The Girondin leader's face was a mask of conflicted emotion.

"Exile," Vergniaud declared, his voice steady.

Étienne clenched his jaw. Despite his efforts, some remained obstinate. He scanned the chamber for others.

"Jean-Baptiste Clauzel," the clerk announced.

Clauzel stood, casting a furtive glance in Étienne's direction. "Death," he whispered.

Étienne allowed himself a small exhale. The man had heeded his earlier 'advice.'

The roll call proceeded, the tally edging ever closer to a majority for execution. Yet, the margin was slim. Every vote counted.

"Camille Desmoulins," came the call.

Desmoulins rose slowly. His eyes met Étienne's across the room—an unreadable expression passing between them. "We will enforce imprisonment until we achieve peace," he declared.

Étienne felt a surge of irritation. Foolish idealism. Desmoulins was a lost cause.

Finally, the last vote was cast. The president conferred briefly with the clerks before announcing the result.

"By a majority of one vote, the sentence is death."

A collective breath seemed to escape the assembly. Reactions varied—some deputies bowed their heads, others exchanged grim nods. The Montagnards appeared resolute while the Girondins whispered among themselves, discontent clear.

Étienne felt a wave of triumph tempered by the narrow margin. It had been perilously close—too close. His manipulations had secured the outcome, but the fragility of his position was starkly apparent.

As the assembly adjourned, he made his way through the throng, deflecting both congratulatory remarks and sullen glares. He needed a moment of solitude.

Exiting into the cold air, he hastened towards the Seine. The river flowed dark and steady, its surface mirroring the slate-grey sky. He leaned against the stone railing, allowing the chill to clear his mind.

"Étienne."

He turned to see Olympe de Gouges approaching, her features etched with a mixture of concern and reproach. "Madame de Gouges," he acknowledged.

"So, it is done," she said softly.

"It is," he affirmed.

She searched his face. "And are you satisfied?"

He met her gaze unwaveringly. "I am content that justice will be served."

"Justice," she echoed, a note of bitterness in her voice. "At what cost? The soul of the Republic?"

He frowned. "The Republic is stronger for this decision. We have eliminated a threat."

"You have set a precedent for bloodshed to an end," she retorted. "Where does it stop?"

"With the enemies of the people," he replied curtly.

She sighed, a weary sound. "Be careful, Étienne. In seeking to destroy monsters, you risk becoming one yourself."

Before he could respond, she turned and walked away; her figure soon swallowed by the fog that drifted off into the river.

Her words unsettled him more than he cared to admit. He had recognised the growing danger of his manipulations—the thin line he tread between orchestrator and oppressor. But doubt was a luxury he could ill afford.

"Étienne!"

He glanced up to see Maximilien Robespierre approaching, his expression troubled. "Maximilien," he greeted.

Robespierre joined him at the railing. "The margin was slim," he remarked.

"Indeed," Étienne agreed. "But sufficient."

Robespierre's gaze was distant. "I cannot help but feel a sense of foreboding."

"You mustn't dwell on it," Étienne counselled. "We acted out of necessity."

"Necessity," Robespierre mused. "A word that justifies much."

Étienne regarded him carefully. "Have you doubts?"

Robespierre shook his head slightly. "No. But I am wary of the path we forge. Each step seems to lead us deeper into darkness."

"Darkness is often the prelude to dawn," Étienne offered.

Robespierre managed a faint smile. "Ever the pragmatist."

They stood silently for a moment, the sounds of the city muffled by the enveloping cold.

"Be vigilant, Étienne," Robespierre said finally. "These are perilous times."

"Always," Étienne assured him.

As Robespierre departed, Étienne remained by the river, his reflection distorted in the rippling water. An acute awareness of the precariousness of his position overshadowed the exhilaration of securing the verdict. He had manipulated allies and adversaries alike, weaving a web that now threatened to ensnare him.

The execution of Louis Capet would mark a turning point—but towards what end? The revolution devoured its own with alarming ease. He thought of Danton's reservations, Desmoulins's idealism, Olympe's warnings. Their voices formed a dissonant chorus in his mind.

"Power is a fickle companion," he murmured.

Returning to his apartment as dusk settled, he found a sealed letter waiting for him. Breaking the wax, he recognised Marat's scrawled handwriting.

Citoyen Corbeau,

Our efforts have borne fruit. Yet whispers of dissent abound within our ranks. We must remain vigilant. There are those who question our methods.

—Marat

Étienne crumpled the note thoughtfully. Not only did the seeds of unrest spread among the populace, but they also sowed them within the very heart of the revolution. His manipulations had achieved their immediate goal but at the cost of trust and camaraderie.

He sat at his desk, the shadows lengthening around him. The candlelight flickered, casting uncertain light upon the papers strewn before him.

> *18 January 1793,*
>
> *A victory secured, but the ground beneath us shifts like sand. I have pushed hard, perhaps too hard. The fragility of alliances weighs upon me. The revolution demands sacrifices, yet I wonder how much more we can yield before we fracture entirely.*

He closed the journal, extinguishing the candle. The room plunged into darkness, mirroring the uncertainty that gnawed at his resolve.

As he lay awake that night, Étienne contemplated the abyss he had edged towards. The path ahead was treacherous, fraught with unseen perils. Yet, he could not turn back. We had invested too much and burned too many bridges.

"Forward," he whispered into the void. "There is no other way."

The revolution churned on, unforgiving, and he stood at its epicentre— alone amid the tumult he had helped unleash.

• • •

The grey dawn of 20 January 1793 broke over Paris with a sullen stillness, as if the city itself held its breath in anticipation. Étienne Corbeau stood on the steps of the National Convention, his gaze sweeping over the gathering crowds. His coat barely shielded him from the biting chill in the air.

"20 January 1793," he whispered to himself, the date etching itself into his memory as a pivotal moment in the revolution he had so fervently championed. The execution of Louis Capet was all but assured, yet an uneasy restlessness gnawed at him. He had manoeuvred the pieces into place, but the victory felt as cold as the winter morning enveloping the city.

The streets teemed with Parisians, their faces a mosaic of emotions— anger, hope, fear. The Sans-culottes were out in force, their tricolour cockades bright spots of colour against the drab backdrop of the buildings. Murmurs rippled through the crowd, snatches of conversation reaching Étienne's ears.

"Justice at last," one man proclaimed, his fist raised defiantly.

"Will this truly change anything?" a woman questioned, her voice tinged with scepticism.

Étienne turned away, ascending the steps and entering the grand hall of the Convention. Inside, the atmosphere was taut, the air thick with anticipation and an undercurrent of something darker—doubt, perhaps, or trepidation. Deputies clustered in small groups, their hushed conversations ceasing as he passed.

He caught sight of Maximilien Robespierre seated alone, his usually composed demeanour marred by a furrowed brow. Étienne approached him, pulling a chair beside him.

"Maximilien," he greeted softly.

Robespierre looked up, his eyes reflecting the weight of their shared burden. "Étienne. The hour is nearly upon us."

"Indeed," Étienne replied, his gaze drifting to the vacant speaker's podium. "We've worked tirelessly for this moment."

"Yet, I find little solace in it," Robespierre confessed. "The execution of a king… it feels like a profound rupture."

Étienne studied him. "A necessary one. To forge a new France, we must sever the ties to the old regime completely."

Robespierre sighed. "I understand that in principle. But the cost—I'm wondering if we can bear it."

Before Étienne could respond, Georges Danton joined them, his presence as commanding as ever. "Gentlemen," he said, attempting a smile that didn't reach his eyes. "Are we ready to make history?"

"As ready as one can be," Robespierre answered.

Danton clapped a hand on Étienne's shoulder. "You've been instrumental in this, Étienne. Your dedication is admirable."

Étienne forced a thin smile. "I simply did what was necessary."

"Did you?" a voice interjected.

They turned to see Camille Desmoulins standing nearby, his expression a mix of disapproval and sadness. "At what point does 'necessary' become 'ruthless'?"

Étienne's eyes narrowed. "I did what others lacked the courage to do."

Desmoulins shook his head. "You've alienated allies and sown seeds of discord. This path leads to a dark place."

"Spare us the melodrama," Étienne retorted. "The Republic demands decisive action."

"Enough," Robespierre intervened gently. "We cannot afford infighting now."

Desmoulins held Étienne's gaze a moment longer before turning away. "History will judge us all," he whispered.

An uneasy silence settled over the trio. Danton cleared his throat. "We should take our seats. The session is about to begin."

As they moved towards their places, Étienne felt a prickle of unease. The room seemed to pulse with unspoken tensions, alliances fraying at the edges. He had noticed the sidelong glances and whispered conversations that ceased when he approached. Isolation wrapped around him like a heavy and constricting cloak.

The president of the Convention called the assembly to order. *"Citoyens,* we gather today to render the final decision on the fate of Louis Capet. Let each deputy stand and declare their vote openly, in the spirit of transparency and unity."

One by one, the deputies rose. The chamber echoed with a litany of voices:

"Death."

"Exile."

"Imprisonment."

As the roll call progressed, the tide was unmistakable. The majority favoured execution. When Étienne's name was called, he stood with conviction.

"Death," he pronounced firmly, his voice carrying through the hall.

He sat down, a hollow sensation settling in his chest. This was the outcome he had laboured for, yet satisfaction eluded him. Instead, a spectre of doubt loomed at the edges of his consciousness.

They announced the final tally: a definitive vote for execution. A murmur swept through the assembly—relief for some, despair for others. Étienne glanced around, noting the varied reactions.

Robespierre appeared stoic, yet his clenched jaw betrayed inner turmoil. Danton stared ahead, his expression inscrutable. Desmoulins sat with his head bowed, a shadow of defeat upon him.

The session adjourned amid a flurry of movement. Deputies departed in clusters, some engaging in heated debates, others slipping away in silence. Étienne remained seated, the bustle around him fading into a blur.

"Congratulations," a voice drawled sarcastically.

He saw Olympe de Gouges standing beside him, her eyes piercing. "You've achieved your goal."

Étienne met her gaze. "A necessary step for the Republic."

"Is that what you tell yourself?" she challenged. "That sacrificing your humanity serves the greater good?"

He bristled. "Do not presume to lecture me, Olympe. Idealism without action is mere fantasy."

"And action without conscience is tyranny," she retorted. "You've become a stranger to those who once called you an ally."

He stood abruptly. "If others lack the resolve to do what's needed, that's their failing, not mine."

She sighed softly. "Be careful, Étienne. The path you're on is lonely."

As she walked away, her words lingered uncomfortably. He dismissed them with a shake of his head, but the seed of disquiet had already taken root.

Exiting the Convention, he found the sky had darkened and heavy snow beginning to fall. Flakes settled on his coat, melting into dark spots that mirrored his mood. He made his way through the streets, the crunch of snow underfoot the only sound in the muffled quiet.

A scaffold loomed at the Place de la Révolution—a stark silhouette against the bleak horizon. Workers moved about it like ants, making final preparations. The sight should have filled him with a sense of accomplishment, yet he felt only emptiness.

"Is this what victory feels like?" he wondered.

A familiar figure approached—Jean-Paul Marat, his intense gaze alight with enthusiasm. "Étienne, I've been looking for you."

"What is it, Marat?"

"The people are restless," Marat said, his voice edged with excitement. "They demand more than the king's execution. They seek purges of all traitors."

Étienne regarded him warily. "We must be cautious. Unchecked zeal can lead to chaos."

Marat scoffed. "Now is not the time for caution. We must seize the momentum."

"At what cost?" Étienne asked—echoes of Olympe's warning surfacing.

Marat's eyes narrowed. "Have you lost your nerve?"

"I've not," Étienne replied sharply. "But we must ensure the Republic doesn't consume itself."

Marat waved a dismissive hand. "Your hesitation is disappointing. If you won't act, others will."

He strode away, leaving Étienne alone in the falling snow. The exchange left a bitter taste. He was caught between extremes—too radical for the moderates, too restrained for the zealots.

Continuing his walk, he found himself outside Café Procope. Warm light spilt onto the street from its windows, and the murmur of conversation was inviting. He entered, shedding his coat and ordering a coffee.

Seated in a corner, he sipped the bitter brew, the warmth failing to thaw the chill within. Snatches of dialogue drifted to him.

"Did you hear? Danton is distancing himself from the radicals."

"Desmoulins has published a new pamphlet calling for clemency."

"Marat grows more unhinged by the day."

Étienne realised his name was absent from their discussions—a disconcerting anonymity. He had become a shadow, influential yet unseen, his deeds recognised, but his person disregarded.

"Mind if I join you?" a voice interrupted his thoughts.

He looked up to see Jacques-Louis David, the painter, standing beside the table.

"Of course," Étienne gestured to the empty seat.

David settled in, his eyes keen. "You've been hard to find lately."

Étienne tersely stated, "I have been busy."

David studied him. "They have set the execution. Your efforts were instrumental."

"So I've been told."

"Yet you don't seem pleased."

Étienne shrugged. "I expected to feel… more."

David nodded thoughtfully. "Such is often the case with ambitions fulfilled."

They sat in silence for a moment. Then David spoke again. "There are whispers, Étienne. Some question your methods."

"I'm aware," he said flatly.

"Be cautious," David advised. "The tide of public opinion is fickle. Today's hero can become tomorrow's villain."

Étienne met his gaze. "Do you doubt me as well?"

"I merely observe," David said gently. "Isolation can be perilous in times like these."

"Perhaps," Étienne conceded, though inwardly, he bristled at yet another warning.

They parted soon after, and Étienne returned to the streets, the snow now a thick blanket muffling the city's heartbeat. He wandered, thoughts churning.

He had achieved his goal, yet the victory rang hollow. The alliances he once relied upon frayed, straining or severing his relationships. The potential for backlash loomed—a shadow he could not ignore.

As night fell, he stood on a bridge overlooking the Seine. The river flowed dark and silent beneath him, its surface punctuated by the occasional drift of ice. He leaned on the railing, the cold seeping through his gloves.

"Was it worth it?" he asked aloud, the question swallowed by the darkness.

He thought of Robespierre's haunted eyes, Danton's wary distance, and Desmoulins's open disdain. The revolution he had given himself to was a beast with insatiable hunger, and he wondered if he would be one of its casualties.

"Étienne Corbeau," he murmured to himself. "Architect of change, or harbinger of ruin?"

The wind picked up, cutting through him. He straightened, pulling his coat tighter. There was no turning back. He had chosen his path and would see it through, whatever the cost.

Returning home, he lit a single candle, its feeble glow casting long shadows. He sat at his desk, quill in hand, and wrote.

20 January 1793,

The king's fate has been determined. Yet, the triumph I expected eludes me. I stand surrounded by achievements but bereft of solace. Isolation encroaches, and I sense the undercurrents of dissent swirling around me.

I have become a stranger to those I once called comrades. Perhaps they cannot comprehend the necessity of my actions. Or perhaps I have misjudged the price of ambition.

The revolution advances, but at what personal cost? I fear I may have sown the seeds of my undoing.

He paused, the ink pooling at the tip of the quill. With a heavy sigh, he set it aside and extinguished the candle.

In the enveloping darkness, Étienne lay awake, the silence of the night pressing in. They decided, but the repercussions were only beginning to unfold.

He closed his eyes, uncertain what the dawn would bring, yet resolute in facing it.

The die was cast, and the path ahead, though fraught with peril, was one he would navigate alone.

• • •

The dawn of 21 January 1793 broke bleak and grey over Paris, a pallid sun struggling to pierce the thick clouds that hung oppressively low. Étienne Corbeau stood amidst the throng at the Place de la Révolution, the chill air biting his cheeks. The square was a sea of humanity—Sans-culottes in their striped trousers, bourgeois citizens bundled against the cold, soldiers in uniform—all drawn by the gravity of the day's event.

"21 January 1793," Étienne murmured to himself. The date was etched indelibly in his mind, and today marked the culmination of his efforts: the execution of Louis Capet, the deposed King Louis XVI. He felt a cold satisfaction settle within him, a vindication of his chosen relentless path.

The guillotine loomed ahead, a stark silhouette against the dreary sky. Its wooden frame was dark and imposing, the blade gleaming dully. Around it, soldiers formed a cordon, their muskets held at the ready. The crowd's murmur ebbed and flowed, a restless energy pulsing through the masses.

Beside Étienne stood Maximilien Robespierre, his typically composed visage tense and drawn. He gazed at the scaffold with an intensity that betrayed his inner turmoil. Étienne observed him sidelong, noting the tightness around his mouth, the furrow etched deep between his brows.

"Are you unwell, Maximilien?" Étienne inquired, his tone measured.

Robespierre started slightly as if pulled from a reverie. "I am… contemplative," he replied. "This is a momentous occasion."

"Indeed," Étienne agreed. "A decisive step towards the new Republic."

Robespierre's eyes flickered with uncertainty. "And yet, I cannot help but feel the weight of this act. The execution of a king… it is unprecedented."

Étienne's gaze hardened. "Louis Capet is but a man, stripped of title and privilege. Justice demands his death."

"Justice," Robespierre echoed softly. "Yes, of course."

A hush fell over the crowd as a carriage approached, its wheels crunching over the frosted ground. Louis Capet emerged, his hands bound, a simple white shirt and breeches replacing the finery he once donned. His face was pale but composed, and his eyes scanned the crowd with a mixture of resignation and defiance.

Étienne felt no pity as he watched the former monarch ascend the steps to the scaffold. The king's downfall was necessary—a symbol to shatter the vestiges of tyranny that clung stubbornly to France.

As Louis attempted to address the crowd, a drumroll drowned out his words. The executioner guided him to the bascule, securing him in place. Moments, they stretched interminably as the blade hovered, suspended like the pendulum of fate.

Then, with a swift release, the blade fell. A collective gasp rippled through the crowd, followed by an eerie silence. The executioner lifted the severed head, displaying it to the masses. Some cheered, others crossed themselves, and a few wept openly.

Étienne felt a surge of triumph, cold and sharp. The deed was done. The Republic had asserted its authority irrevocably.

Beside him, Robespierre turned away, a shadow passing over his features. Étienne sensed their widening chasm—a divergence of conviction and conscience.

"Does this not bring you relief?" Étienne asked, a hint of challenge in his voice.

Robespierre hesitated. "It brings finality, but at a cost I am still grappling with."

"Such hesitation is unbecoming," Étienne remarked coolly. "We must be resolute."

Robespierre's gaze hardened as he said, "Do not mistake reflection for weakness, Étienne. We should never diminish the gravity of taking a life—any life."

Étienne dismissed the rebuke with a slight shrug. "The king's death was necessary for the greater good."

"Perhaps," Robespierre conceded. "But we tread a perilous path when we become desensitised to such acts."

Before Étienne could respond, Georges Danton approached his expression sombre. "It is done, then," he said quietly.

"Yes," Étienne affirmed. "France is free from the shackles of monarchy."

Danton sighed deeply. "Let us hope this ushers in the peace and unity we desperately need."

Étienne sensed the undercurrents of doubt in both men, an unease that threatened to undermine their resolve. "We have struck a decisive blow against tyranny," he asserted. "Now we must focus on solidifying the Republic."

Danton regarded him thoughtfully. "Not everyone shares your enthusiasm, Étienne. There is talk of unrest in the provinces, dissent among the people."

"Then we must address it with firm leadership," Étienne retorted. "Hesitation will only breed further instability."

Robespierre exchanged a glance with Danton. "We should reconvene at the Convention," he suggested. "There is much to discuss."

As they made their way through the dispersing crowd, Étienne noticed the sidelong glances cast his way—the whispers trailed in his wake. Allies avoided his gaze, while others regarded him with thinly veiled suspicion.

He felt the weight of isolation pressing upon him, a realisation that his single-minded pursuit had erected barriers between himself and those he once considered comrades. The cold satisfaction of the king's death waned, replaced by a creeping sense of unease.

They parted ways at the steps of the Convention. Danton and Robespierre drifted towards a deputies' cluster, leaving Étienne alone. He watched as they engaged in hushed conversation, their expressions grave.

"Étienne."

He turned to see Olympe de Gouges approaching, her eyes reflecting a complex mix of emotions—sadness, disappointment, perhaps even pity.

"Olympe," he acknowledged curtly.

She studied him for a moment before speaking. "So, the king is dead."

"Yes," he replied. "Justice has been served."

"Has it?" she challenged gently. "Or have we merely traded one form of tyranny for another?"

He bristled. "Your sentimentality blinds you. The king was a symbol of oppression."

"And what do you symbolise now?" she asked pointedly. "A man willing to sacrifice anything—and anyone—in pursuit of his ideals?"

Étienne's jaw tightened. "I do what is necessary for the Republic."

"At the expense of your humanity?" She shook her head sadly. "I fear you have lost yourself, Étienne."

He felt a flash of anger. "Spare me your lectures. The time for idealistic notions is over."

"Perhaps," she said softly. "But remember this: a revolution that devours its principles will inevitably consume itself."

Before he could plan a retort, she turned and walked away, leaving him with her words echoing uncomfortably in his mind.

Entering the Convention hall, he found the atmosphere tense. Deputies clustered in tight groups, their conversations halting as he passed. The sense of camaraderie that once permeated these walls had eroded, replaced by suspicion and division.

He took his seat, scanning the surrounding faces. Jean-Paul Marat caught his eye, offering a curt nod. Marat's gaze was feverish, a zeal that bordered on fanaticism. Étienne wondered if he saw himself reflected in the man's unyielding stare.

Maximilien Robespierre ascended the podium, calling the session to order. Maximilien Robespierre ascended the podium and delivered a measured speech, calling for unity and vigilance against external threats. Yet, there was a restraint in his words, a caution that had not existed before.

As discussions unfolded, Étienne found himself increasingly sidelined. People either gave a lukewarm reception or entirely deflected his proposals. Allies he had counted on were evasive, their support waning.

"Perhaps they lack the stomach for what must be done," he thought, attempting to dismiss the growing disquiet.

After the session adjourned, he approached Robespierre. "Maximilien, a word?"

Robespierre regarded him with a guarded expression. "What is it, Étienne?"

"I sense reluctance among the deputies," Étienne began. "We need decisive action to maintain momentum."

Robespierre nodded slowly. "True, but we must also be cautious not to alienate the populace. The execution has stirred mixed reactions."

"Which is why we must show strength," Étienne pressed. "Any sign of weakness could embolden our enemies."

Robespierre's gaze hardened slightly. "Strength is not solely shown through force. We must balance firmness with wisdom."

Étienne felt a flicker of frustration. "Hesitation will only lead to disorder."

"Perhaps," Robespierre allowed. "But an uncompromising stance may fracture us further."

There was a moment of strained silence. Étienne realised the gap between them had widened—a divergence of philosophies that seemed irreconcilable.

"Very well," Étienne said tersely. "I see we differ on this matter."

Robespierre inclined his head. "We all seek the Republic's prosperity, albeit through different means."

As they parted, Étienne felt the total weight of his isolation. He had navigated the treacherous waters of revolution with singular focus but now found himself adrift, the alliances he had forged eroding beneath him.

Walking the streets of Paris, he observed the city's shifting mood. Posters denouncing various factions plastered the walls while rumours of conspiracies and betrayals circulated like a plague.

He passed a group of Sans-culottes engaged in heated debate. Snippets of their conversation reached him.

"… can't trust the Convention anymore…"

"… they've become as bad as the aristocrats…"

"… Marat says we need to purge the traitors…"

Étienne quickened his pace, unease coiling in his gut. The very revolution he had fought to advance was fracturing, and he could feel himself slipping into the chasm opening beneath it.

Reaching his apartment, he closed the door firmly behind him, the solitude both a comfort and a reminder of his estrangement. He sat at his desk, the familiar surroundings offering little solace.

21 January 1793,

The king is dead. A new chapter begins, yet I find myself on an uncertain footing. The realisation that I stand increasingly alone taints the satisfaction I expected.

Robespierre grows distant, his ideals diverging from mine. Danton is cautious, Desmoulins openly hostile, and Marat teeters on the edge of fanaticism.

Olympe's words haunt me. Have I lost sight of the very principles that ignited this revolution? Or is this the inevitable price of progress?

He put down the quill, rubbing his temples. The weight of his actions pressed upon him, a tangible burden he could no longer ignore.

A knock at the door startled him. He hesitated before answering. Opening it, he found a young courier, his clothes worn but neat.

"Monsieur Corbeau?" the boy inquired.

"Yes," Étienne confirmed.

"A letter for you," the boy said, handing over a sealed envelope.

"Merci," Étienne replied, offering a coin in return.

Closing the door, he broke the seal and unfolded the letter.

Citizen Corbeau,

We request your presence at a meeting tomorrow evening. The meeting will cover matters of great importance to the Republic.

— Antoine

Antoine was a leader among the more radical elements of the Sans-culottes. Étienne felt a flicker of intrigue mixed with apprehension.

"Perhaps an opportunity to regain influence," he mused.

Yet, a nagging doubt lingered. The landscape was shifting beneath his feet, alliances morphing into something unrecognisable.

He retired for the night, sleep elusive. His thoughts churned, a vortex of ambition, doubt, and a creeping sense of foreboding.

The execution had been a pivotal moment, but the aftermath was proving more complex than expected. The clear path he once saw was now obscured, fraught with unseen dangers.

As he drifted into a fitful slumber, Étienne could not escape the unsettling awareness that the revolution he had helped shape was evolving beyond his control. The repercussions of his choices were only beginning to unfold.

• • •

The morning of 23 January 1793 dawned with a bleak chill that seeped into the very bones of Paris. Étienne Corbeau stood at the window of his modest apartment, gazing out over the city as a thin veil of mist clung to the rooftops. Two days prior, the execution of Louis Capet had sent ripples of shock and exhilaration through the populace, and now the capital simmered with a volatile mix of fear and empowerment.

"23 January 1793," Étienne muttered, his breath fogging the glass. The date marked a new chapter—not just for France, but for his own ambitions.

The king was dead, and in the ensuing chaos, opportunities abounded for those astute enough to seize them.

He turned away from the window, his eyes settling on the scattered papers on his desk. Pamphlets, notes, and correspondence lay in disarray—a testament to his frenetic pace. Among them was a letter from Antoine, the Sans-culotte leader, inviting him to a clandestine meeting that evening. Étienne felt a flicker of anticipation. Aligning himself with the more radical elements could bolster his influence, albeit at a risk.

Donning his coat and tricolour cockade, he left the apartment and stepped into the bustling streets. The air was thick with tension. Citizens gathered in tight knots, their voices hushed but urgent.

"Have you heard? The Austrians are advancing on the border," one man whispered.

"Traitors lurk among us," another warned. "We must be vigilant."

Étienne navigated through the crowds, his mind already strategising how to manipulate these fears to his advantage. Étienne could leverage the threat of foreign invasion to merge power and justify harsher measures against dissenters.

He made his way to the Café de Foy, a popular haunt for revolutionaries and intellectuals alike. Inside, people could feel the charged atmosphere. Jean-Paul Marat sat at a corner table, his piercing gaze scanning the room. Spotting Étienne, he beckoned him over.

"Étienne," Marat greeted, his voice a husky undertone. "The tides are turning. The people are restless."

"Indeed," Étienne replied, taking a seat opposite him. "The execution has stirred the pot. Uncertainty breeds opportunity."

Marat leaned forward, his eyes gleaming with enthusiasm. "We must haste. Root out the counter-revolutionaries before they undermine all we've achieved."

"I couldn't agree more," Étienne said smoothly. "I have information on certain deputies whose loyalties are… questionable."

Marat's expression sharpened. "Names?"

Étienne produced a folded parchment from his coat pocket. "A list of those who have been in contact with *émigrés*, or who have spoken against the Convention's decisions."

Marat scanned the document, his lips curling into a satisfied smirk. "This is invaluable. With your permission, I'll publish their names in *L'Ami du Peuple*. Let the masses know who conspires against them."

"By all means," Étienne acquiesced. "Transparency is vital."

As they parted ways, Étienne felt a surge of grim satisfaction. By feeding Marat's paranoia, he could eliminate rivals and tighten his grip on the revolutionary machinery. Yet, a nagging unease tugged at the edges of his consciousness. Marat was a volatile ally—one who could turn just as quickly.

Leaving the café, Étienne headed towards the Tuileries, where the National Convention was in session. The grand corridors echoed with hurried footsteps and urgent whispers.

"Étienne," a voice called out.

He turned to see Camille Desmoulins approaching, his face drawn and weary. "Camille," Étienne acknowledged coolly.

"We need to talk," Desmoulins insisted, his gaze earnest. "The executions—the purges—this can't continue unchecked."

Étienne raised an eyebrow. "I wasn't aware you had grown so timid."

"This isn't about timidity," Desmoulins retorted. "It's about reason. We've become the very thing we sought to overthrow."

Étienne felt a flash of irritation. "Spare me the moralising. These measures are necessary to protect the Republic."

"At what cost?" Desmoulins pressed. "Innocent lives? Our humanity?"

"Collateral damage," Étienne said dismissively. "A regrettable but unavoidable consequence."

Desmoulins shook his head. "You're playing a dangerous game, Étienne. The tides can turn swiftly."

"Is that a threat?" Étienne's eyes narrowed.

"A warning," Desmoulins replied. "For old times' sake."

As Desmoulins walked away, Étienne felt a prickling at the back of his neck. Paranoia? Perhaps. But in these times, vigilance was a survival skill.

Entering the assembly chamber, he spotted Maximilien Robespierre conversing with Louis de Saint-Just. The latter caught Étienne's eye and gave a brief nod. Robespierre's demeanour, however, remained distant.

"Robespierre," Étienne greeted as he approached.

"Étienne," Robespierre replied curtly.

"I trust we're all aligned with the need for decisive action against internal threats?" Étienne probed.

Robespierre exchanged a glance with Saint-Just before responding. "While security is paramount, we must ensure fear does not overshadow justice."

"Fear is a powerful motivator," Étienne countered. "It unites the people against common enemies."

"But at what price?" Saint-Just interjected. "A society governed by fear is fragile."

Étienne sensed the conversation was futile. "I see our perspectives differ. I hope we can collaborate for the Republic's sake."

"Of course," Robespierre said, though his tone lacked conviction.

As the session began, Étienne observed the proceedings critically. Factions were becoming more pronounced, debates more acrimonious. He noted those who opposed his views, mentally cataloguing potential obstacles.

The meeting concluded with little resolution. Exiting the Convention, Étienne felt the weight of unseen eyes upon him. Paranoia gnawed at his composure. He recalled Desmoulins's warning, Olympe de Gouges's admonitions, and the subtle distancing of Robespierre and others.

Dismissing his unease, he focused on the task ahead—the meeting with Antoine and the Sans-culottes. As night fell, he made his way to a discreet location in the Marais district. The building was unremarkable, its façade blending seamlessly with its neighbours.

Inside, there was a charged atmosphere. Antoine greeted him with a firm handshake. "Étienne, glad you could join us."

"Always a pleasure," Étienne replied, scanning the room. A dozen men were present, their expressions hardened by struggle and conviction.

Antoine began the discussion. "The people grow impatient. They demand action against those who would betray the revolution."

"Agreed," Étienne said. "We must act swiftly to quell any counter-revolutionary activities."

One man, Jacques, spoke up. "Rumours circulate that certain members of the Convention are plotting with foreign powers."

Étienne nodded. "I've heard similar whispers. We need evidence to act decisively."

"Perhaps we don't need evidence," another interjected. "Suspicion alone should warrant action."

A dangerous suggestion, but one Étienne could utilise. "While I advocate for justice, we cannot afford hesitation."

Antoine eyed him thoughtfully. "Are you willing to support more… direct measures?"

"Define *direct*," Étienne prompted.

"Eliminating threats before they materialise," Antoine said evenly.

Étienne considered this. Aligning with such radical elements could expedite his goals, but the risks were considerable. "I'm open to discussing strategies that protect the Republic."

A satisfied murmur rippled through the group. The group laid out plans—lists of targets, methods of execution, and means to incite public support.

As the meeting concluded, Antoine pulled Étienne aside. "Your influence is invaluable. With your backing, we can cleanse the Republic of its enemies."

"I'll do what's necessary," Étienne affirmed.

Stepping back into the night, the cold air contrasted the heated intensity inside. He pulled his coat tighter, senses alert. Footsteps echoed behind him—a mere passerby or something more sinister?

He quickened his pace, instinctively moving his hand towards the small dagger concealed within his coat. The footsteps persisted. Turning a corner, he pressed himself into a shadowed alcove, waiting.

A figure emerged—a young woman's features obscured by a hood. She paused, glancing around before continuing. Étienne exhaled slowly. Paranoia was getting the better of him.

Returning to his apartment, he bolted the door and lit a candle. The flickering light cast long shadows, heightening his unease. He sat at his desk, attempting to organise his thoughts.

23 January 1793,

The aftermath of the king's execution presents both opportunity and peril. Alliances shift like sand, and trust is a scarce commodity. I must tread carefully yet decisively.

Desmoulins and others grow wary—potential obstacles that may need to be addressed. The Sans-culottes offer a means to an end, but their methods could spiral beyond control.

I must remain vigilant. The line between caution and paranoia blurs, but survival depends upon my ability to navigate these treacherous waters.

A sudden knock at the door startled him. Heart pounding, he rose cautiously. "Who is it?" he called out.

"Étienne, it's me," a familiar voice replied.

He relaxed slightly and opened the door to reveal Olympe de Gouges. Her eyes searched his face with a mix of concern and resolve.

"Olympe," he said, surprised. "What brings you here at this hour?"

"I needed to speak with you," she said, stepping inside uninvited. "Things are escalating dangerously."

He closed the door behind her. "I'm aware of the tensions. All the more reason to remain steadfast."

"That's precisely why I'm here," she insisted. "Your name is being whispered among those who seek to purge the Convention. You're not as untouchable as you believe."

Étienne felt a chill unrelated to the weather. "Who have you been speaking to?"

"I have my sources," she replied. "I'm trying to warn you. This path you're on leads to ruin."

He scoffed, though unease gnawed at him. "I appreciate your concern, but I can handle myself."

"Can you?" she challenged. "You're surrounded by shadows, enemies masquerading as allies. Trust me, Étienne, before it's too late."

He met her gaze, the weight of her words pressing upon him. "What would you have me do?"

"Step back," she urged. "Reassess your alliances, your actions. It's not too late to change course."

He hesitated, the façade of confidence wavering. "Perhaps you're right," he conceded quietly.

A flicker of relief crossed her face. "Good. We can steer this revolution back towards its true ideals."

"One step at a time," he said, a hint of a smile touching his lips.

She placed a hand on his arm. "Be careful, Étienne. The storm is far from over."

As she left, he locked the door, her warning echoing in his mind. Paranoia tightened its grip, and every creak and shadow was a potential threat.

He returned to his desk, but the words on the pages blurred. Sleep eluded him as he grappled with the realisation that the chaos he had sown was now encircling him.

Dawn found him still awake. The candle burned low. The city stirred outside, oblivious to his inner turmoil.

"23 January 1793," he whispered again. The date marked not just a turning point for France but perhaps the beginning of his own unravelling.

• • •

The chill of 31 January 1793 settled over Paris like a shroud, the air heavy with the lingering scent of wood smoke and unease. Étienne Corbeau strode purposefully along the cobblestone streets, his coat drawn tight against the biting wind. The city was a hive of whispered conversations and furtive glances, where shadows seemed to harbour secrets and every alleyway could conceal a conspirator.

He made his way to the Hôtel de Ville, where the Committee of Public Safety convened an emergency session. The recent execution of Louis Capet had sent shockwaves through the nation, and the fragile equilibrium of the revolution teetered on a knife's edge. Factions were forming, loyalties shifting like sand, and Étienne knew that decisive action was imperative.

Entering the grand chamber, he surveyed the assembled deputies. Faces etched with fatigue and suspicion turned towards him. Maximilien Robespierre stood near the centre of the room, his pale complexion stressed by the dim candlelight. His eyes held a fiery intensity, a man grappling with the weight of responsibility and moral quandaries.

"Étienne," Robespierre greeted him with a curt nod. "We were wondering if you would join us."

"My apologies," Étienne replied smoothly. "Matters of some urgency detained me. But I am here now, ready to serve the Republic."

Robespierre gestured for him to join the circle of deputies. Georges Danton leaned against a table, his robust frame and forceful presence dominating the space. Camille Desmoulins stood nearby, his expression wary. Jean-Paul Marat sat scribbling furiously in his ever-present notebook, his eyes flickering between the speakers.

"The situation grows dire," Robespierre began, his voice measured yet laced with tension. "Reports of counter-revolutionary activities increase daily. We must consider more stringent measures to safeguard the revolution."

Étienne seized the moment. "I concur, Maximilien. Our leniency encourages the enemies of the Republic. We must act decisively or risk losing all we have fought for."

Desmoulins frowned. "But at what cost? Are we to sacrifice the very principles of liberty and justice in the name of security?"

Étienne met his gaze unflinchingly. "Liberty cannot flourish without order. Justice demands that we protect the people from those who would subvert our cause."

Danton stroked his chin thoughtfully. "There is merit in both arguments. We must be cautious not to become the tyrants we despise."

Marat interjected, his voice sharp. "Caution is a luxury we can ill afford. The guillotine must remain busy if we are to root out the traitors among us."

Robespierre raised a hand to quell the rising tension. "Perhaps there is a path that balances the necessity of virtue."

"Maximilien, you have always been a beacon of integrity," Étienne said, leaning forward. "Your guidance is crucial in these tumultuous times. But we recognise we need firmness and could expand the Law of Suspects to grant us the authority we need."

Robespierre regarded him thoughtfully. "You propose increasing the scope of arrests?"

"Precisely," Étienne affirmed. "We need the power to detain those who pose a threat without the hindrance of bureaucratic delays."

Desmoulins shook his head. "This sounds perilously close to despotism."

"Despotism in defence of liberty," Étienne retorted, "is no vice."

Robespierre's eyes narrowed as he considered the proposal. "I am reluctant to endorse measures that could infringe upon the rights we have fought to establish."

Étienne softened his tone. "Maximilien, think of the greater good. We cannot let scruples hinder the protection of the Republic. You have the influence to steer us towards a safer future."

There was a pause as Robespierre weighed his words. Finally, he spoke. "Very well. I will draught a proposal for the Committee to consider. But it must include safeguards to prevent abuse."

Marat scoffed. "Safeguards? The only safeguard we need is vigilance."

"Vigilance tempered with justice," Robespierre insisted.

Étienne suppressed a smile. He had sown the seeds; now, he needed only to nurture them. The conversation shifted to logistical matters, but his mind was already racing ahead, contemplating the implications of Robespierre's agreement.

As the meeting adjourned, Étienne approached Robespierre privately. "Maximilien, your commitment to the Republic is admirable. Together, we can ensure its survival."

Robespierre regarded him with a hint of weariness. "I hope you have placed your confidence well, Étienne. These are treacherous waters we navigate."

"Fear not," Étienne assured him. "We are charting a course towards a stronger France."

Leaving the Hôtel de Ville, Étienne felt a chill unrelated to the winter air. Successfully nudging Robespierre towards adopting more extreme measures stirred a disquiet within him. He could see the transformation in Robespierre—the gradual hardening of his ideals, the flicker of zealotry kindled by necessity.

He walked through the winding streets, the gas lamps casting pools of flickering light. The city seemed to hold its breath, teetering between hope and despair. Passing a group of Sans-culottes, he overheard their fervent discussions.

"Robespierre is the incorruptible," one declared. "He will lead us to victory."

"Yes," another agreed. "But we must purge the enemies within."

Étienne quickened his pace. The hunger he had helped ignite was spreading, and an undercurrent of instability came with it. He had intended to use Robespierre as a tool for his ambitions, shaping him to enact the policies Étienne believed necessary. But now he wondered if he had unleashed forces beyond his control.

Arriving at his apartment, he found a letter slipped under the door. Breaking the seal, he recognised the elegant handwriting of Olympe de Gouges.

Étienne,

I fear the path you tread leads only to darkness. The measures being proposed threaten the very fabric of our society. I implore you to reconsider before it is too late.

— Olympe

He crumpled the letter, tossing it onto the table. Her warnings had become tiresome, yet they resonated with the nagging doubt that gnawed at the edges of his conscience.

That evening, he attended a gathering at Madame de Staël's salon. The room was filled with revolution luminaries—philosophers, artists, politicians—all engaged in animated discourse. The atmosphere was lighter here, a stark contrast to the grim deliberations of the Committee.

"Étienne!" Madame de Staël greeted him warmly. "It has been too long."

"Madame," he bowed slightly. "Your gatherings are a balm in these troubled times."

"Come, join us," she beckoned. "We were just discussing the role of virtue in governance."

He found himself seated next to Jacques-Louis David, the renowned painter. David's keen eyes missed little, and he curiously regarded Étienne.

"You seem preoccupied," David observed. "Troubles weighing upon you?"

"Merely the burdens of responsibility," Étienne replied.

"Ah, the eternal struggle between ideals and pragmatism," David mused. "Tell me, do you believe the ends justify the means?"

Étienne hesitated. "In matters of state, one must make tough choices."

David nodded thoughtfully. "But at what cost to one's soul?"

Before Étienne could respond, a hush fell over the room as news arrived—Marat had published another scathing article in *L'Ami du Peuple*, calling for increased purges.

The room buzzed with concern. "This will only incite more violence," someone remarked.

Étienne felt a knot tighten in his stomach. The instability he had helped foster was escalating. Marat's influence among the masses was significant, and his radicalism could push the revolution into chaos.

Leaving the salon, he walked the streets deep in thought. The shadows seemed longer, the alleys darker. He had manipulated events to his advantage, but the unfolding reality was perilous.

Passing the river Seine, he paused on a bridge, gazing at the dark waters below. Reflections of the city lights shimmered on the surface, distorted by the current.

He recalled Rousseau's words, whose philosophies had inspired so much revolutionary thought: "Man is born free, and everywhere he is in chains."

Was he now forging new chains for himself and others? Had his pursuit of power blinded him to the consequences of his actions?

A noise behind him jolted him from his reverie. Turning sharply, he saw only a stray cat darting across the cobblestones. His paranoia was growing, a byproduct of the very instability he had sown.

Returning home, he sat at his desk, the flickering candle casting shadows that danced ominously on the walls. He reached for his journal.

31 January 1793,

I have guided Robespierre towards measures to strengthen the Republic—or so I believed. Yet, a disquiet stirs within me. I see in him a reflection of my magnified and potentially uncontrollable ambitions.

Have I created a force that I cannot even direct? The people's power grows, with it, the risk of descending into anarchy. I must tread carefully, lest I become a casualty of the revolution I seek to shape.

He closed the journal, the weight of his realisations pressing upon him. Sleep would not come quickly this night.

As the city settled into an uneasy slumber, Étienne gazed out into the darkness, caught between ambition and the dawning awareness of the monster he might have unleashed.

In the distance, the bells of Notre Dame tolled midnight, each chime echoing like a sombre reminder of time slipping inexorably forward, carrying him towards an uncertain fate.

CHAPTER SEVEN: (1793-1794)
SHATTERED IDEALS

Étienne Corbeau stood at the window of his modest apartment overlooking the Rue Saint-Honoré, his gaze fixed on the crowds below. Citizens moved frenetically, their faces etched with enthusiasm and fear. Posters emblazoned with revolutionary slogans plastered the walls, while the distant tolling of bells marked the passing of another tumultuous day.

"27 July 1793," Étienne mused aloud, his fingers tracing the chipped paint on the windowsill. The date signified more than just the relentless march of time; it heralded his ascent within the inner sanctum of the revolution. As a critical advisor to the Committee of Public Safety, he now wielded influence that few could fathom. Yet, a gnawing dissatisfaction lingered—a craving for recognition that authority alone could not satiate.

He turned away from the window, the dim light casting long shadows across his cluttered desk. Papers lay strewn about—edicts awaiting approval, lists of suspected counter-revolutionaries, correspondence from various factions jockeying for favour. Among them rested a worn copy of Rousseau's The Social Contract, its pages dog-eared and annotated. Étienne picked it up, flipping through the familiar passages, seeking solace or justification for his path.

A sharp knock at the door interrupted his thoughts. *"Entrez!"* he called out, placing the book aside.

The door creaked open to reveal Louis Antoine de Saint-Just, his youthful face betraying none of the burdens they both shared. Clad in the sombre attire befitting his station, Saint-Just carried an air of icy determination that Étienne found both admirable and unsettling.

"Étienne," Saint-Just greeted him with a curt nod. "The Committee convenes shortly. Robespierre requests your presence."

"Of course," Étienne replied, smoothing the front of his waistcoat. "Is there a specific agenda?"

Saint-Just's eyes flickered with a hint of something unreadable. "Matters of internal security. The Girondins continue to stir dissent from their enclaves. We must address these threats decisively."

"Agreed," Étienne affirmed. "I shall join you momentarily."

As Saint-Just departed, Étienne felt a tightening in his chest. The Committee of Public Safety had become the de facto government, its reach extending into every facet of French society. With near-absolute power, they had the authority to enact laws, oversee the military, and suppress opposition—all in the Republic's name.

Yet, the corridors of power were fraught with peril. Alliances shifted like the winds, and whispers of betrayal lurked in every corner. Étienne knew that his position, though influential, was precarious.

He gathered his notes and donned his hat, stepping out into the sweltering afternoon. The streets were alive with activity—vendors hawking wilted produce, orators extolling the virtues of the revolution, children darting between the crowds, oblivious to the undercurrents of danger.

As he approached the Tuileries Palace, repurposed now as the seat of the revolutionary government, he couldn't help but notice the increased presence of guards. Their stern faces and tightly gripped muskets were a stark reminder of the volatility that simmered beneath the surface.

Inside, the grand hall buzzed with the low hum of urgent conversation. Étienne navigated the labyrinth of officials and deputies, going to the chamber where the Committee assembled. The heavy wooden doors swung open to reveal a room suffused with tension.

Maximilien Robespierre sat at the head of the table, his austere appearance stressed by the starkness of his surroundings. His sharp and penetrating eyes settled on Étienne as he entered.

"Ah, Corbeau," Robespierre intoned. "We were just discussing the latest reports from the Vendée."

Étienne took his seat. "The Royalist insurrections persist?"

"Regrettably," Robespierre confirmed. "Their defiance threatens the very foundation of the Republic."

Georges Danton leaned forward, his robust frame nearly engulfing the table. "Perhaps we should consider a more measured approach. The blade cannot solve every problem."

Jean-Paul Marat scoffed from his corner, his sallow face twisted in disdain. "Danton, your reluctance borders on treason. Mercy is a luxury we cannot afford."

Étienne observed the exchange, sensing an opportunity. "We must balance justice with expedience," he interjected.

Robespierre nodded thoughtfully. "Well said, Corbeau. The Law of Suspects grants us the means. We must employ it judiciously."

Camille Desmoulins, seated beside Danton, shifted uncomfortably. "The Law of Suspects has become a tool of oppression. Mere accusations are sweeping away innocent men and women."

Saint-Just fixed him with an icy stare. "Innocence is a malleable concept in times of revolution. The safety of the nation supersedes individual grievances."

Tension crackled in the air. Étienne could sense the fissures widening between them. "Perhaps," he suggested carefully, "we could establish clearer guidelines to prevent abuses by creating a committee within the Committee, so to speak, that reviews cases before taking action."

Robespierre considered this. "An internal oversight could prove beneficial. It would show our commitment to justice while maintaining security."

Marat bristled. "Bureaucracy will be our downfall. Swift action is essential."

"Swift, but not reckless," Étienne countered. "We must preserve the integrity of the revolution."

Robespierre raised a hand to forestall further argument. "Enough. We shall take Corbeau's proposal under advisement. Now, to the matter of provisioning the army…"

As the meeting progressed, Étienne felt a disquiet settle over him. Realising that he was navigating a treacherous landscape tempered the exhilaration of wielding power. They scrutinised every word and gesture, as potential missteps could prove fatal.

After the session adjourned, he walked alongside Danton and Desmoulins. The oppressive heat had given way to a stifling evening, the air thick with the promise of a storm.

"Your suggestion was prudent," Danton remarked. "Though I suspect it will do little to stem the tide of bloodshed."

"One can hope," Étienne replied. "We must strive to uphold the principles that sparked this revolution."

Desmoulins cast him a sceptical glance. "Principles? Or ambitions?"

Étienne met his gaze evenly. "Are the two mutually exclusive?"

"Perhaps not," Desmoulins conceded. "But ambition unchecked can corrupt even the noblest of causes."

Danton sighed heavily. "We are all caught in a maelstrom of our own making. Caution and courage must walk hand in hand."

They parted ways at a crossroads, the shadows lengthening as twilight descended. Étienne made his way to a small café, seeking respite in solitude. The establishment was nearly empty, save for a few patrons lost in their cups.

He took a seat by the window, ordering a carafe of wine. As he sipped the bitter red, he contemplated the precariousness of his position. He craved recognition—not just the whispered acknowledgements within the Committee, but public acclaim. Yet, he knew that visibility brought risk. The guillotine did not discriminate between the famous and the obscure.

A familiar voice interrupted his reverie. "Étienne, brooding alone? That's unlike you."

He looked up to see Olympe de Gouges standing beside his table, her eyes reflecting curiosity and concern. "Olympe," he greeted her with a faint smile. "What brings you here?"

"I might ask you the same," she replied, taking a seat without invitation. "These are dangerous times to be alone with one's thoughts."

"Sometimes solitude is necessary," he mused. "A chance to reflect."

"Or to hide," she suggested gently.

He raised an eyebrow. "Hide? From what?"

"From the consequences of one's actions," she said pointedly. "I've heard troubling rumours about the Committee's intentions."

He sighed. "Rumours are the currency of fear. We are striving to protect the Republic."

"At what cost?" she pressed. "Liberty cannot thrive under the shadow of terror."

He felt a flicker of irritation. "Idealism is a luxury we can ill afford. Pragmatism must guide us."

"Pragmatism need not trample upon humanity," she countered. "You were once a man of vision. Now, I fear you are becoming a man of expedience."

He looked away, the weight of her words pressing upon him. "You judge me harshly."

"I judge what I see," she said softly. "And I see a man at war with himself."

Silence settled between them, thick and uncomfortable. Finally, she rose. "Take care, Étienne. The path you tread is dangerous."

As she departed, he stared into his wine, the crimson liquid swirling like blood. Her admonitions stirred the unease that had been gnawing at him. The power he wielded was intoxicating yet fraught with danger. He trapped himself in a web of his own making, and each thread dragged him further into the abyss.

Leaving the café, he wandered the streets aimlessly. The surrounding city was restless—dogs barked in the distance, muffled voices drifted from shuttered windows, and a sense of foreboding hung in the air.

Passing by the Place de la Révolution, he gazed upon the guillotine silhouetted against the night sky. The instrument of justice—or was it vengeance? The distinction blurred more each day.

"Étienne Corbeau," he whispered to himself. "Architect of change, or harbinger of destruction?"

The wind picked up, carrying the faint strains of a mournful melody played on a distant violin. He shivered though the night was warm.

As he returned to his apartment, he resolved to tread carefully. Ambition had carried him far, but it could just as quickly be his undoing. Trust was scarce, and allies could become adversaries in the blink of an eye.

"27 July 1793," he reflected as he closed the door behind him. The date marked his rise within the Committee and the tightening noose of suspicion and danger.

He sat at his desk, the flickering candle casting shadows that danced mockingly upon the walls. Reaching for his quill, he wrote the scratch of pen on paper, a slight comfort amidst the uncertainty.

> *Power is a double-edged sword. Wielded without caution, it can turn upon the bearer. I must carefully navigate these treacherous waters, for I do not want the very forces I seek to command to consume me."*

As the night wore on, Étienne pondered the path ahead. The Reign of Terror loomed—a storm of his own inadvertent creation. And in the eye of that storm, he stood alone, grappling with the realisation that the greatest threat might not come from without but from within.

• • •

Étienne sat in his dimly lit office within the Committee of Public Safety, the flickering candlelight casting elongated shadows on the walls cluttered with maps and decrees. Beads of sweat traced lines down his temples as he hunched over a parchment, quill in hand, compiling yet another list of those deemed enemies of the Revolution.

"2 August 1793," he noted absently, the date anchoring him to the gravity of his task. Names flowed from his pen like a river of ink: merchants accused of hoarding grain, aristocrats hiding under assumed identities, even former allies whose loyalties now seemed suspect. Each name was a thread in the intricate web he wove, a tapestry of fate that only he could unravel.

A soft knock at the door disrupted his concentration. *"Entrez,"* he called, not looking up.

Louis Antoine de Saint-Just entered, his youthful face was a mask of stern resolve. Clad in the austere garb of a true revolutionary, his dark eyes surveyed the room before settling on Étienne. "Working tirelessly as ever, I see," he remarked.

Étienne glanced up, a faint smile tugging at the corner of his mouth. "The Revolution waits for no one, *mon ami.* There is much to be done."

Saint-Just approached the desk, his gaze falling upon the list. "Another compilation of the condemned?"

"Those who threaten the Republic," Étienne corrected. "We cannot afford complacency."

Saint-Just nodded thoughtfully. "Agreed. The enemies within are as dangerous as those at our borders. Perhaps more so."

"Precisely why we must act decisively," Étienne affirmed. He leaned back, studying Saint-Just's expression. "I trust you to share my commitment to purge these elements?"

"Without hesitation," Saint-Just replied. "But we must ensure our actions are beyond reproach. The people must see justice, not vengeance."

Étienne arched an eyebrow. "Justice is a matter of perspective. To some, our actions may seem harsh."

"Then we must frame them appropriately," Saint-Just countered. "As necessary measures to preserve liberty."

A silence settled between them, heavy with unspoken understanding. Étienne saw in Saint-Just a kindred spirit who grasped the complexities of wielding power in turbulent times. An alliance with him could prove helpful.

"Perhaps we should collaborate more closely," Étienne suggested. "Our combined efforts could streamline the process."

Saint-Just regarded him for a moment before a faint smile appeared. "I was thinking the same. Together, we can ensure the Revolution stays its course."

"Excellent," Étienne said, feeling a surge of satisfaction. "Shall we meet later to discuss specifics?"

"At dusk," Saint-Just agreed. "I shall bring the latest reports from the provinces."

As Saint-Just departed, Étienne returned to his list, the quill scratching feverishly against the parchment. Yet, a disquiet gnawed at the edges of his mind. He had contributed to constructing the formidable machinery of terror, but could he maintain control over it?

The door swung open again, this time without a knock. Jean-Paul Marat entered, his sallow skin and intense gaze giving him a spectral appearance. "Corbeau," he rasped, "I hear you're compiling lists."

"Information gathering is crucial," Étienne replied evenly.

Marat approached the desk, peering at the names. "You have a talent for identifying traitors."

"I merely observe patterns others overlook."

Marat's eyes flickered with something akin to suspicion. "Be careful, Étienne. In times like these, scrutiny is unavoidable."

"Are you implying something?" Étienne asked, his tone sharpening.

"Only that vigilance applies to all," Marat said cryptically. "Even those within the Committee."

Before Étienne could respond, Marat turned and left as abruptly as he had arrived. Étienne felt a chill despite the oppressive heat. Marat's words echoed ominously in his mind.

He pushed the thought aside, focusing instead on the task at hand. The afternoon wore on, the candle burning low as shadows lengthened. As dusk approached, he gathered his documents and went to a secluded room where he and Saint-Just had agreed to meet.

Saint-Just was already there, poring over a map spread across the table. "Timely as ever," he remarked without looking up.

"Old habits," Étienne replied. "What have you found?"

Saint-Just gestured to the map. "Reports show increased activity among Royalist sympathisers in the south. We need to pre-empt any insurrection."

"Agreed," Étienne said, scanning the marked locations. "We should despatch agents immediately."

"I've already arranged it," Saint-Just informed him. "But we need to address dissent within the Convention as well."

Étienne met his gaze. "You refer to Danton and Desmoulins?"

"They question our methods," Saint-Just said, a hint of irritation in his voice. "Their influence could undermine our efforts."

"Perhaps it's time to curtail their interference," Étienne suggested carefully.

Saint-Just considered this. "An open move against them could fracture the Committee."

"Not if we proceed discreetly," Étienne countered. "Gather evidence of any misdeeds. Present an irrefutable case."

A slow smile spread across Saint-Just's face. "Your pragmatism is refreshing."

They spent the next hour strategising, their plans weaving a complex net to trap any who opposed them. Yet, as they delved deeper into their machinations, Étienne couldn't shake the lingering unease.

Emerging into the night air, he parted ways with Saint-Just. The streets were quieter now, the usual bustle subdued by an unspoken dread that permeated the city. As he walked, he noticed footsteps behind him. Glancing over his shoulder, he saw only fleeting shadows.

"Paranoia," he muttered, quickening his pace. But the feeling persisted. Every rustle of leaves, every distant laugh, seemed laden with menace.

Reaching his apartment, he bolted the door and lit a candle. The warm glow did little to dispel the shadows that clung to the corners. He sat at his desk, but the words on the documents before him blurred.

"Have I set in motion forces beyond my control?" he wondered aloud. The very system of terror he had helped orchestrate was a double-edged sword. Today, he wielded it, but tomorrow, it could turn against him.

A sudden knock startled him, the sound echoing ominously. "Who is it?" he called, instinctively reaching for the letter opener on his desk.

"It's Danton," came the gruff reply.

Reluctantly, Étienne opened the door. Georges Danton filled the doorway, his imposing figure casting a shadow over Étienne.

"May I come in?" Danton asked though he was already stepping inside.

"By all means," Étienne said, masking his irritation.

Danton surveyed the room, his eyes lingering on the scattered papers. "Busy night?"

"Always," Étienne replied. "To what do I owe the pleasure?"

"I thought we should talk," Danton said, his tone unusually serious. "There are concerns about the direction the Revolution is taking."

"Is that so?" Étienne replied coolly. "Whose concerns?"

"Many within the Convention," Danton admitted. "Including myself. The purges intensify, and innocent people are caught in the crossfire."

"In times of upheaval, sacrifices are inevitable," Étienne said dismissively.

Danton's eyes hardened. "Sacrifices? Or are we simply merging power under the guise of justice?"

Étienne met his gaze unflinchingly. "Mind your insinuations, Danton."

"I'm merely voicing what others are too afraid to say," Danton retorted. "We risk becoming tyrants ourselves."

"Perhaps you lack the resolve necessary for these times," Étienne said sharply.

"Or perhaps I still keep my humanity," Danton shot back. "Be careful, Étienne. The same blade you wield can fall upon you."

With that, Danton turned and left, leaving Étienne alone with his racing thoughts. The warning hung in the air, a stark reminder of his position's precariousness.

He sank into his chair, the weight of the day pressing upon him. Allies were becoming adversaries, and trust was a rare commodity. Even his alliance with Saint-Just felt fragile, a partnership built on mutual ambition rather than genuine loyalty.

2 August 1793,

The Revolution devours its own. The machinery of terror I've helped construct moves with a life of its own, indifferent to those who set it in motion. I must tread carefully lest I become trapped in its gears.

He closed the journal, extinguishing the candle. Darkness enveloped the room, mirroring the void growing within him.

As he lay awake, the sounds of the city filtered through the open window—the distant rumble of carts, the occasional shout, the murmur of a populace caught in the throes of uncertainty.

Étienne realised that the path he had chosen was a treacherous one, lined with shadows and echoes of betrayal. Once a beacon of hope, the Revolution had become a labyrinth of fear and ambition.

And in the heart of that labyrinth, he stood alone, realising that the terror he unleashed could very well be his undoing.

• • •

The dawn of 16 October 1793 broke with an eerie stillness over Paris. Étienne stood at the edge of the Place de la Révolution, the chill in the air seeping through his heavy woollen coat. The assemblage of citizens—Sans-culottes, bourgeoisie, and curious onlookers alike—pressed around him, their murmurs a subdued cacophony beneath the leaden sky.

"16 October 1793," Étienne whispered to himself, the date echoing in his mind with a weight he couldn't quite articulate. The guillotine loomed ahead, its silhouette stark against the grey morning. Today, Marie Antoinette, the former queen, would meet her fate—a culmination of the Revolution's relentless march towards egalitarianism or perhaps its descent into unbridled brutality.

Beside him, Louis Antoine de Saint-Just stood with customary stoicism, his sharp features betraying nothing of his inner thoughts. "The crowd is restless," he remarked, his voice barely audible above the ambient noise.

"They sense the gravity of the moment," Étienne replied, his eyes fixed on the distant platform where the executioner prepared his instruments with methodical precision.

Saint-Just glanced at him sidelong. "Do you harbour any reservations about today?"

Étienne hesitated. "Reservations? No." Étienne hesitated and said, "We must safeguard the Republic."

"Indeed," Saint-Just agreed, though a flicker of something—doubt, perhaps—passed across his face before it hardened once more into resolve.

The sound of trundling wheels drew their attention as a crude cart emerged from the Rue Saint-Honoré, escorted by armed guards. Marie Antoinette sat within, her once-regal bearing diminished but not extinguished. Clad in a simple white chemise, her hair shorn and greying, she gazed ahead with a composed demeanour that belied the disgrace of her circumstances.

The crowd surged forward, a mix of jeers and silent scrutiny. Étienne felt a knot tighten in his stomach. He had witnessed countless executions, each one a testament to the Revolution's unyielding pursuit of justice—or vengeance. Yet today felt different, an unease gnawing at the edges of his consciousness.

"She maintains her dignity," observed Maximilien Robespierre, who had joined them unnoticed. His pale complexion appeared almost translucent in the diffused light.

"Dignity," Saint-Just scoffed softly. "A last act of defiance, perhaps."

Étienne studied Robespierre's profile, noting the tension in his clenched jaw. "Do you believe this is necessary, Maximilien?"

Robespierre's eyes remained fixed on the procession. "Necessity is a construct we invoke to justify our actions. The people demand justice."

"Justice," Étienne echoed, tasting bitter on his tongue.

A hush fell over the crowd as Marie Antoinette ascended the steps to the scaffold. The executioner, Sanson, guided her to the plank, his movements practised and devoid of ceremony. She attempted to step around his foot and stumbled slightly.

"Pardonnez-moi, monsieur," she murmured, her voice carrying across the silent square.

Étienne felt a chill that had nothing to do with the autumn air. Her simple apology, a vestige of courtly manners, struck a discordant note amidst the stark reality of her impending death.

The blade fell swiftly, a flash of steel followed by the dull thud signalling the end. A collective exhalation rippled through the crowd—some cheered, others remained silent. Étienne stood immobile, a hollow sensation settling in his chest.

"Another enemy of the Republic vanquished," Saint-Just declared, turning away.

Robespierre lingered a moment longer before nodding curtly. "We should return to the Convention. There is much to discuss."

As they moved away from the square, Étienne struggled to articulate the disquiet that plagued him. The execution should have been a triumph, reaffirming the Revolution's ideals. Instead, it felt like a nadir, a point from which there might be no return.

"Does this not sit well with you?" came a voice to his left.

He turned to see Olympe de Gouges matching his stride, her eyes searching his face. "Olympe. I hadn't expected to see you here."

"I could say the same," she replied. "Though I suppose your presence is more requisite than mine."

He attempted a wry smile. "Duty calls."

"At what cost, Étienne?" she pressed gently. "The line between justice and cruelty blurs more each day."

He glanced ahead to ensure Robespierre and Saint-Just were out of earshot. "The Revolution demands sacrifices."

"An oft-repeated refrain," she sighed. "Tell me, when does the ledger balance? How many more must perish before we deem the Republic secure?"

He hesitated. "I don't have that answer."

"Maybe it's time for you to seek it," she suggested, "before the bloodshed causes us to lose the very ideals we fought for."

He watched as she disappeared into the crowd, her words resonating uncomfortably. The streets seemed narrower, the buildings looming oppressively as they returned to the Convention.

Inside the austere halls, the atmosphere was taut. Deputies spoke in hushed tones, casting wary glances at one another. Étienne saw that Saint-Just was already absorbed in a stack of documents when he sat beside him.

"Plans for the new Tribunal," Saint-Just explained without looking up. "We aim to expedite proceedings against those accused of counter-revolutionary activities."

"Efficiency is commendable," Étienne remarked, though his mind was elsewhere.

Robespierre addressed the assembly, his voice measured but infused with an undercurrent of urgency. "*Citoyens,* the events of today mark a significant juncture. We must remain vigilant. The enemies of the Republic are relentless, both within and beyond our borders."

Georges Danton stood, his imposing figure commanding attention. "While I share concerns for our nation's security, we must temper justice with mercy. The guillotine cannot be our sole instrument of policy."

Murmurs of agreement and dissent rippled through the chamber. Étienne noted the narrowing of Saint-Just's eyes, a telltale sign of his growing impatience.

"Mercy is a noble concept," Saint-Just retorted, rising to his feet. "But naivety can be fatal. The Republic's survival hinges on our resolve to eliminate threats decisively."

Danton's gaze hardened. "Resolve should not equate to tyranny, *Monsieur Saint-Just.*"

Before tensions could escalate further, Robespierre intervened. "Let us not fracture over semantics. Our collective aim is the Republic's preservation."

The session continued, but Étienne found it increasingly difficult to focus. Images of the execution replayed in his mind—the swift descent of the blade, the finality of it all. Was this the justice they had envisioned? Or had the Revolution spiralled into something unrecognisable?

After the assembly adjourned, he sought refuge of his office. The familiar scent of parchment and ink offered scant comfort. He sank into his chair, absently fingering a letter opener.

A soft knock interrupted his solitude. "Come in," he called.

Camille Desmoulins entered cautiously. "Am I disturbing you?"

"Not at all," Étienne gestured for him to sit. "What brings you here?"

Desmoulins settled into the chair opposite. "I wanted to discuss the increasing severity of our measures. We're growing concerned that we've lost sight of our original purpose."

Étienne studied him. "And what do you believe our original purpose was?"

"Liberté, égalité, fraternité," Desmoulins replied without hesitation. "Not a perpetual cycle of executions."

"Strong actions are sometimes necessary to uphold those ideals," Étienne countered.

Desmoulins leaned forward. "But when do strong actions become oppressive? When do we become the very tyrants we overthrew?"

Étienne felt a surge of irritation but also a pang of doubt. "What would you propose?"

"A reassessment," Desmoulins said earnestly. "A return to due process, to reasoned debate rather than swift condemnation."

"You're treading on dangerous ground," Étienne warned softly. "Misunderstandings could arise from such sentiments," Étienne warned softly.

Desmoulins met his gaze steadily. "Perhaps they need to be heard, regardless of the risk."

Before Étienne could respond, Desmoulins rose and departed, leaving a heavy silence in his wake.

Alone once more, Étienne contemplated the shifting sands beneath his feet. The machinery of the Revolution had become a juggernaut, its momentum seemingly beyond control. He had played no small part in its acceleration, but now he questioned whether he could—or should—attempt to slow it.

A sudden weariness enveloped him. He retrieved a quill and parchment to organise his thoughts, but the words eluded him. Instead, he sketched aimless lines, the ink forming dark pools on the page.

16 October 1793,

Today, the execution of Marie Antoinette has stirred a disquiet I cannot ignore. The Revolution's path grows ever more treacherous, its ideals overshadowed by an insatiable appetite for retribution.

A knock at the door startled him. Expecting another visitor, he called out, "Yes?"

To his surprise, Jacques-Louis David entered, his artist's portfolio tucked under one arm. "Étienne, I hope I'm not intruding."

"Not at all," Étienne replied, gesturing for him to sit. "What brings you here?"

David placed his portfolio on the desk, opening it to reveal sketches of the day's events. "I thought you might find these of interest."

Étienne examined the drawings—stark, evocative renderings of the execution. "They're powerful," he acknowledged. "You capture the essence of the moment."

David nodded. "But to what end? Art should inspire, not merely document atrocity."

"Perhaps it can serve as a mirror," Étienne suggested. "Reflecting society back upon itself."

"Or as a warning," David countered. "That we risk losing our humanity."

Étienne met his gaze. "Do you believe we're beyond redemption?"

"Not yet," David said quietly. "But the edge grows ever closer."

They sat in contemplative silence before David gathered his sketches. "I won't keep you longer. Thank you for your time."

After David left, Étienne felt an overwhelming sense of isolation. The walls of his office seemed to close in, the air heavy and stifling.

He stood abruptly, needing to escape the confines. Stepping out into the corridor, he nearly collided with Robespierre.

"Étienne," Robespierre greeted him, a hint of surprise in his eyes. "I was just coming to see you."

"Is something amiss?" Étienne asked.

"Not at all," Robespierre assured him. "I wanted to discuss the upcoming proposals for the Tribunal."

"Of course," Étienne replied, though his enthusiasm felt forced.

They walked together, but their usual camaraderie felt strained. Robespierre seemed preoccupied, his gaze distant.

"Maximilien," Étienne ventured, "do you ever question the path we've taken?"

Robespierre paused, regarding him thoughtfully. "Doubts are a natural companion to responsibility. But we must remain steadfast."

"At the expense of our conscience?" Étienne pressed.

Robespierre's eyes narrowed slightly. "Conscience must align with duty. Personal misgivings cannot hinder the Republic's progress."

Étienne nodded slowly. "I see."

"Is there something you wish to convey?" Robespierre asked pointedly.

"No," Étienne lied. "Merely seeking clarity."

"Very well," Robespierre replied, though a note of suspicion lingered in his tone. "We shall discuss the proposals tomorrow."

As Robespierre departed, Étienne felt a chill run through him. Their unspoken undercurrents hinted at a widening rift that could have dire consequences.

Returning to his quarters, he realised that the Revolution had become an entity unto itself—voracious, unyielding, and indifferent to the ideals that had birthed it. The guillotine's shadow loomed large, and none was beyond its reach.

"Unchecked power," he mused aloud. "A force that consumes all in its path."

He sank into a chair, the weight of his realisations pressing upon him. The path ahead was perilous, and he stood at a crossroads.

As night enveloped Paris, Étienne grappled with the inescapable truth: the Revolution he had helped forge was now a storm threatening to engulf him.

• • •

The bleak morning of 31 October 1793 cast a pall over Paris, shrouded in a mist that clung to the narrow alleyways like a spectre. Étienne Corbeau stood by the window of his modest apartment, gazing out at the labyrinth of rooftops. The distant tolling of a church bell echoed through the damp air, a sombre reminder of the gravity of the times.

"31 October 1793," he murmured, the date imprinting itself upon his consciousness. The Revolution had entered a new phase where allegiances shifted like sand, and trust was a currency in short supply. He felt the weight of his machinations pressing upon him—a spider trapped in his own web.

A sharp rap on the door jolted him from his reverie. *"Entrez,"* he called, turning to face his visitor.

Louis Antoine de Saint-Just stepped inside, his youthful features hardened by their shared burdens. Clad in austere black, his piercing eyes held a cold intensity. Without preamble, he announced, "The Committee has summoned us." "Robespierre wishes to discuss matters of utmost importance."

Étienne nodded, slipping on his coat. "Then we should not keep him waiting."

As they walked through the damp streets towards the Tuileries, Étienne sensed an unspoken tension between them. "The air is thick with rumours," he ventured. "Whispers of dissent within our ranks."

Saint-Just's jaw tightened. "Danton grows increasingly troublesome. His calls for moderation undermine our efforts."

"Indeed," Étienne agreed. "He has become a liability—a potential threat to our foundations."

Saint-Just glanced at him sharply. "You speak of treason."

"I speak of necessity," Étienne replied coolly. "The Republic cannot afford half-measures."

They arrived at the grand chambers of the Committee of Public Safety, the atmosphere inside as oppressive as the weather outside. Maximilien Robespierre sat at the head of the table, his pale complexion and steely gaze exuding an aura of unassailable authority. Around him, the other members settled into their seats—some anxious, others inscrutable.

Robespierre began without ceremony. *"Citoyens,"* the Revolution faces threats from foreign enemies and from within. Some would steer us from our course, questioning the measures that ensure our survival."

Georges Danton leaned back in his chair, his robust frame radiating a confidence that bordered on arrogance. "If by '*those*' you mean me, Maximilien, then let us dispense with veiled accusations."

Robespierre's eyes flickered. "If the shoe fits, Danton."

A murmur rippled through the assembly. Étienne examined the exchange, sensing an opportunity. "Perhaps," he interjected, "we should consider the impact of dissenting voices on our unity. The people look to us for decisive leadership."

Danton fixed him with a piercing stare. "And what would you suggest, Corbeau? Silence all who dare to offer a differing perspective?"

"Not silence," Étienne replied evenly. "But responsibility. In times of crisis, discord can be as lethal as any blade."

Camille Desmoulins shifted uncomfortably beside Danton. "Surely, open debate strengthens our cause rather than weakens it."

Saint-Just's voice cut through the air like a knife. "Debate is a luxury we can ill afford when the Republic hangs in the balance."

Danton slammed his palm on the table. "This is madness! We've become a tribunal of tyrants!"

Robespierre's expression hardened as he said, "Mind your tongue, Danton. We do not take accusations of tyranny lightly."

Étienne sensed the moment sowed the seeds of doubt. "Perhaps we should investigate any activities that might compromise our objectives. For the good of the Republic."

Danton's eyes narrowed. "Is that a threat, Corbeau?"

"A precaution," Étienne replied. "If your conscience is clear, you have nothing to fear."

The tension in the room was palpable. Robespierre glanced between them before addressing the assembly. "We shall adjourn for now. Reflect upon your duties to the Republic."

As the members dispersed, Étienne caught Robespierre's arm. "Maximilien, a word?"

Robespierre regarded him with a measured gaze. "What troubles you, Étienne?"

"Danton's rhetoric grows increasingly volatile," Étienne began. "I fear he may incite division when we must stand united."

Robespierre sighed. "Danton is… passionate. But he has been a stalwart of the Revolution."

"Passion unchecked can lead to recklessness," Étienne pressed. "I believe he is engaging in clandestine meetings, possibly undermining our efforts."

Robespierre's eyes sharpened. "Do you have proof?"

"Not yet," Étienne admitted. "But I can get it. For the sake of transparency."

Robespierre hesitated before nodding slowly. "Very well. Discreetly, Étienne. We cannot afford unfounded allegations."

"Of course," Étienne assured him.

Leaving the Committee chambers, Étienne felt a mix of triumph and trepidation. Manipulating Robespierre was delicate; the man was wise, and any misstep could be disastrous.

A familiar figure approached him as he stepped out into the fading light of day. Olympe de Gouges stood beneath a lamppost, her eyes reflecting concern. "Étienne, may we speak?"

He inclined his head. "Always a pleasure, Olympe."

She fell into step beside him. "I couldn't help but notice the growing animosity between you and Danton."

"Differences of opinion," he replied dismissively.

"Is that all?" she queried. "Or is there more at play?"

He glanced at her, weighing his words. "The Revolution demands tough choices."

"Be careful, Étienne," she warned softly. "In seeking to eliminate threats, you may become one yourself."

He offered a thin smile. "I appreciate your concern, but I assure you, my actions serve the greater good."

"Just remember," she said, "you can easily cross the line between justice and vengeance."

She departed, leaving him with her cautionary words echoing in his mind. Étienne shook off the unease and went to a discreet tavern on the Rue du Temple.

Inside, the dimly lit establishment buzzed with low conversations. He spotted a man seated alone in a corner—Antoine, a Sans-culotte with connections to Paris's underbelly.

"Antoine," Étienne greeted him, sliding into the opposite seat. "I have a task for you."

Antoine's eyes gleamed with interest. "Always at your service, *citoyen.*"

"I need information on Danton," Étienne stated. "His associates, his movements—anything that could be significant."

Antoine nodded slowly. "Danton, eh? That's a dangerous game."

"Are you unwilling?" Étienne challenged.

"For the right price, I'm willing to risk much," Antoine replied with a sly grin.

They negotiated terms before Étienne left, stepping back into the night. The streets were quieter now, the usual bustle subdued. He felt the weight of his actions settling upon him, a gnawing doubt taking root.

Returning home, he found a letter slipped under his door. Breaking the seal, he recognised the elegant script of Camille Desmoulins.

Étienne,

We need to talk. Urgently.

— Camille

Étienne sighed, crumpling the note in his fist. Desmoulins' interference was an unwelcome complication. He resolved to deal with it in due course.

The following day, 1 November 1793, dawned with a biting chill. Étienne made his way to the Committee's meeting room, the atmosphere fraught with unspoken tensions.

Robespierre was already present, deep in conversation with Saint-Just. They paused as Étienne approached.

"Good morning," Étienne offered.

"Étienne," Robespierre acknowledged. "We were discussing recent developments."

Saint-Just fixed him with a mysterious gaze. "Rumours circulate about Danton's activities."

"Indeed," Étienne replied. "I have gathered some information that may be pertinent."

"Let us hear it," Robespierre prompted.

Before Étienne could proceed, the doors swung open, and Danton strode in, his presence commanding the room. "I trust I'm not interrupting?"

"Not at all," Robespierre said coolly.

Danton's eyes flicked between them. "I sense a chill in the air. Perhaps we should clear it."

"Transparency is always advisable," Étienne remarked.

Danton smirked. "Then, by all means, lay your cards on the table."

Étienne hesitated. The confrontation was unfolding sooner than expected. "There are concerns regarding your recent engagements."

"Concerns?" Danton echoed. "Or accusations?"

"Call them what you will," Saint-Just interjected. "The Republic cannot tolerate subversion."

Danton's demeanour shifted, a steely edge entering his voice. "I have given everything to this cause. Those who manipulate from the shadows will not judge me."

"Enough," Robespierre commanded. "This discord serves no one. Danton, an inquiry will exonerate you if there is nothing to hide."

Danton glared at them. "Very well. Let the Committee do as it must. But remember, the guillotine has a voracious appetite."

He stormed out, leaving a heavy silence in his wake.

Robespierre turned to Étienne. "Ensure that the investigation is thorough and impartial."

"Of course," Étienne agreed, though he sensed that someone had already compromised impartiality.

As the day wore on, the ramifications of his actions crystallised. The inner circle was fracturing, suspicions festering like an open wound. Étienne found himself increasingly isolated, his alliances tenuous at best.

That evening, he met with Antoine in a secluded alley. The information provided was damning—meetings with suspected Royalists, financial discrepancies, whispers of conspiracy.

"This will suffice," Étienne said, handing over a pouch of coins.

"Be careful," Antoine warned. "Danton is a formidable man."

"I can handle him," Étienne replied curtly.

Returning home, he felt a hollow victory settling within him. The elimination of Danton would remove a rival, but at what cost? The Revolution was devouring itself, and he was complicit in the feast.

He sat at his desk, penning a report to present to Robespierre. Each word felt like a nail in a coffin—not just for Danton, but perhaps for himself as well.

1 November 1793,

The path we tread grows ever narrower, bordered by the abyss on either side. Trust erodes, and the shadows lengthen. I have started irreversible events.

As he sealed the document, a profound weariness overcame him. The toll of his machinations weighed heavily, the spectre of retribution looming ever closer.

He gazed out the window at the darkened streets of Paris, the city's heartbeat a distant echo. The Revolution had become a maze of mirrors, each reflection more distorted than the last.

And in the centre stood Étienne Corbeau—a man trapped by his ambitions, the architect of his potential downfall.

• • •

On December 7, 1793, the chill of Paris cut through the narrow streets like an unseen blade. Étienne Corbeau pulled his cloak tighter around his shoulders as he navigated the labyrinthine alleys of the Marais district. The city had transformed into a landscape of shadows and whispers, the once-vibrant heart of the Revolution now beating with a frantic, fearful pulse.

As he passed shuttered windows and bolted doors, Étienne could not ignore the palpable tension in the air. Conversations ceased as he approached; wary eyes peered from behind curtains before vanishing into darkness. People no longer wore the tricolour cockades with pride; instead, they seemed to use them as talismans against an unseen enemy.

The Reign of Terror was no longer an abstract concept discussed in the hallowed halls of the Committee of Public Safety; it was a living force that stalked the streets, leaving a trail of dread in its wake.

He reached the Place de la Révolution, where the guillotine stood as a grim sentinel against the grey winter sky. The square was eerily quiet, devoid of the crowds that had once gathered to witness the latest execution. Even the ever-present Sans-culottes were scarce, their enthusiasm dampened by the relentless tide of bloodshed.

Étienne approached a small group huddled near a vendor's cart, their faces etched with fatigue and suspicion. *"Bonsoir,"* he offered, attempting a cordial tone.

The men exchanged glances before one replied cautiously, *"Bonsoir, citoyen."*

"News from the front?" Étienne inquired, gesturing vaguely to suggest he was merely a concerned citizen.

The man shrugged. "Rumours abound, but who can say what is true these days?"

Another muttered, "Best to keep one's head down and avoid attention."

Étienne felt a pang of unease. "Surely, as patriots, we must remain informed."

The first man eyed him warily. "Information can be a dangerous commodity."

Sensing he would glean nothing further, Étienne nodded politely and moved on. Their guarded demeanour was emblematic of a populace gripped by fear—a fear he had helped instill. The realisation gnawed at him like a persistent rat on the walls of his conscience.

Making his way to the Café Procope, he hoped to find some semblance of normalcy within its familiar confines. The warm glow of candlelight spilt onto the cobblestone street, offering a brief respite from the cold. Inside, the atmosphere was subdued, conversations hushed and tinged with anxiety.

He spotted Camille Desmoulins seated alone at a corner table, his usually vibrant countenance dulled by exhaustion. Étienne hesitated before approaching. "May I join you?"

Desmoulins glanced up, surprise flickering across his features before he gestured to the empty chair. "By all means."

They sat silently for a moment, the weight of unspoken words hanging heavily between them. Finally, Étienne ventured, "The city feels different."

Desmoulins sighed. "The air is thick with fear. Neighbours turn on one another; friends become strangers. This is not the France we envisioned."

Étienne studied his companion's face, noting the lines etched by worry. "Change is seldom without cost."

"Cost?" Desmoulins echoed bitterly. "We have mortgaged our souls for the illusion of security. The guillotine claims more lives each day, and for what? To satiate the insatiable?"

"You speak dangerously," Étienne cautioned.

Desmoulins met his gaze unflinchingly. "Perhaps danger is the only language left to us. I have written a new pamphlet—*Le Vieux Cordelier*. It calls for an end to the Terror."

Étienne felt a jolt of alarm. "They could interpret such sentiments as counter-revolutionary."

"Only by those who benefit from the perpetuation of fear," Desmoulins retorted. "I will not stand idly by as our nation devours itself."

Before Étienne could respond, the café door swung open, admitting a gust of cold air and Louis Antoine de Saint-Just. His eyes scanned the room, narrowing as they settled upon the two men. He approached with purposeful strides.

"Camille, Étienne," he greeted curtly. "A cosy meeting."

Desmoulins offered a strained smile. "Merely sharing thoughts between old friends."

"Thoughts best kept discreet," Saint-Just replied, his gaze lingering pointedly on Desmoulins.

Étienne intervened. "We were discussing the morale of the people. There is concern that the constant vigilance may be—"

"Necessary," Saint-Just interrupted. "Vigilance is the bulwark of the Revolution."

Desmoulins stood abruptly. "If you'll excuse me, I have matters to attend to."

As he departed, Saint-Just took his vacated seat. "He grows reckless," he observed.

Étienne sighed. "He is passionate. Perhaps we can guide his energies more productively."

"Compassion is a weakness we cannot afford," Saint-Just declared. "Robespierre shares my concerns."

Étienne felt a chill that had nothing to do with the weather. "What are you implying?"

"That measures may need to be taken," Saint-Just said evenly. "For the greater good."

An uncomfortable silence settled between them. Finally, Étienne said, "We must be cautious not to alienate those who have been steadfast allies."

"Allies can become adversaries overnight," Saint-Just replied, rising to leave. "Remember that, Étienne."

Left alone, Étienne stared into his untouched cup of coffee, the dark liquid reflecting his troubled visage. The Revolution had become an Ouroboros, consuming itself in an endless cycle of suspicion and retribution. He could no longer ignore his role in shaping this grim reality.

Stepping back into the street, he wandered aimlessly, his thoughts a tumultuous whirl. The grand ideals that had once ignited his soul now seemed distant, obscured by the fog of paranoia that enshrouded the city. He recalled Rousseau's words: "Man is born free, and everywhere he is in chains." How cruelly ironic that the chains now were of their forging.

As he crossed the Pont Neuf, he gazed upon the Seine, its dark waters flowing inexorably towards an unseen horizon. The river seemed a fitting metaphor for the Revolution—unstoppable, indifferent, capable of both sustaining life and sweeping it away.

"Étienne."

He turned to find Olympe de Gouges approaching, her features illuminated by the flickering lamplight. "Olympe," he acknowledged, managing a faint smile.

"You seem lost in thought," she observed.

"These are contemplative times," he replied.

She joined him at the railing. "The people are afraid. Even the bravest whisper in hushed tones."

"I've noticed," he admitted. "It's as though the entire city holds its breath, waiting for an inevitable calamity."

She regarded him thoughtfully. "And what of you? Do you feel the encroaching danger?"

He hesitated before answering. "I am not immune to the atmosphere."

"Nor should you be," she said gently. "You have influence, Étienne. Perhaps it's time to use it to temper the flames rather than fan them."

He sighed. "I fear it may be too late for that."

"It's never too late to act with integrity," she insisted. "The Terror cannot sustain itself indefinitely. It will either consume everything or collapse under its weight."

He looked away. "I have started certain events that cannot be easily reversed."

"Then perhaps it's time to chart a fresh course," she urged. "Before the tide turns irrevocably against you."

Her words resonated with the doubts that had been gnawing at him. "I will consider what you've said."

"See that you do," she replied, her tone softening. "For all our sakes."

As she walked away, Étienne remained by the river, the cold seeping into his bones. He thought of the countless lives altered or extinguished by the machinery of fear he had helped construct. The Revolution had promised liberty and equality yet had delivered a different tyranny.

Making his way back to his lodgings, he noticed posters plastered on the walls—lists of names marked for arrest and slogans exhorting citizens to report any suspicious activity. Children played in the shadows, their laughter tinged with a nervous edge. Even the street vendors conducted their business with furtive glances over their shoulders.

He entered his apartment and lit a candle, the small flame casting elongated shadows that danced along the walls. Sitting at his desk, he opened a journal and wrote.

7 December 1793,

Fear has become the currency of our society, exchanged at every glance and whispered conversation. I cannot escape the reality that I have been both an architect and a captive of this climate. A relentless pursuit of security—a security that eludes us still has eclipsed the ideals we once cherished.

I see now that the Terror is not a means to an end but has become an end in itself. It perpetuates because it feeds on the very fear it creates. And I, in my ambition and blindness, have been complicit in unleashing this force upon the world.

What remains to be done? Can one man alter the course of such a formidable tide? Or is redemption a folly reserved for the naïve?

A knock at the door startled him. "Who is it?" he called out.

"Jacques-Louis David," came the reply. "May I come in?"

Étienne opened the door to admit the artist, who carried a portfolio under his arm. "To what do I owe this visit?"

"I wanted to share something with you," David said, unrolling a sketch on the table. It depicted a figure standing alone amidst a storm, the winds tearing at his clothes as he faced an indistinct but menacing shape.

"It's powerful," Étienne remarked. "What does it represent?"

"Isolation," David explained. "The plight of those who, willingly or not, find themselves at odds with the forces they've helped unleash."

Étienne met his gaze. "An apt metaphor."

David nodded. "I thought you might appreciate it."

"Is this a warning?" Étienne asked.

"Perhaps," David replied. "Or perhaps merely an observation. Art reflects life, after all."

They stood in silence, the weight of unspoken truths hanging between them. Finally, David rolled up the sketch. "I should be going."

"Thank you for sharing this," Étienne said.

As the door closed behind the artist, Étienne felt a profound sense of isolation. The walls of his world were closing in, and avenues that once seemed clear were now fraught with peril.

He returned to his journal, adding a final line:

The shadows lengthen, and I must decide whether to step into the light or allow myself to be consumed by the darkness I have helped create.

Extinguishing the candle, he sat in the enveloping gloom, the distant sounds of the restless city filtering through the night. Sleep eluded him as the enormity of his situation pressed down like a suffocating shroud.

The Reign of Terror had taken on a life of its own, and Étienne Corbeau found himself trapped within the very nightmare he had woven—a man haunted by the echoes of his choices, standing at the precipice of an uncertain fate.

• • •

On the morning of March 30, 1794, a sharp wind cut through the streets of Paris. Étienne stood at the window of his apartment overlooking the Rue Saint-Honoré, watching as the city stirred to life beneath a sky the colour of tarnished silver. The distant tolling of church bells marked the hour, each chime resonating with a foreboding that settled heavily in his chest.

A knock at his door shattered the stillness. *"Entrez,"* Étienne called out, turning to face his visitor.

Louis Antoine de Saint-Just entered, his sharp features etched with a grim resolve. Clad in the austere attire befitting a Committee of Public Safety member, his presence carried the weight of authority. "Étienne," he began without preamble, "the Committee convenes within the hour. Your attendance is required."

Étienne studied him for a moment. "Is there a particular matter of urgency?"

Saint-Just's gaze was unreadable. "We will provide you with information in due course."

With a curt nod, he departed, leaving Étienne with a gnawing sense of unease. The cryptic summons boded ill, and he couldn't shake the feeling that something monumental was about to unfold.

He dressed quickly, donning his coat and tricolour sash, the fabric feeling heavier than usual upon his shoulders. As he stepped into the bustling street, the cacophony of daily life did little to dispel the shadows lurking at the edges of his mind. Vendors called out half-heartedly, their voices subdued; citizens moved hurriedly, eyes cast downward.

The journey to the Tuileries repurposed as the seat of the revolutionary government was familiar, yet today, each footfall seemed laden with warning. The grand hall greeted him with an atmosphere as tense as a drawn bowstring. Deputies clustered in tight knots, their murmured conversations halting abruptly as he passed.

Maximilien Robespierre stood at the head of the assembly chamber, his pallid complexion and austere expression rendering him almost statuesque. His eyes flicked towards Étienne, offering no hint of acknowledgement or welcome.

Taking his seat, Étienne glanced around the room. Georges Danton was conspicuously absent, as was Camille Desmoulins. An icy tendril of dread coiled within him.

Robespierre's voice cut through the murmur like a knife. "*Citoyens*, we gather today to address matters of grave importance concerning the security of the Republic."

A hush descended as all eyes turned towards Saint-Just. He stepped forward, holding a parchment tightly in his grasp.

"Evidence lights," Saint-Just declared, "implicating certain individuals in activities counter to the interests of the Revolution."

A ripple of unease swept through the chamber. Étienne felt his pulse quicken, a cold sweat forming at his temples.

"Georges Danton and Camille Desmoulins stand accused of conspiracy and corruption," Saint-Just continued. "Their actions threaten to undermine all we have striven to achieve."

A murmur of shock and disbelief erupted. Étienne's gaze darted to Robespierre, whose expression remained impassive.

"I have ordered arrests," Robespierre announced. "Justice will be served."

Étienne's throat constricted. He recalled his own role in sowing seeds of doubt against Danton, manipulating events to sideline a rival. Yet now, witnessing the culmination of those machinations, an unsettling ambivalence struck Étienne.

The session adjourned amidst a flurry of agitation. As the deputies dispersed, Étienne made his way towards Robespierre. "Maximilien," he began cautiously, "may I have a word?"

Robespierre regarded him coolly. "Is there something you wish to discuss, Étienne?"

He hesitated. "Danton's arrest… it seems a drastic measure. Are we certain of his guilt?"

A flicker of irritation crossed Robespierre's features. "The evidence is compelling. We cannot afford hesitation."

"Of course," Étienne conceded. "I merely question whether this course strengthens or fractures our unity."

"Tolerating treachery will not preserve unity," Robespierre replied sharply. "Remember where your loyalties lie."

Étienne inclined his head. "As always, to the Republic."

Robespierre held his gaze for a moment longer before turning away, leaving Étienne with a profound sense of isolation.

Exiting the Tuileries, he meandered through the streets, the cityscape a blur of greys and muted colours. Danton's arrest resonated deeply, stirring a disquiet that unsettled the foundations of his convictions.

Approaching the Place de la Révolution, a gathering crowd drew him. At the centre stood a line of carts flanked by soldiers—the grim procession of the condemned. His heart clenched as he recognised Danton among them, his formidable presence undiminished even in chains.

Their eyes met across the distance. For a fleeting moment, Étienne saw a flicker of recognition, perhaps even accusation, in Danton's gaze. Then the moment passed as the carts lurched forward, bearing their human cargo towards the inevitable.

"Étienne."

He turned to find Olympe de Gouges at his side, her expression a mirror of his turmoil. "You heard," he said hollowly.

"All of Paris has heard," she replied. "This is a turning point from which we may not return."

He swallowed hard. "Danton… he was a pillar of the Revolution."

"And now they abandoned him," she said bitterly. "No one is safe, don't you see? The very mechanisms we've built now consume indiscriminately."

Étienne looked away. "I never intended for this."

"Intentions matter little when the consequences are so dire," she admonished gently. "You must take care, Étienne. The tide turns swiftly."

He met her gaze. "What would you have me do?"

"Speak out," she urged. "Use your influence to stem this madness before it engulfs us all."

He shook his head. "It's not that simple. To oppose the Committee is to invite suspicion upon oneself."

"Then perhaps courage is required," she challenged. "Or will you wait until the noose tightens around your neck?"

Her words struck deep. As she walked away, he grappled with the stark reality of his situation. The fortress of power he had helped construct now resembled a prison, its walls closing in with each passing day.

Later, he found himself at the Café Procope, seeking solace in its familiar confines. The usual patrons were absent, and the atmosphere subdued. He spotted Jacques-Louis David seated alone, sketching absently on a scrap of parchment.

"Mind if I join you?" Étienne asked.

David gestured to the empty chair. "By all means."

They sat in companionable silence for a while before David spoke. "These are dark times."

"Indeed," Étienne agreed. "The fabric of the Revolution unravels."

David sighed. "I once believed art could capture the essence of this grand upheaval—a testament to our ideals. Now, I fear it merely chronicles our descent."

Étienne studied the artist's weary features. "Do you think we've lost our way?"

"I think," David replied slowly, "that the path has become obscured by shadows of our own making."

They lapsed into silence once more. Étienne nursed his drink, the liquid offering little warmth against the chill settling within him.

As evening fell, the city quieted down, and the streets emptied. Passing a news kiosk, he saw posters bearing Danton's likeness, denouncing him as a traitor. The swiftness with which the tide had turned was staggering.

Entering his abode, he lit a single candle, its feeble glow casting elongated shadows that seemed to mock him. He sat at his desk, quill in hand, but the words would not come. The journal before him remained blank, an empty canvas reflecting his inner void.

30 March 1794,

Today, I witnessed the unravelling of what remnants of certainty I had held. Danton's arrest signals more than the fall of a comrade; it heralds the dissolution of any illusion of safety. The mechanisms of fear and suspicion operate with a momentum all their own, indifferent to the hands that set them in motion.

I stand on a precipice, isolated and uncertain. The structures I've helped build now cast a shadow that threatens to envelop me. Trust is a scarce commodity, and I question those around me and the fabric of my beliefs.

No one is safe. Not even I.

He set down the quill, a heavy sigh escaping his lips. The walls of his apartment seemed to close in, the air thick and suffocating.

A sudden knock at the door jolted him. His pulse quickened. "Who is it?" he called, striving to steady his voice.

"Maximilien," came the reply.

Étienne hesitated before opening the door. Robespierre stood on the threshold, his expression inscrutable. "May I come in?"

"Of course," Étienne stepped aside.

Robespierre entered, his gaze sweeping the room. "I wanted to speak with you privately."

"About?"

"Danton's associates are under scrutiny," Robespierre stated. "Given your previous interactions, I thought it prudent to discuss any… pertinent information."

Étienne felt an icy knot tighten in his stomach. "I assure you, my loyalties have never wavered."

Robespierre held his gaze. "I trust that is the case. However, these are precarious times. Transparency is essential."

"Ask what you will," Étienne replied, masking his unease.

They spoke for some time, Robespierre probing with questions that danced on the edge of accusation. Étienne parried as best he could, but the undercurrent was clear: suspicion had extended its reach.

As Robespierre rose to leave, he touched Étienne's shoulder. "Be vigilant," he advised. "The Republic demands unwavering commitment."

"Always," Étienne agreed, the word hollow in his mouth.

When the door closed behind him, Étienne sank into a chair, his composure unravelling. The veneer of control he had maintained was cracking, the isolation of his position laid bare.

He became aware with stark clarity that he had entangled himself in the web he had helped create. The Revolution's appetite for purity spared no one; he was but another thread in its intricate tapestry—easily severed.

The candle flickered, casting fleeting shadows that danced like spectres along the walls. Étienne stared into the wavering flame, the enormity of his predicament settling upon him like a shroud.

"30 March 1794," he whispered into the silence. "I am alone."

Outside, the city of Paris slumbered fitfully, its citizens' dreams troubled by undercurrents of fear and uncertainty. Within his solitary refuge, Étienne Corbeau faced the dawning realisation that the terror he had helped unleash was now poised to claim him as its next victim.

• • •

The bleak dawn of 5 April 1794 crept over Paris, the sun a wan disc shrouded by sullen clouds. Étienne Corbeau stood at his window, gazing out over the labyrinthine streets that sprawled beneath him. The city, once alive with the enthusiasm of revolution, now seemed suffocated by an invisible pall.

He could sense the growing tension and the undercurrent of fear that wound through every alley and boulevard.

The Reign of Terror had tightened its grip, and even those who had once been at the heart of the revolution now found themselves trapped in its relentless machinery.

A sharp knock at his door pulled him from his reverie. *"Entrez,"* he called, facing whoever might intrude upon his solitude.

Louis Antoine de Saint-Just entered his youthful face, a mask of stern determination. Clad in his customary dark attire, he moved with an almost spectral grace.

"Étienne," Saint-Just began, his eyes narrowing slightly, "Robespierre requests your presence at the Committee of Public Safety. There are matters to discuss."

Étienne felt a flicker of unease. "Of course," he replied, masking his apprehension. "Is there a particular issue at hand?"

Saint-Just hesitated ever so slightly. "Maximilien did not elaborate. But he seemed… preoccupied."

"Very well," Étienne said, donning his coat and tricolour sash. "I shall accompany you."

As they stepped out into the chill morning air, Étienne couldn't shake the feeling that something was amiss. The streets were tranquil, the usual bustle of vendors and labourers subdued. The very air seemed heavy, laden with unspoken anxieties.

"Have you noticed a change in the Robespierre of late?" Étienne ventured as they walked.

Saint-Just glanced at him sharply. "In what sense?"

"He appears more guarded, more… distrustful," Étienne replied carefully. "As though he sees enemies in every shadow."

Saint-Just's expression remained inscrutable. "These are challenging times. Vigilance is essential."

"Indeed," Étienne agreed, though inwardly, he wondered how far that vigilance extended.

They arrived at the Tuileries, the grand palace now repurposed as the nerve centre of revolutionary governance. The guards filled the corridors, their faces wearing stern masks.

Inside the Committee chamber, Maximilien Robespierre stood at the head of the long table, his pale complexion and piercing eyes giving him an almost otherworldly appearance. He looked up as they entered, his gaze settling on Étienne with an intensity that sent a chill down his spine.

"Étienne," Robespierre said evenly. "Thank you for coming."

"Always at your service, Maximilien," Étienne replied, taking his seat.

The room was sparsely populated; only a few key members were present, and the atmosphere was thick with tension.

"I have received reports," Robespierre began, his fingers steepled before him, "that certain elements within our ranks may not be as steadfast in their commitment to the Republic as they profess."

Étienne felt his pulse quicken. "What sort of elements?"

Robespierre's gaze bored into him. "Individuals who question the necessity of our measures. Who entertains doubts about the path we have chosen?"

"Surely," Étienne ventured cautiously, "healthy discourse is vital to the strength of the Revolution."

"Discourse, yes," Robespierre allowed, "but dissent breeds discord. Discord leads to weakness."

Saint-Just leaned forward. "We ensure that all who serve the Republic do so with unwavering dedication."

Étienne nodded slowly. "Of course. But we must also guard against the perils of unfounded suspicion."

Robespierre's eyes narrowed. "Are you suggesting that my concerns are without merit?"

"Not at all," Étienne replied quickly. "Merely that we must balance vigilance with reason."

A heavy silence settled over the room. Finally, Robespierre spoke. "I trust that your loyalty remains absolute, Étienne."

"Without question," Étienne affirmed, though a knot of apprehension tightened in his chest.

"Very well," Robespierre said, rising from his seat. "We shall reconvene later. There is much to consider."

As the meeting dispersed, Étienne lingered, his thoughts a tangled web of anxiety. He caught up with Jacques-Louis David, who was gathering his papers.

"Jacques," Étienne said quietly, "have you noticed a change in Robespierre?"

David glanced around before replying. "He grows more isolated, more severe. The weight of his responsibilities, perhaps."

"Or perhaps something more," Étienne mused. "A creeping paranoia."

David sighed. "These are dangerous times to speculate, my friend."

"Indeed," Étienne conceded. "But one cannot help but wonder where it will lead."

Later that afternoon, Étienne wandered the streets of Paris, seeking solace amid the familiar sights and sounds. But everywhere he turned, he saw signs of mounting tension—the furtive glances, the hushed conversations that ceased as he approached.

He entered a small bookshop tucked away on a quiet street, the scent of parchment and leather a comforting balm. As he browsed the shelves, a voice spoke softly behind him.

"Étienne."

He turned to see Olympe de Gouges, her eyes reflecting a mix of concern and resolve.

"Olympe," he said, surprised. "I did not expect to find you here."

"I might say the same," she replied, offering a faint smile. "These days, one must choose one's company carefully."

"Wise counsel," Étienne agreed. "How have you been?"

She regarded him thoughtfully. "I could ask you the same. Word is that Robespierre grows more mistrustful by the day."

Étienne glanced around nervously. "Careful, such talk can be dangerous."

"Truth often is," she said quietly. "But we cannot remain silent. The Revolution devours its own, Étienne. You see that."

He sighed heavily. "I am all too aware. But what would you have me do? To oppose him openly is to invite peril."

"Perhaps," she said, stepping closer, "but remaining complicit is surrendering your integrity."

He met her gaze. "And what of you? Your writings have not gone unnoticed. You tread a fine line."

She smiled wryly. "I have never feared speaking my mind. Though I admit, the stakes are higher now."

They stood silently for a moment, the weight of unspoken fears hanging between them.

"Be careful, Olympe," Étienne said at last. "These are treacherous times."

"And you as well," she replied softly. "Perhaps more than you know."

As she departed, Étienne felt a deepening sense of isolation. The walls were closing in, and he could no longer discern friend from foe.

That evening, he returned to his apartment, the shadows lengthening as dusk settled over the city. He sat at his desk, pen in hand, but the words eluded him.

A sudden knock at the door jolted him from his thoughts. His heart pounded as he approached cautiously.

"Who is it?" he called.

"It's Camille," came the muffled reply.

Étienne opened the door to find Camille Desmoulins standing there, his expression grave.

"May I come in?" Camille asked.

"Of course," Étienne said, stepping aside.

Once inside, Camille wasted no time. "I fear for you, Étienne."

Étienne raised an eyebrow. "Whatever do you mean?"

"Robespierre grows suspicious of everyone," Camille explained. "He sees betrayal in every shadow."

"I am aware," Étienne replied. "But I have been nothing but loyal."

"Loyalty is no shield," Camille warned. "Danton thought himself safe, and we know how that ended."

Étienne felt a chill. "What are you suggesting?"

"Distance yourself," Camille urged. "lie low. Perhaps even consider leaving Paris for a time."

Étienne shook his head. "To flee would only arouse suspicion."

"Then tread carefully," Camille insisted. "There are whispers that your name has come up in discussions."

"Whispers?" Étienne echoed. "From whom?"

Camille hesitated. "I cannot say more. Just… be vigilant."

Camille's departure left Étienne grappling with a gnawing dread. If Camille felt the need to warn him, the situation would must be dire indeed.

He paced the room, considering his options. Distancing himself might indeed draw unwanted attention, yet remaining close to Robespierre as his paranoia intensified was equally perilous.

He considered seeking counsel from Louis Antoine de Saint-Just but dismissed the idea. Robespierre's inner circle had too much influence over Saint-Just, and any sign of uncertainty could be deadly.

He could appeal to Jacques-Louis David, but what could the artist do?

Desperate for clarity, he sat down and wrote in his journal.

5 April 1794,

The storm clouds gather, and I find myself at the eye of the storm. Robespierre's mistrust spreads like a contagion, tainting all it touches. I sense his gaze upon me, weighing my every word and action.

To distance myself may provoke suspicion; to remain is to dance on a razor's edge. There are no safe harbours left.

I consider the path that led me here—the choices made, the alliances forged and broken. I have been both an architect and pawn in this grand design, but now the design unravels.

Is there a way out? Or is this the inevitable culmination of all that has come before?

I do not know.

All I know is that the shadows lengthen, and time runs short.

He set down the pen, exhaustion washing over him.

A sudden thought struck him—perhaps he could seek Madame de Staël. Her salons were still a hub of intellectual discourse, albeit more discreetly these days. She might offer advice or even help.

But was it too risky? Interpreting any overt move as collusion could be dangerous.

As night fell, Étienne sat alone, the flickering candle casting wavering shadows across the walls. The silence was oppressive, broken only by the distant sounds of the city—a city held in fear.

He realised with a sinking heart that there was no simple path. Every option was fraught with peril.

"5 April 1794," he whispered into the darkness. "I stand upon the precipice, and the abyss gazes back."

Sleep eluded him as he wrestled with his thoughts, each more troubling than the last.

With dawn would come new challenges and perhaps new dangers.

For now, all he could do was wait and hope that when the time came, he would find the courage to face whatever fate had in store.

• • •

The oppressive heat of 10 June 1794 settled over Paris like a shroud, the air thick with the scent of sweat and fear. Étienne stood on the steps of the Convention, watching as a restless crowd milled about the Place de la Révolution. The faces that once shone with hope and enthusiasm now bore the skeletal shadows of suspicion and despair. The Revolution, it seemed, had devoured the last remnants of its mercy.

"10 June 1794," Étienne murmured to himself, the date echoing ominously. They had just decreed the Law of 22 Prairial, stripping away the last vestiges of judicial fairness. Trials would proceed without witnesses or defence counsel, and the guillotine's blade would fall swifter than ever.

"Étienne," a voice called from behind.

He turned to see Jacques-Louis David approaching, his artist's smock replaced by the sombre attire befitting a deputy. "Jacques," Étienne greeted him. "A dark day, is it not?"

David nodded, his eyes reflecting a weariness that seemed to have settled upon them all. "The Law of 22 Prairial will change everything."

"Indeed," Étienne replied. Étienne replied, "They have abandoned justice in favour of expedience."

David placed a hand on Étienne's shoulder. "Are you attending the session this afternoon?"

"I suppose I must," Étienne sighed. Étienne sighed, expressing his fear of what further measures may be proposed.

As they entered the convention hall, a volatile mix of tension and resignation charged the atmosphere. Deputies whispered in tight clusters, casting wary glances towards the front, where Maximilien Robespierre stood conferring with Louis Antoine de Saint-Just.

Robespierre ascended the podium, his gaze sweeping over the assembly. "*Citoyens,* the enemies of the Revolution, multiply by the day. We must act decisively to protect the Republic from those who would see it destroyed."

A murmur rippled through the hall. Étienne exchanged a glance with David, noting the unease on his friend's face.

"The Law of 22 Prairial," Robespierre continued, "will enable us to eradicate treachery swiftly and without obstruction. Let no one doubt our resolve."

Étienne felt a knot tighten in his stomach. The legislation was a carte blanche for unchecked executions, a mechanism that would speed up the already rampant cycle of violence.

As the session adjourned, Étienne made his way towards Robespierre. "Maximilien," he called out.

Robespierre turned, his eyes narrowing slightly. "Étienne. What is it?"

"May we speak privately?" Étienne asked.

Robespierre regarded him for a moment before nodding. They stepped aside into a quiet alcove. "What concerns you?"

"This new law," Étienne began carefully. "Do you not fear that in removing the safeguards of justice, we risk condemning the innocent alongside the guilty?"

Robespierre's expression hardened. "In times of revolution, innocence is a luxury we can ill afford. The Republic's survival is paramount."

"But at what cost?" Étienne pressed. "We have already seen the consequences of hasty judgments. Families torn apart, lives ended without a fair trial."

Robespierre's gaze grew cold. "Your hesitation troubles me, Étienne. Do you doubt our cause?"

"I question only the methods, not the ideals," Étienne replied, feeling a chill creep up his spine.

"Be cautious," Robespierre warned. "Doubt is the seed of dissent."

Étienne watched as Robespierre walked away, a figure growing more isolated atop his self-constructed pedestal of virtue. The man who once championed justice had become a judge of fear.

Leaving the Convention, Étienne wandered through the streets. The surrounding city seemed cloaked in a suffocating silence, the usual vibrancy of Paris subdued under the weight of the Terror. Posters plastered on walls proclaimed the latest enemies of the state, names familiar and unknown.

He stood before the closed doors and dark windows of Café Procope, a stark symbol of the stifled intellectual life. Memories flooded back of animated discussions held within its walls; debates fuelled by passion and possibility. Those days felt like a lifetime ago.

"Étienne!"

He turned to see Olympe de Gouges hurrying towards him, her eyes filled with urgency. "Olympe," he greeted her. "It's been too long."

She gripped his hands. "I fear for you," she said. "For all of us. The new law…"

"I know," he interrupted gently. "It heralds a grim chapter."

She pleaded, stating, "Justice is being dismantled, and we cannot stand by and watch. You have influence. Use it to oppose this madness."

Étienne shook his head. "Robespierre will not tolerate dissent. To speak against him now is to invite one's demise."

"Since when did you become so resigned?" she challenged. "The Étienne I knew would have fought for what is right."

He looked away, shame and frustration knotting within him. "Perhaps that man no longer exists."

She released his hands, her expression softening. "It's not too late, Étienne. We must find the courage to act."

Before he could respond, a squad of National Guardsmen marched past, their presence a stark reminder of the ever-watchful eyes upon them. Olympe pulled her cloak tighter around her. "Be careful," she whispered. "They say anyone could be next."

As she disappeared into the crowd, Étienne felt a profound loss. The ideals they had once shared seemed like distant echoes, drowned out by the relentless drumbeat of the guillotine.

He continued walking until he reached the banks of the Seine. The river flowed steadily, indifferent to the turmoil that gripped the city. Sitting on a bench overlooking the water, he tried to reconcile the path that had led him here.

"Étienne Corbeau," a voice interrupted his thoughts.

He turned to see Camille Desmoulins approaching, a melancholy smile upon his lips. "Camille," Étienne replied. "I heard about your release."

"For now," Camille said, sitting beside him. "But I fear it is only a reprieve."

They sat in silence for a moment before Camille spoke again. "The Revolution has lost its soul, Étienne. We sought liberty, and instead, we have forged new chains."

Étienne nodded slowly. "I cannot argue with that."

"I've been writing," Camille continued. "An appeal to reason, a plea for clemency. But I fear it falls on deaf ears."

"Robespierre will see it as betrayal," Étienne warned.

"Perhaps," Camille admitted. "But I cannot remain silent."

Étienne looked at his friend, seeing the determination etched in his features. "Take care, Camille. The stakes are higher than ever."

"As they have always been," Camille replied. "But some things are worth the risk."

As dusk settled, they parted ways. Étienne felt the weight of their conversation pressing upon him. The Revolution had become a monster of their own making, and he was complicit in its creation.

Returning to his apartment, he lit a candle and sat at his writing desk. The flickering flame cast long shadows across the room, mirroring the darkness that had settled within his heart.

10 June 1794,

Today marks the end of mercy. The Law of 22 Prairial has stripped away any pretence of justice, leaving only the cold machinery of death in its wake. I have stood by as friends become foes, as the very hands that once upheld their corrupt ideals.

Now I realise that we have trapped ourselves in a cycle of violence, one that feeds upon itself and spares no one.

> *I cannot escape the haunting faces of those lost—Danton, whose voice once rallied the masses;*
>
> *What remains for me? To continue down this path is to lose what little remains of my humanity. Yet, to oppose it is to risk everything.*
>
> *I am adrift in a sea of uncertainty, the shores of reason and justice receding into the distance.*

A knock at the door startled him. His heart raced as he approached cautiously. "Who is it?"

"It's Jacques," came the muffled reply.

He opened the door to find Jacques-Louis David standing there, his expression grave. "May I come in?"

"Of course," Étienne said, stepping aside.

David entered, glancing around the dimly lit room. "I won't stay long. I wanted to warn you."

"Warn me?"

"Robespierre grows increasingly suspicious," David explained. "He questions the loyalty of those closest to him."

Étienne felt a cold dread settle upon him. "I've done nothing to warrant his distrust."

"That may not matter," David cautioned. "The new law allows for accusations without evidence. No one is safe."

"What do you suggest?" Étienne asked, his voice barely above a whisper.

"Be cautious," David urged. "Watch your words and actions. Perhaps distance yourself from those under scrutiny."

Étienne nodded numbly. "Thank you for telling me."

As David left, the reality of his situation crystallised. The Revolution had turned upon itself, and its unforgiving grasp caught him.

He extinguished the candle and stood by the window, gazing into the night. The city lay cloaked in darkness, the silence punctuated by distant sounds that echoed like prophecies of doom.

"10 June 1794," he whispered. "The end of mercy, the end of hope."

Étienne knew then that the forces he had helped unleash trapped—bound him. There was no clear path to redemption, only a choice between collaboration and resistance, each fraught with peril.

As the stars emerged in the inky sky, he felt the weight of his choices bearing down on him. He pondered how much blood would be spilt before the dawn of a new era—or if such a dawn would ever come—while the cycle of violence continued without showing signs of abating.

In the quiet solitude of his chamber, Étienne Corbeau faced the stark truth: the Revolution he had once believed in had become a harbinger of destruction, and he was powerless to halt its relentless advance.

CHAPTER EIGHT: (1794)
MASKS OF LOYALTY

Paris was under pressure on July 10th, 1794, as the air became dense with the scent of dust and discontent. Étienne Corbeau stood on the balcony of his modest apartment overlooking the Rue Saint-Honoré, watching as the city simmered beneath the relentless sun. Below, vendors half-heartedly hawked their wares while citizens moved with a lethargy born of exhaustion and fear.

He turned away from the railing, the murmurs of the street fading as he retreated into the dim coolness of his parlour. Papers littered the wooden table—reports, decrees, lists of names marked for salvation or doom. Étienne's eyes skimmed over them without focus. His thoughts were elsewhere, fixed upon the fractures spreading within the Convention.

A sharp rap on the door jolted him from his reverie. *"Entrez,"* he called out.

The door swung open to reveal Louis Antoine de Saint-Just, his youthful face betraying nothing of his inner machinations. Clad in his customary black coat, his pale blue eyes regarded Étienne with curiosity and caution.

"Étienne," Saint-Just began, his voice measured, "Robespierre has called for a meeting this afternoon. Your presence is required."

Étienne forced a thin smile. "Of course. Any sign of the agenda?"

"Matters of security," Saint-Just replied cryptically. "There have been… developments."

"Developments?" Étienne echoed, masking his apprehension.

Saint-Just's gaze lingered momentarily before he added, "Best discussed in person. Be at the Hôtel de Ville by three."

"Très bien," Étienne agreed.

As Saint-Just departed, closing the door softly behind him, Étienne exhaled slowly. The veneer of control he maintained was thinning, and he could feel the tension tightening like a noose around his neck. He knew Robespierre's paranoia had escalated; the man saw enemies in every shadow, traitors behind every whispered conversation.

Crossing the room, Étienne settled into a worn armchair, the leather cool against his skin. He considered his options. Aligning himself with Robespierre had once seemed the surest path to influence, but now it felt like standing on the edge of a crumbling precipice. The Committee of Public Safety had become a cauldron of suspicion, and loyalties shifted with the capriciousness of the wind.

A knock sounded once more, lighter this time. *"Oui?"*

The door creaked open, and Camille Desmoulins peeked inside, his eyes bright despite the shadows beneath them. "Are you receiving visitors, *mon ami?*"

"Camille," Étienne said, surprised. "Please, come in."

Desmoulins slipped inside, closing the door behind him. He moved with restless energy, fingers tapping against his thigh. "I had to speak with you."

"What brings you here?" Étienne asked, motioning for him to sit.

Camille remained standing. "There's a tide turning within the Convention. More and more deputies are questioning Robespierre's methods—the endless purges, the unchecked power."

Étienne studied him carefully. "And you? Where do you stand?"

"I believe the Revolution has lost its way," Desmoulins confessed, his voice barely above a whisper. "We sought liberty, equality, fraternity. Instead, we've birthed a regime of terror."

"You tread dangerous ground," Étienne cautioned.

Camille met his gaze. "Perhaps. But silence is a greater risk now. Discussions are happening—plans to challenge Robespierre's authority."

"Who is involved?" Étienne pressed.

Desmoulins shook his head. "I cannot say. Not yet. But I wanted you to know. I thought… perhaps you'd understand."

Étienne leaned back, weighing his words. "You're asking me to join this dissent?"

"I'm asking you to consider where your true loyalties lie," Camille replied earnestly. "To France, or to a man who sees himself as its sole saviour?"

A flicker of unease stirred within Étienne. Aligning with Robespierre's enemies was a dangerous gambit, but remaining at the mercy of his suspicions was equally fraught.

"I'll think about it," Étienne said finally.

Camille offered a faint smile. "That's all I ask."

As Desmoulins departed, Étienne felt the walls of his apartment close in around him. His precarious position was becoming untenable. He found himself caught between the tightening fist of Robespierre's regime and the rising tide of those who would see it dismantled.

He knew he had to act.

The Hôtel de Ville loomed ahead, its stone façade baking under the afternoon sun. Étienne arrived just before three, the streets abuzz with rumours and speculation. Inside, the air was cooler but thick with tension. Deputies milled about, their conversations hushed.

He spotted Maximilien Robespierre standing apart, his usually composed features etched with strain. The once meticulous attire now seemed to hang loosely, his skin pale against the dark fabric.

"Robespierre," Étienne greeted him with a slight bow.

"Corbeau," Robespierre acknowledged, his eyes scanning the room. "We have much to discuss."

"Saint-Just mentioned developments?" Étienne prompted.

Robespierre fixed him with a piercing stare. "There are those within the Convention who conspire against the Republic. Traitors who would undo all we've achieved."

Étienne maintained a neutral expression. "Do we know who they are?"

"Names have surfaced," Robespierre replied cryptically. "But I trust in your loyalty to help root them out."

"Of course," Étienne agreed, though his mind raced.

"Be vigilant," Robespierre advised, placing a hand on Étienne's shoulder. "These are dangerous times."

As the meeting began, Étienne observed more than taking part. The deputies were restless, their gazes avoiding direct contact with Robespierre. Louis Antoine de Saint-Just delivered a report on internal security, his tone flat but underscored by an undercurrent of menace.

"Saint-Just declared "We must deal with any who oppose the will of the people swiftly." "There can be no room for hesitation."

Étienne felt a chill despite the heat. The words were a thinly veiled threat, and he could see the unease ripple through the assembly.

After the session adjourned, Jacques-Louis David approached him. A furrowed brow marred the artist's usual stoicism. "Étienne, a word?"

"Certainly," Étienne replied.

They stepped aside into a quiet corridor. "Have you noticed the shift?" David asked.

"It's hard to miss," Étienne conceded.

"Robespierre tightens his grip, but the more he squeezes, the more slips through his fingers," David observed. "There's talk of action—decisive action."

Étienne regarded him cautiously. "Are you involved in these talks?"

David hesitated. "I am… aware of them."

"Then you know the risks," Étienne said.

"Risks we may have to take," David countered. "For the good of France."

Étienne sighed, the weight of his predicament pressing upon him. "I fear we stand upon a razor's edge."

"Perhaps," David agreed. "But I wanted you to know. You must choose a side."

As David departed, Étienne remained rooted to the spot. The surrounding corridors bustled with activity, yet he felt isolated, adrift in a sea of uncertainty.

He left the Hôtel de Ville as dusk settled, the sky ablaze with hues of orange and crimson. The streets were quieter now, the city's usual hum dampened by the oppressive atmosphere.

Passing a group of Sans-culottes, he overheard snippets of their conversation—discontent with the shortages, frustration with the endless demands of the Revolution.

"All this sacrifice, and for what?" one man grumbled. "We traded one tyrant for another."

Étienne quickened his pace, the words echoing uncomfortably in his mind. The disillusionment was widespread, and he realised that the Revolution's foundations were eroding beneath them.

Returning to his apartment, he lit a single candle, the flickering flame casting long shadows across the walls. He sat at his desk, quill poised above parchment, but hesitated.

10 July 1794,

The tide shifts. Robespierre's grip weakens even as he seeks to strengthen it. Whispers of rebellion grow louder, and I find myself at a crossroads. To remain loyal is to risk being swept away by the inevitable storm. To align with his enemies is to gamble with fate.

I am frustrated by this precarious position, a pawn in a game where the rules change without warning. Yet, I cannot ignore the signs. The Revolution devours its children, and I must act to avoid being among them.

But which path to choose?

He set down the quill, rubbing his temples. The air in the room felt stifling, the candle's flame consuming the oxygen as indeed as the Revolution consumed hope.

A sudden knock startled him. His heart leapt into his throat. "Who is it?" he called, striving to steady his voice.

"Olympe," came the muffled reply.

He exhaled, relief washing over him. Opening the door, he found Olympe de Gouges standing there, her eyes reflecting concern.

"May I come in?" she asked.

"Of course," he said, stepping aside.

She entered, glancing around the dimly lit room. "I heard about the meeting today," she began. "Tensions are high."

"An understatement," Étienne remarked.

She faced him, her expression earnest. "You must be careful. Robespierre trusts no one, and those who were once allies are now suspect."

"I am well aware," he replied.

"Have you considered your options?" she pressed.

"I have," he admitted. "But the risks are significant on either side."

"True," she conceded. "But inaction is a choice in itself."

He met her gaze. "What would you have me do?"

"Follow your conscience," she said softly. "Stand for what you believe is right."

He sighed. "I fear that may lead me to ruin."

"Perhaps," she acknowledged. "But living in fear is no life at all."

As she departed into the night, Étienne felt the weight of her words settle upon him. He knew she was right, yet the path ahead was uncertain.

He returned to his desk, staring at the unfinished journal entry. Dipping his quill once more, he added,

I must decide soon. The currents of dissent swell around me, and neutrality is no longer an option. My survival depends on the choices I make in the coming days.

May I find the courage to choose?

Extinguishing the candle, he sat in the darkness, the city's distant sounds a melancholic symphony. Étienne Corbeau, once a man of ambition and cunning, now entangled in a web of his own making.

The Revolution's wheel turned relentlessly, and he stood at the fulcrum, teetering between survival and oblivion.

•••

From his modest apartment, Étienne Corbeau observed the Rue Saint-Honoré on 17 July 1794, as the city below came to life under a sky tainted with silver hues. The streets below were a hive of restless energy—vendors shouting half-heartedly, Sans-culottes patrolling with a vigilant eye, citizens scurrying about with anxious glances over their shoulders.

The Revolution had reached a dangerous precipice, and Étienne could feel the tension tightening like a noose around his neck. Maximilien Robespierre's grip on the Committee of Public Safety had grown ever more constrictive, his paranoia seeping into every crevice of the government like a poisonous vapour.

A sharp rap on the door jolted him from his thoughts. *"Entrez,"* he called, smoothing the front of his waistcoat as he turned to face his visitor.

Louis Antoine de Saint-Just entered, his angular features etched with a severity that belied his youth. Clad in sombre black, he moved with the calculated precision of a man accustomed to wielding power.

"Étienne," Saint-Just began without preamble, "Robespierre expects you to attend an emergency meeting at the Hôtel de Ville."

Étienne felt a flicker of apprehension. "Has something occurred?"

"Matters of security," Saint-Just replied tersely. It seems we must heighten our vigilance. "

"Très bien," Étienne nodded. "I shall make my way there promptly."

As Saint-Just departed, closing the door with a decisive click, Étienne released a slow breath. The undercurrents of distrust had grown stronger, and he knew Robespierre's gaze had settled uncomfortably upon those closest to him.

He donned his coat and tricolour sash, the fabric heavy against his skin. Stepping out into the sweltering afternoon, he navigated the winding streets towards the Hôtel de Ville. The city seemed to hold its breath, the air thick with unspoken fears.

Upon arrival, the grand hall was abuzz with subdued murmurs. Deputies clustered in tight knots, their faces drawn and pale. Étienne caught sight of Jacques-Louis David, who offered a brief nod before turning away to converse in hushed tones with another delegate.

Robespierre stood at the head of the room, his piercing blue eyes surveying the assembly with a disquieting intensity. His usually immaculate attire appeared slightly dishevelled, and a sheen of perspiration clung to his brow.

"Citoyens," Robespierre began, his voice slicing through the murmurs like a blade. "The Republic is under threat as never before. Traitors lurk among us, their treachery masked by feigned loyalty."

A ripple of unease passed through the crowd. Étienne felt his stomach twist.

"We must act decisively," Robespierre continued, "to root out these enemies of the Revolution. No one is beyond suspicion."

Étienne glanced at Louis Antoine de Saint-Just, who stood impassively beside Robespierre. The atmosphere was taut, and the air seemed to vibrate with tension.

"Maximilien," Étienne ventured cautiously, stepping forward. "Perhaps it would be prudent to consider measured responses. A careful investigation might—"

Robespierre's gaze snapped to him, eyes narrowing. "Do you question the necessity of swift action, Corbeau?"

"Not at all," Étienne replied smoothly. "I merely suggest that in our zeal to protect the Republic, we ensure that justice remains our guiding principle."

A murmur of agreement fluttered through a few deputies, but the majority remained silent, eyes cast downward.

"Justice," Robespierre echoed, his tone icy. "Justice demands that we be unrelenting against those who would betray us."

"Certainly," Étienne acquiesced. "Yet, unchecked purges may sow fear among the innocent, weakening the foundations we seek to strengthen."

Robespierre studied him for a long moment. "Your concern is noted," he said, his voice devoid of warmth. "We shall discuss this further."

The meeting adjourned shortly after that, deputies dispersing like leaves caught in a sudden gust. Étienne felt a hand grasp his arm.

"Bold move," Camille Desmoulins whispered, his eyes alight with admiration and caution.

Étienne forced a wan smile. "Desperate times, *mon ami.*"

"Be careful," Desmoulins warned. "Robespierre's patience wears thin, and his memory is long."

"I am well aware," Étienne sighed. "But we cannot continue down this path of relentless executions."

"Then perhaps it's time to act," Desmoulins suggested, his voice barely audible above the din. "There are those within the Convention who share our sentiments."

Étienne raised an eyebrow. "And you trust them?"

"As much as one can in these times," Desmoulins admitted. "But unity may be our only shield."

"Let us speak more privately," Étienne agreed.

They made their way to a secluded nook, the sounds of the Hôtel de Ville fading into a distant hum.

"Robespierre's list of enemies grows by the day," Desmoulins began. "No one is safe. We must move before he tightens the noose further."

Étienne nodded thoughtfully. "I attempted to broach the subject of moderation, but he is resolute—obsessed, even."

"Then we must curtail his influence," Desmoulins pressed. "For the sake of the Republic."

"Do you propose a motion within the Convention?" Étienne asked.

"Perhaps," Desmoulins said. "But it would require the support of key figures."

"Have you approached others?" Étienne inquired.

"Discreetly," Desmoulins replied. "There's a growing faction willing to oppose him, but fear keeps many silent."

Étienne rubbed his chin. "I must consider the implications."

"Time is of the essence," Desmoulins urged. "Delay may cost us dearly."

As they parted ways, Étienne felt the weight of his predicament pressing upon him. Aligning against Robespierre was fraught with peril, yet inaction seemed equally hazardous. His survival hinged on a delicate balance of courage and cunning.

Exiting the Hôtel de Ville, he was greeted by the oppressive heat and the cacophony of the city. The Seine glittered lethargically under the sun, its waters offering no respite from the turmoil that gripped the nation.

He went to the *Jardin des Tuileries*, seeking a moment of quiet contemplation amidst the manicured hedges and gravel paths. Because of the oppressive weather and pervasive atmosphere of dread, the gardens were sparsely populated, with the usual crowds deterred.

Seating himself on a wrought-iron bench beneath a linden tree, Étienne closed his eyes, allowing the faint rustle of leaves to soothe his frayed nerves.

"Lost in thought, monsieur?"

He opened his eyes to find Olympe de Gouges standing before him, a hint of a smile on her lips. Clad in a simple muslin dress, she exuded a calm that belied the chaos surrounding them.

"Olympe," he greeted her, gesturing for her to sit. "A rare pleasure in these times."

She took a seat beside him. "I heard about the meeting. Word travels swiftly."

Étienne sighed. "Robespierre grows more unyielding by the day. His talk of further purges is… alarming."

"And yet you dared to question him," she observed.

"Someone must," he replied. "Though I fear I may have overstepped."

"Perhaps," she acknowledged. "But your courage may inspire others."

"Or paint a target on my back," Étienne countered.

She regarded him steadily. "You are at a crossroads. To remain passive is to agree to tyranny. To act carries its own risks."

"I am keenly aware," he said ruefully. "But I can't see the path forward,"

"Then allow me to offer clarity," she said, her tone firm. "The Revolution has devoured too many of its children. It is time for an alternative course—a return to the principles we once held dear."

"And you believe that is possible?" he asked.

"I must," she replied. "Otherwise, we will lose everything," she replied.

Étienne looked out over the gardens, the wilting flowers a melancholy reflection of his fading hope. "I shall consider your words."

"Do more than consider," she urged, rising to her feet. "Act."

As she walked away, her figure receding into the afternoon haze, Étienne felt a stirring of resolve. The scales had tipped, and indecision was no longer tenable.

When he returned to the city centre, the sun was beginning to descend, casting elongated shadows across the boulevards. The faces of the people he passed bore the same weariness, the same haunted look of those who had witnessed too much suffering.

Reaching his apartment, he found a sealed letter slipped under his door. Breaking the wax seal, he read the terse message:

"We request your presence at Madame de Staël's salon this evening. Discretion is paramount."

There was no signature, but the elegant script was familiar. Étienne's heartbeat quickened. Madame de Staël's gatherings were renowned for their intellectual enthusiasm and, more recently, for harbouring those who opposed the current regime.

As twilight enveloped the city, he went to her residence on the Rue du Bac. The salon was a haven of candlelit brilliance, the air filled with the murmur of hushed conversations and the scent of jasmine.

Madame de Staël greeted him warmly, her eyes sparkling with intelligence. "*Monsieur Corbeau*, welcome."

"Madame," he bowed slightly. "I am honoured by your invitation."

She guided him towards a quiet corner. "We find ourselves in tumultuous times," she began. She stated we need the voice of reason.

"I fear reason holds little sway of late," Étienne replied.

"Perhaps," she conceded. "But change often begins with a single step."

Throughout the evening, he engaged with various attendees—intellectuals, politicians, artists—all complaining about the direction of the Revolution. The undercurrent of dissent was palpable.

As the gathering drew to a close, Étienne felt a newfound clarity. The threads were weaving together—a network of individuals poised to challenge Robespierre's tightening grasp.

Returning home under a canopy of stars, he pondered the path ahead. The risks were significant, but so too were the potential rewards. His survival depended not only on action but on aligning himself with those who sought to restore balance.

Seated once more at his desk, he penned a last entry for the day:

17 July 1794,

Robespierre's paranoia deepens his calls for further purges, a chilling harbinger of what may come. I tested the waters of moderation, only to find them treacherous.

I realise now that to safeguard my future, I must act decisively. The tides of dissent swell, and I must choose whether to be swept away or to navigate them towards a new horizon.

Courage and caution must walk hand in hand. The time for hesitation has passed.

He set down his quill, the faint glow of dawn beginning to lighten the edges of the sky. Étienne Corbeau, once a shadowy manipulator behind the scenes, now stood on the brink of a pivotal choice.

The Revolution churned on, indifferent to the fates of those caught within its grasp. But perhaps he could steer its course towards a destiny less marred by blood and fear.

As sleep finally claimed him, Étienne knew that the days ahead would test the very fabric of his character—and that his actions might well determine not only his fate but that of a nation teetering on the edge of oblivion.

• • •

Étienne navigated the maze streets of the Marais district, his footsteps echoing softly against the shuttered façades of once-bustling shops. The city had muted its usual vibrancy, and a pervasive sense of unease, mirroring the turmoil within his own mind, filled the air instead.

"23 July 1794," Étienne whispered to himself, the date a constant drumbeat in his thoughts. Time was running thin, and the delicate balance he maintained teetered on the edge of collapse. The Revolution had become a serpent devouring its own tail, and he stood perilously close to the jaws.

He reached an inconspicuous doorway tucked between a dilapidated bookshop and a closed café. After quickly glancing over his shoulder to ensure he was not followed, he rapped a specific pattern against the weathered wood. A moment later, the door creaked open just enough to reveal a pair of wary eyes.

"Nom de code?" the doorman demanded in a hushed tone.

"Liberté," Étienne replied softly.

The door swung open, allowing him entry into a dimly lit corridor. As he descended a narrow staircase, the faded tapestries on the walls muffled the sound of his footsteps. At the bottom, a heavy curtain parted to reveal a spacious cellar converted into a clandestine meeting place.

A dozen figures clustered around a long wooden table strewn with maps and documents. Candlelight cast flickering shadows across their faces, obscuring features and lending an air of secrecy. Among them, Étienne recognised notable members of the Convention: Jean-Lambert Tallien, Joseph Fouché, and even the usually reticent Paul Barras.

"Ah, Corbeau," Tallien greeted him with a tight smile. "We were wondering if you'd reconsidered."

"Hardly," Étienne replied, taking an empty seat. "But one cannot be too cautious these days."

"Indeed," Fouché muttered, his eyes darting about as if expecting Robespierre himself to materialise from the shadows. "The walls have ears."

Barras leaned forward, his sharp features illuminated by the candle's glow. "We have much to discuss, and time is of the essence."

Étienne nodded. "What is the current state of our… endeavour?"

Tallien spread a map of Paris across the table, pointing to key locations marked in red ink. "Support is growing within the Convention. Many are disillusioned with Robespierre's tyranny. The Sans-culottes, however, remain unpredictable."

"Robespierre's hold on the Committee of Public Safety is weakening," Barras added. "But he still has the loyalty of Saint-Just and Couthon."

Étienne felt a flicker of unease at the mention of Louis Antoine de Saint-Just. "Saint-Just is as resolute as ever," he remarked. "It will not be easy to sway him," he remarked.

"Then we must act swiftly," Fouché insisted. "Before they can tighten their grip further."

"Agreed," Étienne said. "I have information that could prove invaluable."

All eyes turned to him. "Go on," Tallien prompted.

"Robespierre plans to address the Convention in two days' time," Étienne revealed. "He intends to denounce several members, accusing them of conspiracy and treason."

A murmur rippled through the group. "Do you know who is on this list?" Barras asked urgently.

Étienne hesitated before responding. "I believe many of us in this room are among those he seeks to condemn."

Fouché cursed under his breath. "Then our timeline speeds up."

"Precisely," Étienne agreed. "We must pre-empt his move."

Tallien's expression hardened. "We need to rally as many deputies as possible. If we can turn the Convention against him, we can strip him of his authority."

"But we must be cautious," Barras warned. "Robespierre still has allies who would defend him vehemently."

Étienne leaned forward. "I can provide a list of his key supporters and their weaknesses. With this, we can undermine their influence."

Fouché eyed him sceptically. "And how did you come by such sensitive information?"

Étienne met his gaze evenly. "I've spent months cultivating relationships within the Committee. My position affords me certain… privileges."

"You're taking a significant risk," Tallien observed.

"As are we all," Étienne countered. "But it's a risk worth taking."

A tense silence settled over the group before Barras spoke again. "Very well. We move forward with the plan. Étienne, your information will be crucial."

They spent the next hour detailing their strategy, voices low and measured. They distributed assignments and discussed contingencies. Étienne contributed where he could, all the while calculating how to position himself to survive, regardless of the outcome.

As the meeting adjourned, Tallien pulled Étienne aside. "I must admit, your agreement to join us surprised me," Tallien said as he pulled Étienne aside.

"Desperate times," Étienne replied with a faint smile. "Robespierre's paranoia grows by the day. It's only a matter of time before he turns on me."

"True enough," Tallien conceded. "But be wary. Trust is a scarce commodity."

"Understood," Étienne said. "I trust you'll keep our arrangement confidential."

"Of course," Tallien assured him, though his eyes betrayed a hint of calculation.

Étienne emerged from the clandestine meeting place and the cool night air greeted him. The city seemed to exhale around him, the oppressive heat of the day giving way to a restless energy. He pulled his coat tighter, navigating the shadowed streets with practised ease.

As he approached his apartment, a figure stepped from the alcove of a nearby doorway. "Étienne," a familiar voice called softly.

He turned to see Olympe de Gouges, her expression a mix of concern and curiosity. "Olympe," he acknowledged, masking his surprise. "What brings you here at this hour?"

"I could ask you the same," she replied, arching an eyebrow. "You've been scarce of late."

"Pressing matters," he said vaguely.

She studied him for a moment. "There's talk of plots within the Convention. Dangerous whispers."

Étienne felt a prick of apprehension. "Rumours abound in these times."

"These are more than rumours," she insisted. "Please, be careful. The tides are treacherous."

"I appreciate your concern," he said sincerely. "But I assure you, I am taking all the precautions."

She stepped closer, lowering her voice. "I've heard that Robespierre intends to make a move against several deputies. If you're involved in any counteractions, you must tread lightly."

He met her gaze, weighing his words. "Sometimes, one must take risks to effect change."

"Just make sure you calculate those risks," she urged. "I'd hate to see you caught in the crossfire."

"I'll do my best," he promised.

They parted ways, and Étienne ascended the stairs to his apartment. Once inside, he secured the door and lit a solitary candle. The flame cast elongated shadows across the walls, mirroring the duplicity that had become his existence.

He sat at his desk, quill poised over parchment.

23 July 1794,

Tonight, I have bound myself to a course from which there may be no return. The conspirators believe I am one of them, and perhaps I am. Yet, I cannot shake the feeling that I am but a pawn in a larger game.

Providing the information was a calculated move. Should the plot succeed, I will have secured my position in the new order. If it fails, I must ensure there is no trace of my involvement. Balancing on this razor's edge is perilous, but necessity dictates my actions.

I have no illusions about those I align with. Ambition drives us all, and trust is but a veneer. I must remain vigilant.

A soft knock at the door interrupted his writing. His heart leapt into his throat. Who could call at this hour?

"Who is it?" he called, keeping his tone steady.

"Louis Antoine," came the muffled reply.

Étienne's pulse quickened. He extinguished the candle and moved cautiously towards the door. Opening it just a crack, he peered to see Saint-Just standing in the dimly lit corridor.

"May I come in?" Saint-Just asked, his expression unreadable.

"Of course," Étienne said, stepping aside.

Saint-Just entered, glancing around the darkened room. "Forgive the late hour," he began. "But matters of urgency have arisen."

"What concerns you?" Étienne inquired, masking his unease.

"There are rumours of dissent within the Convention," Saint-Just stated. "Robespierre is assembling a list of those suspected of conspiracy."

Étienne felt a chill run down his spine. "Do we know who is involved?"

"Not yet," Saint-Just replied. "But vigilance is paramount. I trust your loyalty remains unwavering."

"Naturally," Étienne affirmed. "My commitment to the Republic is absolute."

"Good," Saint-Just said, his gaze piercing. "We cannot afford any more betrayals."

"Agreed," Étienne nodded.

After a moment's silence, Saint-Just turned to leave. "Stay alert," he advised. "These are dangerous times."

As the door closed behind him, Étienne released a breath he hadn't realised he'd been holding. The visit was a stark reminder of the tightrope he walked. Any misstep could prove fatal.

Returning to his desk, he added to his journal entry:

Saint-Just suspects something, or perhaps he merely seeks to intimidate. Either way, the walls are closing in. I must keep all traces of my involvement with the conspirators hidden.

The days ahead will be decisive. I must be prepared for any outcome.

He secured the journal in a hidden compartment beneath the floorboards and retired to bed, though sleep eluded him. The city's sounds drifted through the open window—the distant murmur of voices, the clatter of a carriage on cobblestones, the faint strains of a melancholy tune played on a violin.

As dawn approached, Étienne lay awake, his mind a maelstrom of plans and contingencies. The Revolution had become a crucible, and he was being tested as never before.

"23 July 1794," he whispered into the predawn light. "The plot thickens, and I am trapped within it. May fortune favour the bold."

With that, he rose to face whatever the new day would bring, resolute in his determination to survive the storm that threatened to consume them all.

• • •

The heat of 26 July 1794 bore down upon Paris, the sun a relentless disc in a cloudless sky. Étienne Corbeau stood at the window of his apartment overlooking down on the city below, watching as it stirred beneath the weight of anticipation. The air was tense, whispers of impending upheaval threading through the narrow streets like invisible tendrils.

A knock at the door pulled Étienne from his reverie. "Entrez," he called out, turning to face the visitor.

Camille Desmoulins entered, his usually vibrant demeanour subdued. Dark circles shadowed his eyes, and his clothes hung loosely on his frame. "Étienne, have you heard?" he asked urgently.

"About Robespierre's address?" Étienne replied. "Yes, it's the talk of the city."

Desmoulins nodded, running a hand through his messy hair. "He intends to make vague accusations against members of the Convention, hinting at a grand conspiracy without naming names."

Étienne's jaw tightened. "A dangerous tactic. He risks alienating even his allies."

"Precisely," Desmoulins agreed. "The deputies are on edge, fearing they may be the next targets of his paranoia."

Étienne gestured for him to sit. "This could be the opportunity we've been waiting for."

Desmoulins sank into a worn armchair. "If we move carefully, yes. But we ensure the majority stands with us."

"The tide has been turning," Étienne observed. "Robespierre's increasingly erratic behaviour has sown seeds of doubt."

Desmoulins leaned forward, his voice barely above a whisper. "Are you prepared to commit fully to the plan?"

Étienne met his gaze steadily. "I am. For the sake of France, and our own survival."

A flicker of relief crossed Desmoulins' face. "Good. We meet tonight at Tallien's residence to complete our course of action."

"I'll be there," Étienne affirmed.

As Desmoulins departed, Étienne felt a weight settle upon his shoulders. His path was fraught with peril, but indecision was no longer an option. Robespierre's hold on the Revolution had become a stranglehold, and the time to act was now.

The afternoon sun cast long shadows across the grand façade of the Convention hall. Inside, a palpable sense of unease charged the atmosphere. Deputies shuffled into their seats, hushed conversations punctuated by furtive glances towards the podium where Robespierre would soon speak.

Étienne took his place among the ranks, his gaze sweeping the assembly. He noted the tension etched on familiar faces—men who had once stood resolute now appeared uncertain, their loyalties wavering.

The chamber fell silent as Maximilien Robespierre ascended the podium. Clad in his customary austere attire, he surveyed the gathered deputies with an inscrutable expression.

"Citoyens," Robespierre began, his voice resonating through the hall. "The Republic stands at a crossroads. Enemies of the Revolution lurk among us, disguised as patriots but harbouring treacherous intentions."

A murmur rippled through the assembly. Étienne exchanged a glance with Joseph Fouché, who raised an eyebrow in silent acknowledgement.

"These conspirators," Robespierre continued, "seek to undermine our efforts to return France to the clutches of tyranny. But we shall not allow it. We must remain vigilant."

"Name them!" a voice called out from the back of the hall.

Robespierre paused, his gaze hardening. "I will reveal their identities in due time," Robespierre assured as his gaze hardened. "For now, let this serve as a warning to those who would betray the Revolution."

The unease gave way to anger among the deputies. Étienne could sense the shifting mood—a blend of fear and resentment. Robespierre had cast suspicion upon them all by refusing to specify his accusations.

"Is this justice?" Jean-Lambert Tallien stood, his voice cutting through the disquiet. "To levy accusations without evidence, to threaten without due process?"

Robespierre's eyes narrowed. "Those who are innocent have nothing to fear."

Tallien retorted, "You endanger us all with your veiled threats."

A chorus of assent echoed through the chamber. Étienne seized the moment, rising to add his voice. "We cannot allow fear dictating our actions. Transparency and justice must prevail if we are to maintain the integrity of the Republic."

Robespierre's composure faltered ever so slightly. "It appears the conspirators reveal themselves through their protestations."

The tension escalated, murmurs growing into open dissent. Étienne felt a surge of determination. Robespierre had overplayed his hand, and the assembly was turning against him.

Louis Antoine de Saint-Just rose beside Robespierre. "We must maintain order," declared Louis Antoine de Saint-Just, his youthful face stern. "The safety of the Republic supersedes individual grievances."

But the tide had shifted. More deputies stood, voicing their objections. The chamber descended into chaos as accusations and rebuttals flew.

Étienne caught sight of Jacques-Louis David, who gave a subtle nod—the moment had come to commit fully.

He stepped forward, projecting his voice above the clamour. "*Citoyens*, this discord serves only to weaken us. We must address these concerns directly. I propose Robespierre provide concrete evidence of these alleged conspiracies or retract his statements."

A swell of agreement met his proposal. Robespierre's face flushed with anger. "You dare question my integrity, Corbeau?"

"I question any action that undermines the principles we vowed to uphold," Étienne replied firmly.

Robespierre's gaze burned with intensity. "Beware, Étienne. Your words tread dangerous ground."

"Perhaps," Étienne conceded, "but silence in the face of injustice is a greater danger."

The chamber erupted in a cacophony of voices. Saint-Just attempted to regain control, but the momentum had shifted irrevocably. Deputies gathered around Étienne, Tallien, and Fouché, forming a united front.

Robespierre, isolated on the podium, seemed to grasp the precariousness of his position. "You are all deceived," he shouted, desperation creeping into his tone. "The enemies of the Revolution manipulate you!"

"Enough!" Tallien declared. "We demand accountability. Unfounded accusations will not hold the Convention hostage."

Étienne felt a strange mix of exhilaration and apprehension. The die was cast, and there was no turning back.

That evening, the conspirators convened at Tallien's residence, a grand townhouse discreetly tucked away on a quiet street. The luxury of the surroundings stood in stark contrast to the day's turmoil.

As plans solidified, people clinked glasses of wine softly. Étienne listened intently as Barras outlined the strategy. "We move tomorrow. Barras plans to put forth a motion to arrest Robespierre and his closest allies. We have the numbers now."

"What of the military?" Fouché inquired. "Robespierre may attempt to rally the National Guard."

"Contingencies are in place," Tallien assured him.

Olympe de Gouges appeared at Étienne's side, her eyes reflecting relief and concern. "You've committed yourself fully," she observed.

"It was necessary," he replied. "Robespierre sealed his fate with that speech."

"Be cautious," she warned. "Desperate men are capable of desperate actions."

He offered a faint smile. "I believe we all are desperate in these times."

She placed a hand on his arm. "When this is over, perhaps we can heal the wounds inflicted upon our nation."

"Perhaps," he agreed, though a shadow of doubt lingered.

As the gathering dispersed, Étienne lingered in the parlour, gazing into the flickering flames of the fireplace. Desmoulins joined him, his face contemplative.

"Do you think we've done the right thing?" Desmoulins asked quietly.

"We've taken a necessary step," Étienne replied. "Whether it's right remains to be seen."

Desmoulins sighed. "The Revolution consumes us all."

"Then let us hope we can redirect its course before it's too late," Étienne said.

They parted ways, and Étienne stepped out into the night. The air had cooled slightly, a gentle breeze carrying the distant sounds of the city—

laughter, a baby's cry, the clatter of a carriage over cobblestones. Life continued amidst the upheaval.

Returning to his apartment, he settled at his desk, the familiar ritual providing a semblance of normalcy. He opened his journal and wrote.

26 July 1794,

Robespierre's speech today was the catalyst we needed. His vague accusations have turned the Convention against him, and I have committed myself fully to the conspiracy. The path ahead is fraught with uncertainty, but action was imperative.

I cannot deny a lingering unease. While I believe in the necessity of our actions, how we achieve our ends weighs heavily upon me. The Revolution has become a labyrinth of moral complexities, and I am no longer sure where I stand.

Tomorrow will be decisive. The course in France will change tomorrow.

He set down the quill, fatigue washing over him. The candle's flame danced erratically, casting elongated shadows that seemed to mock his introspection.

A sudden knock at the door startled him. His heart quickened. "Who is it?" he called out.

"Jacques-Louis David," came the reply.

Étienne exhaled, rising to admit his friend. "Jacques, what brings you out this hour?"

David entered, his expression grave. "I thought you should know—Robespierre is aware of the opposition mounting against him. He's convened a meeting at the Hôtel de Ville tonight."

Étienne's pulse quickened. "Do you think he'll attempt a countermove?"

"It's possible," David acknowledged. "We must be prepared."

"I'll alert the others," Étienne said. "Thank you for informing me."

David nodded. "Take care, Étienne. The stakes have never been higher."

As David departed, Étienne felt the moment's weight settle upon him. The final act was unfolding, and he was a central player.

He penned a brief note to Tallien detailing the new information and dispatched it with a trusted courier. Then, he returned to his desk, gazing out the window at the city bathed in moonlight.

"26 July 1794," he whispered. "The die is cast. May fortune favour us."

Sleep eluded him as he contemplated the consequences of his actions. The Revolution had been a crucible, forging and destroying in equal measure. He wondered whether he had lost a part of himself in striving to save the Republic.

As dawn approached, Étienne prepared to face the day that would determine not only his fate but also the future of France.

• • •

The morning of 27 July 1794 dawned with the air thick with anticipation and the scent of impending upheaval. Étienne Corbeau stood at the window of his apartment overlooking the city, watching as it stirred awake. The sky was a bruised palette of greys and purples, the sun struggling to pierce through the haze.

A sharp knock at the door pulled him from his thoughts. *"Entrez,"* he called out, turning to face the visitor.

Joseph Fouché entered swiftly, his eyes alert and movements brisk. Clad in a simple dark coat, he exuded an air of quiet determination. "It is time," he announced without preamble.

Étienne nodded, his expression unreadable. "The others are in place?"

"Yes," Fouché confirmed. "Tallien and Barras are rallying the deputies. The Convention will convene shortly."

"Très bien," Étienne replied, reaching for his coat and tricolour sash. "We must ensure everything proceeds as planned."

As they stepped out into the street, the sounds of the city enveloped them—vendors setting up stalls, children laughing, the distant rumble of carts over cobblestones. Yet beneath the mundane, an undercurrent of tension thrummed, palpable to those attuned to it.

"Robespierre suspects nothing?" Étienne asked as they navigated the winding streets towards the Tuileries Palace.

Fouché shook his head. "He believes he still holds sway over the Convention. His arrogance blinds him."

A faint smile tugged at the corner of Étienne's mouth. "Then his downfall will be even more complete."

They arrived at the Convention hall, where deputies were already gathering in clusters, their conversations hushed but intense. Étienne could see the mix of fear and resolve etched on their faces. He exchanged nods with Jean-Lambert Tallien and Paul Barras, who stood near the entrance, their expressions grave.

Inside, the atmosphere was electric. The deputies took their seats, the murmur of voices dwindling as Maximilien Robespierre ascended the podium. Clad in his customary austere attire, he surveyed the assembly with a cold, penetrating gaze.

"Citoyens," Robespierre began, his voice resonating through the chamber. "The Republic stands on the precipice of greatness, yet enemies within seek to undermine our hard-won achievements."

Étienne watched him intently, noting the slight tremor in his hands and his jaw's tautness. Robespierre continued, "I have a list of traitors who conspire against the Revolution here."

A murmur rippled through the assembly. This was the moment they had expected.

"Enough of these baseless accusations!" Tallien exclaimed, rising from his seat. "We tire of your tyranny, Robespierre. You have become the very despot we fought to overthrow."

Robespierre's eyes flashed with anger. "You dare challenge me, Tallien? Perhaps your name tops this list."

Others joined in, voices overlapping.

"Liberty cannot survive under your oppressive hand!"

"We demand justice and the rule of law, not fear!"

Étienne stood, his voice cutting through the din. "Robespierre, your reign of terror has fractured the very foundation of our Republic. It is time for a change."

Robespierre glared at him, a mix of disbelief and fury contorting his features. "You too, Corbeau? After all, have we achieved something together?"

"There is no achievement in tyranny," Étienne replied coolly. "The Revolution belongs to the people, not any one man."

Chaos erupted as deputies shouted accusations and demands. Louis Antoine de Saint-Just moved to his side, his face a mask of steely resolve.

"This assembly is out of order," Saint-Just declared. "We must restore decorum."

But the momentum had shifted irreversibly. Guards entered the chamber at Tallien's signal, heightening the tension.

"I propose we arrest Robespierre and his accomplices and hold them accountable for their actions," proclaimed Tallien.

"Seconded!" came voices from across the hall.

Robespierre's face paled. "This is treason," he hissed. "You will all pay dearly."

Étienne felt a detached satisfaction watching the scene unfold. There was no remorse, only a recognition that this was the course. Survival demanded ruthlessness.

As the guards approached, Robespierre attempted to rally his supporters. "*Citoyens*, will you allow this injustice? Stand with me against these traitors!"

Étienne caught sight of Jacques-Louis David, who stood silently observing. Their eyes met briefly, an unspoken understanding passing between them. David nodded subtly before turning away.

The session adjourned amid the tumult. Deputies spilt into the corridors, the weight of their actions settling upon them.

Outside, the sun blazed overhead, indifferent to the human dramas beneath it. Étienne stepped into the glaring light, blinking as his eyes adjusted.

Camille Desmoulins approached his expression, a mix of relief and uncertainty.

"It's done, then," Desmoulins said quietly.

"Yes," Étienne affirmed. "Robespierre is finished," Étienne affirmed.

Desmoulins sighed. "I cannot help but feel we've merely traded one form of chaos for another."

"Perhaps," Étienne acknowledged. "But we must seize control to steer the Republic towards stability."

Desmoulins regarded him thoughtfully. "And at what cost, Étienne? How many more must fall for this elusive stability?"

Étienne met his gaze unflinchingly. "As many as necessary. Sentiment has no place in the harsh realities we face."

Desmoulins shook his head. "I fear for the soul of our nation and yours."

Before Étienne could respond, Olympe de Gouges approached, her eyes searching his face. "Is it over?"

"For Robespierre, yes," he replied.

"And for you?" she pressed.

He offered a mirthless smile. "Survival requires certain sacrifices."

She frowned. "At the expense of your humanity?"

"My humanity is a luxury I cannot afford," he retorted.

She looked away, disappointment clear. "Be careful, Étienne. The path you're on leads to a hollow victory."

He watched her walk away, a fleeting pang of something resembling regret stirring within him. But he dismissed it. Emotions were liabilities he could ill afford.

That evening, Étienne attended a gathering of the new power brokers at Barras's residence. The mood was cautiously celebratory.

"To the Republic," Tallien toasted, raising his glass. "May we guide her towards a brighter future?"

"To the Republic," voices echoed.

Étienne sipped his wine, the taste bitter on his tongue. Conversations buzzed around him—plans for restructuring the government, discussions of potential threats, alliances being forged and broken in moments.

Fouché sidled up beside him. "You seem pensive, Corbeau."

"Merely contemplating the work ahead," Étienne replied.

"Indeed," Fouché agreed. "Power vacuums are dangerous. We must act swiftly to merge control."

Étienne nodded. "Agreed. We cannot allow factions to destabilise what we've achieved."

"Precisely," Fouché said, a calculating gleam in his eye. "There is room for those with vision and fortitude."

Étienne recognised the unspoken offer. "I appreciate your confidence."

"Think about it," Fouché suggested before moving on to another conversation.

As the night progressed, Étienne felt increasingly detached. The victory felt hollow, the celebrations empty. He had survived, yes, but at what cost? The faces of those he had betrayed flickered in his mind—Robespierre's shock, Desmoulins' disillusionment, Olympe's disappointment.

Excusing himself, he left the gathering and entered the cool night air. The streets were quieter now, and the earlier fervour diminished. He wandered, the sounds of the city fading into the background.

He found himself by the Seine, the river's dark waters reflecting the moon's pale glow. Leaning against the stone parapet, he gazed into the depths, his thoughts as murky as the currents below.

"27 July 1794," he murmured. "I have secured my survival, yet I stand alone."

He recalled the enthusiasm of the Revolution's early days—the ideals, the camaraderie, the sense of purpose—and how far they had strayed from those aspirations.

Returning to his apartment, he settled at his desk and opened his journal.

---

27 July 1794,

Today, I contributed to Maximilien Robespierre's downfall. I feel no remorse for my betrayal; it was a calculated necessity. The Revolution demands ruthlessness, and I have embraced it.

Yet, as I reflect upon the events, hollow echoes within me, tainted by the realisation that I have become what I once despised. The Revolution devours its own, and I am both witness and participant.

Survival is paramount, but at what cost to the soul? I find myself isolated, the connections that once grounded me severed by my hand.

Perhaps this is the price of power—an existence of solitude and suspicion.

Time will tell if it was worth it.

He closed the journal, the weight of his actions settling upon him like a shroud. The flickering candle cast long shadows across the room, mirroring the darkness creeping into his spirit.

As Étienne Corbeau extinguished the flame and lay down to rest, he realised that securing his survival required him to sacrifice a part of himself that he could never reclaim.

The Revolution churned on, indifferent to his inner turmoil. And as sleep eluded him, he stared into the abyss of his own making, acutely aware of the emptiness that awaited him.

• • •

Étienne stood atop the steps of the Église de la Madeleine on the fateful day of 27 July 1794, its imposing columns casting long shadows across the Place de la Révolution. From this vantage point, he could observe the unfolding drama without being trapped in its immediacy. The distant murmurs of the crowd reached him—a low, restless hum that mirrored the turmoil within his mind.

Below, the Convention was in chaos. Deputies surged through the streets, their faces etched with a volatile mix of fear and enthusiasm. The National Guard, previously loyal to Robespierre, now hesitated; their allegiances fractured. Étienne watched as a contingent of guards marched towards the Hôtel de Ville, where Robespierre and his remaining allies had retreated.

Beside him, a woman adjusted her shawl, glaring at the unfolding spectacle. *"Quel désordre,"* she muttered.

"Indeed," Étienne replied absently, his gaze fixed on the distant figures. He could make out the distinctive silhouette of Louis Antoine de Saint-Just, standing resolute beside Robespierre on the balcony of the Hôtel de Ville. Their expressions were defiant, but there was a palpable tension—a realisation that the tide had irrevocably turned against them.

A sudden commotion rippled through the crowd as soldiers stormed the building. Shouts and the clatter of muskets echoed across the square. Étienne felt a surge of adrenaline, yet an unexpected emptiness tempered it. He had orchestrated this moment, but the expected satisfaction eluded him.

"Vive la Révolution!" someone shouted nearby, their voice a shrill note against the din.

Étienne turned away from the scene, descending the steps with measured strides. The cobblestones beneath his boots felt unsteady as if reflecting the instability of the times. He navigated the labyrinthine streets, the sounds of upheaval fading behind him.

Passing the shuttered windows of once-thriving shops, he could not help but notice the pervasive air of desolation. Paris, the heartbeat of the Revolution, seemed drained of vitality—a city caught in exhaustion.

He went to the *Jardin des Tuileries*, seeking respite among the wilted greenery. Only a few people populated the gardens, and the usual bustle was subdued. Finding an empty bench beneath a sagging chestnut tree, he sat down heavily.

"Is this victory?" he mused aloud, the words tasting bitter. The sacrifices made, the alliances forged and broken—all had led to this juncture. Yet, instead of triumph, he felt an unsettling void.

Footsteps approached, and he glanced up to see Jacques-Louis David standing before him, his attire dishevelled and eyes shadowed with fatigue.

"Étienne," David greeted him quietly. "I thought I might find you here."

"Jacques," Étienne acknowledged. "The city is aflame with rumours."

"They have apprehended Robespierre," David confirmed, sitting beside him. "Saint-Just as well. It is over."

Étienne nodded slowly. "So it seems."

David studied him for a moment. "You do not appear relieved."

"Should I be?" Étienne countered. "One tyrant falls, and another will rise to take his place. The cycle is unending."

"Perhaps," David conceded. "But we must hold on to hope that change is possible."

"Hope is a fragile thing," Étienne remarked, his gaze distant. "Easily shattered by the realities of power."

They lapsed into silence, the weight of unspoken thoughts settling between them. Finally, David rose. "Take care of yourself, *mon ami.* These are uncertain times."

"And you, Jacques," Étienne replied, watching the artist walk away, his figure blending into the mosaic of shadows.

Alone once more, Étienne allowed his mind to wander. Memories surfaced—conversations with Robespierre in dimly lit rooms, the fierce ideals they once shared. He recalled the intensity of Robespierre's gaze and the conviction in his voice. And now, that same man was in chains, his fate sealed by the revolution he sought to steer.

A flicker of doubt ignited within Étienne. Had he been too ruthless? Too willing to sacrifice others for his preservation? The questions twisted like thorny vines around his conscience.

"Regrets, *monsieur?*" a voice interrupted his reverie.

He turned to see Olympe de Gouges standing nearby, her expression inscrutable. Clad in a simple gown, she exuded a quiet strength that belied the turmoil.

"Merely reflections," he responded guardedly.

She approached, her gaze steady. "Robespierre's fall was inevitable, but the manner of it… It leaves a bitter taste, does it not?"

Étienne considered her words. "He became a danger to the Republic. Action was necessary."

"Perhaps," she allowed. "But at what cost to ourselves? To you?"

He met her eyes. "Survival demands tough choices."

"Survival at the expense of one's soul is a hollow victory," she retorted gently.

He looked away, the truth of her statement piercing through his defences. "Do you judge me, Olympe?"

"I seek to understand," she replied. "We all carry burdens. I wonder if yours has become too heavy to bear alone."

Étienne sighed, the weight of exhaustion pressing upon him. "Isolation is the price of ambition, it seems."

"It need not be," she offered. "There is still time to rediscover the ideals we once held dear."

He shook his head slowly. "Those ideals feel like distant echoes, drowned out by the machinations of power."

She placed a hand on his shoulder. "Do not let the darkness consume you, Étienne. The Revolution brought enlightenment, not despair."

He gave a wan smile. "You have always been the beacon amidst the shadows."

"Then let me guide you back to the light," she implored softly.

Before he could respond, a distant bell tolled, its sombre notes resonating through the evening air. Olympe withdrew her hand, a hint of sadness in her eyes. "I must go. Take care."

As she departed, Étienne felt a profound sense of loss—a realisation that in his pursuit of survival, he had distanced himself from the very connections that gave life meaning.

Rising from the bench, he meandered through the gardens, the fading light casting elongated shadows that seemed to reach out like spectral hands. The surrounding city was a mosaic of contrasts—beauty intertwined with decay, hope entangled with despair.

He found himself near the banks of the Seine, the river's dark waters reflecting the first glimmers of starlight. The gentle lapping of waves against the stone embankment provided a melancholic melody.

"Is this what I sought?" he wondered aloud. "A victory devoid of joy, a future shrouded in uncertainty?"

The faces of those he had outmanoeuvred swam before his eyes—Robespierre, who held unwavering conviction;

He recalled the passage from Rousseau: "Man is born free, and everywhere he is in chains." He did not miss the irony. In breaking the chains imposed by others, had he forged new ones for himself?

As night enveloped the city, Étienne made his way back to his apartment. The familiar surroundings felt alien, the walls closing in like a confining embrace. He lit a candle, the flame casting a feeble glow that barely pierced the darkness.

Seated at his desk, he opened his journal, the blank pages waiting to absorb his thoughts.

---

27 July 1794,

The very forces Robespierre sought to control arrested him, thus ending his reign. I watched from afar as the culmination of my schemes unfolded, yet the satisfaction I expected eludes me.

The victory feels hollow, a façade that crumbles upon closer inspection. In my quest for survival and influence, I have isolated myself and severed ties that once anchored me to a shared purpose.

I cannot escape the gnawing question: was it worth it? The power, the manoeuvring, the betrayals—do they amount to anything of substance?

Perhaps Olympe is right. Perhaps I have sacrificed too much of myself.

But I cannot reverse the actions I have taken. I am left to navigate the consequences of my choices, to confront the emptiness that shadows me.

The Revolution churns on, indifferent to individual fates. And I, Étienne Corbeau, am but a solitary figure adrift in its turbulent currents.

Though I cannot see the path clearly, I must find a way forward.

He set down the quill, a heaviness settling in his chest. The candle flickered, its flame wavering as if mirroring his own uncertainty.

A sudden knock at the door startled him. He hesitated before rising, a sense of foreboding creeping in. "Who is it?" he called out.

"Camille Desmoulins," came the muffled reply.

Surprised, Étienne opened the door to reveal Desmoulins standing in the dimly lit corridor. His friend's eyes were weary, yet held a glimmer of something akin to hope.

"May I come in?" Desmoulins asked.

"Of course," Étienne replied, stepping aside.

They settled into chairs by the window, the sounds of the night filtering in—a distant murmur of voices, the clip-clop of a horse's hooves on cobblestone.

"I wanted to see how you were faring," Desmoulins began. "It's been a tumultuous day."

"That it has," Étienne agreed. "And you? How do you feel about it all?"

Desmoulins sighed. "Conflicted. Robespierre's downfall was necessary, but I cannot help but mourn the loss of what we once believed in."

"Beliefs have a way of eroding under the weight of reality," Étienne observed.

"Perhaps," Desmoulins conceded. "But I refuse to let go entirely. There must be a way to rebuild, to steer the Revolution back towards its original ideals."

Étienne regarded him thoughtfully. "You still possess that unwavering optimism."

Desmoulins smiled faintly. "Someone must. Otherwise, what was it all for?"

A silence settled between them, not uncomfortable but reflective. Finally, Desmoulins stood. "I won't keep you. I merely wanted to remind you that you're not alone, Étienne. Despite everything."

"Thank you," Étienne said sincerely. "Your friendship means more than you know."

As Desmoulins departed, Étienne felt a small measure of solace. Perhaps Étienne didn't lose everything. Perhaps we could mend connections and rediscover purpose.

He returned to his journal, adding a final line:

> *Tonight, a glimmer of light pierces the darkness. I am reminded that isolation is a choice, not an inevitability. The cost of my ambitions has been steep, but redemption may yet be within reach.*
>
> *Tomorrow, I shall seek an alternative path.*

Extinguishing the candle, he gazed out into the night. The city slept, but the first hints of dawn were painting the horizon with soft hues of gold and rose.

Étienne Corbeau, anti-hero and architect of his own fate, closed his eyes, allowing the quiet hope of renewal to settle within him.

The Revolution's wheel turned ceaselessly. But perhaps, just perhaps, there was room for transformation—for both himself and the nation he had sought to shape.

• • •

The hesitant sun of 28 July 1794 cast a wan light over Paris, its rays filtered through a pall of smoke and dust that seemed to hang perpetually above the city. Étienne Corbeau stood amidst the throng gathered at the Place de la Révolution, his features shadowed beneath the brim of his hat. The air was thick with a morbid anticipation, a collective breath held as the final act of a protracted tragedy prepared to unfold.

"28 July 1794," he murmured to himself, the date echoing in his mind like a sombre tolling bell. The Revolution had come full circle, and he was here to witness the demise of a man who had once embodied its vibrant spirit.

The guillotine loomed ahead, a stark silhouette against the pale sky. Around him, vendors hawked stale bread and diluted wine, their voices hollow amid the low hum of the crowd. The scent of unwashed bodies mingled with the odour of fear and sweat, creating an oppressive atmosphere that pressed upon his senses.

A woman nearby clutched a small child to her breast, whispering a prayer. *"Dieu nous protégé,"* she breathed.

Étienne glanced at her before returning his gaze to the scaffold. The National Guard formed a cordon around the platform, their expressions inscrutable beneath tricolour cockades. He recognised some of them—faces hardened by months of unrest, eyes dulled by the relentless march of death.

The guards led forth the prisoners, causing a ripple of movement through the assembly. Maximilien Robespierre emerged, his once austere demeanour now marred by pain and resignation. A bloodied bandage wrapped his shattered jaw—a grim testament to a failed attempt at escape through death. Beside him walked Louis Antoine de Saint-Just, his youthful features set in a mask of stoic defiance.

Étienne felt a tightening in his chest as he watched Robespierre ascend the steps with faltering steps. This was the Incorruptible, the architect of so much hope and so much terror. Now reduced to a spectacle, a cautionary emblem of the very forces he had unleashed.

"Thus falls the mighty," a voice murmured beside him.

He turned to see Camille Desmoulins, his face etched with a mixture of sorrow and grim satisfaction. "Camille," Étienne acknowledged softly. "I did not expect to find you here."

Desmoulins offered a faint smile. "And yet, here we both are. Perhaps it's fitting—we who have walked this path together should witness its inevitable conclusion."

Étienne nodded, his gaze returning to the scaffold. "A last act in this relentless tragedy."

As the executioner prepared the blade, a hush settled over the crowd. The drumroll began—a steady, ominous beat that seemed to echo the pounding of Étienne's own heart. They guided Robespierre to the plank, his movements mechanical. For a fleeting moment, his eyes met Étienne's across the expanse—a gaze that held a myriad of unspoken words, accusations, perhaps even a plea.

"Do you feel anything?" Desmoulins asked quietly.

Étienne hesitated. "I thought I might feel relief or perhaps vindication. But now… only emptiness."

Desmoulins sighed. Friend and foe alike, the Revolution consumes all.

As the blade fell with swift finality, a collective gasp rose from the assembled masses upon the display of Robespierre's severed head. The drum ceased, leaving a profound silence in its wake—a void where sound dared not intrude.

Étienne closed his eyes, the image seared into his memory. Another life extinguished in the name of liberty, equality, fraternity. Yet the ideals felt hollow, tarnished by the very bloodshed intended to uphold them.

"How many more must die before it ends?" he whispered.

Desmoulins placed a hand on his shoulder. "Perhaps this is the turning point. The end of the Terror."

"Or merely a pause before the next cycle of violence," Étienne replied bitterly.

As the crowd dispersed, the macabre spectacle concluded, life resumed its relentless pace. Vendors packed away their wares, conversations rose in subdued tones, and the city breathed once more.

"Walk with me," Étienne suggested.

They threaded their way through the labyrinthine streets, the cacophony of Paris enveloping them—the clatter of carriage wheels, the distant strains of a street musician's melody, the murmur of countless voices blending into a discordant symphony.

"Do you recall when it all began?" Étienne mused. "The fervour that ignited the hearts of men, the unshakeable belief that we could forge a new world."

Desmoulins smiled wistfully. "The day I stood upon a café table and rallied the people to arms. It feels like a lifetime ago."

"A different world entirely," Étienne agreed. "We were idealists then, untainted by the realities of power."

"And now?" Desmoulins prompted.

"Now, I wonder if we have become the very thing we sought to destroy."

They paused on the Pont Neuf, leaning against the stone balustrade as they gazed upon the Seine's languid flow. The river mirrored the sky's melancholy hues, its surface marred only by the occasional ripple of a passing boat.

"Do you regret your choices?" Desmoulins asked.

Étienne considered the question. "Regret implies the possibility of change. I did what I believed was necessary to survive. But I cannot ignore the emptiness that accompanies this so-called victory."

Desmoulins nodded thoughtfully. "Perhaps we lost ourselves along the way, traded our souls for fleeting power."

"Is redemption possible?" Étienne wondered aloud. "Can we reclaim the ideals we once held, dear?"

"Only if we choose to," Desmoulins replied. "The path forward is ours to shape. Should we have the courage?"

They stood in contemplative silence, the weight of their reflections heavy yet shared. Étienne felt a flicker of something—hope, or perhaps the mere acknowledgement of possibility.

As they resumed their walk, Desmoulins spoke. "I plan to resume my writings, to use words to heal rather than to inflame."

"Words have power," Étienne agreed. "Perhaps more enduring than the blade."

"Join me," Desmoulins suggested. "Let's strive to mend what we have broken," Desmoulins suggested.

Étienne offered a faint smile. "I will consider it."

Their paths diverged as Desmoulins took his leave, disappearing into the warren of streets. Étienne continued on, his steps unhurried, his thoughts a tumultuous current.

He found himself drawn to the Luxembourg Gardens, seeking solace among the manicured lawns and sculpted hedges. The tranquillity of the surroundings starkly contrasted with the inner turmoil he was grappling with.

Seating himself on a wrought-iron bench beneath a canopy of linden trees, he watched as children chased one another. Their laughter was a poignant reminder of innocence untainted by the world's cruelties. A painter nearby captured the scene with deft strokes, his canvas a vibrant testament to moments of fleeting joy.

"Beautiful, isn't it?" a voice remarked.

He turned to see Olympe de Gouges approaching, her eyes reflecting a quiet empathy. "Olympe," he acknowledged. "It is indeed."

She sat beside him, the rustle of her skirts blending with the whisper of leaves. "I heard about today."

"News travels swiftly," he noted.

"Especially such news," she replied. "How do you feel?"

"Adrift," he confessed. "As though I've reached the summit only to find the view obscured by fog."

She studied him thoughtfully. "Perhaps the journey was flawed, the path leading not to elevation but to isolation."

"Isolation," he echoed. "An apt description."

"You are not beyond redemption, Étienne," she said gently. "The Revolution need not define you entirely."

He glanced at her, a flicker of vulnerability crossing his features. "I fear I've strayed too far."

"It's never too late to seek a different course," she insisted. "The ideals we fought for still hold value, tarnished though they may be."

He sighed. "I question whether those ideals can withstand the weight of reality."

"Only if we allow them to be overshadowed," she countered. "We must be the custodians of our own principles."

A silence settled between them, the sounds of the garden enveloping their introspection. Finally, Étienne spoke. "Thank you, Olympe. Your words offer a glimmer amidst the shadows."

She smiled softly. "I believe in you, even if you struggle to believe in yourself."

As she rose to leave, she placed a hand lightly on his shoulder. "Take care, Étienne. The path ahead is yours to choose."

He watched her depart, a sense of both longing and resolve stirring within him. Perhaps there was a way to reconcile the man he had become with the ideals he once cherished.

Returning to his apartment as dusk painted the sky in hues of amber and rose, he settled at his desk. The familiar scratch of the quill against parchment provided a semblance of order amidst the chaos.

28 July 1794,

Today, I bore witness to the execution of Maximilien Robespierre—a man of unwavering conviction, undone by the very revolution he sought to shepherd. I stand amidst the ashes of our aspirations, questioning the worth of all that has transpired.

The cycle of violence continues unabated, each act begetting another in a relentless march towards oblivion. I am left to ponder the cost of my ambitions—the alliances betrayed, the moral compromises embraced.

Yet, amid the desolation, there are whispers of hope. Conversations with Camille and Olympe remind me that the human spirit endures that redemption remains within reach should one choose to grasp it.

I cannot change the past, but perhaps I can influence the future. It is a fragile thread, but it is one I am compelled to follow.

The Revolution has devoured many, but it need not consume all.

He set down the quill, a sense of quiet determination settling over him. The soft candlelight illuminated the room, transforming the threatening shadows into merely present ones.

A soft knock at the door drew his attention. Rising, he opened it to reveal Madame de Staël, her eyes alight with curiosity.

"Madame," he greeted her with a slight bow. "This is an unexpected honour."

She smiled graciously. "I thought it prudent to check on one of our most intriguing minds during these turbulent times."

"Please, come in," he offered.

They engaged in a discourse that spanned the philosophical to the personal, her insights probing yet compassionate. "The Revolution is but a stage," she mused. "The genuine test lies in what we build upon its foundations."

"I fear the foundations are unstable," Étienne remarked.

"Then it is our duty to strengthen them," she countered. "Through reason, through art, through a recommitment to the principles that ignited the flame."

As she departed, Étienne felt a renewed sense of purpose. The path ahead was uncertain fraught with challenges, yet he no longer felt adrift.

He returned to the window, gazing out over the city as the first stars emerged. Paris breathed beneath him, a mosaic of light and shadow, hope and despair intertwined.

"28 July 1794," he whispered. "A day of endings, and perhaps, the genesis of a new beginning."

Étienne Corbeau, once an architect of turmoil, now contemplated the possibility of becoming a catalyst for restoration. The Revolution's cycle need not define him; the emptiness he felt could be the space from which to cultivate something enduring.

He embraced the uncertainty and resolved to navigate the complexities with a renewed commitment to the ideals that once guided him.

The future beckoned—a canvas awaiting the strokes of intention and action. And for the first time in a long while, Étienne felt prepared to engage with it entirely.

•••

The sultry afternoon of 31 July 1794 enveloped Paris in a haze, the air heavy with the lingering scents of smoke and uncertainty. Étienne Corbeau stood on the balcony of his modest apartment overlooking the Rue Saint-Honoré, observing the ebb and flow of the city's life below. The din of the marketplace mingled with the distant tolling of church bells, creating a discordant symphony that echoed the tumultuous state of the nation.

Étienne sipped a cup of lukewarm coffee, its bitterness a fitting accompaniment to his thoughts. He contemplated the recent decrees issued by the Convention—abolishing the Law of 22 Prairial, releasing many political prisoners, and curbing the powers of the Committee of Public Safety. The architects of the Terror were being purged, and a cautious optimism flickered among the populace.

Yet, for Étienne, the shifting sands of power signalled a treacherous landscape. The alliances he had forged were fragile, contingent upon mutual benefit rather than genuine trust. With Robespierre gone, the balance of influence had tilted, and new players emerged to vie for dominance. However, remnants of pro-Robespierre factions still lurked in the shadows, their loyalty unwavering despite the fall of their leader. Rumours of clandestine meetings and covert operations to reclaim their lost power reached Étienne's ears, heightening his vulnerability.

A knock at the door interrupted his reflections. Setting down his cup, he moved to answer.

"Étienne," Camille Desmoulins greeted him with a wan smile. "May I come in?"

"Of course," Étienne replied, stepping aside. "I was just pondering the state of affairs."

"As are we all," Camille remarked, removing his hat and running a hand through his untamed hair. "The Convention is a hive of activity. They've declared an end to the Terror's excesses."

Étienne gestured for him to sit. "And do you believe them?"

Camille sighed, settling into a worn armchair. "I want to. The people are weary of bloodshed. There is talk of restoring liberties, of healing the wounds inflicted upon our nation."

"Talk is plentiful," Étienne observed. "Action is another matter."

Camille regarded him thoughtfully. "You sound sceptical."

"Merely cautious," Étienne corrected. "We've seen how swiftly tides can turn. Those who were allies yesterday may become adversaries tomorrow."

"True," Camille conceded. "But perhaps we steer the Revolution back towards its original ideals."

Étienne leaned against the mantelpiece, the flickering light of the hearth casting shadows across his features. "And who will lead this resurgence? The likes of Tallien and Barras? They are as ambitious as any, their motives clouded by self-interest."

Camille's eyes flickered with a hint of frustration. "Not everyone is driven solely by ambition, Étienne. There are those who genuinely seek to mend our fractured society."

"Perhaps," Étienne allowed. "But one must navigate carefully. The political landscape is fraught with hidden snares."

A silence settled between them, each lost in their own thoughts. Finally, Camille spoke. "They asked me to contribute to a new publication—an effort to promote reconciliation and reason," Camille said.

"Your words have always held power," Étienne acknowledged. "Perhaps they can inspire change where actions have failed."

Camille offered a faint smile. "Would you consider joining me? Your insights could lend weight to our cause."

Étienne hesitated. "I am uncertain my voice would be welcome. There are those who view me with suspicion."

"All the more reason to speak," Camille urged. "To dispel doubts, to show your commitment to a better future."

Étienne considered the proposition. "I will think about it."

As Camille departed, Étienne returned to the balcony, the city's bustle continuing unabated. He knew that accepting Camille's offer would align him with a faction that, while noble in intent, might lack the political clout to protect him. Yet remaining aloof carried its own risks—isolated, he could become an easy target for those seeking scapegoats in this new order.

Joseph Fouché, who appeared unannounced at his door, interrupted his thoughts.

"Étienne," Fouché greeted him with a measured nod. "May we speak?"

"Certainly," Étienne replied, masking his surprise. "What brings you here?"

Fouché entered, his sharp gaze taking in the surroundings. "The Convention is undergoing significant changes. The Committees are being restructured, and new appointments are imminent."

"And you have a proposal?" Étienne surmised.

"An opportunity," Fouché corrected. "Your skills and experience could be invaluable in the reformed government."

Étienne raised an eyebrow. "I thought my associations might render me unsuitable."

Fouché waved a dismissive hand. "Past affiliations are of little consequence if one proves adaptable. The key is to align oneself with the prevailing winds."

"Meaning aligning with you," Étienne inferred.

Fouché smiled thinly. "We share a pragmatic approach. Ideals are commendable, but survival hinges on understanding the realities of power."

Étienne regarded him steadily. "And what role would you envision for me?"

"A position within the Committee of General Security," Fouché suggested. "Your acumen would be a valuable asset."

"Monitoring internal threats," Étienne mused. "Maintaining order."

"Precisely," Fouché confirmed. "In these times, stability is paramount."

Étienne weighed the offer. Accepting could secure his position, yet it tethered him to a man whose loyalties were as fluid as the Seine.

"I will need to consider," he replied carefully.

"Do not tarry," Fouché advised. "Decisions are being made swiftly."

After Fouché's departure, Étienne found himself at a crossroads. Camille's offer represented a path towards redemption and the restoration of principles he once held dear. Fouché's proposition, however, offered security and influence in a volatile environment. Yet, the looming threat of pro-Robespierre elements—those still loyal to the fallen leader and eager to exact retribution—forced Étienne to reconsider his options. The whispers of conspiracies and the sightings of familiar faces in suspicious gatherings indicated that danger was far from over.

He ventured out into the streets, seeking clarity amid the city's pulse. The cafés bustled with animated discussions. Citizens debated passionately, their voices a tapestry of hope and scepticism. But beneath the surface, Étienne sensed the undercurrents of fear and suspicion—residual loyalties that could turn deadly.

Entering the *Café de la Régence*, he spotted Olympe de Gouges seated by a window, engrossed in writing. She looked up as he approached.

"Étienne," she greeted warmly. "Join me."

He took a seat opposite her. "You seem absorbed."

"Penning a new pamphlet," she explained. "Advocating for the rights of all citizens, regardless of gender or station."

He smiled appreciatively. "Your resolve is unwavering."

"Now more than ever," she affirmed. "The Revolution must encompass true equality."

He hesitated before confiding, saying, "I have been presented with choices—paths that could define my future."

She regarded him with a knowing gaze. "Fouché has approached you."

"Yes," he admitted. "As has Camille, in a different capacity."

"And you," she concluded, "are experiencing inner conflict."

"Indeed," he acknowledged. "One offers influence and security, the other a chance to reclaim lost ideals."

She leaned forward. "Power without purpose is hollow, Étienne. You've seen where ambition untempered by conscience leads."

He nodded thoughtfully. "Your counsel is, as always, invaluable."

She smiled softly. "Follow the path that aligns with who you wish to become, not merely who you have been."

As evening descended, Étienne wandered along the banks of the Seine, the river reflecting the city's shimmering lights. He contemplated the intricate dance of shadows and illumination, a metaphor for his choices. The residual threat of pro-Robespierre factions made staying in Paris increasingly perilous. The remnants of the Terror were not quickly silenced, and any misstep could spell disaster.

Returning home, he resolved to act. He wrote Camille, declining his offer to contribute to the publication. He recognised that genuine change required more than manoeuvring within the corridors of power; it demanded a commitment to principles—a willingness to shape the discourse. Simultaneously, he drafted a polite decline to Fouché, expressing gratitude but wanting to pursue a different path. The decision was clear: remaining in Paris was no longer safe. To protect himself and those he cared about, Étienne knew he had to flee.

He penned a final entry in his journal:

31 July 1794,

The Convention moves to dismantle the apparatus of the Terror, ushering in a new chapter. I stand at the threshold of choices, defining my role in this evolving landscape. "I choose to align with those who seek to heal and restore rather than merely to wield power. It is a risk that aligns with a rekindled sense of purpose.

Navigating this changed environment will require care, but I embrace the uncertainty with a resolve anchored in the ideals that first ignited the Revolution. "Perhaps, in contributing to the shaping of thought and the promotion of reason, I can find redemption and a measure of peace.

He set down the quill, a sense of clarity settling over him. The path ahead was uncertain, but he felt aligned with a purpose beyond survival for the first time in a long while. However, the lingering threat of pro-Robespierre elements meant that staying posed a significant risk. Étienne made the difficult decision to leave Paris, knowing that his departure would be met with resistance from those still loyal to the old guard.

As he prepared to flee, the weight of his choices pressed upon him. The ambition that had once driven him to influence the course of the Revolution now necessitated his departure to preserve his life and sanity. Étienne knew that escaping Paris was not just a matter of physical distance but a symbolic severance from his past misdeeds and the chaos they had wrought.

He packed his few belongings swiftly, ensuring no trace of his presence remained. The night air was calm as he slipped through the narrow streets, blending into the shadows of gaslit lanterns. The city that had been his battleground was now a labyrinth he needed to navigate with utmost caution.

As Étienne left Paris behind, he felt fear and liberation. The journey ahead was uncertain, but it was a necessary step towards survival and, perhaps, eventual redemption. The city lights faded in the distance, replaced by the starlit expanse of the countryside, offering a glimmer of hope amidst the darkness of his tumultuous journey.

With one final glance back at the city that had shaped and shattered him, Étienne Corbeau set forth into the unknown, determined to forge a new path away from the shadows of his past and the lingering threats that still sought his downfall.

CHAPTER NINE: (1795)
SHATTERED FAÇADES

The bleak winter landscape stretched endlessly before him, a tapestry of barren fields and skeletal trees shrouded in mist. Étienne Corbeau—now known as Pierre Blanchet—stood at the threshold of his modest cottage on the outskirts of Montferrand, the chill of 12 February 1795 seeping into his bones. He pulled his threadbare coat tighter around his slender frame, his once-refined attire replaced by the plain garments of a provincial merchant.

The village was far from the tumultuous streets of Paris he had navigated with cunning and ambition. Here, the air was thick with the scent of damp earth and wood smoke, a stark contrast to the smoke of gunpowder and the metallic tang of fear that had pervaded the capital. Yet, despite the tranquillity of his surroundings, a relentless unease gnawed at him—a phantom lurking in the shadows of his mind.

"Bonjour, Monsieur Blanchet!" a voice called out.

He turned to see Madame Dupont, the innkeeper's wife, shuffling along the muddy path with a basket of linens on her ample hip. The cold had flushed her cheeks, and wisps of greying hair escaped her bonnet.

"Bonjour, Madame Dupont," he replied with a forced smile.

"Are you settling in well?" she inquired, her eyes crinkling at the corners. "It's rare to see unfamiliar faces in our little corner of the world."

"Oui, très bien," Étienne lied smoothly. "The village is peaceful, and the people are kind."

"That's good to hear," she nodded approvingly. "If you need anything, ask."

"Merci beaucoup," he said, inclining his head.

As she continued on her way, Étienne felt a pang of guilt. The villagers saw him as Pierre Blanchet, a reclusive merchant seeking solace in the countryside. They knew nothing of his true identity, of the intrigues and betrayals that had propelled him to the heart of the Revolution—and subsequently cast him out.

He retreated indoors, the door creaking shut behind him. The interior had sparse furnishings, including a worn table, a solitary chair, and a narrow bed tucked against the wall. A fire crackled weakly in the hearth, offering scant warmth against the encroaching cold. He moved to the window, the panes frosted at the edges and peered out cautiously.

Every rustling branch, every distant footfall set his nerves on edge. Paranoia had become his constant companion, a shadow he could not escape. He feared that at any moment, agents of the Convention—or worse, remnants of Robespierre's supporters—would descend upon him, exacting retribution for his past deeds.

"Mon Dieu," he whispered, running a hand through his unkempt hair. "Is this to be my existence? A prisoner of my making?"

He recalled the heady days of influence and intrigue—the corridors of power where he had once walked confidently, manipulating events to his advantage. The faces of those he had outmanoeuvred haunted him: Maximilien Robespierre, whose execution he had orchestrated; Louis Antoine de Saint-Just, steadfast to the end; even Camille Desmoulins, whose idealism had both inspired and confounded him.

Now, stripped of title and standing, he grappled with the stark reality of anonymity. The weight of isolation pressed upon him, each passing day a reminder of his fall from grace.

A sudden knock at the door jolted him from his reverie. His heart raced, the sound echoing ominously in the quiet space.

"Who is it?" he called out, striving to steady his voice.

"It's Lucien," came the muffled reply. "Lucien Moreau."

Étienne exhaled slowly. Lucien was the village's blacksmith—a burly man with a ruddy complexion and a genial disposition.

He opened the door cautiously. "Bonjour, Lucien."

"Pierre!" Lucien beamed. "I hope I'm not disturbing you."

"Not at all," Étienne assured him. "What brings you here?"

"I noticed your fire's low," Lucien said, gesturing towards the chimney. "Thought I'd bring you some extra logs. Winter's not done with us yet."

"That's very kind of you," Étienne replied, a genuine warmth touching his tone. "Please, come in."

They entered the cottage, and Lucien set the logs beside the hearth. "It's the least I can do," he said. "You're part of our community now."

Étienne managed a faint smile. "I appreciate your generosity."

Lucien glanced around the sparse room. "You're a quiet one, aren't you? Keeps to himself, the villagers say."

"I suppose I'm used to solitude," Étienne admitted.

"Well, if you ever fancy a pint and some company, the inn's always lively," Lucien offered. "We could use another voice to argue politics with old Bertrand."

"Politics?" Étienne's gaze sharpened involuntarily.

"Aye," Lucien chuckled. "Bertrand fancies himself an expert on the Revolution, though I reckon he's full of hot air."

Étienne's stomach tightened. "I prefer to leave politics behind," he said carefully. "Too much strife for my liking."

"Can't blame you there," Lucien nodded. "These are uncertain times."

"Indeed," Étienne agreed.

An awkward silence settled before Lucien clapped his hands. "Well, I won't keep you. Just remember, you're not alone here."

"Merci, Lucien," Étienne said sincerely. "Your kindness means more than you know."

As the blacksmith departed, Étienne felt a flicker of something resembling hope—a slight reprieve from his isolation. Yet, the mention of politics had reignited his anxiety. He wondered how much the villagers knew and how long he could maintain his façade.

He moved to the small desk in the corner, retrieving a worn journal from a hidden compartment. Flipping to a blank page, he wrote:

12 February 1795,

The days blur together in this place, each a mirror of the last. I exist as Pierre Blanchet, a shadow of the man I once was. The anonymity is both a refuge and a torment. I am haunted by the ghosts of my past—decisions that, while necessary, have left indelible marks upon my soul.

Lucien's kindness is a stark contrast to the duplicity I have known. Yet, I cannot fully embrace it. Trust is a luxury I cannot afford. The spectre of retribution looms ever-present.

I question whether redemption is possible or if I am condemned to this half-life, a phantom hiding from the Revolution I helped shape.

He set down the quill, rubbing his temples wearily. The weight of his thoughts was suffocating. Engaging with the villagers could ease his solitude, but the risk of exposure was too significant.

A sudden gust rattled the windowpanes, and Étienne's gaze snapped towards the sound. Through the distorted glass, he thought he glimpsed a figure lingering at the treeline's edge—an indistinct yet unsettling silhouette.

He blinked, and the figure was gone. "Imagination," he muttered, though his pulse quickened. The paranoia tightened its grip, feeding on his isolation.

Determined to regain composure, he stoked the flames, dancing shadows across the walls. He settled into the chair, drawing a tattered book from the shelf—Voltaire's *"Candide."* The familiar prose offered a semblance of comfort, a connection to a world beyond his self-imposed exile.

As the hours slipped by, the words blurred on the page. Fatigue tugged at his eyelids, but sleep remained elusive. The silence of the night amplified every creak, every whisper of wind. He couldn't shake the sensation of being watched, of unseen eyes observing his every move.

"Get a hold of yourself," he chastised softly. "Fear is the enemy."

Yet, logic did little to quell the unease. He considered the possibility that someone had recognised him, that whispers of his true identity had reached even this remote village.

"Tomorrow," he resolved, "I will make discreet inquiries."

He extinguished the lamp, darkness enveloping the room. Lying on the narrow bed, he stared into the void, his mind a maelstrom of doubt and regret.

"12 February 1795," he whispered into the emptiness. "How far I have fallen?"

As he finally fell asleep, fragmented images plagued his dreams—a guillotine's blade gleaming under a pale sun, faces twisted in accusation, and a crowd's roar swelling to a deafening crescendo.

The dawn would bring no respite, only the continuation of his silent battle—a man caught between the shadows of his past and the uncertainty of his future.

• • •

The pale sun of 20 February 1795 struggled to penetrate the low-hanging clouds that draped over the village like a threadbare cloak. Étienne Corbeau, masquerading as Pierre Blanchet, stood at the edge of the modest market square, his breath visible in the crisp morning air. He watched villagers shuffle between stalls, their faces etched with the harsh winter's hardships and the Revolution's lingering aftermath.

"Pierre! Over here!" called a familiar voice.

He turned to see Lucien Moreau waving enthusiastically, his broad shoulders wrapped in a woollen coat dusted with snowflakes. Beside him stood Thérèse Dubois, the baker's daughter, her cheeks rosy beneath a knitted bonnet. Thérèse had developed an attraction towards Étienne, which made him uneasy as he feared being found out. Solitude was his most trusted companion.

"Bonjour, Lucien," Étienne replied, forcing a smile as he approached. *"Mademoiselle Dubois."*

"Bonjour, Monsieur Blanchet," Thérèse said shyly, averting her gaze.

"We were just discussing the latest shipment of flour," Lucien explained. "Thérèse's father secured a decent supply despite the shortages."

"That's fortunate," Étienne remarked. "Reliable provisions are scarce these days."

"Indeed," Thérèse agreed softly. "Perhaps you'd like to try our fresh bread? I could set aside a loaf for you."

"That's very kind," Étienne replied, though the thought of another coarse peasant loaf did little to lift his spirits. "I may stop by later."

"Excellent!" Lucien clapped him on the back. "By the way, a few of us are gathering at the inn tonight. A chance to warm ourselves with some *vin chaud* and good company. You should join us."

Étienne hesitated. The inn was the village's social hub, where tongues loosened, and curiosity thrived—a risky environment for someone guarding secrets. Yet, his isolation was becoming unbearable, the walls of his cottage closing in like a prison.

"Perhaps I will," he conceded. "It would be good to get to know more of the villagers."

"Splendid!" Lucien beamed. "We'll expect you after sundown."

As they parted ways, Étienne wandered through the market, the smells of cured meats and aged cheeses mingling with the earthy aroma of root vegetables. He observed the villagers with a detached eye—their simple exchanges, their uncomplicated lives. A pang of bitterness tightened his chest. Once, he had been at the epicentre of power, shaping the destiny of France. Now, he haggled over the price of turnips with toothless farmers.

"Pierre!" a voice interrupted his thoughts.

He glanced up to see Bertrand Lefevre, the old cobbler, hobbling towards him. Bertrand's rheumy eyes gleamed with mischief beneath bushy eyebrows.

"Good day, Monsieur Lefevre," Étienne greeted him politely.

"Have you heard the news from Paris?" Bertrand asked, his voice a conspiratorial whisper.

"I've not," Étienne replied cautiously. "I keep to myself."

"Ah, but this is worth hearing," Bertrand insisted. "They say the National Convention is in disarray. Factions forming, power shifting. Some even whisper of a Royalist resurgence!"

"Is that so?" Étienne feigned indifference though his pulse quickened.

"Mark my words," Bertrand continued, wagging a gnarled finger. "The Revolution isn't over. There's talk of new leaders rising, men understanding people's needs."

"Let's hope they bring stability," Étienne said, keen to end the conversation.

"Indeed," Bertrand agreed. "Perhaps you could join us at the inn tonight? We will discuss it further."

"I've already received an invitation," Étienne replied. "I may see you there."

"Excellent," Bertrand grinned, revealing a gap-toothed smile. "A man of your intellect would add much to the debate."

As Bertrand shuffled away, Étienne felt a knot of anxiety tighten in his stomach. The last thing he desired was to be drawn into political discourse, yet declining too many invitations could arouse suspicion.

Returning to his cottage, he stoked the fire and settled into the creaking chair by the hearth. The solitude that once offered refuge now felt oppressive. He retrieved a folded letter from a concealed compartment—a message smuggled from Paris weeks ago.

"Étienne," it read. "The tides are changing. Your name surfaces in whispers. Caution is imperative. Trust no one."

The letter bore no signature, but he recognised the elegant script of Olympe de Gouges. Despite their complicated history, she had extended this discreet warning, a lifeline.

He crumpled the letter in frustration. The spectre of his past clung to him like a persistent shadow. No matter how far he fled, the consequences of his actions pursued him.

As dusk settled, casting long shadows across the snow-laden ground, Étienne prepared to venture to the inn. Donning his coat and a worn hat pulled low over his brow, he stepped into the crisp evening air. The village was aglow with lantern light, the soft murmur of voices drifting from the warmly lit windows.

Pushing open the heavy door of the inn, a wave of heat and the pungent aroma of spiced wine greeted him. The interior bustled with activity—

farmers, tradesmen, and their families gathered around rough-hewn tables, laughter and animated conversation filling the space.

"Pierre! Over here!" Lucien called from a corner table.

Étienne weaved through the crowd, nodding politely as he passed. He sat beside Lucien, across from Bertrand and Thérèse, who offered a shy smile.

"A mug of *vin chaud* for our friend!" Lucien declared to the barmaid.

"Merci," Étienne said, adjusting to the convivial atmosphere.

"So, Pierre," Bertrand began, leaning forward. "What's your take on the current state of affairs? Surely a man of your background has insights."

"I'm afraid I'm rather disconnected from politics these days," Étienne replied. "My interests lie elsewhere."

"Come now," Bertrand pressed. "Everyone has an opinion. Do you think the Directory will stabilise France?"

Étienne chose his words with precision. "I hope for peace and prosperity, like any citizen. The nation has endured enough turmoil."

"A diplomatic answer," Lucien chuckled. "But perhaps wise."

"Sometimes caution is prudent," Étienne said, sipping the mulled wine.

"Well, I think we need strong leadership," Bertrand huffed. "Someone to unite the factions and restore order."

"Let's not dampen the evening with heavy talk," Thérèse interjected gently. "Tell us, Monsieur Blanchet, what brought you to our village?"

"A desire for quiet and simplicity," Étienne replied. "I spent too many years amidst the chaos of the city."

"A sentiment I can understand," Lucien nodded. "Life here may be modest, but it's honest."

Étienne managed a genuine smile. "There's a certain charm to it."

As the evening progressed, he relaxed slightly, the warmth of the fire and the wine loosening his guarded demeanour. The villagers shared stories of harvests, festivals, local legends, and family histories. For a fleeting moment, he almost felt a part of their world.

Yet, beneath the surface, a simmering resentment lingered. He resented the simplicity others cherished, the mundane routines that defined their lives. He, who had once influenced the fate of a nation, now debated crop yields and weather patterns.

"Are you all right, Pierre?" Thérèse asked softly, noticing his distant expression.

"Tired," he lied. "Perhaps the wine is stronger than I'm accustomed to."

She laughed lightly. "It has a kick. Would you like some water?"

"That would be lovely," he admitted.

As she rose to fetch a pitcher, Étienne's gaze drifted towards the window. Outside, the darkness pressed against the glass, distorted reflections mingling with the shadows. For a split second, he thought he saw a figure standing across the street, cloaked and still. His heart lurched, but when he blinked, the apparition was gone.

"Here you are," Thérèse said, placing a cup of water before him.

"Merci," he replied, forcing a smile.

"You're quite the enigma, Monsieur Blanchet," she remarked. "The villagers are curious about you."

"Am I that mysterious?" he asked lightly.

"Not mysterious, perhaps," she considered. "But there's a sense that you've seen much and carry stories untold."

He met her gaze. "We all have our stories."

"Indeed," she agreed. "Perhaps one day you'll share yours."

"Perhaps," he echoed.

As the gathering dispersed, Lucien clapped him on the shoulder. "I'm glad you joined us tonight, Pierre. It does one good to be among friends."

Étienne nodded. "Thank you for inviting me. It was… enjoyable."

"Don't be a stranger," Lucien grinned. "You're part of our community now."

"Goodnight," Étienne said, bidding farewell to the remaining patrons.

Stepping into the chilly night, he drew a deep breath, the air sharp in his lungs. The village was quiet, save for the distant hoot of an owl. He rushed towards his cottage, the sense of being watched prickling at the back of his neck.

Upon reaching his door, he fumbled with the key, glancing over his shoulder. The street was empty, yet the feeling of unseen eyes persisted.

Once inside, he bolted the door and lit a candle, its flickering glow casting long shadows. He then securely latched the windows.

"You're letting fear consume you," he muttered to himself. "There is no one here."

Yet, as he prepared for bed, the bitterness resurfaced. He resented the villagers' simplicity, their contentment with so little. He despised the anonymity that cloaked him, reducing him to a footnote in a rural backwater.

"Is this to be my life?" he questioned aloud. "A forgotten man, hiding among those who cannot comprehend the world's complexities beyond?"

Sleep eluded him as he stared at the ceiling, the silence oppressive. Memories of his past—triumphs and transgressions—swirled in his mind. The grandeur of Paris, the intoxicating allure of influence, and the delicate dance of power seemed like echoes from another existence.

"20 February 1795," he whispered. "A date of no significance, in a place of no consequence."

As dawn's first light crept through the shutters, Étienne realised that his bitterness was a poison, eroding what little solace he might find. Yet, his past trapped him — by his choices and the revolution he had helped to forge.

He rose from the bed, exhaustion weighing upon him. Perhaps today, he would reconcile his present with his past, or maybe he would continue to exist in this liminal space—a phantom among the living.

Either way, the world outside continued unabated, indifferent to his inner turmoil.

• • •

The first light of 1 March 1795 filtered through a veil of mist that clung to the village like a lingering phantom. Étienne Corbeau—still cloaked in the guise of Pierre Blanchet—stood at his window, gazing out at the quiet street below. The cobblestones glistened with the residue of an early morning drizzle, and the air carried the crisp scent of impending spring.

As he sipped his lukewarm coffee, Étienne noticed an unfamiliar figure entering the village square. The man was of medium build, his posture erect, and he led a weary horse laden with saddlebags. He wore a dark, travel-stained coat and a wide-brimmed hat that shadowed his features. The villagers paid little heed to newcomers—it was not uncommon for traders or travellers to pass through—but something about this man stirred a disquiet within Étienne.

He watched intently as the stranger tethered his horse outside the inn and disappeared through its heavy wooden door. A knot of unease tightened in Étienne's stomach. "Who are you?" he muttered under his breath.

A knock at the door startled him. Setting down his cup, he composed himself before opening it to reveal Thérèse Dubois, the baker's daughter's cheeks flushed from the brisk air.

"Bonjour, Monsieur Blanchet," she greeted with a warm smile. "Father asked me to bring you this." She extended a small basket covered with a linen cloth.

"Thank you, *Mademoiselle Dubois,*" Étienne replied, accepting the offering. The aroma of freshly baked bread wafted up, momentarily soothing his nerves. "Please convey my gratitude to your father."

"I will," she said, her eyes lingering on his face. "Are you well? You seem… unsettled."

"I'm all right," he assured her. "Just a restless night."

She hesitated before speaking again. "We have a recent visitor in the village. Have you seen him?"

"I noticed someone arriving this morning," Étienne admitted cautiously. "Do you know who he is?"

"Pierre Duval is his name," she informed him. "He's taken a room at the inn. A trader, perhaps."

"Perhaps," Étienne echoed, masking his apprehension.

"Well, if you need anything, you know where to find us," Thérèse offered, her gaze earnest.

"You're very kind," he replied, managing a faint smile.

As she departed, Étienne closed the door and leaned against it, his mind racing. Pierre Duval. The name meant nothing to him, yet the coincidence of sharing a first name was unsettling. He unwrapped the bread and tore off a piece, though his appetite had waned.

Determined to quell his rising paranoia, he ventured into the village. Donning his coat and hat, he stepped into the damp morning. The air was fresh, carrying the distant sounds of livestock and the chatter of villagers beginning their day.

He approached the market square, intending to appear casual in his inquiry about the newcomer. Near the blacksmith's forge, he encountered Lucien Moreau, his muscular frame silhouetted against the glow of the forge's fire.

"Pierre!" Lucien called out, wiping his sooty hands on a rag. "What brings you out so early?"

"Just taking a walk," Étienne replied. "I heard we have a visitor."

"Ah, yes. Monsieur Duval," Lucien confirmed. "Passed through the forge earlier. Needed a shoe replaced on his horse."

"Did he mention his business?" Étienne probed, striving for nonchalance.

"Said he's travelling south," Lucien replied. "Seemed pleasant enough, though a bit reserved."

"Did he say where he's from?"

"Not specifically," Lucien mused. "But his accent—sounds like he's from the north, perhaps Normandy."

Étienne's unease deepened. Normandy was a region rife with Royalist sympathies and pockets of resistance against the Revolutionary government. "Interesting," he remarked.

Lucien studied him curiously. "Is everything all right, Pierre? You seem preoccupied."

"Just a lingering headache," Étienne lied. "Perhaps the change in weather."

"Take care of yourself," Lucien advised. "If you need a tonic, Madame Rousseau has remedies that work wonders."

"I'll keep that in mind," Étienne said, offering a polite nod before continuing.

He approached the inn, its exterior worn but welcoming, tendrils of smoke curling from the chimney. Peering through the window, he glimpsed Pierre Duval seated at a corner table, a tankard before him and a map spread out. The man appeared absorbed in his thoughts, occasionally making notes in a small ledger.

Étienne's mind raced with possibilities. Did Duval merely travel, or did someone send him to find Étienne? The notion that his past had finally caught up sent a chill down his spine. He withdrew from the window, retreating into the anonymity of the street.

"You're being irrational," he chastised himself quietly. "Not every stranger is a threat."

Yet, the seed of suspicion had been planted and it took root quickly. He would gather more information, but discretion was paramount.

As he wandered towards the edge of the village, he encountered *Madame Rousseau*, the local herbalist, tending to her garden despite the lingering chill.

"Good morning, *Monsieur Blanchet*," she greeted without looking up, her hands deftly pruning dried stems.

"*Madame Rousseau*," he acknowledged. "Preparing for spring?"

"Always work to be done," she smiled. "Nature waits for no one."

"Indeed," he agreed, appearing casual. "Have you met the recent visitor at the inn?"

"Briefly," she replied, glancing up. "He purchased some herbs from me. Seemed knowledgeable about their uses."

"Is that so?" Étienne remarked, his curiosity piqued.

"Few men take an interest in such things," she noted. "But he knew exactly what he wanted."

"What did he purchase, if I may ask?"

"Valerian root and some dried lavender," she said. "Common enough for aiding sleep."

"Perhaps a troubled traveller," Étienne suggested.

"Perhaps," she echoed, studying him with perceptive eyes. "You seem unsettled yourself."

"Just restless," he deflected. "Thank you for the conversation."

"Anytime," she replied, returning to her work.

Étienne continued his aimless walk, the overcast sky mirroring his mood. His thoughts circled endlessly—was he overreacting, or was there a genuine cause for concern? The details accumulated: Duval's arrival from the north, interest in herbs, and solitary demeanour.

Returning to his cottage, he found a folded piece of parchment slipped under the door. His heart pounded as he picked it up, unfolding it with trembling hands.

Pierre Blanchet,

We should speak. We should exercise discretion. Meet me at the old chapel at dusk.

—P.D."

Étienne's breath caught in his throat. The initials confirmed his fears. Duval knew of him, perhaps even his true identity. But what did he want? Blackmail? Retribution? Or was this a trap laid by those seeking vengeance?

He paced the room, the walls seeming to close in. Options raced through his mind: flee the village, confront Duval, seek help. Yet, whom could he trust? The villagers were kind but unaware of his past. Involving them could endanger them and expose them further.

As dusk approached, Étienne weighed his choices. Running would confirm his guilt and potentially draw more attention. Confronting Duval might provide answers but also pose a significant risk.

"Face the unknown," he resolved, steeling himself. "Better to understand the threat than live in perpetual fear."

He concealed a small dagger beneath his coat—a precaution from his days in Paris. The old chapel lay on the outskirts of the village, a relic of bygone times, its stone walls weathered and ivy-covered.

The path was quiet, the fading light casting long shadows. As he approached the chapel, he scanned the surroundings, alert for movement. The heavy wooden door stood ajar, a sliver of darkness beckoning.

Entering cautiously, he allowed his eyes to adjust. Candles flickered on a makeshift altar, casting a dim glow. Pierre Duval stood at the far end, his features obscured by shadow.

"Monsieur Blanchet," Duval greeted, his voice echoing softly. "Thank you for coming."

"Why have you summoned me?" Étienne demanded, his hand resting near the concealed dagger.

"I believe we have mutual interests," Duval replied, stepping forward. His face became clearer—a man in his thirties, with keen grey eyes and a scar tracing his jawline.

"I don't know what you mean," Étienne said guardedly.

"Come now, Monsieur Corbeau," Duval said evenly. "Or do you prefer your alias?"

Étienne's blood ran cold. "You have me at a disadvantage."

Duval smiled faintly. "I represent parties who are keenly interested in your… talents."

"Parties?" Étienne echoed. "What parties?"

"Let's just say they are influential and share your disillusionment with current affairs," Duval explained. "They believe you could be an asset."

"I'm done with politics," Étienne asserted. "That life is behind me."

"Is it?" Duval challenged. "Hiding in a village, under a false name, consumed by paranoia—is that truly living?"

Étienne bristled. "What choice do I have? My past ensures I am hunted."

"Aligning with us could provide protection," Duval offered. "A chance to reclaim purpose."

"And if I refuse?"

Duval's expression hardened slightly. "I would advise against that. Duval's expression hardened slightly as he advised against that."

Étienne weighed his words. The veiled threat was obvious, yet the opportunity could be a lifeline—or a noose.

"I need time," he said finally. "To consider your proposal."

"Of course," Duval agreed. "But do not delay. Time is a luxury we cannot afford."

"How will I contact you?" Étienne inquired.

"I will find you," Duval assured him. "Return to your cottage and act as though this meeting never occurred."

With that, Duval extinguished the candles, plunging the chapel into darkness. Étienne heard his footsteps recede, leaving him alone in the silence.

He exited the chapel, the night air sharp against his skin. The encounter left him unsettled—uncertain whether he had found an ally or stepped into a deeper peril.

Back at his cottage, he lit a lamp and sat at his desk, his mind a whirlwind. He retrieved his journal and wrote:

1 March 1795,

A stranger arrives, and with him, the spectres of my past resurface—Pierre Duval—a man who knows more than he should, offering a path fraught with unknowns. My paranoia was not unfounded. I stand at a crossroads once more.

Do I accept his offer, risking entanglement in new schemes, or do I flee, abandoning even this tenuous refuge? The walls close in, and I feel the weight of my choices pressing upon me.

The Revolution's shadows are long, and I cannot outrun them forever.

He set down the quill, exhaustion washing over him. The candle's flame wavered, casting flickering shadows that danced across the walls.

"Sleep will not come easily tonight," he murmured.

As he extinguished the light, Étienne lay awake, the darkness filled with unspoken threats and the relentless whisper of uncertainty. Faced with a decision that could redefine his fate—or seal it—the phantom he had become now had to choose.

• • •

Étienne Corbeau's mounting despair was mirrored by the relentless blanket of grey that pressed down upon the village on 10 March 1795. The air was thick with the promise of rain, the kind that seeped into the bones and refused to let go. From his cottage window, Étienne watched as the world outside moved with a languid pace, each moment stretching into the next with unbearable slowness.

Since his unsettling encounter with Pierre Duval, the days they had blurred together in a haze of anxiety and doubt. Étienne's thoughts spiralled endlessly, each one a thread pulling at the frayed edges of his sanity. The village, once a reluctant refuge, had become a labyrinth of unseen threats and whispered conspiracies.

He paced his cottage's small confines, the floorboards creaking beneath his restless steps. Shadows clung to the corners, deepening as the light struggled to penetrate the gloom. The familiar surroundings felt alien now, the walls closing in like a vice.

"Mon Dieu," he muttered, running a trembling hand through his dishevelled hair. "This cannot continue."

A sudden knock at the door jolted him, his heart leaping into his throat. He froze, every muscle taut, listening intently. The knock came again, gentle yet insistent.

"Pierre? It's Thérèse," called a soft voice from the other side.

He exhaled slowly, the tension ebbing just enough for him to move. Composing himself, he opened the door to find Thérèse Dubois standing there, concern etched upon her delicate features.

"Bonjour, Mademoiselle Dubois," he greeted her, forcing a smile.

"Bonjour, Monsieur Blanchet," she replied, her eyes searching his face. "I hadn't seen you at the bakery lately. Father sent me to check on you."

"That was kind of him," Étienne said, stepping aside. "Please, come in."

She entered hesitantly, her gaze flickering around the cluttered room. "Are you unwell? You look… tired."

While avoiding her eyes, he admitted, "I've been preoccupied." "Matters of business."

"Of course," she nodded, though her expression betrayed scepticism. "We've all been worried. Even Lucien mentioned your absence."

"I hadn't realised my presence was so missed," he said, a hint of bitterness creeping into his tone.

"You're part of our community," Thérèse insisted gently. "We care about you."

He sighed, the weight of her sincerity pressing upon him. "I appreciate your concern. Truly."

She offered a small smile. "Perhaps you might join us at the inn tonight? It might do you good to be among friends."

"I don't think that would be wise," he replied hastily. "I've much to attend to."

Her brow furrowed. "Is there something you're not telling me?"

Before he could respond, a movement outside caught his attention. He glimpsed Pierre Duval through the window, standing across the street, watching intently. Their eyes met briefly before Duval turned away, disappearing into an alley.

Étienne's pulse quickened. "I… I must go," he stammered, grabbing his coat.

"Go? Where?" Thérèse asked, bewildered.

"There's something I need to address," he said, ushering her towards the door. "Forgive me."

"Pierre, wait—" she protested, but he had already closed the door behind them, locking it with a decisive click.

He hurried down the street, the damp air clinging to his skin. The village seemed to wrap around him, familiar landmarks distorted by his heightened alarm state. He turned corners at random, attempting to shake the unseen gaze he felt upon him.

The sound of footsteps echoed behind him. Glancing over his shoulder, he saw only empty streets and shuttered windows. Yet the sensation of being followed persisted, a prickling at the nape of his neck.

He ducked into an alleyway, pressing himself against the rough stone wall. His breath came in ragged gasps; each inhale laced with the scent of wet stone and decay.

"You're losing your grip," he whispered to himself. "Get a hold of yourself."

"Talking to shadows, Monsieur Corbeau?" a voice drawled from the darkness.

Étienne's blood ran cold. Pierre Duval emerged from the shadows, a sardonic smile on his lips.

"What do you want?" Étienne demanded, masking his fear with indignation.

"I thought we had an understanding," Duval replied casually. "Yet you seem intent on avoiding me."

"I gave you my answer," Étienne retorted. "I'm not interested in your proposition."

Duval tutted softly. "You misunderstand. Refusal was never an option."

Étienne's hands clenched into fists. "You cannot force me into your schemes."

Duval's eyes gleamed with a predatory light. "Perhaps not by choice. But circumstances can be… arranged."

"Is that a threat?"

"Consider it an opportunity," Duval said smoothly. "Your talents are wasted here. Join us, and you can reclaim a measure of your former influence."

"I've left that life behind," Étienne insisted, though his voice wavered.

Duval stepped closer, his tone hardening. "You cannot escape your past. The Revolution may have changed faces, but the game remains the same. Power is there for the taking—for those bold enough to seize it."

Étienne recoiled. "At what cost? More bloodshed? More betrayal?"

"Such is the price of progress," Duval shrugged. "Surely you, of all people, understand that."

A surge of anger flared within Étienne. "I understand that I've had enough of shadows and daggers. Leave me be."

Duval regarded him with a bitter smile. "Very well. But know this— declining our offer does not absolve you of consequence. Others may not be as forgiving."

Before Étienne could respond, Duval turned on his heel and vanished into the maze of alleys.

Shaken, Étienne leaned against the wall, the damp seeping through his coat. The village around him felt suddenly oppressive, the quaint façades masking hidden dangers.

He returned to his cottage under the gathering gloom, the skies unleashing a steady drizzle that pattered against rooftops and cobblestones. Upon entering, he bolted the door and drew the curtains tightly shut.

His hands trembled as he lit a candle, the flickering flame casting distorted shadows. The isolation weighed heavily upon him; the silence filled with the echoes of his fears.

He extended his hand towards his journal. With unsteady fingers, he wrote:

10 March 1795,

The walls are closing in. Duval's presence is a relentless reminder that my past refuses to remain buried. His words linger like a toxin, seeping into my thoughts. I can no longer distinguish between reality and the phantoms of my mind.

Every face in the village seems a mask, every glance a scrutiny. Thérèse's kindness feels like pity, Lucien's camaraderie a façade. I am untethered, adrift in a sea of doubt.

> *Isolation has become my prison, yet I cannot bear the thought of re-entering the world I left behind. The choices before me are bleak—align with those who would use me or continue this descent into madness.*

A sudden knock at the door caused him to spill ink across the page. His heart pounded violently against his ribs.

"Pierre? It's Lucien. Are you home?" called the muffled voice.

Swallowing hard, Étienne steadied himself. "One moment," he called out, attempting to mask the tremor in his voice.

He opened the door a fraction, peering out. Lucien stood there, concern clear in his eyes.

"Thérèse said you seemed unwell," Lucien began. "I wanted to check on you."

"I'm fine," Étienne lied. "Just under the weather."

Lucien frowned. "You've been avoiding everyone. Is something troubling you?"

"Not at all," Étienne replied tersely. "I appreciate your concern, but I need rest."

Lucien hesitated. "If you need anything—"

"Thank you," Étienne interrupted, closing the door before the conversation could continue.

He leaned against the door, his breaths shallow. The veneer of normalcy was slipping, his carefully constructed façade crumbling under the weight of paranoia.

"Think, think," he muttered, pressing his palms to his temples. "There must be a way out."

The candle sputtered, casting erratic shadows that seemed to mock his turmoil. Visions of Paris flickered in his mind—the grand boulevards, the heated debates within the Convention, the faces of those he had outmanoeuvred and betrayed.

He remembered Olympe de Gouges, her piercing gaze and unyielding principles. What would she think of him now? A man undone by his own machinations, hiding in a remote village, pursued by real and imagined spectres.

"Perhaps I deserve this," he whispered. "A fitting end for an architect of chaos."

Outside, the rain intensified, a relentless drumbeat against the roof. The sound enveloped him, amplifying his isolation.

He considered fleeing—packing what little he had and disappearing into the night. Yet, where would he go? The reach of those who sought him was vast, and the world beyond was fraught with dangers unknown.

A sudden realisation settled upon him with crushing weight. His own mind trapped him, not Duval or any external force. The unravelling had begun, and he was powerless to stop it.

He sank to the floor, the damp seeping through his trousers, and let the darkness wash over him. The candle flame extinguished, plunging the room into shadow.

"10 March 1795," he whispered into the void. "Étienne Corbeau fades into obscurity, a phantom consumed by the fears he once instilled in others."

As the night wore on, the boundaries between reality and illusion blurred, and Étienne surrendered to the abyss, his grip on sanity slipping away like sand through clenched fingers.

• • •

The morning of 15 March 1795 dawned with a deceptive serenity, the pale sun casting a muted glow over the tranquil countryside village of Montferrand. Étienne Corbeau—having long left Paris and adopted the guise of Pierre Blanchet—stood at the threshold of his secluded cottage, the crisp air filling his lungs. Despite the idyllic surroundings, an ominous weight pressed upon him. The events of the past weeks had frayed his nerves to the brink; Pierre Duval's enigmatic presence continued to gnaw at his sanity like a relentless spectre.

Étienne had fled the chaos of Paris weeks earlier, seeking refuge in Montferrand to escape the lingering pro-Robespierre factions still prowling the capital. With its narrow cobblestone streets and tightly-knit community, the village offered a semblance of peace he desperately craved. Yet, the tranquillity was superficial, masking the ever-present threat of discovery. Duval had already confronted him about his true identity, leaving Étienne to grapple with the uncertainty of Duval's intentions.

Determined to reclaim some semblance of control, Étienne resolved to understand what Duval truly wanted from him. The uncertainty was unbearable, and he could no longer endure the insidious doubt that had taken root in his mind.

He made his way towards the village inn, the muddy streets slick beneath his boots from the previous night's rain. Villagers went about their routines, exchanging pleasantries and casting curious glances his way. Thérèse Dubois' curiosity was piqued when she offered a tentative wave from the bakery doorway, but he pretended not to notice, his focus singular.

As he approached the inn, the scent of fresh bread and burning wood wafted through the open door. Inside, a handful of patrons lingered over breakfast, their conversations indistinctly murmuring. At a corner table sat Pierre Duval, poring over a spread of documents, his expression unreadable.

Summoning his courage, Étienne crossed the room, each step heavy with anticipation. Duval looked up as he approached, a fleeting shadow of recognition crossing his features before settling into a polite smile.

"Bonjour, Monsieur Blanchet," Duval greeted, inclining his head. "Would you join me?"

Étienne hesitated for a fraction before pulling out a chair. "I thought it was time we had a proper conversation," he said, his tone measured.

"Indeed?" Duval arched an eyebrow. "And what prompts this sudden interest?"

Étienne studied him, searching for any sign of duplicity. "We've shared this village for weeks now yet remain strangers. It strikes me as odd."

Duval chuckled softly. "In a place like this, one values privacy. But I'm not opposed to a bit of company."

A barmaid approached, setting down a steaming mug before Étienne. "Compliments of the house," she said with a smile.

He nodded absently, his gaze never leaving Duval. "Your travels," Étienne began cautiously. "What brings you to our quiet corner of the world?"

"Business," Duval replied smoothly. "I trade in goods that require discretion and careful handling."

"Discretion," Étienne echoed. "An admirable quality."

Duval sipped his drink thoughtfully. "And you, Monsieur Blanchet? What path led you here?"

Étienne felt a prickle at the back of his neck, a silent reminder of their previous encounter. "A desire for simplicity," he said. "To leave behind the chaos of the Revolution."

"A sentiment I understand well," Duval remarked. "These are turbulent times."

"Yes," Étienne agreed, leaning forward slightly. "Turbulent indeed. One never knows whom to trust."

Duval met his gaze evenly. "Trust is a rare commodity."

Étienne's patience frayed. "Let's dispense with the pleasantries," he said tersely. "I need to understand what you want from me."

Duval leaned back, his expression inscrutable. "Straight to the point, I see. Very well. You and I both know why I'm here. Étienne"

Étienne took a deep breath, the tension palpable between them. "Explain yourself, Duval."

Duval's eyes softened slightly, a hint of empathy breaking through his professional façade. "You possess knowledge and connections that could be invaluable in stabilising the Republic and preventing further chaos. I'm here to offer you a place within the new order—a chance to redeem yourself."

Étienne felt a surge of conflicting emotions—relief at the prospect of redemption but also deep-seated mistrust. "And what if I refuse?"

Duval's smile was measured, devoid of malice. "Refusal would make you a target. Pro-Robespierre elements are still active, seeking retribution against those associated with the Reign of Terror. Aligning with me offers protection and a way to mitigate past actions."

Étienne glanced around the inn. The nearby Sans-culottes, identifiable by their practical long trousers and red caps, gesturing emphatically in groups, their presence a constant reminder of the Revolution's enduring fervour. The National Guard marched past, their uniforms crisp, faces solemn, embodying the fragile stability the Convention sought to maintain.

He understood then the gravity of Duval's offer. Accepting meant aligning himself with a faction striving to rebuild and stabilise, but it also meant exposing himself further to political machinations and power struggles. Refusing meant risking exposure and retribution from those still clung to the old ideals.

"Why trust me?" Étienne asked, his voice low. "What assurance do I have that your intentions are pure?"

Duval's expression hardened slightly. "Because I have no use for deceit. I aim to restore order and ensure that the Revolution's true ideals are upheld—liberty, equality, fraternity. Your cooperation would be mutually beneficial."

Étienne weighed his options. The lingering pro-Robespierre elements were not quickly silenced, and staying in Paris posed a significant risk. The only viable option to protect himself and those he cared about was to flee the city and seek refuge elsewhere.

But now, having already fled to Montferrand, Étienne faced a new dilemma. Duval's presence in the village meant his past was not easily left behind. The serene façade of the countryside did little to mask the undercurrents of danger that still swirled around him.

A sudden commotion erupted outside the inn as Étienne prepared to decline Duval's offer. Étienne glanced towards the door, spotting a small group of pro-Robespierre sympathisers congregating, their expressions intent and hostile. The danger was imminent.

"I can't accept," Étienne said firmly, rising from his seat. "I left Paris to protect myself and those I care about."

Duval stood as well, a hint of disappointment in his eyes. "It's unfortunate, Étienne. But perhaps our paths will cross again under different circumstances."

Before Étienne could respond, Duval nodded curtly and departed, leaving Étienne with urgency and resolve. He knew that time was of the essence; the pro-Robespierre factions were closing in, and remaining in Montferrand was no longer safe.

He exited the inn, the cold morning air hitting him like a slap. His heart raced as he navigated the narrow streets, every shadow and alleyway a potential hiding spot for his pursuers. The village that had once offered refuge now felt like a labyrinth he needed to escape swiftly.

Thérèse Dubois, ever the steadfast companion, caught up to him near the bakery. Her eyes searched his, filled with concern. "What's wrong? Why did he call you Étienne? Why are you leaving so abruptly?"

He hesitated, the weight of his decision pressing upon him. "I can't stay here, Thérèse. They're looking for me; if I remain, it won't just be me at risk."

She placed a reassuring hand on his arm. "We can find a way to leave together. You don't have to face this alone."

Étienne looked into her eyes, finding a flicker of hope amidst the turmoil. "Are you sure? It's dangerous."

She nodded firmly. "I won't abandon you. Let's go now before it's too late."

They hurried through the labyrinthine streets, slipping into the shadows cast by the gaslit lanterns. Étienne guided her towards a discreet back alley, where a trusted associate awaited with a horse-drawn carriage ready to whisk them away from the village's confines.

As they mounted the carriage, Étienne took one last look at the inn, now a distant memory. The weight of his decisions bore down on him, the futility of his ambition now painfully apparent. The drive that propelled him into the heart of the Revolution was the same force that now necessitated his escape for survival.

"15 March 1795," he thought grimly. "The day Étienne Corbeau stepped from the shadows and into the unknown."

With Thérèse by his side, he felt a flicker of determination ignite. Perhaps, in fleeing Montferrand, he could find a way to reconcile with his past and forge a new path—not defined by deceit and isolation but by the fragile bonds of trust he had formed.

As the carriage rolled towards the horizon, Étienne Corbeau accepted that his ambition had led him astray. Now, he sought not just survival but a chance to find peace beyond the tumultuous legacy of the Revolution.

The carriage moved swiftly, leaving the village behind. The countryside stretched before them, a landscape of rolling hills and dense forests bathed in the early morning light. Étienne glanced back once more, the silhouette of Montferrand fading into the distance, replaced by the promise of an uncertain future.

"Where to now?" Thérèse asked quietly, her voice steady despite the chaos surrounding them.

Étienne looked forward, the road ahead winding into the unknown. "There's a safehouse near the border," he replied. "Few know of its existence, and it should keep us hidden from any who seek us."

Thérèse nodded, her resolve unwavering. "Then let's make sure we get there quickly."

As the carriage sped along the winding path, Étienne reflected on the choices that had led him here. The alliances forged in desperation, the betrayals born of ambition, and the relentless pursuit of power had culminated in this moment of escape. He recognised the futility of his actions, the hollow victories that had only deepened his isolation.

With Thérèse's unwavering support, he felt a flicker of hope amidst the darkness. Perhaps, in leaving Paris and Montferrand, he could find a way to reconcile with his past and forge a new path—one not defined by deceit and isolation but by the fragile bonds of trust he had formed.

As the carriage rolled towards the horizon, Étienne Corbeau accepted that his ambition had led him astray. In fleeing Paris, he sought not just survival but a chance to find peace beyond the tumultuous legacy of the Revolution.

• • •

Étienne Corbeau and Thérèse Dubois had sought refuge in the dense forest, as the bleak dawn of 18 March 1795 crept over the horizon, casting elongated shadows. The hunting lodge, once a sanctuary of tranquillity, now felt like a confining cell. The air was thick with the scent of damp wood and lingering smoke from the dying embers of their meagre fire.

Étienne sat by the fogged window, his gaze fixed on the indistinct shapes beyond. Sleep had eluded him for days, his mind a turbulent sea of fragmented memories and unrelenting dread. Every rustle of leaves, every distant snap of a twig sent a jolt of alarm through his weary body.

"Étienne," Thérèse's gentle voice broke the heavy silence. "You must rest. You've not slept since we arrived."

He turned to face her, shadows etched beneath his eyes. "Rest?" he echoed hollowly. "How can I rest when they could be upon us at any moment?"

She approached cautiously, laying a comforting hand on his shoulder. "We've seen no sign of pursuit. Perhaps they've abandoned the search."

He pulled away abruptly. "You don't understand. They won't stop—not until they've found me."

Thérèse sighed, concern deepening the lines on her brow. "Who are 'they,' Étienne? The villagers? Duval? Please, help me understand."

He raked a trembling hand through his hair. "It's not just them. It's everyone—anyone who knows what I've done."

She knelt beside him, her eyes searching his. "Then tell me. Let me share this burden."

He looked away, his voice barely above a whisper. "My past is a labyrinth of betrayals and ambition. I played the game of power, and now the ghosts of those I've wronged haunt me."

"Haunted how?" she pressed gently.

"Visions," he admitted reluctantly. "Faces of the condemned, voices of the silenced. They plague my thoughts day and night."

Thérèse hesitated before speaking. "Perhaps it's guilt manifesting—your mind's way of seeking atonement."

He laughed bitterly. "Atonement? There's no redemption for the likes of me."

"That's not true," she insisted. "Everyone has the capacity for change."

He stood abruptly, moving away from her. "You don't know the depths of my deeds, Thérèse. The Revolution consumed us all, but I... I will sacrifice anything—anyone—for the illusion of control."

She rose to her feet, determination hardening her voice. "Then confront it. Acknowledge your past, and perhaps you can heal."

He spun to face her, anger flashing in his eyes. "Heal? While being hunted like an animal? While my mind unravels? It's too late for that."

A heavy silence settled between them, the crackling of the fire the only sound. Thérèse stepped forward cautiously. "You're not alone in this," she said softly. "Let me help you find a way forward."

He shook his head, frustration and despair clouding his features. "I can't drag you down with me. You should have stayed in the village."

"I am here," she reminded him firmly. "I won't abandon you now."

Étienne's gaze softened momentarily before hardening once more. "I need some air," he muttered, grabbing his coat and pushing past her.

Outside, the morning chill bit at his skin, but he welcomed the sensation—it grounded him, pulling him momentarily from the abyss of his thoughts. He wandered among the towering trees, their barren branches reaching skyward like skeletal fingers.

"18 March 1795," he murmured to himself. "A date of no significance, yet here I stand on the precipice of madness."

The whispers began soft, indistinct murmurs at the edge of his consciousness. As he pressed deeper into the woods, they grew louder, more insistent.

"Traitor."

"Blood on your hands."

"Justice awaits."

He clutched his head, pressing his palms against his ears to silence them. "Leave me be!" he cried out, his voice echoing among the trees.

A figure emerged from the mist ahead—a familiar silhouette clad in austere attire. Étienne's breath caught in his throat. "Robespierre?" he whispered incredulously.

The apparition regarded him with cold, unblinking eyes. "You betrayed the Revolution," it intoned.

"No," Étienne protested weakly. "I did what was necessary."

"At what cost?" the figure pressed. "You orchestrated my downfall, sent countless to their deaths."

"It was for the greater good," Étienne insisted, his voice trembling.

Another figure appeared beside the first—Camille Desmoulins, his once-vibrant eyes now dull and accusatory. "We believed in you, Étienne. You led us astray."

"I tried to save us!" Étienne exclaimed, backing away.

More faces materialised—Olympe de Gouges, her gaze filled with disappointment; Jean-Paul Marat, his visage twisted in anger; nameless others whose lives had intersected with his in the Revolution's tumult.

They chorused, "We cannot absolve your sins."

"Enough!" Étienne shouted, stumbling backwards. He tripped over an exposed root, falling to the damp forest floor. The impact jolted him, and when he looked up, the apparitions had vanished.

Chest heaving, he lay there, the cold seeping into his bones. Reality blurred at the edges, and he no longer trusted his senses.

A rustling nearby snapped him back to alertness. He scrambled to his feet, eyes darting wildly. "Who's there?"

Thérèse emerged cautiously from behind a tree, her expression a mix of fear and concern. "It's me," she said softly. "I heard you shouting."

He stared at her, uncertainty flickering across his face. "Did you… did you see them?"

"See who?" she asked gently.

"The ghosts," he whispered. "They were here."

She approached slowly, extending a hand. "There's no one here but us."

He shook his head vehemently. "No, they were real. They spoke to me."

She placed a hand on his arm. "You're exhausted, Étienne. Your mind is playing tricks."

He pulled away. "You think I'm mad."

"I think you're tormented," she corrected. "Please, let me help you."

He looked into her eyes, searching for deception but finding only earnest compassion. A wave of weariness washed over him, and his shoulders sagged. "I don't know what's real anymore," he admitted hoarsely.

"Come back to the lodge," she urged. "You need rest."

Reluctantly, he allowed her to guide him back. Inside, she coaxed him to sit by the fire, offering herbal tea. "Madame Rousseau taught me this blend," she said softly. "It might help calm your nerves."

He accepted it with a shaky hand, the warmth seeping through the cup into his fingers. "Why are you doing this?" he asked after a moment.

"Because I care," she replied.

He stared into the flickering flames. "I don't deserve your kindness."

"That's not for you to decide," she said gently. "Everyone deserves compassion."

He sipped the tea, the bitter taste grounding him. Silence settled between them, not uncomfortable but heavy with unspoken thoughts.

After a while, he spoke again. "When I was in Paris, I thought I could shape the world. That my actions, however ruthless, served a higher purpose."

"And now?" she prompted.

"Now I see only the wreckage I've left behind," he confessed. "Lives destroyed, trust shattered. Perhaps these visions are my penance."

"Perhaps they're a sign that you must forgive yourself," she suggested.

He shook his head. "Forgiveness seems an impossible notion."

"Nothing is impossible," she countered. "But you must confront your past honestly."

He glanced at her, a glimmer of hope flickering in his eyes. "How does one atone for so much?"

"One step at a time," she said. "By making different choices, here and now."

He considered her words, the fog in his mind lifting ever so slightly. "I don't know if I have the strength."

"You don't have to do it alone," she reminded him.

A faint smile tugged at the corners of his mouth. "You're remarkably stubborn."

"So I've been told," she replied with a gentle smile.

The wind picked up outside, rattling the shutters and causing the flames to dance erratically. Étienne felt a stirring within—a fragile resolve taking shape.

"Perhaps there is a way forward," he mused aloud.

Thérèse placed a reassuring hand over his. "We'll find it together."

Just then, a distant sound echoed through the forest—the unmistakable bark of dogs and muffled voices.

Étienne stiffened, all colour draining from his face. "They're coming," he whispered.

Thérèse stood, her eyes widening. "We need to move."

He nodded, adrenaline surging. "Gather what you can. We'll head east, towards the river."

They hastily packed their scant belongings, the sense of urgency sharpening their movements. As they slipped out into the twilight, the sounds of pursuit grew louder.

"Stay close," Étienne instructed, leading the way through the tangled underbrush.

They navigated the forest by practising stealth, but the terrain was unforgiving. Branches snagged at their clothes, the ground uneven beneath their feet.

A shout rang out behind them. "There they are!"

Panic surged. Étienne grasped Thérèse's hand. "Run!"

They broke into a sprint, the forest blurring around them. The river's distant glimmer beckoned—an escape route. But the pursuers were gaining, the baying of hounds drawing ever nearer.

As they reached the riverbank, Étienne scanned desperately for a means to cross. A fallen tree spanned the rushing water—a precarious bridge.

"Go!" he urged Thérèse.

She hesitated. "What about you?"

"I'll be right behind you," he promised.

She nodded, carefully stepping onto the makeshift crossing. Étienne waited until she was halfway across before following.

Midway, the shouts intensified. A gunshot cracked through the air, splintering the tree trunk near his feet.

"Faster!" he called to Thérèse.

They reached the opposite bank, scrambling onto solid ground. Without pausing, they plunged back into the forest, the river now serving as a temporary barrier.

As darkness enveloped them, they slowed their pace, lungs burning and limbs aching.

"We can't keep this up," Thérèse gasped.

Étienne nodded grimly. "We need to find shelter."

They pressed on until they stumbled upon a rocky outcrop, a shallow cave offering minimal protection. Collapsing inside, they huddled together, the weight of exhaustion pressing down.

"Thank you," Étienne whispered after a long silence.

"For what?" Thérèse murmured.

"For not giving up on me," he replied.

She rested her head against his shoulder. "We're in this together."

As they drifted into an uneasy sleep, Étienne's mind remained restless. The faces of the past stayed at the edges of his consciousness, but their voices sounded muted. Thérèse's steady presence beside him anchored him to the present, a fragile tether holding him from the abyss.

"18 March 1795," he thought. "Perhaps not a date of significance to the world, but a turning point for me."

The path ahead remained uncertain, fraught with dangers both tangible and imagined. Yet, amidst the chaos, a glimmer of purpose emerged—a chance to confront his demons and perhaps, in some measure, find redemption.

• • •

The biting chill of 25 March 1795 hung in the air, a lingering remnant of winter refusing to yield to spring's embrace. Étienne Corbeau trudged along the muddy path that snaked through the forest, each step heavy with uncertainty. The canopy above was a lattice of bare branches, skeletal fingers clawing at the overcast sky. Beside him, Thérèse Dubois walked in contemplative silence, her presence a fragile tether anchoring him to reality.

"How much further?" she asked softly, her breath forming pale clouds that dissipated into the cold.

"Not far," Étienne replied, his voice strained. "There's an abandoned mill by the river. We can find shelter there."

They had been on the move for days, evading unseen pursuers and the ghosts of Étienne's past. Sleep came only in snatches, haunted by vivid nightmares that blurred the line between memory and madness. The relentless march had taken its toll; his once sharp features were now gaunt, eyes shadowed by exhaustion.

As they emerged from the thicket, the mill appeared—a crumbling stone structure perched precariously by the churning river. Its waterwheel was still coated in moss and ivy, a relic of forgotten industry.

"Wait here," Étienne instructed, gesturing for Thérèse to stay back. He approached cautiously, scanning the surroundings for any sign of life. Before beckoning her forward, Étienne made sure that the area was deserted.

Inside, the mill offered scant protection from the elements but was dry and hidden from prying eyes. They settled near a corner where remnants of an old hearth provided a semblance of comfort.

Thérèse unpacked a small bundle of provisions. "We have enough bread and cheese for a few days," she said, trying to sound optimistic.

Étienne nodded absently, his mind elsewhere. The silence between them was thick with unspoken fears.

"Étienne," she began tentatively, "we can't keep running indefinitely. Perhaps we should seek help."

He glanced at her sharply. "From whom? The authorities would sooner see me guillotined."

"Not everyone is an enemy," she insisted. "There are those who oppose the excesses of the Revolution, who might offer refuge."

He sighed heavily. "Trust is a luxury I cannot afford."

Before she could respond, a faint sound echoed outside—a twig snapping underfoot. Étienne stiffened his senses on high alert.

"Did you hear that?" he whispered.

Thérèse strained to listen. "Perhaps an animal?"

He shook his head. "Stay here."

Drawing a dagger from his belt, Étienne edged towards the entrance. The cold air greeted him like a slap as he stepped outside, eyes scanning the treeline.

"Show yourself," he demanded, his voice low but firm.

A figure emerged from behind a gnarled oak—Pierre Duval, his hands raised in a gesture of peace. He wore the same travel-worn coat, his expression inscrutable.

"Peace, *Monsieur Corbeau*," Duval called softly. "I mean you no harm."

Étienne's grip tightened on the dagger. "You have a peculiar way of showing it."

Duval took a cautious step forward. "May I approach?"

"That depends on your intentions."

"I come with a warning," Duval said earnestly. "Some seek you—people with less forgiving motives."

Étienne studied him warily. "How did you find us?"

"It wasn't easy," Duval admitted. "But I've had practice in such matters."

"Why should I believe anything you say?"

Duval sighed. "Because we share a common cause, whether you accept it."

Thérèse appeared at the doorway, concern etched on her face. "Étienne, what's happening?"

He gestured for her to stay back. "This is the man I told you about."

Duval offered a polite nod. "*Mademoiselle Dubois*, I presume?"

She glanced between them. "What do you want?"

"To help," Duval replied. "Though I suspect my arrival is unwelcome."

Étienne's eyes narrowed. "You admitted recognising me in the village. Why wait until now to reveal yourself?"

Duval met his gaze steadily. "Because circumstances have changed. News travels swiftly. Word of your disappearance has reached influential ears."

"Whose ears?" Étienne demanded.

"Factions within the Convention," Duval explained. "Those eager to root out remnants of the previous regime."

Étienne's jaw tightened. "So, you're one of their agents?"

Duval shook his head. "I operate independently. My loyalties are… flexible."

"Convenient," Étienne scoffed.

"Believe what you will," Duval said calmly. "But know this: others are on your trail. Less discreet, more ruthless."

Thérèse stepped forward. "If what you say is true, why help us?"

Duval's gaze softened. "Because chaos breeds opportunity. And perhaps, deep down, I believe in second chances."

Étienne laughed bitterly. "A romantic notion from a mercenary."

"Call me what you like," Duval replied. "But the reality remains—you cannot stay here."

Étienne weighed his options, the weight of Duval's words settling upon him. "And where do you suggest we go?"

"South," Duval said. "To Marseille. The port city offers anonymity and passage to elsewhere."

"Escape France entirely?" Thérèse asked, her eyes widening.

"It's your best chance," Duval affirmed.

Étienne considered the proposition. The idea of leaving his homeland stirred a mix of relief and sorrow. "And what do you gain from this?"

Duval smiled faintly. "Perhaps I tire of the endless machinations. Or maybe I see a value in keeping you alive."

"Forgive me if I remain sceptical," Étienne retorted.

"Understandable," Duval conceded. "But time is not on your side. I've delayed your pursuers, but they will not be far behind."

Thérèse looked at Étienne, her expression pleading. "We can't keep running blindly. Maybe he's right."

Étienne exhaled slowly. "Assuming we agree, how do we reach Marseille undetected?"

"I have a wagon hidden nearby," Duval offered. "We can travel as a family—husband, wife, and brother."

Étienne arched an eyebrow. "A convenient plan."

"One that has worked before," Duval assured.

Silence stretched as Étienne grappled with the decision. Trusting Duval went against every instinct honed by years of deceit. Yet, the alternative was a slow march towards inevitable capture.

"Very well," he said at last. "But know this—if you betray us, I won't hesitate to ensure you regret it."

Duval inclined his head. "Understood."

They gathered their belongings quickly. As they prepared to leave, Étienne pulled Thérèse aside.

"Are you certain about this?" he asked quietly.

She met his gaze firmly. "We have little choice. And perhaps it's time to start anew."

He nodded a hint of gratitude in his eyes. "You've shown more courage than I deserve."

"Let's focus on reaching safety," she replied gently.

The trio set off through the forest, following a narrow path between ancient oaks and tangled underbrush. The air was tense with unspoken mistrust, but necessity bound them together.

After an hour's trek, they arrived at a small clearing where a modest wagon, hitched to a sturdy mule, awaited them. The vehicle was unremarkable—weathered wood and faded paint—a perfect guise for their journey.

"Climb aboard," Duval instructed. "We need to maintain a steady pace."

As they settled in, Étienne couldn't shake the feeling of stepping deeper into a web he couldn't see. Duval took the reins, and with a flick, the mule pulled them onto a rutted track that led southward.

Hours passed in relative silence, the rhythmic creak of the wagon wheels the only constant. Thérèse dozed fitfully beside Étienne, her head resting on his shoulder. He gazed at the passing landscape—fields giving way to rolling hills, the terrain gradually shifting as they progressed.

"Tell me," Étienne finally said, breaking the quiet. "How did you truly find us?"

Duval glanced back. "As I mentioned, I have resources. And you left a trail—subtle, but there for those who know where to look."

"Are you always this evasive?"

Duval chuckled softly. "Old habits die hard."

"Why leave the village without alerting the others?" Étienne pressed.

Duval's expression grew sombre. "Because despite my initial intentions, I saw the fear in your eyes. I recognised a man haunted by his past, not a threat to be eliminated."

Étienne absorbed this silently. "And the people searching for me—how close are they?"

"Closer than I'd like," Duval admitted. "Which is why we must maintain our pace."

As dusk approached, they stopped to rest the mule and respite briefly. Thérèse stretched her limbs, the weariness clear.

"How much further to Marseille?" she inquired.

"Another few days if we keep moving," Duval replied.

Étienne walked a short distance away, lost in thought. The gravity of their situation settled heavily upon him. Exile was daunting, yet the idea of a fresh start held a glimmer of appeal.

Thérèse joined him, her eyes reflecting the fading light. "What are you thinking?"

He sighed. "That perhaps this is the only path left."

"Do you regret it?" she asked softly.

He considered her question. "Parts of me do. But I've spent so long looking over my shoulder. Maybe it's time to face forward."

She smiled gently. "I believe in second chances."

He met her gaze, a flicker of hope igniting. "Perhaps together, we can find a way."

Duval's urgent call interrupted their moment. "We need to move. Riders approaching."

The alarm jolted them into action. They hastily returned to the wagon as distant figures appeared on the horizon, silhouettes against the dying sun.

"Can we outrun them?" Étienne asked.

"We can try," Duval responded, snapping the reins. The mule surged forward, the wagon lurching as it picked up speed.

The chase intensified, the riders gaining ground. Étienne's heart pounded, a mix of fear and adrenaline coursing through his veins.

Thérèse gripped his hand tightly. "Hold on," he urged.

As they approached a fork in the road, Duval suddenly turned onto a narrower path obscured by overhanging branches.

"This way leads to an old smugglers' route," he explained breathlessly.

The riders thundered past the fork, failing to notice their abrupt detour. Relief washed over them as the sounds of pursuit faded.

"That was close," Thérèse whispered.

Duval slowed the mule to a steady trot. "We should be safe for now."

Étienne regarded him with a newfound respect. "Perhaps I misjudged you."

Duval offered a wry smile. "You're not the first."

They continued in relative peace as night enveloped the countryside. The stars emerged, pinpricks of light in the vast darkness.

Thérèse leaned into him. "Perhaps it's the start of a new chapter."

He wrapped an arm around her, a tentative embrace. "One can hope."

Duval glanced back, his eyes reflecting the starlight. "Rest while you can. Tomorrow brings new challenges."

As they settled, Étienne felt the weight of his past lift ever so slightly. The path ahead remained uncertain, but he allowed himself a sliver of optimism for the first time in years.

"Thank you," he said quietly to Duval.

The man nodded. "We all have our ghosts, Monsieur Corbeau. It's how we confront them that defines us."

Étienne gazed upward, the vast expanse of the night sky reminding him of the world beyond his fears. With Thérèse by his side and an unlikely ally leading the way, he dared to imagine a future where his past no longer held dominion.

As sleep finally claimed him, the wagon creaked into the unknown, carrying with it the fragile hopes of redemption and the possibility of a reclaimed life.

• • •

The pale morning sun of 28 March 1795 struggled to pierce the veil of mist that clung to the landscape, casting an ethereal glow over the rolling fields outside Marseille. Étienne Corbeau sat atop a weathered stone wall, gazing out towards the distant spires of the city that promised refuge yet whispered of uncertainty. The salty tang of the Mediterranean hung in the air, starkly contrasting to the dense forests and muddy paths they had traversed.

Thérèse Dubois approached quietly, her footsteps barely audible on the dew-soaked grass. "We've made good time," she remarked, offering a tentative smile. "By midday, we'll be within the city walls."

Étienne nodded absently, his eyes fixed on the horizon. "Indeed," he murmured. "Marseille awaits."

Pierre Duval emerged from behind the wagon, adjusting the brim of his hat against the sun's glare. "Our journey's end is in sight," he announced. "I've contacts in the port who can secure passage for us."

"Passage to where?" Étienne inquired, his tone edged with resignation.

Duval made a suggestion, saying, "Perhaps we could go to Spain, or if necessary, we could go further afield to places where they don't ask questions and where histories can be easily rewritten."

Étienne sighed deeply. "Histories are not so easily discarded," he said. "They have a way of clinging to you, no matter how far you run."

Thérèse placed a gentle hand on his arm. "We've come this far," she encouraged. "A new beginning is within reach."

He turned to face her, the shadows under his eyes more pronounced in the morning light. "Thérèse, I've been fooling myself," he confessed. "Believing I could simply shed my past like a serpent's skin. But it follows me like a spectre."

Duval glanced between them, his expression unreadable. "We all carry burdens," he remarked. "It's how we shoulder them that defines our path forward."

Étienne shook his head slowly. "You don't understand. My actions—my ambition—have wrought ruin not just upon myself but upon others. Innocents caught in the crossfire of my schemes."

Thérèse's eyes searched his face. "What are you saying?"

He stepped down from the wall, his boots sinking into the soft earth. "Perhaps it's time I stop running," he declared. "Face the consequences of my deeds."

Duval frowned. "That's noble but hardly practical. Surrendering yourself won't undo the past."

"No," Étienne agreed. "But it might prevent further harm."

Thérèse clasped his hand. "I won't let you do this," she insisted. "We started this journey together."

He met her gaze, a mixture of gratitude and sorrow in his eyes. "You've shown me kindness beyond measure," he whispered. "But I cannot, in good conscience, drag you deeper into my abyss."

"You're not dragging me anywhere," she retorted. "I'm here by choice."

Duval cleared his throat. He cautioned, "The authorities have a reputation for lacking mercy. If you turn yourself in, there's little hope for a fair trial."

Étienne offered a faint smile. "Justice may be elusive, but perhaps accepting my fate is the only way to find peace."

Thérèse's grip tightened. "And what of us? What of the future we could build together?"

He looked away, the weight of her words pressing upon him. "A future built on falsehoods is no future at all."

Silence enveloped them; the distant sounds of the awakening city carried on the breeze. Finally, Duval spoke. "If this is your decision, I won't stand in your way. But ponder the ramifications."

Étienne nodded. "I have. And it's the only path that feels… right."

Thérèse's eyes glistened with unshed tears. "I can't accept that," she whispered. "There's always another way."

He reached out, brushing a stray lock of hair from her face. "You've given me hope when I had none," he said tenderly. "But my past is a shadow that will darken any life I touch."

She pulled back, anger flashing in her eyes. "So that's it? You'd rather martyr yourself than fight for a chance at happiness?"

"It's not martyrdom," he insisted. "It's a responsibility."

Duval shifted uncomfortably. "We should decide quickly. Lingering here increases our risk."

Étienne straightened his shoulders, resolve hardening his features. "Then I must go."

Thérèse shook her head vehemently. "I won't let you do this alone."

He gave her a sad smile. "You must. Your life shouldn't be bound to the fate of a man condemned by his own choices."

She opened her mouth to protest, but no words came. The reality of his decision settled between them like an insurmountable wall.

Duval stepped forward. "If you truly intend to surrender, at least allow me to accompany you part of the way. There may yet be options we haven't considered."

Étienne considered the offer before nodding. "Very well."

They gathered their belongings in silence. The wagon remained behind a relic of a journey that had led them to this crossroads. As they walked towards Marseille, the city loomed larger, its labyrinthine streets and bustling ports a testament to the lives that continued unabated, indifferent to their plight.

They became absorbed in the throng of merchants, sailors, and townsfolk as they passed through the city gates. The cacophony of voices and the scent of spices mingling with the sea air created a sensory tapestry that contrasted with the isolation of their recent days.

Duval guided them towards a quiet alleyway. "There's an inn nearby," he said. "We can rest there and plan our next steps."

Étienne shook his head. "No more delays. I need to find the local magistrate."

Thérèse grabbed his arm. "Please, Étienne. At least give us a chance to find another solution."

He gently extricated himself from her grasp. "Every moment I delay puts you both at greater risk."

They went through winding streets to the magistrate's office, an imposing stone building guarded by stern-faced soldiers. Étienne paused at the steps, taking a deep breath.

"This is madness," Thérèse whispered, her voice trembling. "Don't do this."

He turned to her one last time. "Live your life free from my shadows," he implored. "Find happiness."

Before she could respond, he ascended the steps, Duval at his side. The guards eyed them warily as they approached.

"I am Étienne Corbeau," he announced, his voice steady. "I wish to speak with the magistrate."

One guard raised an eyebrow. "The Étienne Corbeau? From Paris?"

"The same," he confirmed.

The guards exchanged glances before one gestured towards the door. "Wait here."

As they stood in the foyer, the weight of his decision settled entirely upon him. Duval leaned in. "Are you certain about this? There's still time to walk away."

Étienne met his gaze. "I've never been more certain."

Moments later, a clerk appeared, his expression a mix of curiosity and apprehension. "Monsieur Corbeau, the magistrate will see you now."

Duval placed a hand on his shoulder. "I'll be nearby if you need me."

Étienne nodded. "Thank you, Pierre. For everything."

He followed the clerk into a dimly lit chamber, the air heavy with the scent of ink and old parchment. The magistrate, a gaunt man with sharp features, regarded him from behind a cluttered desk.

"Monsieur Corbeau," he began. "Your reputation precedes you."

Étienne stood tall. "I answer for my actions."

The magistrate steepled his fingers. "An unusual choice. Few come willingly."

"Running no longer serves a purpose," Étienne replied.

The magistrate studied him for a long moment. "Very well. We shall record your testimony. Justice will take its course."

As the formalities began, Étienne felt a strange sense of calm. The fear that had consumed him for so long ebbed, replaced by a quiet acceptance.

Hours later, as dusk settled over Marseille, Étienne found himself confined to a modest cell. The sounds of the city filtered through the small window—distant laughter, the creak of ship masts, the hum of a world continuing unabated.

Footsteps echoed in the corridor. Thérèse appeared at the door, her face pale but determined.

"How did you get in here?" he asked, surprised.

"I persuaded the guard," she said. "I had to see you."

He approached the bars separating them. "You shouldn't be here."

"I couldn't leave without saying goodbye," she whispered, tears welling in her eyes.

He reached through the bars, his fingers brushing against hers. "I'm sorry for everything."

She shook her head. "I don't regret a moment. You showed me courage and kindness."

He smiled softly. "Perhaps in another life…"

She placed a finger to his lips. "No regrets. Promise me you'll hold on to hope."

He hesitated before nodding. "I promise."

A guard cleared his throat, signalling the end of their brief reunion. Thérèse squeezed his hand one last time before turning away and disappearing down the dim corridor.

As night enveloped the cell, Étienne sat on the narrow cot, gazing up at the sliver of the moon visible through the window.

"28 March 1795," he mused aloud. "A day of endings and, perhaps, beginnings."

He closed his eyes, the myriad voices of his past quieted at last. Though the future remained uncertain, he found solace knowing that he had taken responsibility for his life—a step towards redemption, however small.

Outside, the city of Marseille thrummed with life, oblivious to the solitary man who had faced his fate. Étienne Corbeau, once consumed by ambition and fear, now embraced the uncertainty ahead, his journey a testament to the complexities of the human spirit.

• • •

The grey dawn of 9 April 1795 enveloped Paris in a shroud of mist, the Seine's waters reflecting the muted hues of a city still healing from its scars. Étienne Corbeau sat in the dim confines of a modest carriage, his wrists bound with a coarse rope that chafed against his skin. The muffled sounds of the bustling streets seeped through the wooden panels, a stark reminder of the world outside—a world he had once influenced but now observed from behind a veil of disgrace.

As the carriage jolted over uneven cobblestones, Étienne gazed through the small window, catching fleeting glimpses of familiar landmarks. The spires of Notre Dame loomed in the distance, piercing the morning haze like silent sentinels. Memories flooded his mind—heated debates within the National Convention, clandestine meetings in shadowed alcoves, the zeal of a populace hungry for change. Those memories tasted bitter, laced with the irony of his current plight.

The previous days had unravelled with cruel efficiency. After surrendering in Marseilles, Étienne's escorts brought him to Paris under heavy guard. The journey had been swift, his captors offering little in the way of conversation.

The carriage lurched to a halt, pulling Étienne from his reverie. The door swung open, revealing a pair of stern-faced soldiers clad in the Republic's blue and red uniforms.

"Out with you," one barked, his eyes devoid of sympathy.

Étienne stepped onto the damp street, the morning air's chill biting through his thin garments. Before him stood the imposing façade of the Conciergerie—a fortress that had witnessed the final days of many, including the late Queen Marie Antoinette; he couldn't ignore the irony.

As he entered, the din of the city faded, and he heard the echoing footsteps along stone corridors. The scent of mildew and cold stone filled his nostrils. They arrived at a small chamber where a clerk sat behind a wooden desk, quill in hand.

"Name?" the clerk inquired without looking up.

"Étienne Corbeau," he replied, his voice steady.

The clerk's quill paused mid-stroke. He glanced up, eyes widening slightly. "The Étienne Corbeau?"

Étienne offered a faint, sardonic smile. "The same."

The clerk cleared his throat, regaining his composure. "Charges: conspiracy against the Republic, abuse of power, and complicity in the atrocities of the Reign of Terror."

"Noted," Étienne said quietly.

They escorted him to a cell—a small, damp room with a narrow cot and a barred window that offered a sliver of the sky. The door clanged shut behind him, the metallic echo resonating like a final decree.

Alone with his thoughts, Étienne paced the confined space. His reflection in the tarnished metal of a water basin caught his eye—a visage marked by fatigue and the stubble of neglect. The man who stared back was far from the polished figure who had once stridden confidently through the halls of power.

"How the mighty have fallen," he murmured to himself.

Time passed indistinctly. The distant sounds of other prisoners and the occasional footsteps of guards patrolling the corridors broke the monotony only. As daylight waned, the clatter of keys announced a visitor.

The door swung open to reveal François Louvet, his expression inscrutable. He carried a small lantern, its glow casting elongated shadows across the cell.

"Good evening," Louvet greeted, his tone formal.

"Is it?" Étienne replied dryly. "I hadn't noticed."

Louvet gestured to a guard, who placed a stool inside the cell before stepping back. "May I?" Louvet inquired.

Étienne nodded. "By all means. It's not as though I can refuse."

Louvet sat, arranging his coat with deliberate care. "We have scheduled your trial for tomorrow."

"Efficient," Étienne remarked. "I suppose the outcome is already determined."

Louvet met his gaze steadily. "That depends on you."

Étienne arched an eyebrow. "Oh? And how might I influence proceedings from within these walls?"

"By cooperating," Louvet replied. "Provide testimony against others who remain at large. Your insight could be invaluable."

A bitter laugh escaped Étienne's lips. "You wish me to betray former associates for leniency?"

Louvet's expression remained impassive. "Consider it an opportunity for redemption."

"Redemption," Étienne echoed. "A quaint notion."

Silence settled between them, heavy with unspoken tensions. Finally, Étienne sighed. "Tell me, Louvet, do you believe in justice?"

Louvet regarded him thoughtfully. "I believe in the ideals of the Republic."

"And yet, here we are—men who have navigated the murky waters of politics, compromising principles for power."

Louvet bristled slightly. "I have always acted in the best interests of the people."

"As did I," Étienne countered. "At least, that's what I told myself."

"Then you acknowledge your misdeeds?"

Étienne leaned back against the icy wall. "Ambition can blind even the most well-intentioned. In positing a greater good, one might lose sight of the cost."

Louvet stood, adjusting his coat. "Reflect on my offer. It may be your only chance."

As he turned to leave, Étienne called after him. "What became of Thérèse?"

Louvet paused. "She is in good health; she travelled to Paris to witness your trial."

Étienne nodded slowly. "Thank you."

The door closed once more, leaving Étienne enveloped in shadows. He sank onto the cot, the weight of reality pressing upon him. The prospect of betraying others sickened him, yet the allure of survival tugged at the frayed edges of his resolve.

"9 April 1795," he whispered. "A date that may well mark my end."

Sleep eluded him that night. Visions of past acquaintances swirled in his mind—Georges Danton's booming laughter, Camille Desmoulins' fiery speeches, Maximilien Robespierre's piercing gaze. Ghosts of a bygone era, their fates intertwined with his own.

As dawn broke, a pale light seeped into the cell. Étienne stood, stretching his stiff limbs. The sound of approaching footsteps heralded guards.

"It's time," one announced curtly.

They escorted him to a chamber where a modest assembly awaited— a makeshift courtroom adorned with the tricolour flag. As he entered, faces turned towards him, some curious, others hostile. Seated at the forefront was the magistrate, an austere man with stern features and a powdered wig that seemed anachronistic amidst the revolutionary fervour.

"Étienne Corbeau," the magistrate intoned. "You stand accused of grave offences against the Republic. How do you plead?"

Étienne met his gaze unflinchingly. "Guilty, where I acknowledge my actions contributed to the turmoil of our nation."

A murmur rippled through the audience.

The magistrate raised an eyebrow. "An unusual admission. Do you wish to elaborate?"

He took a deep breath. "I was driven by ambition, blinded by the allure of power. In the name of progress, I made decisions that cost lives and sowed discord. For that, I am remorseful."

Louvet observed from the sidelines, his expression unreadable.

The magistrate stated, "I have noted your candour." "However, the severity of your crimes demands accountability. Do you have any last words in your defence?"

Étienne glanced around the room, his gaze settling momentarily on Louvet before returning to the magistrate. "I offer no defence. Only a hope that the Republic may learn from the mistakes of men like me."

The magistrate conferred briefly with his advisors before addressing the court. "Considering the evidence and the defendant's own admission, this tribunal finds Étienne Corbeau guilty of all charges."

A collective sigh emanated from those gathered, a mixture of satisfaction and solemnity.

As they led him away, Étienne experienced a strange sense of calm. A clarity of purpose replaced the uncertainty that had plagued him. Although they led him away, Étienne felt a peculiar sense of calm. He realised that in accepting responsibility; he had reclaimed a fragment of his lost honour.

He sat at the small table; the quill poised over the parchment. Words flowed, unburdened by fear.

To whom it may concern,

I pen these lines not as a plea for mercy but as a testament to a life lived in shades of grey. Ambition drove me to heights I scarcely imagined, yet it also led me down a path strewn with the wreckage of compromised ideals.

I accept the consequences of my actions. Let this serve as a cautionary tale—that positing power, unchecked by conscience, can corrupt even the most ardent of patriots.

To Thérèse, whose compassion was a beacon in my darkest hours—I hope you find peace and happiness untethered by the shadows of my past.

May the Republic forge a future rooted in true liberty, equality, and fraternity.

Étienne Corbeau

9 April 1795

He folded the letter carefully, addressing it to Thérèse's last known residence. Handing it to the guard, he requested its delivery—a last gesture in a world he would soon depart.

As evening fell, the distant tolling of bells marked the passage of time. Étienne sat quietly, gazing through the barred window at the starless sky.

"An ignoble end," he mused. "Yet perhaps fitting."

•••

The dawn of 11 April 1795 broke with a sullen grey over Paris, the sky heavy with clouds that threatened rain but delivered only a damp chill. Étienne Corbeau stood in his cell within the Conciergerie, the ancient fortress that had held so many before him. The cold stone walls seemed to absorb any warmth, leaving a pervasive chill that settled in his bones. He traced a finger along the rough surface of the wall, his thoughts drifting between past and present.

The faint light seeped through the high, barred window, casting long shadows that stretched across the floor like grasping hands. Étienne sat on the narrow cot, his mind a tumult of memories—some sharp and vivid, others blurred at the edges. Faces floated before him: Maximilien Robespierre's intense gaze, Georges Danton's booming laughter, Camille Desmoulins' fiery passion. They were ghosts now, spectres of a time when ideals burned brighter than the reality they faced.

A soft knock interrupted his reverie. The door creaked open, and a young guard entered, his eyes avoiding Étienne's. "Monsieur Corbeau," he said quietly, "it is time."

Étienne nodded, rising with a calm that surprised even himself. "Merci," he replied, his voice steady. He smoothed the front of his worn jacket, the fabric frayed at the cuffs. There was a dignity in the slight gesture, a last assertion of the man he had been.

As he stepped into the corridor, two more guards joined them, flanking him on either side. The silence was thick, punctuated only by the echo of their footsteps against the stone floor. The corridors twisted and turned, a labyrinthine path that seemed to lead deeper into shadow before ascending toward the light.

Emerging into the courtyard, the overcast brightness momentarily blinded Étienne. The air was crisp, carrying the scent of wet leaves and the distant murmur of the city stirring awake. A carriage awaited him—a simple, unadorned conveyance drawn by a single horse whose breath billowed in the cold morning air.

He climbed into the carriage without prompting, settling onto the wooden bench. The guards took their positions, and with a flick of the reins, they set off through the cobbled streets. The city unfolded around them, a tapestry of narrow alleys and broad boulevards, of grand edifices and humble dwellings. Parisians continued their morning routines; some watched the carriage pass, others oblivious to its passage.

Étienne gazed out of the small window, his eyes tracing familiar sights. There was the café where he had met with fellow revolutionaries, plotting and debating into the early hours. The Palais-Royal, its gardens once a haven of lively discourse and clandestine meetings. The Seine, its waters reflecting the muted light as it flowed steadily onward.

He thought of Thérèse and wondered where she was at this moment. Had she received his letter? Would she remember him with kindness or regret? He hoped, at least, that she would understand why he had chosen this path. He could not shift the weight of his actions onto another.

The carriage drew to a halt at the Place de la Révolution, the expansive square dominated by the imposing silhouette of the guillotine. A crowd had gathered. A sea of faces blurred at the edges. Some wore expressions of grim satisfaction, others of detached curiosity. The atmosphere was subdued the chill in the air mirrored by the solemnity of the occasion.

Étienne descended from the carriage, his steps measured and unhurried. The guards escorted him toward the scaffold, their grips firm but not rough. As he mounted the wooden steps, the murmur of the crowd hushed, a collective breath held in anticipation.

At the top stood the executioner, a stout man with a steady gaze. He regarded Étienne with neither malice nor compassion—merely a professional carrying out his duty. The blade of the guillotine gleamed dully, a stark reminder of the finality that awaited.

Étienne turned to face the crowd, his eyes scanning the multitude. He saw workers in their coarse clothing, bourgeois gentlemen with polished boots, women clutching shawls tightly around their shoulders. Among them, he imagined the faces of those he had known—the allies and adversaries who had shaped his journey.

"Citoyens," he began, his voice carrying across the quiet square. "I stand before you, a man who once believed himself a servant of the people. In my pursuit of change, I lost sight of the very ideals I claimed to uphold."

A stir rippled through the crowd, but no one spoke.

"I do not ask for forgiveness, nor do I expect it," he continued. "Let my fate serve as a caution—a reminder that ambition without conscience leads only to ruin."

He paused, the weight of his words hanging in the air. Then, with a nod to the executioner, he signalled he was ready.

The executioner guided him to the bascule, the wooden plank that would hold him in place. Étienne knelt, resting his neck against the icy embrace of the lunette. The smell of sawdust mingled with the faint scent of iron.

Time seemed to stretch, each moment elongated into eternity. Étienne's thoughts drifted to simpler times—a childhood spent in the countryside, the warmth of his mother's smile, the boundless possibilities that had once stretched before him.

"11 April 1795," he thought. "An unremarkable day to mark the end of a life filled with contradictions."

The whisper of the blade slicing through the air was the only sound. It fell swiftly, mercifully, its descent a blur of motion that concluded with a definitive thud.

In the silence that followed, the crowd dispersed, conversations resuming in hushed tones. Life in Paris continued unabated—the vendors calling out their wares, children chasing one another through the streets, the ever-present hum of a city that had grown accustomed to such spectacles.

Among the departing throng, a figure lingered at the edge of the square. Thérèse stood with her hands clasped tightly before her, her face pale but composed. She had watched from a distance, the final moments etching themselves indelibly into her memory. Clutching a small locket that held a strand of Étienne's hair—a keepsake he had entrusted to her—she whispered a silent farewell.

"May you find peace at last," she murmured, turning away as a single tear traced a path down her cheek.

Elsewhere, in the salons and meeting halls, news of Étienne Corbeau's execution spread quickly. Reactions varied—some hailed it as justice served, others viewed it with a resigned acceptance of the Revolution's relentless tide. A few questioned the necessity of yet another death in a cycle that seemed unending.

In the following days, discussions of Étienne's life and deeds became fodder for pamphlets and broadsheets. Writers dissected his motivations, debated his impact, and pondered the legacy he left behind. Some painted him as a cautionary figure—a man consumed by his own aspirations. Others recognised the complexity of his character, acknowledging both his flaws and the genuine desire for progress that had initially driven him.

Jacques-Louis David, the renowned painter and chronicler of the Revolution, considered capturing Étienne's likeness in a sketch—a study of the human cost of political upheaval. But in the end, he set aside his charcoal, choosing instead to focus on the living subjects who continued to shape France's future.

As spring approached, the city settled into a fragile calm. The fervour of previous years had cooled, leaving in its wake a landscape scarred by conflict yet ripe for renewal. The people of France stood at a crossroads, their path forward uncertain but imbued with the hard-won knowledge of experience.

Étienne Corbeau's name gradually faded from public discourse, becoming a footnote in the annals of history. Yet, for those who had known him—for Thérèse, for the colleagues who had walked alongside him—the memory remained. He was a reminder of the perils of unchecked ambition, of the human capacity for both greatness and folly.

In the quiet corners of Paris, where the Seine flowed steadily under stone bridges and the shadows lengthened in the fading light, the echoes of his life lingered—a testament to a man who had reached for the stars but had fallen back to earth, his journey ending as unceremoniously as those he had once condemned.